# MICE AND MEN BOX SET 1

## RUTHLESS KING & QUEEN OF THORNS (THE WAR OF ROSES UNIVERSE)

## LANA SKY

# RUTHLESS KING

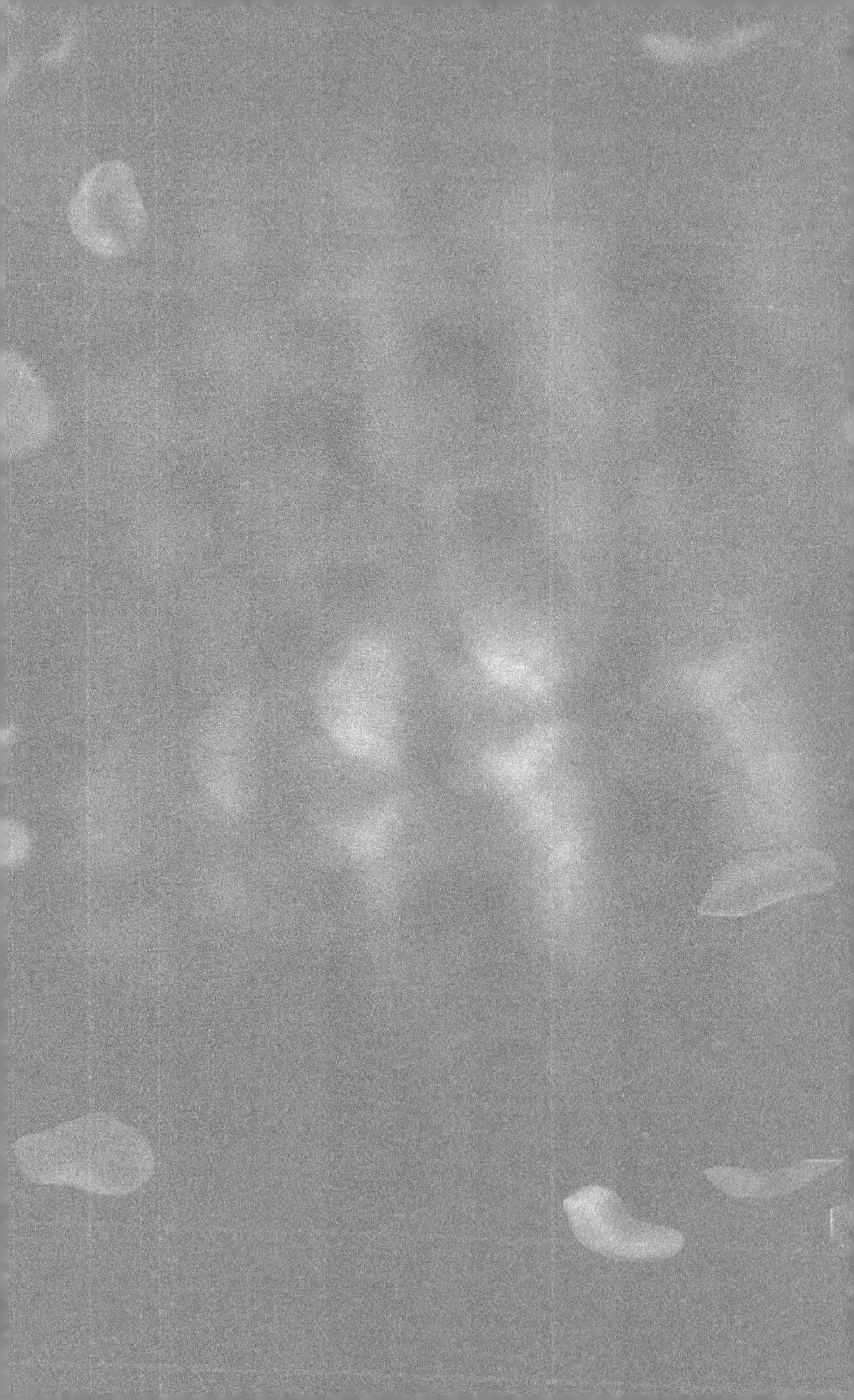

**Ruthless King**

**Ruthless King** By Lana Sky

Copyright © 2020 by Lana Sky
All rights reserved.

No part of this publication may be reproduced, distributed, or transmitted in any form or by any means, including photocopying, recording, or other electronic or mechanical methods, without the prior written permission of the author.

# ACKNOWLEDGMENTS

Thanks so much to everyone who supported this draft along the way, including the many beta readers who provided encouragement! Please keep in mind that this story includes dark, graphic, and explicit content matter that is not suitable for readers under the age of 18—or for readers who are uncomfortable with the following subject matter: age gap relationships, explicit sex, mentions of sexual abuse, and graphic depictions of violence.

# DON

*"Though this be madness, yet there is method in't." ~Hamlet.*

While I wasn't the smartest kid in the world, I had one trait most don't—ambition. Ambitions so grand I envisioned myself one day ruling the world—and I wasn't satisfied with just imagining it. Sure, the dumb fantasies were no different than what most punks aspire to at that age, but I'd wanted more. More than a kid raised in the streets was entitled to.

More than I deserved.

Mama called it "dreaming," thinking too big for my britches but, bless her soul, she was naïve when it came to the way of the world. She never taught me that dreams don't mean shit in the long run, or that success has a price —desperation. You have to take it. With pain, with blood, by any means necessary, you take what you want.

And the easiest way to do that? Through force. Young Donatello learned that violence could garner him whatever he craved. Cars. Booze. Women.

But I also learned that there isn't one damn thing that can't be ripped away afterward. Despite the odds, I'd gotten my wish once, gaining everything I'd dreamed of and more. The funny thing is, I was so fixated on what I lacked, I didn't even know it. Greed was the one constant I knew, and I only ever had one goal. Money. To have more of it than God himself, enough to have this entire city in the palm of my hand. I got that wish too—my name was feared, be it Donatello or the various monikers assigned to me by rivals. *Il Mostro. The Butcher. That Violent Cunt.*

Back then, I'd been stupid enough to assume that fear meant something. That fear equaled power. In his own esteem, the old Donatello was a force to be reckoned with —and if that smug little punk could see the man I am now, he'd scoff, unable to recognize himself.

A man who scrapes for what he has and appreciates every damn cent. Who knows what it means to be humble. To suffer. To bide his time and keep his fucking mouth shut.

This new man ain't no *Butcher*, for damn sure. From crook to legitimate businessman. Hell, it sounds like some shitty fairy tale, but reformed or not, a man never forgets his past. If he's smart, he'll even learn from it.

Now, of all times, I remember a particular piece of advice— coincidentally given to me by the last bastard I ever killed myself. His name didn't matter; he was some balding, pudgy little asshole who read Hamlet once, and thought that made him a fucking intellectual. Funny, because that "intelligence" didn't pan out so well for him in the end. I will give him this much, though—he made an impression on me in a way few have.

*"Though this be madness, there's a method to it, see. Like Shakespeare?"* he'd ranted, right before I'd put a bullet in his skull.

The madness was selling me out. The method? Using back-channel deals to frame me for extortion. In his mind, it all made sense. He wasn't trying to set me up to save his own skin, see? By slithering his way into my inner circle like the lying cunt he was, he was merely doing me a favor by revealing how easy it could be to fuck me over. His betrayal was all for the greater good.

Unimpressed by that genius rationale, I'd reacted the only way I knew how back then.

Fast-forward almost a decade later, and karma gives me a cruel, new perspective. Finally, I understand just what the dumb son of a bitch was getting at. He wasn't smart; hell, he wasn't even trying to be. Logic doesn't mean shit when you're *desperate*; when you have nothing else to fall back on but insanity.

In such a mental state, everything starts looking like a good idea—like what I'm doing right now.

It's insane to stand here before two armed guards, holding a gift wrapped by some lady in a store who assured me a woman would "enjoy such a thoughtful present." She even tied it with a goddamn bow.

It's insane to wear this pathetic smile and pray to God my act holds up.

It's methodical insanity.

"We're Fabio Botelli's guests," I say, gesturing to the slender man beside me. Just like I'd told him, he keeps his mouth shut, his smile as dumb as mine.

One look at these guards, and I know they're no bumbling rent-a-cops. *Ex-soldier* is written all over their stiff posture and the cautious way they glance me over. Considering the reputation of the man who owns this property, I'm not surprised.

Nerves ripple through my belly, catching me off guard. I feel like a punk again, stepping up to the head of the *famiglia* for the first time, wearing my Sunday's best. Little did I know, the dress shirt sported a fucking pizza stain on the collar. Old Giovanni had taken one look at me and scoffed, seeing through my act. He'd turned me away that time, warning that he didn't work with "boys." He only hired men.

This inspection feels no different, though one would hope a couple decades of experience would improve my chances. A week after that initial meeting, I'd returned to Giovanni, but with the added prestige of having shot one of his rivals at point-blank range. Bloodstains carry a bit more weight to them than pizza sauce. The old man had taken me on then and taught me the importance of casting an image. Of sowing a reputation based on fear. He bought me a brand-new shirt, and I made sure never to stain it. Hell, I still have it, a reminder of that valuable lesson.

If he could see me now, Giovanni would shake his head in disbelief. "You look plain, Donny," he'd scold. "You are a lion among men dressed like a fucking sheep."

In this city, aptly named Hell's Gambit, *sheep* wear Italian designer suits and grease their hair to shine. They smile awkwardly before those in authority and simper just long enough to go undetected. Those sheep? They dine with the wolves, a position preferable to figuratively starving. Hell, I'd bleat if I thought it would help.

Luckily that aspect of this ruse doesn't seem necessary. The guards share searching glances, and then one inclines his head. "This way, Sir."

He gestures to the massive oak doors propped open to allow guests inside. With a few tense steps, we're in, joining an advancing line of other guests.

Relief surges through my blood, mingling with the shot of whiskey I'd taken for good luck. I fall into step behind a woman dressed in a black gown and catch sight of myself in a mirror hanging on the wall. A crazy son of a bitch stares back, his eyes only slightly bloodshot, his hair the neatest I've seen it in days. His smile is charming, but the strain in his expression gives it all away—he's desperate. In a sense, he looks like Mr. Hamlet did when he pled for his life before me.

What supposed method might explain this man's madness?

That's easy. Survival.

I'm here because the only other option is to lie down quietly and let the brutality of this city swallow me whole. I can't, not even newly reformed as I am. Luckily, Mischa Stepanov, owner of this massive residence, has done the one thing worth prostrating myself at his mercy. An act powerful enough to change the entire Vanici legacy for the better.

He's decided to present his daughter to the world on a silver platter.

So, call me insane. I'm here, ready to grovel.

And apparently, I'm not the only one. A queue of well-dressed guests extends both ahead of me and behind. On polished shoes and pointy heels, we tread over a floor burnished to shine, and into a home displaying breathtaking gothic architecture. A large central staircase dominates the entryway, and past that is a winding set of corridors capped by vaulted ceilings and grand arches. Eventually, we're herded into a massive grand hall, every bit as impressive as the name would imply. Instantly, I find the rumors were true after all, and this isn't some elaborate trap. The fearsome leader of the Russian mob has decided to throw a birthday party of all things, in honor of his eldest daughter. Fresh roses litter nearly every available inch of space. Soft white accents lessen the intimidating atmosphere cast by the house itself and the security presence out front. As the swell of elegant music reaches my ears, and I spot dedicated servers mingling with trays of food, some of my unease lessens.

"You see, Vincenzo? There's a method to my madness," I tell the boy beside me. He doesn't look convinced, an eyebrow cocked, his mouth flat in a hard line. Balancing the gift on one hand, I flick his nose the way I used to when he was a kid, always giving lip. "Stop your pouting and smile, damn it. You have a *principessa* to charm."

"A princess, huh? You've lost your mind," Vin grumbles while tugging at the collar of his tux. Hell, it might be the first time in years that he's worn one—I know for a fact that he spends more time hiding in the library of his fancy school these days, than dressing to impress. If he didn't share my eyes, and the signature Vanici grin, I'd doubt we were related. My heir, the genius, who'd have thought?

What he makes up for in ambition—to become a doctor, of all things—he lacks in political savvy. Sadly, even a doctor must learn what this world comes down to in the end— filthy, dumb politics.

"It's like a game of chess," I explain for what has to be the millionth time. "You make your connections to stay ahead, or you'll be the pawn in some other motherfucker's game of checkmate."

As usual, he rolls his brown eyes from behind the wire rims of his glasses. Apparently, the ways of the mob aren't as interesting as medicine.

No better time to learn than now.

"This little party could change your entire life," I insist, adopting the gravelly baritone of old Giovanni. "Sonny, with a move like this, you'll be set."

"Set to marry some rich girl? This isn't medieval times, Donny," he says. "People don't do dumb shit like marriages for alliances anymore. You're about a thousand years too late for that."

"And you've been at that pretty-boy school for too long," I snipe. Though I'm the one who insisted he get a degree in the first place. Pride swells in my chest whenever I think back on everything he's accomplished. Graduating from that fancy private school at the top of his class and earning a ticket to one of the world's best universities. Not to mention doing it all without so much as a misdemeanor to his name.

It sounds too good to be true. My boy, the scholar. He's made his mother prouder than I ever did. Though, despite all that knowledge, he's never learned how to wear a thousand-dollar suit like it doesn't itch worse than a motherfucker.

"Look at you." I nudge his shoulder, scowling at his posture. Giovanni would send him away as a lost cause, even if he were covered in blood. "Slouching in designer duds. Disgraceful. My nephew? Bah! You look like you might be a doctor or something."

"And you look like a criminal or something." His quick smile draws a chuckle from me as I ruffle his hair.

"You little smartass. Now, look sharp." I stiffen, sensing several pairs of eyes swivel in our direction. As much as I've joked with him, this isn't a game. "We're here on business, and you need to act the part. I know you've been poring over those doctor books of yours, but let me test your knowledge of the real world."

I fix my gaze on two men standing near the hall entrance, their backs to us. A face alone can be enough to identify a man, but clothing is just as signifying. Burgundy suits stand out amongst the sea of the typical black. Even Vin recognizes the color, and his upper lip curls back from his teeth.

"Going off those hideous outfits, they must be Sigerelli men," he says.

"Good." I nod in approval.

As if on cue, the two men turn in our direction. Both Vin and I nod in a greeting that is promptly returned. Forcing a smile, I mutter, "We like them because…"

"They helped you launder your dirty money through their luxury car dealership," Vin recites as crisply as if reading from a goddamn book. "Back when you were a crook."

I can't deny him another laugh. "Good boy. Old friends can prove to be valuable, even to someone on the straight and narrow. Now, who are they?" I nod to a couple across the room. Between the diamonds draped over the slender, brunette woman, and the quality of her male counterpart's suit, they could purchase the entire Sigerelli stock for fun.

"Hooked nose, a scar on his chin… He's Giovanni Rossi. Runs a casino, but that's just his day job," Vin murmurs around his own fake grin. "Pompous. A dick. We don't like him."

"That's my boy," I mutter back. Unlike his namesake, this Giovanni is a pathetic whelp, unworthy of the Rossi name. His own father didn't allow him into the fold, but he still has his uses. "Now, tell me *why* we don't like him."

"Because he's not only a dirty crook, but a backstabber," Vin replies under his breath. Spotting us, Giovanni inclines his head in greeting, and Vin's the first one to return it with so much enthusiasm I'd think it genuine if I didn't know any better. "We still show him respect, though," he adds as we approach an unoccupied corner. "Even if he no longer runs the *famiglia*."

"And why is that?" I ask, my head cocked, tone critical.

The answer is so obvious, he shoots me a sideways glance. "Because you keep your enemies closer than your friends."

"Damn right. Speaking of enemies…" My eyes narrow as I spot a figure holding court across the room, and a worrying ripping sound comes from the gift tucked beneath my arm. I grasp it with both hands, fighting to keep my expression neutral. "Who is that?"

I nod in his general direction, though Vin has no trouble seeking him out. A white suit sets this man apart from the rest of the crowd—but not in the way he probably expects.

"Antonio Salvatore," Vin hisses. His handsome façade cracks as his lips twist into a snarl. "He runs the *famiglia* now, but we definitely don't like him because he's a—"

This description, I voice for him. "A sick son of a bitch. Dickhead. And a murderer." Even if I could never prove it. His hallmark is a signature of all the crimes he has a hand in —cruelty, brutality, and callous rage. Turning his head, the bastard catches me staring and winks, puffing up his chest like he's some big man.

A different me would have slit his throat here and now. I just smile. "You stay away from him," I hiss to Vin.

He nods in agreement, only to raise an eyebrow at a sudden thought. "But you haven't spoken about this guy much. Mischa."

He's scanning the massive grand hall of the Stepanov manor —and I don't miss the appreciative gleam in his eye. Despite his studious tendencies, he has enough sense to know power when he sees it on stark display. He's impressed.

And I'm unnerved.

"Why come here if we weren't invited?" he questions, cutting his eyes up to mine, as perceptive as ever. "What makes this Mischa so important you'd drag us here on Uncle Fabio's coattails?"

I turn away, avoiding those searching looks he excels at. The bastard will make a damn good surgeon one day. Or a cop in another universe.

"You don't party, Don," he points out, refusing to let the subject drop. "Ever. Hell, any other day, you'd be sloshed by this time of the night—"

"You want to know why we're here?" I slip my arm around his shoulders and jerk my chin to indicate our surroundings. "Take a look. View more than the surface beauty. Tell me what you see."

I see deceptive white accents and enough fucking roses to choke someone to death on the stench. But beneath that? I see power. The massive hall alone is large enough to fit the entire floor of the hotel Vin and I booked, with room to spare—and it's just a fraction of the manor itself. Well known for his swagger, Mischa spared no expense to celebrate his daughter's exploits. Decadence oozes from every corner of the space, from the ivory tablecloths to even more sprawling floral centerpieces.

I figure it'll take months of showers before I stop smelling like fucking flowers.

But roses aren't enough to sway the men gathered here. No, this gesture of fatherly love serves another purpose entirely. Even someone as disconnected from our world as Vincenzo can instantly pick up on it.

"He must have more money than God," he mutters in awe, and I'm reminded of the boy I used to be who'd craved to own just that. "And a lot of sway to get you to even enter the same mile radius as Antonio Salvatore."

"And then some," I grudgingly admit. "He's only been active in this territory for about six years, but he now controls the entire *mafiya,* which—their exploits combined—gives him a hefty sum of dark money to draw on. Not to mention that his allies outnumber everyone else two to one. Only a fool would dare to challenge him."

And under his control, this city has transformed, forgetting all about the legacy of the *famiglia* and its once feared ex-leader. Or so I'd hoped.

Maybe I'd been the naïve one, thinking that I could quietly return and just meld into the business sector, newly focused on legitimate enterprise. I'd tried that—only to be thwarted at nearly every fucking turn. Someone doesn't want me back, and if I were a betting man, I'd place my money on Antonio Salvatore.

The funny part is that we came up together, both pupils under Giovanni's tutelage. There were three of us once— Antonio, myself, and another man I considered to be my brother, Gino Mangenello. While I went on to lead in the old man's place, Antonio was too busy lusting after everything I had to achieve anything on his own. Some might say he still won in the end. Now he rules over the fragments of the *famiglia,* but it's a shadow of its former glory. Case and point—he's here sniffing after Mischa just like I am.

I'm sure he's done everything he could to scuttle my latest deal, but I managed it regardless, and now I own legitimate shares in the city's port. It isn't much, but it's something, more than enough revenue to fund Vin's education. With a new advertisement campaign, I hope to extend that holding.

And with Mischa Stepanov on my side? No one could stand in my way, and I technically wouldn't be breaking any of the vows I swore to myself all those years ago. Perhaps, just bending them a little.

"A fool would challenge someone like that," Vin agrees, a note of seriousness in his voice. "Which is why we just snuck into his party even though Fabio told you we couldn't come?"

"We didn't sneak in," I counter gruffly. Spying a man dressed in black lurking on the outskirts of the room, I point him out with a grim warning, "Do you really think we'd make it past the front door if we had? Besides, Fabio always says no to everything. He worries worse than you do."

"Fine, we didn't sneak in," he admits. "We just kindly hijacked Uncle Fabio's invitation and spent five grand on a silver mirror to impress some crime lord's daughter."

"It's a nice gift," I say grudgingly, eyeing the pale blue wrapping paper and its nice white bow. The saleslady was right—it looks fitting for any princess, be her legitimate royalty or not. Meeting Vin's disapproving stare, I shrug. "Here is another lesson for you—in this world, my boy? You've got to pay to play."

"What would you call it? A down payment on my future?" His sneer reveals his true thoughts on that statement, but I smirk, satisfied. At least he's thinking like me for once.

"Exactly. And you might like this girl. I hear she studies in Vienna, at a school just as fucking pretentious as yours." He purses his lips at that, but I know him well enough to sense he's intrigued. Vinny admires smarts the way most men do tits. "She's a musician too. Blond. Beautiful, and—"

"And she's the kind of girl who has her father throw her some stuffy ass party for clout."

I bark out a laugh. Every now and again, he reminds me that beneath the book smarts, he's one hundred percent Vanici. "Like that makes a difference? Now, look sharp!" Ruffling his hair again, I shove him forward.

Speaking of his future, the time for jokes is over. Switching to a sterner tone, I tell him, "No heiress will pick you out of the crowd if you stick to me like a baby up his mother's skirt. Take this gift and go mingle—" I hand him the box. "And stop slouching. Remember who you are. Vanicis cower before no one."

"Except Mischa Stepanov."

"Hey!" I smack him on the back so hard he coughs. "No one. You got that?"

"Whatever you say, Don," he mutters under his breath. Nonetheless, he strolls off with his head held high, the way I taught him.

The same way my father taught me—Vanicis always keep our fucking chins up. You make eye contact with only those who matter. Shove your way past anyone bold enough or dumb enough to stand in your way.

Bow to no one.

We may not have much, but we are Vanici.

Daughter of a Stepanov or not, this *mafiya* princess will be lucky to have him. Willow is her name, and the things I told Vin weren't all bullshit. They say she's blond like her father. Thin. A swan, apart from the family of raptors she sprung from. For what it's worth, they've kept her out of the public eye, limiting the information known about her. I hear she's beautiful, at least. Like Vin, she runs in better social circles than the criminals her family controls, attending the best schools in the world.

Even if he won't admit it, Vincenzo deserves a woman like that. With his pretty pianist wife, he can play doctor all he wants, and an alliance with the Stepanovs will give him a hand up in the world I would have killed to possess at his age. Nestled in their powerful orbit, he'll be untouchable.

More importantly, he won't have to scrape like me.

He won't be like me.

The only problem?

As Vincenzo stated, we weren't exactly invited.

Why? I'd be a fool not to consider the most obvious of reasons—my reputation has preceded me, even after all these years. It would certainly explain why the man has rebuffed all my attempts to meet and why Fabio balked when I even suggested attending this little party.

Perhaps Mischa doesn't want to associate with such a monster, though from the rumors, he's no saint either. The same man who singlehandedly fought a bloody war for over a decade doesn't seem like the type to shy away from an old phantom from the past. Besides, if the man saw me as a real threat, I doubt we would have made it past security at all.

They're professional, the kind of men it costs good money to keep. Loyal. Subtle. Intimidating. A least twenty men cover this room alone. Dressed in black, they stand guard at strategic positions throughout as a constant reminder of the vigilance a man like Mischa lives under—and for a good reason. In our world, even a girl's debutante party could invite danger.

Danger I know well. Unease prickles my skin as I watch Vin meld into the assembled crowd of criminals and socialites. It's comical in a sense—politicians and crime lords alike, all gathered to kiss the ring of one man.

And, as if on cue, he appears beneath an archway at the back of the hall, drawing everyone's notice.

I stiffen at the sight of him, but not out of fear. Hell, maybe it's jealousy? Some men need whiskey to make it through the night while others…

They bask in the bosom of family like something out of a fucking sitcom. Despite his reputation, I've only seen him in person a handful of times. Tall, built like a bear with the cruelty and wit to match, he requires no introduction, nonetheless. Basking in the attention, he starts forward, a beautiful brunette on his arm. A mature grace gives her a poise I doubt a nineteen-year-old girl would possess. His wife, I presume.

They say she too comes from a powerful web of families—the proud, ruthless Vasilevs and the callous Winthorps. Standing beside a man nearly twice her size, she looks every bit the welcoming hostess I'm sure she is.

But no sane woman could live with a man like him without possessing some ruthlessness of her own. Even my Olivia, with her soft, gentle ways, had a temper. Mischa's wife, I'm sure, is no different—and the elegance of this soiree is no doubt in part to her efforts. Though, judging from the size of her belly, Mischa looks well on his way to expanding his brood of daughters to display.

My jaw clenches as I take a step forward and consider approaching him now. Would he really refuse a direct meeting here?

In theory, he shouldn't. Donatello the Butcher is dead. Brick by brick, he rebuilt his life in the sun—and I don't intend to look back. Though while my days in the *famiglia* are over, I still have something to offer Mischa and his *mafiya*—an alliance. For peace. For stability.

For outright greed.

With Mischa's resources and my assets, we could secure this city for years to come with plenty of spoils for us both.

Emboldened by that thought, I take another step, tracking the couple across the room to a raised dais festooned with white roses. Clearing my throat, I adjust my collar and try to compile a fitting greeting.

*"Hello, Mischa. Thank you for presenting your daughter on a silver platter? Have you met my nephew?"*

Not exactly tactful, but it might do. So intent on my quarry am I, I don't realize someone's beside me until they grab my forearm, triggering years of instinct. My hand slaps against my pocket before I even remember that I'm unarmed. Those empty fingers curl into a fist regardless, poised to attack in any way possible. Tense, I jerk my head around and sigh.

"I thought I told you that you were not welcome," a man scolds. One look at him, and some of the tension drains from my muscles. Some. Rather than prepare to fight, I brace for a scolding like a boy caught by his mama with his hand in the cookie jar.

"Don't look so grumpy, Fabio," I gruffly reply, shrugging him off. "It's a party. Don't tell me you're tired already, old man?"

Though he's my age, thirty-five, he looks older. Gray has already started to color his auburn hair, a testament to his gift for worrying, though the trait is a double-edged sword. His obsession over detail makes him a sought-after accountant employed by everyone from the governor, to Mischa Stepanov himself.

"If it makes you feel better, I promise to be on my best behavior, scout's honor." I slap a hand over my chest for emphasis. "Trust me, Mama. You don't have to be up my ass tonight. Relax, I'm here for business."

"I wouldn't have to be 'up your ass'—" He grimaces with distaste at the wording. "If you weren't swaggering about the place, drawing notice. I saw how you looked at Antonio Salvatore. The least you could do is be subtle."

"This is me subtle, Fabio," I say, though I submit to letting him herd me toward the back of the room where we're more hidden among the crowd. Eyeing him, I'm forced to admit, "You look good tonight. Aiming to snag this Stepanova for yourself?"

He cuts a confident image in a tailored black tux, his hair perfectly coifed. It's easy to overlook the fact that he barely comes to the middle of my chest. For what he lacks in stature, the man more than makes up for in reputation.

No one in this room is more respected.

"At least you remembered her name," he grouses while snatching a glass of champagne from the tray of a passing server.

"The adding an 'a' at the end for a woman?" I gloat, pleased with myself. "This old dog can learn some new tricks."

"That's the simple way of putting it. These Russians are sticklers for respect. Though like that matters any to you." He takes a hearty sip from his glass as his cheeks flush pink. In a hoarse whisper, he confesses what has him so frazzled, "Even after all the years I've known you, you always manage to surprise me. Really, Don? Sneaking into the home of the head of the *mafiya* on my invitation. I'll be lucky if I don't wake up to a horse head in my bed tomorrow."

"He's the *mafiya*, not *famiglia*," I correct. "It's my kind that butcher horses—though Giovanni was partial to severing a finger or two instead. He was an animal lover, you see. I'm sure Mischa would just kill you. Or castrate you outright as a friendly warning."

Wincing, Fabio downs nearly half of his glass in one go. "Thanks for the reassurance, Don. *Cavolo!* Why am I even letting you talk me into this?"

"Because I'm invoking Olivia's name," I say softly. It's a low blow, but desperate times call for desperate measures. Sure enough, Fab's strained frown reveals the appeal hit its mark. "You're too good of a man to resist that," I point out, but in no way am I pleased with myself.

Olivia. I can clearly remember the last fucker I killed... One would think I'd never forget her face. Never.

But as my last dose of whiskey wears off, the painful truth seeps in—I can't even recall what she sounded like.

"She was twice the social charmer you are," Fabio says. Some of the worry lines around his mouth soften. "If only she could see you now. She'd probably piss herself from laughing at the sight of you stuffed into a suit. Could you find no tailor to fit you properly? Though I suppose it's too much to ask for a miracle—"

"Hey! I can't help it that I spent more of my life fighting in the streets than mingling with the upper class," I grumble, tugging at a sleeve of my jacket. Contrary to Fabio's snide remarks, it was expertly tailored by a man I trust, not to mention damn expensive. Alas, fine material and expert craftsmanship can only go so far.

My life didn't offer me the same pampered safety as a Willow Stepanova, or a Giovanni Rossi, who never wielded a weapon in his life.

Wars may begin and end, but battle scars will always remain.

"I should have known you wouldn't be able to resist drawing attention to yourself, even unintentionally," Fabio grouses. "It's in your nature, you damn, prideful Vanicis."

I feel my upper lip quirk into a grin. "Yes, us damned, incredible Vanicis. For all of your worrying, look at Vin." I nod to where he stands. Head held high, he's taken my encouragement to heart, radiating that trademark charm. Joy swells in my chest, overpowering even my own doubts.

My smart boy may have some inclination toward politics yet.

"My God, Donatello," Fabio exclaims, slapping a hand over his chest. "It's been years since I've seen you smile. And the last time you had just killed a man. The blood on your chin negated the effect a little."

"I think every father cracks a grin when he sees his baby boy out in the world." The seriousness of the moment flattens my mouth again. "Forget me. You ask why I came here? For him. I can't protect him forever."

Fabio sighs, inspecting his now empty glass. "There are real fathers out there who don't treat their own sons the way you treat Vin—let alone their nephews. Donella would be proud of you for how you've looked after him. I know she's looking down on us both right now, cursing us to hell and back for letting Vincenzo wear a tie that clashes so harshly with his skin tone. Really, Don? Navy?"

I shrug, gritting my teeth—but he's right. I can hear my little sister nagging from here. Even back when we had pennies to our name, she was so fixated on keeping up appearances. It was that pining for more that cost her her life in the end. When she didn't achieve the fairy tale ending she envisioned for herself, not even her son could keep her from a bottle of pills. One day, she took too damn many.

"A tie is a tie," I snap, shaking my head to banish the memory. "No matter the color, let's just hope it catches the younger Stepanova's eye, huh?"

The girl hasn't made her entrance yet, though I sense her arrival is imminent. Her parents are positioned expectantly by the dais, and an air of impatience buzzes through the shifting crowd. Already, anyone with something to prove has jockeyed for a prime spot near either of the two entrances she's bound to come in through.

"I feel like we're watching one of those animal documentaries about the breeding season," Fab remarks, ever the intellectual.

I'm not so tactful. "Welcome to the world that awaits those of us without wives," I tell him. "It's all one big pissing contest."

Some have gone through greater lengths, it seems. I catch a flicker of movement from above and spy a shadowed hall overlooking this space. An amusing thought makes me chuckle. Could the little *principessa* be lurking up there, gloating over her crowd from above?

From her vantage point, she'll have a good view of the contenders, including a familiar figure who managed to score one of the best spots available.

"Smart lad, Vin," I mutter with pride. "Smart lad."

Finally, a commotion near the back entrance draws my attention, along with everyone else in the room. Visible from beyond the archways, a retinue of people approach, Willow presumably among them. I surprise myself, eagerly craning my neck for a glimpse of this elusive *mafiya* princess along with everyone else.

"Don." I barely register Fabio snatching at my forearm until he digs his nails in. "Don!"

I swivel my head toward him in alarm. That wasn't his usual worrying tone. Constricted, his gaze is focused straight ahead and whatever he sees makes him clench his jaw. "It seems you weren't subtle enough."

Confused, I turn to look in the same direction and instantly find the source of his concern. Mischa Stepanov. Apparently, my party crashing has not gone unnoticed— and judging from his frown, the man has no intention of rethinking his slight.

I'm no pussy. I've stared down grown men armed with way more than a corsage of roses more than once in my life.

And I can safely say that none of those foes ever looked at me the way he does. With raw, searing anger that transforms his expression into a snarl. Funnily enough, I know that look well, seeing it every time I look in the fucking mirror these days.

There's no other word for it—hate.

"Wait here," Fabio mutters before slipping through the crowd. He reaches Mischa within seconds, presumably speaking in that smooth, confident way he excels at.

But even his skills can only go so far.

I know hostility when I see it. Alarm for Vincenzo mingles with anger, festering, building… I have to dig my nails into my palms just to wrestle it under control. I've come too far to fuck up now. Too far…

But only respect for Fabio keeps me from crossing the room and confronting the man directly.

All this time, I've written off his shunning of me as arrogance. To him, I could be just another greedy son of a bitch desperate to lick up his scraps. God knows I ignored more than my fair share of ass kissers when I was the *famiglia's* head.

But now? There is no mistake—he knows damn well who I am. Which rumor or horror story sparked his ire, I wonder? My past? The men I've killed? The crimes I've committed unchecked? Or maybe the man—with his many children— heard about what I did to the one I'd sworn to protect.

*Her.* Even while I look for Olivia at the bottom of every bottle of liquor, another face haunts me at night. Torments me, her dark eyes searching, her lips hollowed around a silent scream. Nothing keeps her away for long. Not booze. Not time. Not prayer.

My little Safiya…

*No!* I fight back her memory as my breathing quickens. Teeth gritted, I refocus every brain cell I have on Mischa. No matter the reason, he's gone out of his way to prove his point. I'm not welcome in his orbit.

"Don?" Vin's already by my side, scanning my face. "What's wrong?"

"Nothing." I snatch the present from him, but even as I force a smile, I know he suspects the truth. "But we need to leave," I murmur as Fabio glances at me with an unmistakable warning. From the corner of my eye, I see that retinue of security start to peel away from the perimeter one by one, converging in our direction. Grabbing Vin's arm, I practically drag him after me. "Now."

"Why? What's wrong?" he asks, but he doesn't resist as I hook my arm around his shoulders and head for the entrance of the ballroom.

"Just a minor hiccup," I say, glancing back to find Fabio following us. "I'll explain later. But who needs a fancy shindig anyway? I'll buy you whatever drinks you want back at the hotel. We should celebrate before you return to London."

He's still frowning, but he's too smart to argue now. Guilt taunts me for bringing him here in the first place. Together, we exit the manor the way we came, skirting the scrutiny of Stepanov agents with every step.

A guard we pass on our way into the foyer touches a headset affixed to his ear, frowning, his gaze on me. Never before have I so bitterly regretted playing by the rules and coming here unarmed. Would Mischa be above mounting an attack right at this moment?

I can't tell. Someone knew to expect our hasty exit, at least. We've barely made it down the front walkway when my driver pulls up. Not of my own employ, he's a hire from the hotel, but judging from his blank expression, I doubt rushing his clients from fancy venues is an unusual occurrence.

"I'll take that, sir," he says, stepping out to retrieve the gift from me and set it in the trunk.

As I climb into the back seat, I make a mental note to tip him extra. Fuck, if he can get us off this property within the next few minutes, I'll employ him my damn self. Fear of Mischa isn't what sparks my impatience. Adrenaline rushes through my veins, making me think more clearly than I have in months. Calculating. The icy way I cringe from these days. Like the world is against me and fighting tooth and nail is the only way out.

It was the dark impulse I'd relied on back in the day. The cruelty that led me to do more than just kill a man. No, I had to make him suffer. Make him bleed.

Ensure that anyone watching would swear then and there to never cross me.

If I were still that man, Mischa's silence would not be tolerated so kindly. I'd march up to the bastard, put a knife to his throat, and demand he faces me like a man and states his issue outright. It's the way things should be fucking done...

"Don?" I don't even realize I've been holding my breath until Vin sprawls out on the seat across from me.

"Some party," he gripes, oblivious to the danger. Or so one might assume by looking at him—but his brown eyes are alert, darting toward the windows at the imposing manor looming above.

Tension stiffens my muscles, and the twisted thoughts come faster. *I've raised Vin too soft. Too weak. He has to learn for himself that nothing in this world comes for free. You've got to fight for it. Rip from the bastard who has it. You win.*

Sweat dribbles down my neck. I'm clutching the end of the seat just to keep myself in this car. I feel like I'm damn near close to exploding from this goddamn suit entirely by the time Fabio wrenches open the door and sticks his head inside.

"Sorry to cut your fun short," he says to Vin. "But I need your uncle to handle some very important business for me. I'll make it up to you, though." He tosses something to him that I can't make out in the dark. "Take my card for the week. Have some fun on me. The kind of fun stuffy Donatello might disapprove of."

"Thank you, Uncle Fabio." Vin grins though I suspect the boy's idea of a good time is far from what Fabio may have in mind.

"I bet you'll find a series of charges from a bookstore," I taunt.

But as Fabio meets my gaze, I realize the true depth of the situation he has the sense to hide from Vincenzo. He's worried. Judging from the prominence of the wrinkles around his mouth, I suspect this little incident will take all of his cunning to smooth over.

I don't even have the chance to ask him why before he leaves, closing the door behind him. Just as quickly, the driver takes off, whisking us away from Stepanov manor with a briskness that significantly improves my chances of offering him a job.

"I would have liked to see what she looked like," Vin says wistfully. "Given all the pomp and circumstance, I bet I dodged a bullet. Rich men tend to overcompensate, and going off the expense of that party, that guy must have a lot to make up for."

He sounds so damn confident that I snort, shocking myself. Gradually, that icy, unfeeling thinking process gives way to the warmth I've clung to all these years. It's like I can breathe again, and I eye the boy, feeling an ache in my chest. If my love for him could grow any more, I'd explode from the force of it by now. God bless him; he's kept me sane.

"You're quiet because you know I'm right," he teases.

"I hear she's beautiful," I counter. Beautiful, rich, and off-limits to him.

*Fuck.* If anything, tonight proved that securing his future won't be as easy as catching the eye of some spoiled debutante.

But I'll find another way.

Any way.

"You have that look again," Vin scolds, crossing his arms, already over the fancy event. His posture slouches as he adjusts his glasses on the bridge of his nose. I recognize that studious expression—the second we return to the hotel, he'll probably sequester himself in his room, eager to pore over whatever medical texts he lugged on the plane ride here.

Just like that, I have to question if he truly is my nephew.

"What look?" I demand.

"The 'woe is me. I'm Donatello, the toughest, saddest son of a bitch in the world. I do things like dragging my Vincenzo to extravagant birthday parties even though I can count the number of times I've worn a suit on one hand.'" He hams up his performance, mocking my voice, and puffing up his chest. "'I beat myself up for every little thing because I don't know how to operate outside of perfection.' You can relax, Don. I'm not mad."

His smile wrings a similar one out of me, and I choke out a noise that could be a chuckle. The little bastard. Ever since he was a boy, he's had a knack for cutting to the heart of a situation and turning it on its head in one go. He certainly turned my world on its head—for the better.

He deserves so much more than I can give him.

More than some spoiled *mafiya* girl.

"You can be sappy when you want to, you know that?" I toss back.

"Yeah. And I'm fairly sure that your matchmaker story was bullshit. Just admit it. I think you wanted her for yourself."

He wags a finger disapprovingly at me. "You're old enough to be her father. That's gross, Don."

"Sure, Vin. I wanted a spoiled little socialite nearly half my age. The girl wouldn't know what to do with me."

"Maybe she could get you a better suit for one?"

"Oh? Is this your way of coming out to me, Vin? Turning down a beautiful, rich brat in the name of fashion? I'd love you all the same if you were gay, you know."

He laughs harder. "No. This is my way of saying you need a woman in your life. At least then I won't have nightmares while I'm at university of you waking up in a pool of booze mixed with your own vomit. It's time to settle down, old man."

"Why settle?" I raise my hands and lean against the leather seat. "I already have an heir to carry on my legacy. Besides, I was married once. What use is another woman? You're all I need, Vincenzo." I'm not laughing anymore. I don't think I've ever been so serious. So earnest. Vin squirms in discomfort, but I don't shy away from adding, "You are my heir. My legacy. The future of the Vanici line rests with you. You will carry it all, and look damn good doing so. I don't need anyone else."

"You do," he says softly. His eyes take on a distant gleam that triggers an ominous dread. I'm tensing before he even whispers her name, "What about Safy?"

Every time, it hits with brutal force, this pain—affecting me more than the remnants of my old icy mindset. I crumple beneath the guilt. Like a wave, it crashes down, drowning out everything else. The need to breathe. Think. I can't even see as the world goes black.

In the midst of that darkness, her face appears in my mind. So innocent. So trusting. My little Safiya.

Only Vincenzo can ever bear to say her name. Why? He doesn't know the truth, believing she died in a horrible accident all those years ago. I fed him that lie myself.

"Don?" I blink to find Vin nearly leaning out of his seat, his eyes on my face. "I'm sorry," he says. "I know you don't like to talk about her."

I look away, fighting the emotions down to the depths of my soul where they belong. The guilt, and the pain, and the regret. Gradually, I forget her—that face, those eyes. I banish her memory—for now. She always comes back.

Every night. Every nightmare. She always returns.

"You're here now," I rasp, turning my attention back to Vin. "You."

He nods solemnly. "You're lucky to have me," he says. "I, at least, know how to wear a suit."

2

---

## DON

*I* barely get one glass of whiskey into Vin before he's already heading up to bed.

"That fancy university has made you soft, whelp," I scold him, horrified by his nearly full drink. "Be thankful that as a doctor, you won't be expected to out drink a Russian informant while trying to secure a deal for a shipment."

He raises an eyebrow. "I thought you were doing everything on the up and up these days?"

I scoff, but he's right. While he's been slaving away to earn those good grades, I've been on my own journey toward self-improvement. The new Donatello Vanici makes his wealth through legal means only. My first step in that direction was securing partial ownership of Hell's Gambit's sole port. The next goal in mind? Plaster the city with enough advertisements to overcome any hostile parties who might be trying to undermine me, be them Antonio Salvatore or Mischa Stepanov himself.

I've already covered the airport to capture any incoming businessmen looking to make connections here. I'd say that in a year, I'll have my own shipping empire. Hell, even without the *mafiya* or the *famiglia* on my side, I'm nearly there anyway. Most of the legitimate commerce flowing into this godforsaken place comes through me.

And I'm proud to say that I haven't stolen or extorted a single dime.

But going on the straight and narrow overnight can't help a man's reputation. There are still plenty of my enemies waiting to strike a blow—from law enforcement to jaded old families. The Salvatores being one of them.

And, as it seems, the Stepanov clan.

"Take Javier when you go up," I command, swiping my hand through Vin's hair. Like a good boy, I'd left the old bodyguard here while at the manor, but I know better than to let Vin wander around alone.

"I don't think I need a nanny, Don," Vin says, but the argument is half-hearted.

"A nanny wouldn't look half as badass holding a gun as Javier," I counter. One of the first professionals I hired after leaving the *famiglia*, I trust the man with my life—more importantly, I trust him with Vin's. "Humor me. If you won't carry a gun on you, at least stick close to someone who will."

He eyes me sideways with far more maturity than a kid twenty-one should possess. "You're drunk, Don." His tone is resigned, belaying a truth that causes me to snatch up my glass rather than face.

He relays it regardless, "Though, to be fair, you're always drunk."

"I prefer the term 'inebriated,'" I counter, saluting him with my drink. At least I'm not falling down pissing myself like my father. A few shots of whiskey on the regular keep me dulled enough to think with some ounce of sanity, let alone sleep until morning. Considering my track record when I was sober, I think it is a fair trade-off. Some nights it actually helps.

Vin disapproves of the habit. "Night, Don," he says in that soft, sad way that makes me flinch with guilt.

"Night, Vinny!" I choke down my drink entirely and call to his retreating back, "As soon as you're married and practicing as some renowned doctor, I won't have to hide behind a bottle ever again."

The sad part? I'm not joking. Maybe then, I'll finally know peace. If my liver holds up, that is. I'm on my third glass when the seat beside me is taken by a figure who wrinkles his nose in disgust.

"How did I know I'd find you here?" Fabio grumbles while waving down the bartender. Rather than hard liquor, he orders a glass of water with a lemon wedge. Typical Fab.

"Shouldn't you be dancing with the younger Stepanova by now?" I ask, raising an eyebrow.

"Stop sulking," Fab scolds. "And for your information, no one got to dance with her. She never showed. At least not before I left."

Frowning, I eye the gilded clock mounted over a fireplace at the other end of the bar. "We left what? Four hours ago?"

He nods, grabbing for the water glass the bartender sets down before him. "Four hours. You should have seen it. We were all milling about like scurrying cockroaches as the *hors d'oeuvres* dwindled. Soon it became a bloodbath for the last glass of champagne. It seems our little Stepanova found other entertainment tonight. A shame." He shakes his head with a wistful sigh. "She was spared a hall of lecherous old men hoping to charm her in pursuit of her father's favor. I'll have you know that poor Antonio Salvatore looked like he might piss himself in disappointment."

I chuckle at the mental image before another takes its place —Salvatore skulking around, hoping to claim the girl for himself. I wouldn't put it past the sick bastard to want someone so young. He can't keep a real woman long enough to tell the difference.

Eyeing Fabio, I ask, "Mischa ever say why I wasn't welcome at his little party?"

I'm more curious than I let on. Anxious too. My foot bounces against the rung of my stool, and those dark thoughts start to gnaw through my alcoholic daze. Virgin mother Mary above, the man is lucky I'm reformed.

"No," Fabio admits, but his grim expression confuses me even more. "I know a death glare when I see it, however. I explained you were my guest, but it did no good. I'd go as far as to say I may have just lost the Stepanov accounts from my clientele because of my association with you."

"Bullshit," I declare, lifting my glass and slamming it against his. "You're the best damn accountant in the game. He'd be a fool to dump you, regardless of your ties to me."

"I'm still convinced you haven't told me everything about what's going on between you two," Fabio suspects, eyeing his lemon wedge. "That look… You don't build up that kind of animosity for nothing. Come clean now, Donatello. You fucked his wife, is that it? She's pretty enough for your tastes with that sweet, wholesome thing and all. If one of Mischa's little whelps is yours, that would explain his feelings a bit."

I scoff at the prospect. "No. Though, if I had, considering how fertile she is, I'd probably have an army of children by now. Then I wouldn't be pining for Mischa's approval, pissing myself with worry every time Vin leaves the country, and I certainly wouldn't be spending my nights at the bar like some pathetic *stronzo*. Bartender!" I flag the man down and shove my empty glass toward him. "Another."

"I'll try to find out," Fabio says softly. "If only to satisfy my own curiosity. The man deals with Salvatore, so it can't be a moral standing. You may be no saint, but I'd bet my soul on you getting into heaven over him."

Even I have to chuckle at that assessment. "Antonio Salvatore may be a cunt, but he's never killed half as many men as I have," I point out. At least not with his bare hands. The pussy prefers to hide behind mercenaries, covering his tracks. Or, as in the case of Gino Mangenello, manipulating others into doing his dirty work. Still, sin is sin, and I've spent my fair share of time in the confessional to be unable to judge anyone.

"It's not a contest, Don," Fab says.

"No. Though if it were, let me add up the score, then. Antonio Salvatore may have gone through four wives in his lifetime, but he lost them all to divorce—"

"His latest one died in a car crash, remember?" Fabio interjects. "The Salieri heiress."

"Yes, but he didn't *fail* them." My voice breaks, but the arrival of a fresh shot of whiskey provides the perfect distraction. I down it and mutter, "He never had to scrape pieces of their brains from his living room floor with his bare hands—"

"God damn it, Don," Fabio exclaims, clearing his throat. He looks visibly pale, though he should. His sister was the woman in question.

My Olivia…

Could I prove that Salvatore was behind the attack that killed her? No. But I more than got my revenge on the sick sons of bitches who carried out the plan. Gino Mangenello suffered the most of them all.

"Another," I demand, striking the counter. But the promise of another drink isn't enough to shut me up. "As vile a cunt as he is, Antonio Salvatore never failed to protect that horrid fucking family of his—"

"Protect?" Fabio sniffs. "The bastard is no father of the year. I've heard more than one rumor about his little girl sporting bruises—the one who lives with him."

"While he may beat his children senseless," I say over him, "he hasn't sold one of them—"

"Enough! Don't even compare yourself to him," Fabio snarls. He levels me with a hallmark stare that serves as one of the many reasons why his reputation is so respected in our circles. Despite all his pomp, Fabio always tells the truth, no matter how cruel it may be. A skill both valued in an accountant as well as a friend.

"What happened wasn't your fault, and you've made the best of it," he insists. "And as for that last thing you mentioned…"

"Selling a child, you mean?" I choke down the rest of my drink and gesture for more. "Vincenzo mentioned her tonight. He whispered her name, and I don't even have the heart to tell him that I'm the reason she's gone."

"You were mad with grief," he says. "That doesn't make it right, but there is no telling what a man would do in that state. I remember how you were back then. God knows, you could have done so much worse…" He shivers, and the horror unfurling across his face is a testament to how hard I've worked to change. Never again will I be that man.

I've gotten clean.

Gotten a soul.

But even so, most days, it feels like God is merely mocking me, testing my patience by the day. What might he throw my way that could finally put me over the edge?

"We all have our lot to live with, Don," Fab says. "Stop punishing yourself. You want to know why? Because even after what you've done, you live with it. You've done your best to repent, and I think you have."

Repent. He makes it sound so damn righteous to forsake the criminal underworld I was raised in. Try to forge a path on the right side of the law. Raise Vincenzo with the skills that will never force him to make the mistakes I did.

"Look at our precious boy," Fabio points out as if reading my mind. "He's studying to be a doctor. *Madonna!* Donella is dancing in her grave."

A tired smile tugs on the corner of my mouth. "She should have married you, you know. Rather than run off with some punk half the man you are. It's the Vanici in us, always leading us to stubborn defiance of our hearts. The only downside is that Vin would have turned out about a foot shorter and two feet wider."

He rolls his eyes and stands, fishing a gold money clip from his suit pocket. "Bah! Vin is fine just the way he is. I wouldn't be half as fanatic a guardian as you are. But as much as you love him, you need to try showing some of that to the man in the mirror."

I scowl at my reflection, barely visible on the polished surface of the bar counter. In that man's dark gaze, I see only evil restrained by sheer willpower. I see violence. A lost soul destined to burn in the fires of hell where it belongs.

Then I blink, and I see a smaller face. Rounder, with wide, searching eyes and a hopeful smile. I don't banish her this time. Reaching out, I stroke the edge of a tiny cheek, feeling only cold, hard wood in response.

"She would be nineteen by now," I say, though I barely hear myself above the surging thump of my own heartbeat. The sound chugs away, mocking me with every steady beat. She's dead, but I still live on. Stubbornly, this body lives, enduring the abuse I've put it through.

"Her birthday was in the spring. Little Safy. Nineteen." I chuckle at the thought of it, picturing her dancing at her own debutante ball. The pain returns like a lance, ripping me apart—but still... My heart keeps beating on. "I promised her once I'd throw her a grand party, can you believe that? She was so excited. God forgive me, I promised her—"

"You've spent too damn long punishing yourself," Fab snarls in disgust. "Enough. I think it's time you strive for a little happiness, huh?"

He sets down a crisp stack of bills. It's more than enough to cover the tab with a hefty tip to spare.

As he turns on his heel, he adds over his shoulder. "Oh, and Vin made me promise not to tell you, but he's already used my card to charge a special gift to help cheer you up. It's in your room."

He winks, and I'm genuinely unnerved. Vin and Fabio's "gifts" are rarely of the desirable variety. But hell, at least I'm distracted by the prospect enough to take another drink and clear my head.

"It better not be another glitter bomb or whatever the fuck those things are called," I grumble, cringing at the memory of the pink sparkles I'd spent weeks trying to wash from my hair the last time the pair felt benevolent enough to give me a present.

Fabio just laughs. "Goodnight."

When I finally tear myself away from the bar, I approach the group of rooms we rented on the hotel's top floor. It was an expense well worth Vin's supposed introduction to high society. I even gave him the pick of the lot with encouragement to enjoy himself with whoever he chose.

Deep down, I know the boy is too much of a goody-goody to take me up on the offer. In contrast to his, my room is a simple suite. I enter it, scanning the narrow space for any hint of Vin's "present."

I don't have to look too hard. On the bed is a silver tray sporting a small white cake, upon which someone wrote in blood-red icing the phrase, "Best Papa." Surrounding it is a crudely formed smiley face crafted out of what appears to be silver condom wrappers and a handful of the best damn cigars money can buy.

"Little bastard," I scoff, swiping my finger through a dollop of icing. I'm smiling as I sample the taste. It isn't bad, though it could be made of shit, and I'd appreciate it no less.

My boy. God bless his devious little soul.

Though maybe more devious than I thought…

A flicker of movement makes me pivot, instinctively reaching for my—still empty—pocket. The lack of a weapon I can easily rectify the second I can get to the safe in the closet. Though, as my eyes narrow over the intruder standing in the corner of the room, I let my hands fall, all thoughts of fighting forgotten.

*Damn.* An appreciative whistle escapes me as I stand straighter and inspect my visitor fully. For the first night in a while, I wholeheartedly regret dulling my senses with so much alcohol.

That's the only explanation for why I might have overlooked the woman watching me from beside the bed. Slender and blond with dark eyes that swallow most of her delicate face, she brings a new meaning to the term present.

"Vinny, Vinny, Vinny," I murmur on a long exhale as my gaze drinks her in. While a bit on the thin side, a tight black dress clings to her like a second skin, revealing more than enough curves to work with. Perky little breasts and a nice round ass to start.

My cock stirs for the first time in weeks, and the sensation triggers a legitimate concern. How long has it been since my last lay?

Too damn long.

"What a damn fine son you are, my boy!" Appreciation thickens my tone, but the blond doesn't simper in gratitude for the compliment.

Instead, she raises her hand, and I stiffen as the light glints off the object she holds. I recognize the shape instantly, and —if anything—my pulse surges faster, excitement heightening my senses to a manic state of amusement.

The little minx has a knife.

# 3

# WILLOW

## TWENTY-FOUR HOURS EARLIER...

One of my composition professors is an accomplished pianist who has performed with various orchestras worldwide. Undeniably talented, he also happens to be a virulent misogynist. Working with him was a trying nine-week-long test of my patience.

I did learn something from him, though—a valuable lesson when it comes to dealing with men outside of my family—most are vain, selfish creatures unable to think beyond a pretty face. It's an aggravating realization to come to, but there's also power in that knowledge.

There is power in destroying some pompous lecher's perceptions of success.

*"A young girl shouldn't be studying music, wasting her beauty away,"* he'd scolded me during our first lesson. *"You should be living your life, thinking pretty thoughts, and finding a husband to whisk you away."*

He'd shouted, of course, presuming that I was deaf instead of mute. With an eyebrow raised in feigned pity, he then suggested I, *"Take a less intense course this semester. I'm disinclined to make any adjustments to compensate for a disability as I don't think it would be fair to the other students. I'm sure you understand, dear."*

I did understand. After all, he had a point. "Compensating" his notoriously ruthless schedule for one lone woman would have been a crime against humanity. So, to ease his concerns, I'd proceeded to play a concerto so complicated he promptly kept his mouth shut for the rest of the class.

"Disabled" or not, I went on to pass that semester with top marks.

Still, I could kick myself for channeling his banal thinking now. Maybe, in some warped, twisted sense of logic, the bastard had a point? On the eve of her nineteenth birthday, a girl should think nothing but pretty, happy thoughts. Fantasies starring men her own age, or silly daydreams, perhaps?

Especially if said girl is rich, well-protected, and healthy. Her life is perfect, and she should be grateful, not fearful. I know firsthand—it could be worse.

Therefore, fully content, someone in my position should be looking toward the future—not at a billboard innocently placed in her path as though fate itself intended it to be there.

Stopping short, I blink several times. Shake my head. I even pinch myself on the wrist so hard the pain lances up my arm.

Nothing makes the sight disappear.

Ironically, I should have been too distracted to even notice such an obscure advert but, for whatever reason, I couldn't miss it.

And it can't be real.

*His* face, staring at me from beneath a glossy veneer, must be the result of some horrific waking nightmare—and it could be… If it weren't for the faint wrinkles around his eyes. I never picture him like this. Aged. Weary, and yet in so many ways, exactly the same. Dark, brooding eyes glowering at the world before him, his mouth curled in a beguiling half-smile.

There's no mistaking him for anyone else—this is Donatello.

Pain rips through my stomach as though I've been punched, building with every new detail I notice. Even in a photograph, vigor screams from his coifed, dark hair and bronzed skin. Both could be the work of Photoshop, yes.

But the man I knew would be too proud to craft such a façade.

It's him. In the background stretches an expanse of water and a succinct title reading: *V Development Group: We build the future you desire.*

A future…

I blink again and rub at my eyes for good measure. This can't be real. Only in my imagination could such a cruel parallel be cast by that one word.

Because by just looking at him, one would never know of the so-called "future," he ripped from me. The life he brutally stole. The beloved friend who put a little girl through unimaginable horror.

Closing my eyes can't erase it. They burn beneath the assault of memories, and it takes everything I have in me to choke them back. Squash the emotions the way my father taught me to.

*"Focus, Mouse,"* Mischa would scold while training me with simple defensive moves in the courtyard of our home. *"You always let your anger get in the way. Move past it! Focus!"*

It was that mindset that drew me to studying music. Sheets of notes required more than just emotion to play effectively. They had to be analyzed rationally, every note carefully planned.

I try to do that now, pushing past the jumbled emotions clawing through my heart.

At the end of it all, one reality remains—I am not that girl anymore. He should mean nothing to the person I am in this moment. This rich, sheltered woman. This accomplished, scholarly musician. Nothing…

But like some lingering infection, he's already inside me anyway, seeping into my veins with every frantic surge of my pulse. The memories descend one after the other, until I'm drowning in them. All I can think about is *him*. Donatello, the man who left me for dead. So sweet, his laugh could infect an entire room of people with joy. One smile from him could charm the sun from the sky.

His love was poison, but as a child, I gladly took every ounce he had to give.

And after seven long years, I've healed from him. Through grit, and luck, and pain, I salvaged the life he tried to destroy. I've found a new family with which to enjoy it. A new protector. A father.

A new life.

Nineteen is a significant birthday in the world I belong to now, denoting so many things—freedom first among them, womanhood overall. The day a girl shakes the bonds of childhood forever and takes her rightful place in society. It may be more symbolic in this case, given my real birthday was months ago—but I am no longer Safiya Mangenello, and Willow Stepanova will achieve this milestone with fanfare.

On this one day, I should be the happiest…

"Miss?" a voice beckons from the exit of this private terminal. I look over to find a man with black hair shorn close to his head, standing at the door. His dark suit and watchful gray eyes set him apart from any other airport customer—even before someone would happen to notice the gun professionally tucked beneath his jacket. He's tall enough that I have to crane my head back to meet his gaze.

For his benefit, I force a smile, but I can't seem to make myself move. Not yet. Slowly, I return my attention to the billboard, praying that it's vanished, only a delusion after all.

Dark, glittering eyes meet mine mockingly, crushing that hope. He's still here—in more ways than one. An address in the corner of the advert refers to a location in Hell's Gambit —a port city so close it's laughable. I scan it over and over, burning every last letter into my memory. Only then do I turn away and continue forward.

With every step, trivial observations creep into my brain, and I gladly let them, trading the past for stupid, nineteen-year-old thoughts. I'm overdressed. It's still stifling hot this early in summer. Sweat slips beneath the collar of my blouse as I exit the airport for the sweltering fresh air. I'd give anything to trade this beige wool skirt and sweater for the light linen shifts I used to wear as a child.

Holding the door for me, my father's trusted bodyguard, Evgeni, stands beside a cart containing many of my suitcases. He smiles the moment I'm in view, but I know him too well. His eyes scan my face with undisguised concern.

"It seems your mood has changed between you stepping off the plane and now," he teases. "I'm sure you heard the news? About your not-so-secret birthday party, that is." He makes a show of cupping his hand around his mouth, his voice a mock whisper. "I think your papa's invited half the world by now."

I blink to show I'm unsurprised, and he chuckles. As suspected, I know. Mischa couldn't keep a secret, even with me out of the country. He's too proud, not to mention unsubtle, in posing many "hypothetical" questions regarding which kind of party ornaments I might enjoy during our video calls.

"You're too smart for your own good," Evgeni remarks as we approach the black car waiting nearby. "If I didn't know better, I'd think you made your flight come in two hours early on purpose. Your papa had a whole grand welcome planned, but you've managed to skirt it. So far, at least." He winks, alluding to the event I've both dreaded and anticipated for weeks.

"Don't be too mad," he says as we approach the sleek sedan my father sent to collect me. He loads my suitcases into the trunk and faces me, rubbing his hands together. "If my daughter got into that fancy school of yours, I think I'd at least throw her a party, even if she hated them."

I smile warily at that, but I can't shake a niggling sense of dread that has loomed over this date for weeks. Mischa means well, I know he does—but he has no idea what the symbolism of this birthday means, not even after seven years since he adopted me.

Nineteen. It's a chilling reminder of everything I've lost. It's a sickening anniversary of the day I became someone else apart from who I was born as. A shadow. A mouse. Someone trapped in limbo between two worlds. Two families.

I can't forget his voice…

*"I will throw you a grand debutante celebration when you come of age, little cucciola. No other shall compare…"*

"I'm not supposed to tell you," Evgeni warns, his voice cutting through the memory. Blinking, I turn to find him watching me in a way that warns distracting me was his goal. "So if you snitch, I'll deny it, but I hear he's gone all out for you, your papa. He even bought a suit. Give it a chance; you may find that you enjoy having a little fun."

He crinkles his mouth, seeming so much younger than a man in his early thirties.

"Come on, let's get going." Clapping his hands, he ushers me into the back of the vehicle and then claims the driver's seat. "And, only for you, I'll let you decide if I let your papa know in advance that you got in early. If you want, you can mount a surprise all your own. Turn the tables, so to speak. Should I call?"

Even the thought of arriving to fanfare and drama makes me cringe.

"Thought so," Evgeni says with a nod.

He takes off toward the countryside, and the sprawling fields and swaths of green forests usher in a nostalgia potent enough to distract from everything else. I've been so desperate for the change in scenery, and a sigh escapes me, soft and wistful. I've missed this place. While away in Vienna, longing for my old home plagued me constantly. The stone manor, with its familiar walls, draped in ivy and the abundant rose gardens dotting the property. I've missed Mischa and his booming laugh, and my mother's soft grace. I've missed the many children who fill the manor with more noise and clamor than the busiest orchestra.

But beneath those charming memories, my past festers. Ripped open by one chance sighting, not even the delightful views from my window can soothe the wound. He corrupts me, creeping into my skull. Donatello, dwelling in a nearby city. It almost seems too cruel to be reality. I've pined for home, but now I wish for nothing more than to be back on the plane.

It's strange. Time used to seem endless when I was a child. Despite how overwhelming a stretch it feels like now, in reality, I'll only have a few short months before I'll be back in Vienna—an education made possible only by the man who took me in when everyone else in my life turned their back.

Mischa deserves my focus, no one else.

"Don't stress about the party," Evgeni calls from the front seat, still troubled by my expression. Apparently, he thinks the party is the cause of my unease, but I don't have the courage to correct him. "It isn't until tomorrow night, after all. If you really don't want it, I'm sure your father would cancel it if you asked him."

He's right, and I purse my lips at the prospect. Mischa would do anything I asked him to—but a man like him isn't the type to plan parties without a reason well beyond some trivial age milestone. Years ago, another man spoke of my far-off debutante debut in more stark terms. *Your ball will be the best in the world,* he'd boasted. *No one will doubt which family you come from.*

Mischa's pride is entwined with this celebration as much as his love is.

As I settle into the back seat, I try to imagine what such a party might look like. Something grand, but presumably no different than any gala or performance I've suffered through this past year. And yet, it promises to be worlds apart from the modest events that peppered my childhood. Before...

My life was even more sheltered than it is now. Most girls would be embarrassed by the lack of traditional milestones, I think. I had no real mother to guide me then—mine was too busy partying. No, my modest presents were always clumsily wrapped by a man who could master a weapon but never understood the concept of a ribbon. Still, he tried if only to make me happy. Even my cakes, he would bake himself, coloring the icing whatever happened to be my favorite hue that year. Without fail, he'd attempt to write my name across the top and always run out of room, forcing him to condense it into his affectionate moniker— Safy. Afterward, he would sing to me in Italian despite his preference that we practice English at home. To make me laugh, he'd sing in as high a pitch as he could, straining his deep baritone so that it comically broke as the song went on. *Happy birthday to you, my Safiya…*

His voice has never left me. Long after he turned his back on me and walked away, I can still hear him, echoing inside my skull. *"Do with her what you will,"* he'd said to the stranger keeping me restrained. *"I don't care."*

My throat thickens as my eyes blur, obscuring my view from the windows. Desperately, I blink back any threat of tears, choking them down. The past is the past—and I made peace with mine a long time ago.

Or maybe I haven't…

The billboard just gives me an excuse to confess the obvious—he will always live in my head, smiling that goofy, deceitful grin while balancing my lopsided cake on one hand and a present on the other.

"Miss Willow?"

I look over to find the back seat door open and Evgeni standing on the other end. The car has stopped, I realize. Before me looms a stoic structure formed of gray stone and creeping ivy.

"We're home," Evgeni says, extending his hand for me. "True to my word, I haven't called to inform anyone. That's bought you a few minutes of peace, but the sooner you face your parents, the sooner everyone else can pretend you won't notice the parade of caterers streaming in through the back."

Eager for a new distraction, I scramble out and crane my neck to take in the house fully. As my gaze drifts over the familiar architecture, my lips quirk, and my heart swells with pride.

"It might not be some fancy university," Evgeni remarks, "but I guess it does hold some charm, doesn't it?"

I nod. Stepanov Manor is relatively old by most standards, lacking the modern embellishments that adorn the fancy mansions of the wealthier students at the conservatory. Even so, its worn stone walls convey a familial softness no other dwelling could come close to. Expansive emerald lawns lush with rose gardens create a world apart from the harsh reality waiting beyond these walls.

It's paradise. Always, when I'm here, it's like being transported to another realm, one where the harsher realities of the world could never encroach. A place where someone like Donatello Vanici doesn't exist, and where my only identity is that of a beloved daughter.

But, as I approach the servant's entrance, I have no delusions about the cost of such peace. Much like my idyllic childhood, all of this security and luxury is made possible by the sheer efforts of one man who rules it all.

And no matter how beautiful it seems…

This paradise is paid for with blood.

# 4

# WILLOW

"Pretend to be surprised," Evgeni warns as he hauls my bags through the servant's entrance. We're alone in this spacious back hallway, but already telltale signs of the impending party are obvious. Stacks of boxes clutter the space, leaving barely enough room to reach the nearby breakroom beside the stairs. An audible commotion warns of a flurry of chaos taking place throughout the house. Paramount among the noises? Child-like shouting.

"Hurry." Evgeni nods to the stairs and winks. "I'll have these brought up and unpacked later. You have maybe five minutes before the others sniff you out, so enjoy it."

I start up the back stairwell feeling my throat tighten. The wooden floors creak beneath my steps as if welcoming me back, and I can't resist trailing my fingers along the worn beige walls. Excitement tinges the air, giving the old structure a renewed sense of wonder. Six months away might as well have been six years. Before I even reach my bedroom on the second floor, I have a grim suspicion as to what might await me. As expected, I've barely pushed my door open when I see it, draped over my bed with loving care.

My hand falls to my side as the door sways, obscuring the sight from view for a split-second before revealing it again in breathtaking glory—a gown fit for any debutante.

I'm immediately flashed back to over seven years ago, the first time someone presented me with a similar dress. That garment had been part of a ruse in which I was meant to smuggle drugs for a criminal. It might as well have been a funeral dress.

The presentation this time is admittedly far different. I creep toward it, tallying up the differences as I go. A soft, creamy off-white, this gown spans the length of my childhood bed. Tentatively, I run my fingers over a bodice formed of delicate interlocking lace and marvel at the feel. Silk, I suspect, buttery soft to the touch.

It's beautiful—but much like my first white dress, the purpose of this newer one is more figurative than anything else. Wearing it, I'll be a dove, finally let loose from her protective cage.

I'll be presented to the world as a Stepanova.

"Do you like it?" a voice calls tentatively from the doorway. I turn to find Ellen, my adoptive mother, standing there, her blue eyes as perceptive as always. "I thought I'd heard someone moving around this wing two hours too early. Welcome home!"

She approaches me, cradling her swollen belly with one hand and her neatly coiled brunette hair with the other. As she eyes the dress, a hesitant smile flits across her lips, making her seem even younger than she already does. If she claimed to be my age, I doubt anyone would be able to tell the difference from a glance. The only flaw in her delicate beauty is a series of faint, silver scars on the left side of her face, strategically obscured by a few loose brown curls.

"I know it's a bit much," she admits, referring to the dress. "I wasn't sure of the style, but Mischa insisted. What do you think?"

Whatever she sees in my expression emboldens her to approach the bed.

Gingerly, she drapes the fabric over her arm before turning to me. "May I?" she asks.

I nod, and she positions the garment against my body, circling to stand behind me. I catch sight of myself in a floor-length mirror in the far corner. The girl I find staring back could be a stranger, but I can't tell if it's because her dress is so beyond my usual fashion scope.

Or because her face is so unnaturally blank.

"It's going to look stunning on you," Ellen murmurs while smoothing a stray bit of hair behind my ear. "You are stunning. I know I've blathered on about it so many times, but..." Her lips strain to conceal another smile. "We are so very proud of you. Mischa can't stop talking about your accomplishments, and the girls were pestering me all week about your arrival. I'm surprised you even made it inside the house without getting ambushed—"

"You're back." As if on cue, a slender boy slips across the doorway, proving her point moot. Whip-thin, with wild blond curls, he's like a miniature version of Ellen. Her smile widens as he draws up to her side.

"Why didn't you tell me she was home already, Aunt Ellen?" he demands, his tone as inquisitive as always.

"Eli, darling, I've only just found out, like you." She pinches his cheek playfully, laughing as he swats her off. Turning to me, she cocks an eyebrow, her gaze skeptical. "It seems Miss Willow thought she could sneak in and circumvent the surprise your papa has planned for her."

"I told him she wouldn't like it," Eli smugly declares, crossing his arms. The motion makes him look older than eleven. He's grown so much since I've been gone. Some of the baby fat has left his cheeks, revealing a bone structure enhancing his resemblance to the woman standing beside him. Wearing a plain white shirt and jeans, he could be a carbon copy of Mischa as well.

More nostalgia constricts my chest. I remember the days we used to play together in these very halls. At night, we'd sneak out to the gardens and race beneath the moon. I couldn't love any brother more, be them related to me by blood or not.

*But he's not the first*, a cruel voice in my mind whispers. I try to ignore the memories, but they unfurl anyway. Those of another boy, older, but no less tolerant of me. Always patient, he used to braid my hair to keep it clean before we played hide and seek. Wide from behind his glasses, his brown eyes only ever radiated kindness and joy. Vincenzo...

"Will?" Eli's voice draws me back, and I find him watching me with that mature curiosity again. Before he can say anything else, I step forward, my arms outstretched. He blinks, but within seconds he's throwing his arms around me as Ellen gently moves the gown out of reach.

"The twins, reunited at last," she says with a wistful sigh.

I smile at the moniker—our combined nickname, despite our difference in ages, setting us apart from the other faction of this growing family. *The little ones.*

And as if conjured by the thought alone, the oldest of said faction comes storming into my room, several inches taller than when I saw him last.

"Get ready, Mama," he declares, placing his hands on his hips. Dark brown curls fall haphazardly into his eyes, the same piercing blue as his mother's. His stern, serious expression is all Mischa, however. "The girls are fussing again, and—Willow!" Argument forgotten, he throws himself toward me, muscling in beside Eli. I extend my arm around him, marveling even more at his height. Not so little anymore, he comes up to Eli's chest, who is already an inch over my modest stature.

"Careful, Ivan," his mother warns. "You'll knock her over. She's only just got home… Oh, not again!"

Cocking my head, I can easily pick up on the sound that triggered her alarm—high-pitched shrieking growing louder by the second. The next figure to teeter through my doorway just so happens to be the source of the noise—a toddler with blond curls and amber eyes wearing a tiny pink dress.

Spotting her mother, she bursts into tears. "Jona kicked me!" she declares, scampering forward to bury her face in Ellen's skirt. "She kicked me and took my doll!"

"It was Aljona's doll," Ivan corrects, pointing a finger at her disapprovingly. "You took it from her first. Then you broke it and gave her the pieces."

"Marnie!" Ellen inclines her head sharply, suddenly stern. "Is that true?"

The little girl stiffens, her cheeks flushing pink with guilt. "She started it."

"Oh, is that so? Where is Jona now?" Ellen asks, smoothing her fingers over her daughter's curls.

Ivan rolls his eyes with an exasperation well beyond his six and a half years. "Where else?"

From behind him, Eli flashes a crooked grin, and I can sense what's on his mind—*nothing's changed.*

"Let's find her and sort this out," Ellen says tiredly. Looking at me, she shrugs. "Would you mind juggling one, while I juggle the other?" She coaxes Marnie toward me.

Sniffling, the girl tugs on my hand until I scoop her into my arms and then proceeds to hide her face in the crook of my shoulder. As I start after Ellen, Marnie lifts her head long enough to murmur, "I missed you, Willa."

I tighten my arms around her, surprised by just how much I missed her too. How I missed them all. My first year away should have been a godsend. For once, I was no longer a burden, free to earn back every bit of kindness Mischa and his wife—my adopted parents—have bestowed upon me.

Now that I'm back, I can't ignore the feeling that's been itching at my psyche long before the resurgence of Donatello.

Doubt.

Guilt.

That unsettling, lingering pain I've tried to suppress for seven years. It's foolish to dwell on anything other than gratitude—I know that. Mischa and Ellen took me in and loved me as their own, but there is no denying the truth lurking underneath. That despite their affection and generosity, I've never really belonged here. It's obvious to anyone looking from the outside in. After all, my age and features set me apart from the Stepanovs in ways that nothing else could. Eli and I were "the twins" for more than just our closeness. We were both misfits in this world.

Cherished, wanted misfits, but still misfits all the same.

"Is your papa in his study, Marnie?" Ellen calls from the base of the grand staircase that serves as the heart of the manor. Lost in thought, I barely manage to catch my footing on the next step.

"I think so," Ivan says, answering for his sister. "And Jona will be hiding behind him, of course."

I chuckle internally, forgetting my dilemma for now. Mischa Stepanov strikes fear into the hearts of most men, and yet his daughters have the poor man wrapped around their fingers.

Sure enough, we round the corner to the mouth of his study and find him sitting at his desk in the center of the massive room, scanning a stack of documents. He's aged slightly, the lines around his mouth growing more pronounced. But with his blond hair hanging loose around his shoulders and dark eyes narrowed in concentration, he's no less formidable than the man I remember. Looking at him, I'd assume he's hard at work if it weren't for the hint of pink fabric peeking from behind his chair.

"Is Aljona with you?" Ellen asks though her raised eyebrow reveals that she's spied the same telling clue I have.

Sighing, Mischa sets his papers aside and steeples his fingers. His brows draw together, enhancing the harsh planes of his face and the effect is admittedly intimidating. Most people only ever see this man, but as his gaze falls over the girl in my arms, his jaw twitches slightly, betraying a rare hint of softness no one could deny. As his eyes cut up to mine, he winks.

"Aljona would like to initiate a peace treaty," he says to Marnie, his voice booming, accent heavy. "Will you hear her terms, Marnie?"

"No!" Marnie grumbles from my chest. "I don't want stupid terms! I want my doll—"

"It was wrong of you to take her doll," Mischa says over her, but a gentle edge lessens his otherwise stern tone. "And it was wrong of her to kick you." He inclines his head, directing his voice to anyone who just so happens to be hiding behind him. "You both acted inappropriately. Therefore, the only way I can see to settle this matter is..." He throws his hands into the air with a sigh of defeat. "I will buy you two new dolls, and you can keep them separate—"

"Mischa!" Ellen shakes her head. From the firm set of her shoulders, I suspect this is just another battle in a longstanding war between them. "You can't keep spoiling them. They'll never learn." Hands on her hips, she raises her voice, "I propose a punishment of no dessert for the both of you."

"No!" With a cry of protest, Marnie wiggles from my arms. At the same time, another girl pokes her head from behind Mischa's chair, scrambling to her feet. Straight brown hair and the fact that she's nearly a foot taller sets her apart from her sister.

"But Mama!" they whine in unison.

"But Mama," Mischa intones with a pained grimace. "Can we not have both punishment and peace?"

He reaches into his pocket and withdraws two brightly colored items that make the girls squeal and crowd him, jumping in excitement.

Ellen scoffs. "Sweets?"

Mischa doesn't seem to catch the disapproval in her tone. "Apologize to your mother, both of you," he demands, unnervingly stern once more.

"We're sorry," the girls sing in unison with twin smiles, the picture of sweetness.

Mischa can't resist, sporting a grin to match. "Now, Mama…" He bats his eyes imploringly, drawing giggles from his cohorts. "One little treat?"

Ellen rolls her eyes. "It doesn't matter what I say. You'll just sneak it to them anyway—but still no dessert."

With their current goodies—two lollipops—the girls don't seem to mind.

"Mine's bigger," Aljona, the older of the two at the age of five, declares, shoving her lollipop into her mouth. She takes off with Marnie, nearly four, right on her heels.

"Not, uh!"

"I'll make sure they don't kill each other," Ivan says before huffing after his siblings. "As payment, I want four lollies, Papa," he calls back.

Mischa chuckles with pride as he watches them go. When he finally returns his attention to his wife, his eyes fall to her stomach rather than her disapproving stare. "How did I do?" he asks innocently.

Crossing her arms, Ellen shrugs. "Better than last time. At least you plied them with candy and not piles of toys. They will drain you dry if you let them. You need to learn to tell them no."

He shrugs indignantly. "I can tell them no—"

"And mean it," Ellen corrects, sliding a hand down to her belly. "Let's hope you practice in time for the next one. Speaking of children, aren't you even going to welcome your oldest home?"

Mischa looks up sharply, breaking into a full beaming grin. "You!" Lurching to his feet, he circles his desk in mere seconds. "What are you doing here early?"

I'm in his arms before I can even explain.

"She snuck in," Ellen says. "Her plane got in early, and Evgeni apparently forgot to call ahead. She's already seen the dress."

"About that..." Mischa pulls back, his face uncharacteristically red. "It's a small gathering, Mouse—"

"Tell her the truth," Ellen goads. "She won't be any less angry when she finds out."

"So...it's more like a ball," he admits with a sheepish grin that undercuts his hardened exterior a second time. His eyes sparkle, and it's painfully apparent how much this event means to him. "Your debutante ball. It's time you were presented to the world for who you are, Willow Stepanova. Especially so all those rich fuckers at the conservatory know that you aren't some random fling."

I wince but force a smile rather than confess that—as far as the men at the conservatory go—no man has expressed interest in me at all, as a fling or otherwise.

"And to share how proud we are of you," Ellen says, gently rephrasing his words. "I tried to keep it casual, but Mischa spared no expense. You'd be surprised by how well he's done. He even designed the centerpieces—"

"Creative investments," Mischa corrects. His calculating frown resembles that of a brooding tactician more than any party planner. "Investments into your future. Hell, even some of those high society bastards will be there."

I can hear the pride in his voice but guilt grips my chest. It must show on my face as well, because Ellen turns to me, brushing her fingers along my cheek.

"What's wrong, darling?"

"She's probably exhausted," Mischa says, returning to his desk. "Go get some rest before the girls decide to demand a year's worth of play from you. But first…" Much as he had with the sweets, he turns around to reveal yet another surprise balanced on his calloused palm—a polished wooden box. "A little present to celebrate your birthday."

"One of many," Ellen corrects with a conspiratorial smile.

He lifts the lid, and I swallow hard at the sight of what lurks beneath it on a bed of blue velvet—a string of pearls finer than anything I've ever owned. I can't take my eyes off them.

"My daughter, the pianist," Mischa says, chuckling in amusement at my expression. He lifts the pearls and returns to me, holding the strand between his fingers. "I must admit that's something I never thought I'd say."

"We are proud of you," Ellen murmurs. Stepping behind me, she lifts my hair from my neck as Mischa secures the necklace around it.

I look down, watching the delicate pearls settle against my collar. In so many ways, my transformation feels complete. Safiya Mangenello is dead and gone. Willow Stepanova stands in her place. And yet, I can't ignore the tiny voice in my head whispering...

*For how long?*

"Now, get some rest." Mischa shoos me off with a wave of his hand. "And you, wife—" he glares at Ellen. "Tell me how we ensure this next one isn't a girl."

I slip into the hall, trailing one hand along the worn, though ornate wallpaper while the other fiddles with the pearls around my neck. Lost in thought, I nearly trip over Eli, crouched within a doorway a few paces from the study. Coincidentally, just within eavesdropping distance.

"What's wrong with you?" he demands, rising to his feet.

I shake my head to indicate nothing, but he frowns, honing his gaze on my face. I have to resist the urge to turn away, revealing the lie for what it is. I'd forgotten how perceptive he can be, even at his age. No one else can read me like he can.

"You've been weird since you got back," he declares, crossing his arms over his chest. "And you're taking this whole party thing well. Any other time, you'd raise hell if Aunt Ellen tried to make you wear a fancy dress."

I feel my eyes widen, and his cheeks redden, negating some of his maturity. "I can say hell," he mutters, glancing nervously over his shoulder. "Sometimes."

I shrug and continue down the hall. Anyone else would accept the gesture as an end to the conversation—but not Eli. Stubbornly, he's right on my heels.

"It's not nothing," he argues as if reading my mind. "The last time Aunt Ellen bought you a dress, you avoided her for two days."

A rebellious act that feels so childish now. Maybe it's the year I've spent away that's reshaped my mindset? Those spoiled, pampered artists corrupted my more practical ways. Gone is the girl who used to play in the mud and eschew the thought of any dresses.

The real world taught her the true cost of freedom. Life is all an act requiring a fitting costume, like any role in a performance would. To belong to this sheltered realm, you follow its few, hallowed rules. You don't fracture the simple, pretty melody you're required to uphold, and your life can be just as beautiful.

Why resist that?

I never have to worry that my tuition will be paid. Protected from the horrors of the world, I have a bodyguard assigned to me at all times. While I was away, Mischa arranged for a hairdresser on-call for performances. My clothing is tailored to my measurements, and the place I call home is an ancestral manor with miles of land to its name.

My future will consist of traveling with the most accomplished musicians before some rich man snags me as his wife, all with my father's permission...

*Liar*, a part of me hisses. The sighting of Donatello just reinforces the opposite reality—Mischa isn't my father. Ellen isn't my mother, and for all their love and kindness, I am not their daughter.

I wasn't Donatello's, either.

My real parents abandoned me at the mercy of a monster who couldn't even do me the courtesy of devouring me himself. He threw me away and never looked back.

I squeeze my eyes shut against the memories. When I reopen them, I'm in my room again, standing before the bed. I finger the dress still lying here, snatching handfuls of the fabric. Maybe it's the color that softens me to it? Or that it's so similar to the dress I'd been meant to wear when Mischa first acquired me.

This arrangement of fabric symbolizes the twisted full circle my life has become—I'm the heiress of an empire that would have chewed me up and spit me back out.

"You can't ignore me, Will."

Eli's here as well, I find, watching me from the doorway. "You've been quiet, too," he admonishes.

I feign surprise and point to my mouth.

He rolls his eyes, unamused. "You know what I mean." He raises his hands, letting his fingers contort. *You just stood there and let them talk around you. You never let anyone talk around you.*

I shouldn't be surprised that he's improved so much with signing despite me being away. Knowing him, he's been practicing.

*I've grown up,* I sign back.

He shakes his head, still motioning with his hands. *No. Something happened. I know it. What's wrong? Did something happen at that stupid school?*

*No.* I insist, turning to stare from the nearest window rather than face him directly.

An education overseas gave me an even more insular upbringing, and while music isn't an exciting profession, it's safe. Much like the most carefully composed concerto, it's beautiful, formed of predictable notes, and contained order. You can stray from the rules only so far and still create something incredible.

Music healed me from hate.

Or perhaps it's become more of a Band-Aid in some ways—one I'm terrified to rip off.

I can't be that scared, angry little girl again.

I won't let even his memory steal my life from me a second time. Shaking my head, I banish him only to discover that Eli's still watching me.

*Will you be at the party?* I ask, changing the subject. *I can ask Mischa to make an exception.*

"It's not him I'm worried about," Eli grumbles out loud, wrinkling his button nose. "Come with me?"

Grateful for the change in subject, I follow him into the hall and into the wing opposite this one where Ellen, Mischa, and the children stay.

"Mama?" Eli calls as we near a suite of rooms. We've barely rounded the corner when a slender woman with long dark hair coiled into a braid appears at the other end of the hall. Anna. A shapeless brown dress helps her to almost blend into the wood-paneled walls. It's her quiet beauty that gives away her resemblance to Ellen, her half-sister. Otherwise, they're as opposite as night and day.

"There you are, darling," she calls, sighing in relief. "Oh, and Willow! I didn't know you were home so soon. Welcome back."

She steps forward to throw her slender arms around me. While she's distracted, Eli chooses this moment to pounce.

"Do you think I could stay up late tomorrow night, Mama?" he asks. "Willow wants me at her party. Please?" He's as shameless as Aljona or Marnie, batting his eyelashes charmingly with a grin to match.

Anna bites her lower lip. "I don't know, darling…" Hesitantly, she runs her fingers through his hair, eventually returning his smile. "I'll think about it."

He throws his arms around her with unbridled joy. "Thank you!"

She kisses his cheek, smoothing his hair one final time. "I suspect you two have a lot to catch up on," she says, winking at me. "I'll let you enjoy your time."

The moment she's out of view, I turn to Eli, signing, *You were worried about her? She would give you the moon if you asked for it.*

He shrugs. "You know she doesn't like being around a lot of people."

He's right. She and Eli reside in the most secluded wing of the manor for a reason. Even during the years I lived here, I could count the interactions I've had with her alone on one hand, and rarely does she join events that aren't restricted to the family. After the death of her father, Ivan, two years ago, she's been even more reclusive.

I've heard Mischa and Ellen mention snippets of her past in hushed whispers; that she had been held captive for years by a rival family.

I've known her to be nothing but kind; however, it's obvious that Eli is her sole devotion. Anyone might think she was his biological mother. Once, a few years ago, I'd gathered up the nerve to ask him: *if Ellen is your mother, why do you call her "Aunt?"*

His answer, as always, portrayed a logic well beyond his young years. "Aunt Ellen doesn't need me as much," he said wistfully. "My mama does."

I didn't know what he meant then. Ellen needed him—anyone with eyes could see that. A lesser woman would have shunned Anna from his life, doing her best to assert herself in her natural role. But as selfless as she is, Ellen knew what he wanted, and was brave enough to make that sacrifice for him.

From Eli's perspective, the reasoning was more childish and, in some ways, tragic. Ellen had more than enough children with Mischa. Anna? She had none. In his analytical brain, that wasn't fair, so he rectified it as only a child could.

"Will?" He grabs my hand, his gaze more piercing than ever. "You zoned out again. Maybe you are tired? Playing music all day would make me want to sleep too." He smiles in that impish way his younger siblings have yet to master.

I roll my eyes and sign, *We can't all be soldiers like you.*

It's a strange thing for a boy to aspire to be—especially one with so much wealth and opportunity at his disposal. On the other hand, it's an obvious outcome to anyone who knows him. While he loves Anna and Ellen, he worships

Mischa, a man who sneers at anything not involving fighting tactics or knives. Or at least he used to. It's strange what children can do to men like him. With Ivan, another dutiful mini-soldier, he was gentle but still stern.

But when Aljona was born, he barely raised his voice in her presence. And when Marnie came? He had the various displays of weapons hanging in his office quietly replaced with paintings.

It wasn't as if the girls made him softer, oh no.

Mischa guards his family jealously. The bigger it grows, the tighter his grip becomes on the world around us. God help the poor men who fall for Jona or Marnie.

Or me.

"I'm going to find the others," Eli declares, apparently bored with our reunion already. "Go get some sleep."

I watch him skip off, and a part of me throbs in a subtle, aching way. I miss the days when I could have raced off with him and wrestled in the dirt with the others. Our gap in ages never really mattered, until one day it did.

And it became more apparent than ever what an anomaly I am in this family. Like an off-note in an otherwise flawless aria. You don't notice it at first—perhaps one might assume it's part of the song. But the more you play the piece, the more pronounced that one note sounds.

Until it's all you can hear, grating above the rest.

Destroying the otherwise harmony.

# 5

## WILLOW

*I* can't sleep for long. Restless, I start to wander the halls, scanning the shadows that drape the hallways and the occasional painting I pass. Judging from the quiet, everyone else is already asleep this time of night, leaving the manor an eerie shell of its daytime chaos. It feels so strange to be alone in the heart of such a bustling hive of activity.

Until suddenly, I'm not. A figure appears near the top of the grand staircase, his silhouette recognizable even in the dark. With a nod of his chin, he beckons me closer. "Mouse," he says, his old childhood nickname for me, given my obvious silence. "Come."

He descends the steps, leaving me to follow him into his study.

"I've had to learn pretty damn quick how to read your expressions," he declares, observing me from behind his desk. I doubt he's even gone to bed yet, considering he's still wearing his clothing from earlier. Sharp with intensity, his dark eyes scan my face. "You're thinking about something, and I doubt it has anything to do with a party," he gruffly surmises. "You and I never mince words, so tell me what's on your mind."

He's right, but I don't even know how to broach this topic. What to say. That I've been thinking too much of the past? Wanting answers I shouldn't pursue.

"I know that look," Mischa grumbles, apparently more perceptive than I've given him credit for. "You have the same look about you that Eli did when he asked me what happened to the bastard who sired him. It's only understandable; you're thinking about the past."

I swallow hard, caught off guard by the admission. Eli never once mentioned his biological father, at least not to me. Mischa has always been "Papa" in his world. As far as I know, his real father had been a monster who separated him from his own mother at birth.

"I'll tell you the same thing I told him," Mischa says gruffly. "I'll answer whatever questions you have, but I will not coddle you, and nothing I may say will ever change my love for you." His eyes shine in the dim glow cast by a sole lamp, and I feel a painful mixture of hope and dread crawl up my throat.

With a wave of his hand, he indicates the leather chair before his desk while he claims the one across from it.

"What is it you want to know?" he asks, folding his hands before him as I sit.

I feel my fingers twitch helplessly, unsure of where to start. Unlike Eli, signing is not his forte, so I reach for a slip of blank paper resting on his desk, and he hands me a pen.

Cautiously I write a single question—what do you know about me?

It's a question I've dreaded proposing for so long. I'm holding my breath in anticipation of his answer.

"About the man who sold you?" he wonders, cutting to the heart of the matter.

I wince. Hearing it out loud triggers a wave of emotions I didn't expect. Pain. Confusion. Sadness. Rage…

*Donatello.* Once upon a time, he could have been known only as the man I admired more than anyone else in the world. The man who labored to acknowledge my birthday every single year in lieu of my parents. Who swore to protect me.

All lies. He'll forever be regarded merely as the man who sold me.

I've never asked Mischa about him, because I never wanted to know just how much my new guardian might know about my past. About Donatello. And if he did know…

Why let him live so close to us, in a city just a car ride away? Why let him live at all? Why let him thrive?

The thoughts are vengeful and childish, but they fester no matter how hard I try to ignore them. Mischa loves me; I know he does—but an irrational sense of betrayal makes it harder to think clearly.

Because if he does care for me so much, then why hasn't he hunted down Donatello on his own? Why hasn't he punished the man who hurt me?

All I can see is his face. His smile, mocking me seven years later.

"Nicolai never told me his name," Mischa says, referring to another man I've strived to forget—Nicolai Baryshnikov, a slave trader, among other things. The same man he unwittingly rescued me from. "What do you remember?"

I lift the pen, pressing the nib to the page, but as the seconds pass, I can't bring myself to write anything more than a faint, hollow line. Shaking my head, I set the pen aside altogether.

"I won't tell you what to feel," Mischa says with a heavy sigh. "But maybe it's for the best that you don't remember."

He rises and approaches me. His hands settle over my shoulders, urging me to my feet, and I'm in his arms again, crushed to his chest.

"You are my daughter," he tells me. "Mine. No one will ever harm you. Never. Do you understand?"

I can only nod, burying my face against his shoulder the way I would when I was a child. My eyes burn, welling with tears I don't have the energy to fight back anymore. They spill down my cheeks unchecked as Mischa withdraws.

"Good girl," he praises, running his fingers through my hair. "Now go. Get some rest."

As I leave, an unexpected sense of relief loosens the tension in my shoulders I wasn't aware of until now. For whatever reason, his ignorance comforts me. It makes it easier to breathe and think ahead as a woman in my position should. Donatello Vanici is dead to me. Tomorrow, I'll be presented to the world as a Stepanova, and I wouldn't have it any other way.

I exit the study with my head held high and nearly run into a slim figure lurking beyond the doorway. Ellen. Her golden-brown hair streams loose down her shoulders, and a white nightgown sets her apart from the darkness around her.

"Willow? What are you doing up?" She strokes my cheeks, her smile strained. "I forgot to tell Mischa about the final arrangements for tomorrow," she says, slipping past me. "Goodnight."

I don't know what it is about her expression that makes me swallow in alarm.

Still, I start down the hall, but as murmuring voices catch my ear, I quietly circle back.

"You were eavesdropping," Mischa scolds, his voice easily reaching me as I falter just beyond the doorway.

"And you were lying," Ellen counters haughtily. "You lied to her. Why?"

"I don't know what you're talking about," Mischa says, but his tone gives him away. Ellen is the only one capable of wringing that gruff, raw baritone from him. Guilt.

"You've known the identity of the man who sold her for seven years," she declares. "In fact, you've been waging a campaign to keep him away from this area—and don't look at me like that. You aren't as secretive as you think when it comes to your business arrangements. Why didn't you tell her? I could understand if you thought she wasn't ready, but we decided together to tell Eli about his—"

"Because he's not dead," Mischa growls. "Eli? He is like you, able to square the past and leave it buried. Mouse? She is like me. I'm sure she remembers him. His name. Everything he did to her—but if he is not acknowledged out loud, he doesn't exist. She can go on living in peace. But if she knows he's still alive? Still breathing, walking, existing in this world. She won't ever let go. Ever. I don't want that for her." His voice breaks, hoarse and hollow. A sudden thump alludes to him striking his desk with a clenched fist, and I imagine Ellen approaching him, wrapping her slender arms around him from behind.

"Tell me what is on your mind," she pleads.

"You once fantasized about a life of peace for us," he says. "And we have it. The children who aren't destined to be casualties in some senseless war. Children who can study music over hatred and fighting. So, if to maintain that peace, I have to lie, I will lie."

"She'll learn about him soon enough," Ellen says softly. "God forbid she runs into him. She's back until September. Don't tell me you plan to lock her away in a tower until then."

"I won't have to," Mischa snaps. "She'll have her pretty party and be distracted until her schooling resumes. She'll be safe. As for now? Donatello Vanici isn't welcome in my territory, and I've made that clear. If the motherfucker didn't own half the damn harbor, I could drive him from the city altogether. From the country. As it stands, I won't let him near her."

"I know you love her," Ellen says, her voice soothing. "But one day, she'll have to face her past."

"Not alone," Mischa declares. "Never alone. And only when she's ready to finally leave it behind."

They grow silent, though it could be the sound of my pulse drowning them out. It surges through my ears, deafening me as I return to my room. My thoughts are a maze of confusion.

Betrayal.

And grim resignation.

Mischa is right.

As long as my past lives, I can't.

# 6

# WILLOW

$\mathcal{M}$orning comes far too soon, and I rise from my bed, having barely slept. My head throbs as snippets of a nightmare still taunt me.

I had been there again. In the home I lived in before ever meeting Mischa, a beautiful manor every bit as storied as this one. Smaller in size but no less comforting, I can remember every inch of it so clearly it hurts.

In that home, I grew so much.

And in that home, I lost everything.

My present should be so much brighter. As if to taunt me, golden daylight streams in through my windows, warming my cheeks. Inside, however, I feel so cold. It's like my thoughts have turned to ice, jagged, and painful.

Maybe Mischa was right? Ignoring the past is the only way forward. As the faint smell of cooking food carries on the air, I'm willing to try.

I get dressed in a sweater and jeans for now, but my debutante dress awaits, hanging from the front of my wardrobe as a glaring reminder of what today signifies. For all intents and purposes, I am nineteen, finally a woman.

Supposedly, I should be freed from the bonds of my childhood…

But dangerous thoughts creep into the silence, countering that narrative. I can't help the comparison—would Donatello have spent as much on his version of my debutante ball? Would he have slaved over every detail and gushed with pride about his planning?

It stings to even imagine it. His smiling face. His sloppily wrapped gifts. The dress he'd design for me…

I don't know how long I've been lost in thought when my door opens and a kind face peeks from behind it.

"You're awake," Ellen says warily. Her blue eyes are unusually guarded, her gray day dress subdued. Is she aware of what I overheard last night? As her gaze fixates on the dress, I can't tell. She crosses to it, fingering a corner of the massive skirt. "I just wanted you to know that today is your day, and I'm so proud of you for humoring us. We know you hate parties. And dresses. And attention—"

I shake my head, cutting her off.

"Yes, but I just want you to know that we didn't plan this on a whim," she insists. "We've…"

She turns away, gazing through the gap in my white curtains to the view revealed beyond my bay windows. The vast stretch of the manor looms below, a yawning mass of emerald green lawns and sheltered forests. What does she see within such a realm? Safety? Or another looming reality that makes her bite her lip and clasp her hands?

One look at the slim fingers symbolizes the violent start to her relationship with Mischa that most wouldn't expect when seeing them now. Rather than sporting a wedding ring as it should, the digit on her left hand itself ends abruptly at the knuckle, severed years ago.

"He's been worried, you know," she admits, her voice soft. "About what your proximity to him might do to your future. If doors might be slammed in your face, that otherwise wouldn't be. He knows he isn't perfect, but you and the other children… You mean the world to him. To give you what he thinks you deserve, he will do anything. I need you to know that. He loves you."

*So he lies to me.* I could assert as much, but I don't. Regardless, I'm startled by the anger building in my chest, so raw it hurts. I try choking it down and grit my teeth against it. Try to rationalize it away—he loves me, I know he does.

But so did Donatello.

"This means a lot to him," Ellen continues, still gazing from the window. "Think of this party as his way of trying to make amends and bridge the gap. He's even planning on wearing a suit. Can you imagine?" She laughs as I attempt to picture it—Mischa in anything other than fatigues or simplistic clothing.

Her amused grin lasts for only a second before she's frowning. "It's funny how things change. There was a time when I would have never imagined him plotting and scheming something other than revenge or retaliation..." She trails off and clears her throat. "Well, get some rest. I'll keep the children away for the day, and later, if you want, I can help you get dressed?"

I nod as she crosses to me and kisses my cheek. "Happy birthday, Willow."

I watch her go as more memories return, but these thankfully don't star Donatello. I can still remember the first day she and I met. Back then, we were nothing more than captives held at the mercy of one man we both love now.

Sometimes it feels like I'm dreaming. That one day I'll wake up, and I'll be that scared little girl again.

More often than not, I used to pray that day would come soon.

At least then, I'd stop dreading it.

# 7

## WILLOW

The day slips away until it's evening before I know it. Night paints the world beyond my windows in hues of navy that serve as a backdrop to a swollen full moon. Already shuffled off to bed, the children's boisterous playing has been replaced with faint music and the bustle of footsteps from down below.

My heart pounds with every new sound to invade—the growing din of numerous voices, along with the musical clangs of silverware and delicate china. The swish of ivory silk as I spin before the mirror and try my best to smile. Ellen's soft gasp as she oversees me, her hands clasped in approval.

"What do you think?" she asks, already wearing her own frothy pink gown.

I observe my reflection in the glass without conveying an answer right away. A stranger looks back at me, her teeth bared in a seemingly painful expression. She looks far from a debutante—just a stone-faced pretender. Large brown eyes stare blankly, and I can't even tell what she might be feeling. Happiness? Contentment? Terror?

I look away from her, eyeing the skirt billowing out around me. Gratitude thickens my throat, and all I can do is finger a section of intricate lace over and over. I've never worn a dress like this. Even for my recitals.

"You look so beautiful," Ellen murmurs. She smooths her hands along my hair, brushing the tresses from my face, but with her next to me, the contrast between us is stark. I barely come to her shoulder, gangly and gaunt with cheekbones that are far too prominent. In comparison, she's willowy and lithe, her beauty unmarred even by the jagged scar on her left cheek, fully displayed with her hair swept into an elegant coil.

I could be self-deprecating if I wanted to, drawing on the few descriptions of myself I've heard from various colleagues while training in Vienna. I'm pretty, they say, but far too serious. My looks alone aren't enticing enough for most of my classmates to broach a conversation with me. According to some, my father may even be a mobster, explaining my need for security and seemingly unlimited funds.

Physically, at least, my nose is longer than Ellen's and blunter. With my thin lips, even my best smile is no comparison to her charming grin. I used to wish she really were my mother. That I was as calm as her. As quiet and strong. Mischa's name alone could make grown men piss themselves, but one word from her could restrain him like nothing else.

In some ways, their relationship is inconceivable. A man with such a capacity for violence, shouldn't be capable of love. A woman so gentle should be unable to tame a monster.

Their love is comparable to the most complex concertos involving a wide range of instruments to perform—intricate and intimidating, but undeniably perfect when played. Some might compare their union to a fairy tale.

Or a curse. If my life has taught me nothing else, it is that peace is fragile, and when it ends—and it always does end —the resulting chaos renders the happier times nothing more than a weapon. One that cuts into your thoughts with every waking moment, subverting any attempt to suppress it. Stubbornly, the past resists, blaring through your thoughts like a shout growing louder by the second. Louder and louder still, until it drowns out everything else.

*Donatello.*

*Donatello.*

*Donatello!*

"You look so surly tonight," Ellen scolds, pinching my cheek. "Is it the style? I can try a different look."

I blink and realize that she's already arranged my hair. A long plait loops around my skull, forming an elegant coif similar to hers.

*It's perfect,* I sign, and her relieved grin only enhances the gentle grace cast by her dress. I don't resist as she smooths the gown over my waist, adjusting the fit. With an appreciative sigh, she stands back.

"You're a woman now," she says wistfully. "It feels like just yesterday when you and Eli would play hide and seek for hours, and when Mischa would braid your hair. Do you remember? With Ivan already in school, the girls will follow before I know it." She cradles her belly. "At least I have one more to savor. Now shall we?"

I start to follow her, entering the hallway. An admirer is already there, wearing a casual shirt and jeans. "You look nice, Aunt Ellen," he chirps.

"Thank you, Eli darling." Ellen ruffles his hair before shooting me a knowing glance. "I'll see you downstairs."

As she leaves, Eli steps forward, his lips pursed. "Mama didn't want me to stay up late," he says to me with a sigh. "She wanted me to tell you happy birthday, though, and give you this." He hands me a beautifully wrapped box.

I open it carefully, and my eyes widen at what I discover inside of it—a delicate pair of gold earrings.

*They're beautiful,* I sign before placing them on my nightstand.

"They're okay," he says with a mischievous grin while taking something from his pocket. "But here is my present. Before you ask, Mischa said I can have it," he explains, holding a small knife on the flat of his palm. "I carved it myself. Do you like it?"

Recognition runs through me as I take in the dagger's familiar shape. It's the same one I used to practice with as a child, running drills to the point of exhaustion under Mischa's discretion. I rub my finger over the polished leather hilt, feeling my heart swell with emotion. Etched there in gold is a single name—Mouse.

"You can use it to stab those rich guys if they get on your nerves," Eli suggests with solemn seriousness. "Papa said I can tell you to 'kick anyone's ass who doesn't treat you right.'"

I reach out, placing my hand over his cheek. With his knife in my grasp, that taunting voice in my head vanishes. I can think again, and I feel so childish for letting the negative thoughts take over in the first place.

"Don't get sappy on me," he scolds, dodging my touch, but his smile is so infectious I'm grinning back. "Now go to your fancy party. I scoped it out, and I bet you'll have to use that knife pretty soon."

I raise an eyebrow, though I doubt he's exaggerating. Nervous energy rides the air, sending my heartbeat racing. Excited butterflies take flight in my stomach, and I sneak one last look at myself in the mirror.

If I squint, I see less of that stone-faced girl from before. A woman instead takes her place. Willow Stepanova. Who might she meet at her own debutante ball?

I honestly have no idea as to the kind of men Mischa would invite. Rich and bold, as Eli claimed? Or a more dangerous breed?

"We should spy on them from the top," Eli offers, extending his arm to me. "That way, you can decide who to stab before you go down."

I gratefully hook my arm around his, letting him guide me down the hall. Even from here, the noise is deafening—murmuring voices and elegant music. Rather than approach the grand staircase, Eli and I creep to a rarely traveled wing that overlooks the grand hall.

The space itself is massive, crowned by an ornate vaulted ceiling. Marble flooring amplifies every sound in the spacious interior. Two hallways on the upper level provide a more private position from which to observe those below.

"Wow," Eli exclaims, sneaking a look over the wooden railing.

I touch his shoulder in silent agreement, too awed to make my own remarks. The full extent of Mischa's planning is breathtaking. Garlands of roses hang from the ceiling along with ivory banners and delicate accents.

"Is that a smile?" Eli teases, wrinkling his nose. "You look pretty, by the way." He tugs on a section of my skirt. "Like a princess. Your knife looks nice too."

And maybe I should embrace that. I'm no longer the little Mouse Mischa rescued or the naïve child before that. I am Willow Stepanova, beloved member of a powerful family.

Mischa is right. The past has to stay dead and buried. I can move on and keep living. I won't let it drag me back.

Leaning over the banister, I take in the new world I'm entering. Already, a sizable number of attendees crowd the room, and I feel a burst of pride for Mischa. He's succeeded where most men fail in forging a new path for himself and for his family. He even stuffed his muscular bulk into a suit, proudly displaying Ellen on his arm.

I grin as I envision him attending one of my musical events in the future. The *mafiya* leader turned lover of music.

Suddenly, his expression hardens, setting my nerves on alert. Confused, I follow the line of his gaze to a man standing near a corner of the ballroom. An unwanted guest?

His back is to me at first, but then he turns.

And time crawls to a stop. As if in a daze, I vaguely note his strikingly tall figure first, before my eyes drift up to his dark brown hair. The firm line of his jaw next. It's like my brain knows to do anything it can to stall before I finally register the rest of his face…

That firm, stoic jaw.

Those eyes.

That smile.

Images slam into my skull one after the other. That same figure in another life. Memories swarm me of crawling onto his lap, relishing his attention. Running my tiny fingers over the expansive planes of his face and understanding, even at that young age, that he looked different than most. His eyes were a rich brown, his nose so stern he could seem more intimidating than thunderstorms—my biggest fear then—and yet a simple quirk of his mouth could transform him into the most comforting presence I'd ever known. Even Mischa can't muster the same level of playful softness.

But Mischa's love was never a lie.

Everything about my past with Donatello Vanici was. A brutal, terrifying, horrifying lie.

I blink rapidly, expecting him to disappear—but he doesn't. I pinch myself, willing him to vanish. My eyes burn but with every tear to fall, blurring my vision, he stubbornly remains.

Oblivious, he tilts his head, allowing the glow from a hanging chandelier to illuminate him in painfully stark detail. He's the man I remember from my childhood, only aged exactly seven years, dressed in a suit that strains against the bulk in his forearms. Dark stubble speckles his chin, and his eyes scan the room as watchful as ever.

Beside him stands another man I recognize despite him having grown several feet, sprouting into a near copy of his uncle. Vincenzo.

"Will?" Eli stage-whispers. "What's wrong?"

His voice snaps me back with a chilling realization that has me gripping the railing, in danger of pitching over it—this isn't a dream.

Or, even more terrifying—I've finally gone insane. Around me, the walls melt, forming a puddle that obscures everyone and everything but him. He's untouchable by the chaos, standing as tall as he did the day he dragged me before Nicolai Baryshnikov and left me for dead.

*"Do what you will with her,"* he'd said. *"I don't care."*

*I don't care…*

And apparently, he hasn't, frolicking like a man without a care in the world, here to attend the birthday party of a girl he thinks he's never met. Does he assume that Willow Stepanova will be as easy to charm as Safiya Mangenello?

As I watch, he goes rigid, his eyes flashing. A vicious sense of triumph roots me in place. I hope he sees me. Notices me. Remembers me…

But without ever looking my way once, he heads for the exit of the ballroom, pulling Vincenzo after him.

I turn away so quickly I nearly trip over the skirt of my gown. There's no way down from here. I can only stagger forward, craning my neck for a view of the figure retreating toward the front of the house.

"Will, what's wrong?" Eli is already by my side, using his hand to steady me. "You look like you've seen a ghost or something."

But I have. There isn't any way to explain the truth to him.

My fingers are shaking too badly to form any coherent reply. It's too hot. The air is too thick. Suffocating.

"Is it the dress?" Eli asks, padding after me as I tear into the upstairs wing. "I'll get Aunt Ellen, and she can—"

I grab his hand, shaking my head no, though I barely register his worried expression. It's like the walls of this home fade, and I'm a child again, unable to see anything beyond the figure retreating from me. I can't even cry out.

All I can do is hate him.

Chase him.

Follow him to the boundaries of a slamming door and watch him leave. Again. I'm shaking as I reach the top of the staircase, waiting for him only to find the foyer devoid of anyone but my father's guards. Then I remember that it will take him minutes to reach this part of the house from the lower level.

"Will?" Eli tugs at my skirt. "What's wrong?"

My fingers are moving before I even realize what I'm signing, *I need you to do me a favor.*

He cocks his head. "What kind of favor?"

*Cover for me.* Surging past him, I cross the wing, entering my room in a rush. I set the knife aside, pacing circles as my mind races.

"What do you mean?" Eli demands, right on my heels. "Where are you going?"

It's the same question I'm asking myself. I don't know. I can't think…

It's like someone else possesses my body, making me claw at the fastenings of my gown Ellen had so lovingly done up. With sheer brute force, I unhook it enough to wrench myself free of the massive skirt. The fabric falls to the floor with a pathetic thud, resembling one of the many roses decorating the main hall.

"Hey!" From the corner of my eye, I see Eli turn his back to me, his neck beet red. "If you didn't like the dress, you could have told them before the party," he scolds.

I can't apologize. I'm too busy reaching for my closet. Throwing open the wooden doors, I rummage through the few items left hanging. I only brought a few things home from school—assorted shirts, skirts, and jeans. Apart from those items lurks one lone black dress at the very back of the cabinet.

My heart pangs as I grab it by the hanger. I wore it to the older Ivan's funeral with a sweater over the top for modesty —it was the only thing in the store that suited my height without requiring inches to be taken off the hem. On me, the dress came just past my knees.

Observing it now, it suits a far different purpose than mourning. It's tight enough to run in. Or stab someone while wearing it and obscure any bloodstains. In a sense, it's the polar opposite of the white dress I'd been given after being abandoned.

This…is a fitting dress to kill Donatello Vanici in.

Teeth bared, I slip it on, still wearing my new white heels.

Why? My brain is on autopilot, racing ahead too quickly for my body to keep up. I keep seeing him, his back to me. Leaving, always leaving…

But following him now would be foolish. Pointless. Unless…

I can find him alone. Unguarded.

To do what?

Silver on my dresser catches my eye, and I lunge for the object, testing my thumb over a sharpened edge. Eli's knife.

"Will…" His voice, trembling with alarm, grates on the anger, making me falter.

I turn to find him watching me, his blue eyes fathomless in the dark. "What are you doing?"

Guilt chokes me for the fear in his gaze. *I have to take care of something,* I sign to him. *Please, just cover for me.*

"Cover? How?"

A part of me knows this is wrong. My fingers are moving anyway. *Make a distraction.*

Pushing past him, I reenter the hall, heading for the staircase. A figure walks by, too perfectly timed to be real. I'm imagining him, storming past two guards stationed near the front door. In this hallucination, I hear him clearly. "We'll return to the hotel."

Rather than descend the main staircase, I skirt around to the servant's wing and out a door that leads to the side of the house. The fact that I run into no one is a testament to the scale of the party Mischa planned. It feels as though everyone, from the servants, to the security detail, is positioned outside to manage the flow of guests.

Only one car awaits out front now; however, its headlights painting the driveway gold against an ebony sky. I crouch behind a row of hedges, inching forward until I'm just paces from the manor's entrance. The car is close enough to touch, a black luxury model.

As if on cue, two men exit the front of the manor and approach the vehicle. The tallest of the pair gestures for the driver and hands him a large box that the man promptly brings to the trunk.

He opens the compartment, placing the box inside, and I don't know what possesses me to grab a rock from the lawn and throw it. The skittering noise draws the driver's attention, and he walks toward it just long enough for me to slip from between two hedges and climb inside the trunk entirely.

Admonishments run through my mind. There's no way no one saw me. What the hell am I doing?

When footsteps approach, I tense in anticipation, knowing I'll be caught.

But the lid slams shut instead, and the sudden darkness has the effect of a bucket of ice water being dumped over my head.

I'm in the same car as Donatello Vanici.

The knife is in my grasp, and I cling to it so tightly it hurts —but I don't drop it.

Instead, I channel another set of memories from my childhood. Mischa, shouting at me as we trained in the yard, his warnings unrelenting.

*"Never let your guard down, Mouse! No matter how exhausted you are, you fight. You win. Now move!"*

With his voice in my head, I feel a strength I've never experienced before, giving me the sense of mind to strain through the dark and get my bearings.

I'll trust this protector over the other two who failed me.

I'll take his words to heart.

I'll fight.

And I will win.

# 8

# WILLOW

We don't travel far from the manor, though every passing second might as well be an eternity. In the dark quiet of the trunk, there is nothing to ground me but the endless motions of the vehicle and muffled snippets of noise. Eventually, a lone shred of logic seeps through the splintered thoughts circling my brain—we could be headed anywhere.

I can't hear any coherent conversation from inside the car—just murmured voices. One overpowers the other, deep and rich. My entire body stiffens in response to it, and I grit my teeth so hard my jaw aches.

He is so close…

He and Vincenzo, a boy I never thought I'd see again. The sight of him hurts the most. Beneath all the festering rage and hate, there is only pain when I think of how our relationship used to be. My Vinny. He is so tall now, embodying his uncle even in stature in a way he never could with his huge eyes and awkward glasses. Does he even remember the little Safy who used to follow him around with the devotion of a puppy?

Did he even care when Don tore that girl away from their world?

I feel strange. Lost. Empty. Like I've ripped off a mask I've been wearing for so long, I'd forgotten it wasn't my real face. Without it, I'm someone nameless devoid of a real identity. A waif with her blond hair falling from its elegant coil, draping her shoulders with random strands.

There is no order to my appearance. No retinue of security or staff to reinforce my supposed importance. Willow Stepanova is an untouchable idea in this moment, and though it hurts like hell to admit it…

I will never be her.

Safiya is growling, thirsting for revenge. That scared little girl from my past is scratching at the boundaries of my control, desperate to be unleashed. The longer I'm so close to these snippets from my past, the harder it becomes to restrain her.

I'm sweating with the effort, tightening my grip over the knife. Finally, the car slows to a stop, leaving me trembling in the aftermath. As if from underwater, I hear the doors opening and the slam of them closing again.

Soon my panting is the only noise to fill the silence. I can't tell if the driver is still nearby, waiting to retrieve the box placed here beside me. Jealousy is an irrational thing to feel, but it crawls through my chest as I make out the professionally wrapped gift. There are no flaws marring it like the presents Donatello once gave me—he didn't do this himself. So desperate to make an impression on Mischa's daughter, he procured only the best.

What gift would he think might impress such a girl?

I finger a corner and then rip at the glossy blue wrapping paper. Beneath is a white box, and inside it, a mirror bright enough to reflect what little light there is and reveal my shadowed reflection.

An inhuman creature stares back, her teeth bared in a feral snarl, her once elegantly styled hair a wild mess.

Finally, I hear a low whistle and then footsteps trailing away from the car. The driver?

I scour the inside of the trunk until I find a release that opens it. Cautiously, I lift the lid, blinking as my eyes adjust to a dim source of light coming from above. From what I can tell, I'm in a garage. Rows of luxurious vehicles are parked beside this one. Through a row of windows, I can make out what seems to be an office where several men mill about.

My heart races as I rise to my knees. Slowly, I slip one foot from the trunk, bracing it against the pavement before I leave the vehicle entirely. Straining to keep out of view, I lower the lid as much as I can without slamming it closed.

Low to the ground, I inch my way forward, scanning the area for any hint of an exit. But there are too many, and a parade of vehicles streams in and out. I don't see Donatello anywhere. With no other options, I stand and approach the office, tugging the remainder of my hair loose. The knife, I tuck within my bra between my breasts, praying that the fall of the material obscures its shape.

"Hey, what are you doing here?" a man demands, calling from the doorway. I flinch as he takes one look at me. Whatever he sees makes him clear his throat, and some of the suspicion in his gaze softens. "Are you lost?"

Relieved, I nod, and he inclines his head toward a silver elevator on the other end of the garage. Above it is a sign reading: *To the Grande Hotel Lobby.* That explains the suit he wears—a crisp, black ensemble nearly identical to the style worn by the other men in the room. It must be a uniform for the drivers hired by the hotel.

"Guest services are that way," he says.

I take a step in that direction, only to turn to him and start to sign. It's random nonsense, but he doesn't know that, flushing pink with confusion.

"I'm sorry," he admits with a pained grimace. "I don't understand sign language."

I mime for a pen and paper, and he ushers me into the office and hands me both. Crouched over a desk, I embody every bit of what I learned about being rich from my classmates. There is a dichotomy to it one must learn to master. It isn't enough to be rude; you have to be delicate as well. There's an art to knowing how to simper and smile with an air of superiority. When to sneer and when to bat your lashes.

In short, you perform no differently than when playing an instrument.

*I lost my card key,* I write. *My uncle is staying at the hotel, and we got separated. Can you tell me what room we're in, please?*

"You haven't tried the front desk?" He eyes me warily and sighs when I shake my head. "Name?"

My hand trembles so badly I can barely form the letters. In the end, I press down hard enough that the nib of the pen tears through the page.

Reading the name, the man raises an eyebrow. "Donatello Vanici?"

"I drove him tonight," another man pitches in from across the room. Seated at a desk with his feet propped on the edge, he eyes me with a raised eyebrow and shrugs. "He hired full service, and there's a package I was supposed to deliver for him tonight. I could take her up."

*I don't mind. Thank you,* I scribble.

With a grunt of acknowledgment, the man rises to his feet. "Wait here, Miss."

He leaves the office to enter the garage, and sweat drips down the back of my neck as I wait.

Eventually, he returns with a questioning frown and an unwrapped gift box tucked beneath his arm. "Damn kids," he grumbles, tugging at the gray tie accenting his black suit. "Someone went through the trunk."

"I'll check the cameras while you write a report," the man near the door grumbles. "Just make sure nothing's stolen. That's the last thing we fucking need around here."

"Quit your bitching," the man with the gift snarls. "Let me take her up first." He jerks his head for me to follow, and I nearly trip in my haste to keep pace.

Together, we enter the elevator, and the man swipes a badge before selecting a floor just a few numbers down from the highest level. Within minutes, the doors open onto a lush hallway accented by blood-red carpet and wood-paneled walls polished to shine.

The driver shuffles forward to a room a few paces down and swipes the card to let me inside.

"Your uncle, huh?" he wonders, inspecting me with a curious expression. "Look, if either of you needs a ride in the future, here is my private card. I'm looking to trade up, if you know what I mean. The pay here is shit." He rummages through his coat and withdraws a plain business card. "If the ride is for you, text this number. You know how to text?"

He grunts when I nod.

"Good. Text this number with your name and where to pick you up, no questions asked. And don't forget to tell your uncle, if he's hiring. Oh, and tell him happy birthday for me." He hands me the present and leaves.

I can't seem to move other than to slip his card where I hid my knife. Or turn away from the surprisingly modest space. My first coherent thought is that the air doesn't smell like him, too crisp and clean.

Apparently, I wasn't the first to find a way in here, either. A cake rests on the king-sized bed, along with small, square items wrapped in shiny silver packaging.

It's so anticlimactic in a sense.

He should be sprawled in a massive penthouse, reveling in his money, unbothered by any skeletons in his past.

But this arena is as fitting as any to finally face him after all this time. Squaring my shoulders, I step inside, closing the door behind me. I drop the present near the entrance and find myself inching toward a row of windows overlooking a view of the busy waterfront.

We must be in the heart of the city. Several skyscrapers surround this building. The nearest one is close enough for me to make out various people exposed by gaps in curtains or blinds. They live their lives regardless, oblivious to being on display.

On a floor roughly equal to this one, I catch a man who seems to be staring intently in this direction. The second I spot him, he shifts out of view.

And I turn away, withdrawing my dagger from its hiding place.

For the first time, I feel a pang of guilt for leaving Mischa and Ellen to wonder where I am.

But after tonight, I'll finally be able to live among them with no more crippling uncertainty.

No more pain.

After tonight, I'll finally be free to become someone else and leave Safiya Mangenello behind for good.

I'll silence Donatello Vanici's memory, one way or another.

# 9

# DON

*V*inny, my sweet, cunning boy. He has taste after all—the little bastard went all out when picking his present for me. She's perfect—a pretty, innocent-looking piece of ass every bit as beautiful as any pampered heiress.

Her dark eyes watch me, so fucking wide. Endless. I'm too drunk to be poetic about it, but if I weren't, I'd describe her in the sexiest terms that get a man's cock throbbing. Mine, at least.

Beautiful.

Dangerous.

Unsettling.

Psychotic.

She has that knife raised high before I even have the sense to pivot out of her reach. Undeterred, she swipes for me anyway, her eyes blazing, teeth bared.

Laughing, I grab her wrist, and she recoils, stumbling into a sideboard in her haste to wrench away from me.

"You aren't a professional," I deduce, sizing her up with a glance. Disappointment melds with the effects of my last whiskey, and my shoulders slump in defeat. So much for my good boy sending a naughty toy my way. "Sexually or otherwise," I suspect, sounding like a child denied a treat. "Not a part of my gift, it seems."

What a damn shame.

A second glance makes it more obvious that she's no whore. She's far too slight for one, no hint of muscle in sight. Her skin is paler than the style these days, and her hair looks to be a natural shade in between blond and brown—no hint of highlights or some shit most escorts adorn themselves with. But her hands give her away—slim, pale, struggling to grip the knife she holds.

She's no assassin, either.

"Revenge, is it?" I ask as she whirls to face me, blade drawn. "Which loved one of yours did I kill? A beloved daddy? A brother? It can't be your mother," I add, easily parrying her next attempt to slash my throat. "I don't kill women."

Her eyes flash at that, and she lunges again, flailing more wildly with her blade.

"So, your mother then," I deduce while twisting on my heel to avoid her attack. Unguarded, she doesn't even try to stop me from gripping her waist, tugging her against me. It's only as her eyes meet mine for a split-second that I realize I've fucked up.

Pain lances through my side, drawing a hiss as I buck out of her range. Shit. I don't even have to look down to know she got me. I can feel the blood already starting to pool beneath this godforsaken suit. Fuck it. What a way to end the night. Hissing in irritation, I swipe at the wound without bothering to inspect it in full.

"So, you are trained, after all," I rasp. "Fuck, playing games, then."

I snatch a handful of her hair, using the grip for leverage to shove her away. Only when I let go, do I realize how rough I've been. She's so thin that in theory, she could go right through the wall. At the last minute, she catches herself with her free hand, already spinning to come at me again.

Even as I brace myself for her next blow, I'm impressed. Someone trained her well.

But her skill eliminates about ten potential motherfuckers off the list of who her employer—or avenged family member—might be. None of those sons of bitches would ever have the balls to train a woman.

"So, I offended your mother," I say, trying and failing to maintain eye contact. Her gaze is a viper, darting around the room in search of an exit. I barely manage to shift my stance enough to keep her from lunging for the door. "Did I fuck her?" I ask, raking my gaze over her body from head to toe. "Don't tell me you're my long-lost daughter."

It's sick, but as my eyes fall over the small breasts peeking beneath the neckline of her dress, I pray to God she's not. Though, fuck. At least then, I'd have a daughter to carry on my legacy in addition to Vin.

Her cheeks flush with fury at the suggestion, her chest heaving. Wrong answer.

"Did I fuck you?" I sound as skeptical as I feel, and the answer seems to be a definitive no. I would remember her. Those eyes. Those lips. Her smell—one inhale and I'm high on the stench—roses.

"Did I hurt you?" I ask, noting the shift in my pitch. I sound damn near genuine. "If I did fuck you and never call, trust me—put the knife down, and I will be more than willing to make it up to you. I was probably drunk."

Very, *very* drunk, I decide as my gaze descends her shapely legs. Piss drunk. Vin had probably snuck something into my drink as a prank—it wouldn't be the first time. His way of trying to convince me to stay sober.

But her eyes narrow, and more color floods her cheeks. Rather than peg her issue, I've insulted her.

And she comes for me again, eyes blazing.

For a heartbeat, she transforms into someone else. Someone even smaller, scrawnier, her honey-colored hair in pigtails, her expression so feral she resembled a stray mutt more than a little girl.

I'm almost startled into saying her name out loud. Almost…

But she's dead. I know because I hand-delivered her to her killer.

Fire slices through the meat of my cheek, drawing my attention to an outstretched pale hand lashing through the air. The little bitch is quick, reaching me before I have the chance to block. She lands a good punch to my chest, already maneuvering her knife to go again.

Grunting, I ram my shoulder into her side, knocking her off balance. Before she can recover, I fist my fingers through that mass of hair, noticing just how damn thick it is. Soft too. Perfect for gripping. Pulling.

To test that theory, I use a handful of it to shove her onto the bed face down and pin her in place, jabbing my knee against the small of her back. I'm not gentle—she should gasp at least. Cry out.

But she doesn't make a sound. Strange. I'm used to the theatrics that tend to color these situations. The screaming. The monologues. The listing of grievances and shouting.

She isn't the first person I've found in my room willing to kill me. Not by a long shot.

Even as she struggles, grappling at the bedsheets with nails drawn, she doesn't say a word. Doesn't make a sound. It's strangely…hot.

A series of thoughts flit across my mind—sick, twisted shit belonging to the old Don. The fucker who would relish in slipping his hand beneath her dress, palming that sweet, ripe little ass and seeing how silent she'd be then.

My hand is already moving, fingering the hem as her limbs quiver just beyond my reach. Groaning, I form a fist and brace it against the mattress beside her instead. As if to mock me, I catch a handful of condoms. The cake, I discover, is already smashed on the floor, having been knocked off the bed.

So much for Vin's present.

"Who do you work for?" I demand of the woman.

She attempts to lift her knife in lieu of giving me an answer. With a sigh, I snatch her wrist, bending it back just shy of painful. She has to go still or risk injuring it. Her eyes cut up to mine, burning so hot it's like they're on fucking fire.

"Tell me, and I'll let you go."

She bares her teeth, desperately trying to buck me off.

I rip the knife from her grasp, eyeing it from end to tip. It's a custom blade, one of damn good quality. Too good to be wasted on a murder, where common sense would dictate it'd have to be tossed or destroyed afterward. No, this has to be personal.

I inspect the blade's leather hilt while running my finger over it for any clue. All I find is a scribbled engraved message in what looks like a child's handwriting.

"Mouse?" I say, reading the inscription out loud. "That some kind of nickname?" When she doesn't answer, I trace the curve of her squirming hip up the length of her back and wind up looking straight into those fiery eyes. "No. You aren't a mouse," I tell her. "I think you're more like a wicked little kitty. A tiger. Huh, *tigre?*"

She rears up as far as she can with her arm still in my grasp. I recognize how her cheeks hollow, but I don't try to avoid the glob of spit she lobs my way. It lands on the corner of my fancy lapel, relegating this suit as yet another casualty of this night.

"If Vin sent you, after all, I wouldn't blame him," I tell the woman, scanning her face for any hint of recognition of the name. She gives me nothing but more perfectly white teeth. Those eyes blaze even hotter, and it doesn't take much of an imagination to guess the insults flying around the inside of that pretty skull.

She can join the club of people I've disappointed.

"So maybe I did try to set him up with some spoiled little bitch. All I want is for the bastard to turn out better than me," I say. "Is that so wrong?"

In so many ways, he already has. Over twenty without a felony to his name. No blood on his hands to speak of. Apart from a pistol for protection, I never even taught the bastard how to shoot a weapon. A real weapon.

And yet my first choice for his father-in-law would be one of the most infamous gun runners this side of hell.

"I want him to be protected," I say in my defense, flicking the knife into the air and catching it by the handle. "Like I never was. I want the kind of security for him that can be provided only by a good name. A name people fear."

And if a side benefit to that happened to be forming an alliance with a powerful family in the process, then so be it.

"I'd do anything for him," I rasp to the silent form flailing beneath me. "I couldn't love him more even if he were my biological son. He is my son. Besides, it's not like I'm asking him to draw blood or enter the Stepanov business. Just—" I break off at the same exact moment the little tiger goes limp.

"Stepanov," I repeat the name deliberately, scouring her body for a reaction. This time, I catch it in slow motion— her entire body tenses. Though she tries to turn away from me, I don't miss how those eyes go wide as her teeth skewer her bottom lip between them. Hard.

"Did Mischa Stepanov send you?" Frankly, I'm asking the question hypothetically more than anything—not that she gives me an answer. Frowning, I wrack my brain, trying to remember if I really had done something to accidentally offend my deadliest rival. More than crashing his little party. More than with just my reputation.

Something egregious enough for him to send a woman after me, wielding a knife etched with the word *Mouse*.

It sounds insane enough in my head that I don't bother entertaining it out loud. So I laugh instead. If Mischa wanted me dead, I know enough of his reputation to have full confidence that he'd do it himself.

She must know him somehow, I deduce as she turns away from me, clawing at the mattress.

"Is he your next target, little *tigre*?" I wonder. My lip quirks at the thought of it—her slender form tangling with a brute like Mischa. But the amusement dies when I picture her dead in the aftermath. Mutilated. In pieces.

Some men don't need rumors to inspire terror in their wake. Not when they leave a body of evidence behind. Mischa Stepanov's body of evidence is terrifying even to those in this business with a mountain of bodies piled in their closets.

To men like me. I wouldn't wish his wrath on my worst enemy.

Not even this snarling, feisty little *tigre*.

She kicks out with her legs, forcing me to apply more pressure to my knee to keep her down. The motion brings me closer to her, and I fully take advantage of this new perspective. Every time she flexes her thighs, a warm sliver of bare skin becomes exposed, brushing the back of my extended leg.

Heat I haven't felt in a long time flares, forcing me to grit my teeth against it. And as if sensing the reaction, she goes limp again, refusing to move a muscle in defiance.

"I can tell you one thing," I say, releasing her arm in favor of stroking through that mane of hair. She tries swiping at my hand with both of hers, but from this angle, she can't reach.

And I have the lion's share of exploration. From her hair, down to her throat. From that slender column of flesh, down to the top of her spine and a defined, muscular little shoulder.

Once again, I was wrong—she's toned as hell, but her overall size helps to disguise the actual strength coiled in the lithe little body.

Strength that she hones in a vicious buck of her hips that nearly succeeds in dislodging me. Keeping her down requires more effort. I'm gritting my teeth, sensing a bead of sweat form on my temple.

For all this exertion, we might as well be fucking.

I adjust my weight to keep her restrained, and an ominous ripping sound issues from my sleeve. Sure enough, the entire goddamn suit gives way next with a metallic ping of a button flying off, landing on the floor. I have no choice but to shrug it off and toss it aside. I snatch at the shirt as well when the damn thing constrains my movements. Using one hand, I rip at the buttons until some of the pressure loosens.

"I'm not going to hurt you," I tell the woman. "Stop resisting, and I'll turn you over to the hotel authorities. They'll probably let you go with a slap on the wrist. Trust me, that's the upside offer. Sorry to put a damper on your little revenge plot, but I'd rather not die today…"

I trail off as her eyes find mine again. So damn piercing. Though she still hasn't said a word, it's like I can clearly hear her voice echoing in my head. Sexy in cadence, shouting obscenities.

"You know," I say in between pants. "It's usually after we fuck that a woman tries to stab me."

In another burst of strength, she contorts her hips, using her slightness to her advantage enough to skirt my knee and flip onto her side. I barely manage to pin her by the shoulders, easily maneuvering my weight on top of her. Skilled or not, she can't fight pure gravity. I'm too damn heavy for her to resist.

And she's so damn small. It's almost too easy to have her immobile, my knees trapping her legs, my weight balanced over her narrow hips. Of all the thoughts to enter my mind, one of sheer practicality takes the cake—if we were fucking, she'd have to be on top. Otherwise, I'd crush her in this position. Break her.

But even now, she's still resisting. Still fighting, her teeth bared, eyes darting around the room, anywhere but me. I don't know what makes me brush my thumb against her chin. She contorts her neck and nearly takes the appendage off, snapping with her teeth.

Our eyes meet, and maybe that was my goal all along. They're amazing, those fucking eyes. In a world where men only make eye contact to intimidate, women to seduce, grifters to lie. It's been a long damn time since anyone has looked at me. Stared without a damn for who I am or what I might do.

To her, I'm not Donatello Vanici, a black-hearted son of a bitch with a past too chilling to escape. Or maybe I am. The way she rages silently, her chest heaving, cheeks flushed, eyes narrowing. Her reaction confirms my previous hunch —this is personal.

But not to avenge someone else.

"What the hell did I do to you, little *tigre*?" I murmur, stroking her cheek again though she recoils so violently a troubling cracking sound issues from her neck. The fact that she's still trying to kick me assuages my worries of any serious injury.

But her reaction proves it.

"I can assure you that whoever you're after, it isn't me. I have never harmed a woman."

Physically at least. Emotional distress could be debated by a handful of scorned lovers, but that isn't her grudge. Now more than before, I'm sure of it—I would have remembered her, drunk, drugged, or not. Those eyes. This scent. That pouty, stubborn pink mouth. I would have recalled this lay. Her size especially. I've never met a woman so delicate, and —judging by the grunt I choke out as her knee slams dangerously close to its intended target—so fierce.

A part of me rails at the decision before I even let her go and stand from the bed. She scrambles into a sitting position, racing to adjust her askew dress. Her heavy breathing alone reveals how exhausted she truly is. That and the fact that she doesn't come for me automatically. So, much like her newly christened namesake, she sizes me up, hunting for a weak point to pounce on.

And there are plenty. Keeping her in my peripheral view, I risk glancing down and hiss in irritation. She nicked me good with her knife, causing a splotch of blood that ruins this shirt and ensures Vin will get to collect on his bet. I managed to rip the top buttons on it, leaving it open and gaping, exposing part of my chest.

"Goddamn it," I snarl, fingering the flopping lapel. "The one damn time I try to keep the son of a bitch intact…" I trail off, fixing my attention on the cause of the destruction.

Before my eyes, the little *tigre* transforms. Her eyes widen in alarm, fixated on my chest. Out of guilt for nicking me? No. I brush my hand over my left pec, and I know what has her attention.

A topic that not even a sexy little hellcat will ever get the chance to defile. I turn my back to her, forsaking the stupidity out of sheer, pathetic pride. Absently, my fingers trace the contours of a marking I've memorized every inch of by heart. My reason for being who I am now. For leaving the old Don behind.

This name is everything I stand for as a new man. A new person. Despite how drunk I get, or how many men like Mischa Stepanov shun me, never will I let myself forget it. I may have failed her when it mattered, but she'll always haunt me. Always.

I will never escape her.

"You can go," I snap to the woman on the bed. Suddenly, playing games with a hellcat isn't so appealing. There's a part of me that will always crave the thrill of the fight. Then there is the man who just wants to rest. To watch Vin marry some spoiled little *mafiya* bitch and live his happily ever after. Everything I've bled and fought for, the horrible shit I've done…

All of it will be worth it for that one moment. It will.

Impatient, I wait for the sound of footsteps. For the door to slam. I give her ample time before I whirl around to find her still crouched on the bed, her eyes like saucers, staring at me as though I'm a ghost. Or a monster. Some horrible mixture in between the two.

And my exhausted fucking brain… It toys with an impossibility too foolish to seriously entertain even for a second. Considering it at all makes me no better than a goddamn masochist. For over seven damn years, I've avoided poking this wound.

Until tonight. Vin's already scraped the surface of the scar by saying her name.

So why not stick a knife in it.

My jaw aches as I pry my lips apart. I know before I say the name that it's useless to suspect this woman could be her. Still, I torture myself. "Safiya?"

An image of her, blurred and distorted after years of suppressing her memory, appears in my mind. A cherub face. Eyes the color of amber. A sweetness unmatched by even the most cheerful incarnation of Pollyanna. She used to love that stupid book. Relished in finding the good in anything, even in the monsters who surrounded her and the parents who, by their actions, condemned her to death. The little girl I sold. The innocent life I ruined. The flame that ignited the creature I've become today.

Safiya Mangenello. Her life is a cross around my neck, my burden to carry until I die. And this woman isn't her. There's none of that sweetness, that innocent, pure joy. None of that yearning to please or her gift for sowing peace.

The Safiya I knew would never wield a blade against someone. Not her, the girl who cradled dying birds in her hands and wished only to play in the mud. It was her gentle spirit that made her so easy to mold and manipulate at will.

It made it even easier to kill her.

"Safiya Mangenello," I repeat hoarsely, watching the woman's face for any shred of acknowledgment. Her lips are pursed, her expression carefully controlled. But she can't hide a subtle flinching. While not Safiya herself, she's heard that name before.

Whoever hired her must have fed it to her. As an example of why I deserve to die? Or maybe as part of some elaborate trick. Pretend to be Safiya. Even imitate her mute nature to get inside my head and make me lower my guard.

There is just one flaw with that plan. Safiya couldn't scream, even if she wanted to. This woman will.

I adjust my grip on the knife, suppressing the tendril of unease warning me to stop. Let her go. Ignore this slight.

But Vin's not here. Without his calming influence, it's easier to entertain the icy thoughts for longer than I normally would. Fuck, I swear I literally see red, flashing across my vision for a split second. From the window? I look over, but apart from the lights in a nearby building, I see no such color.

My fucking head… I didn't drink enough, it seems. Old Don lurks beneath the confines of my fragile sanity, growling like a goddamn animal.

To be fair, she could have gone after me, and I wouldn't care. My life. My reputation. My livelihood. Anything or anyone but my family—what little of it remains, alive or otherwise.

Olivia and our child.

Vincenzo.

Safiya.

They are the few aspects of my life I've deemed off-limits. No one will ever sully them before me.

"Did he tell you to say it?" I demand, gripping the blade so tightly it shakes. "The bastard who hired you? Huh? Did he tell you to pretend to be a mute little girl in some sick, fucking way to get inside my head? Answer me!"

She doesn't. Her eyes remain fixed on my chest, but her expression slips. For a heartbeat, she isn't a tiger anymore. Just a woman, pale, trembling in the shadow of someone more than twice her size.

That look feeds the darkness inside me like a match striking tinder. Crueler fantasies come to life on the edge of my consciousness. I could easily crush her throat in my fist if I wanted to. Pin her down. Prove my point by making her scream… My fingers flex at the thought, and I can't stop myself from taking a step toward her. Then another.

I reach out, but in the end, I grab my jacket, tugging it on despite the loose sleeve.

"Safiya Mangenello couldn't plead for her life," I confess, facing the woman once more. I can't help the way I flinch as the words leave my mouth—that fact has haunted me every waking moment since I betrayed her. "But you will. Tell me who hired you—"

She lurches to her feet in such a display of grace; I almost forget my hate. This pain... As elegant as a dancer, she races toward me, her gaze on my face, her beautiful features displaying pure terror.

I'm too startled to react like I should. I halfheartedly lift the knife, but her hands, soft and outstretched, slam into me first. She's not strong enough to push me down outright—and yet I let her, using the momentum to dive to the floor.

It's something in her eyes, those dark, fucking intense eyes. I can hear her voice again, as if she shouted into my ear, though she never makes an actual sound. *Get down!*

I only have enough sense of mind to curl my arm around her waist, pulling her with me. We barely hit the floor before I have her beneath me, shielding her body as the world explodes. My neck prickles, stung by spraying material. The sound of broken glass shatters the quiet, along with a low, telltale buzz that precedes an explosion of noise in the corner of the room.

"Fuck!"

In addition to finding a beautiful assassin in my room, it's been a while since someone's taken a shot at me, let alone a sniper. I rock onto my knees, staying low to the ground. Only as my gaze falls over the woman do I entertain the possibility that she could be a part of this attempt. Distract me while the shooter takes his aim.

Even as the suspicion enters my mind, her tiny hands grip my forearms, her eyes scanning the room with that tiger-like intensity.

"Stay down," I tell her, watching her stiffen as my mouth brushes her ear. "On my lead, we head for the door. Got it?"

Her mouth tightens, but she nods without meeting my gaze directly.

Tearing my attention from her, I try to take stock of the situation as quickly as possible. The shooter must have aimed twice. One initial shot shattered the window, and another took a chunk out of the wardrobe in the corner of the room. Through the fractured glass, I can only make out the darkened landscape and the nearest row of buildings. One's close enough to be the shooter's nest, and a flicker of movement in a window draws my notice.

"Got you, you sick fuck," I hiss. Keeping close to the ground, I lurch for the door, dragging the girl by her arm. She's quick, keeping pace on her hands and knees—but she runs into me as I stop short with a grim realization.

To open the door, I have to reach for the handle and risk entering the shooter's line of sight. I could always grab the gun from the closet safe, but there's no way I'd have a shot from here—not to mention that any move puts the woman at risk. I eye her and consider the most reckless of solutions —taking the risk anyway, long enough for her to escape.

I tighten my grip on her arm, prepared to shove her back— but already footsteps are racing down the hall.

"Boss?" a familiar voice rings out. I recognize the gruff baritone as belonging to Javier, my personal guard. "Is everything okay in there—"

"Be careful," I warn. "Open the door but keep cover. Sniper."

The handle turns, and the door opens just wide enough for me to shove the girl through. A whizzing noise hums past my ear as wood goes flying.

"Fuck!"

The second the girl moves, I follow her, slamming the door behind me. Lurching to my feet, I discover the other two guards on my detail already running to meet me.

"Send a team to comb the building northeast from here," I demand. "I think I saw the son of a bitch on the same floor with a view facing mine."

One of the men takes off while I turn to Javier. "Where is Vin?"

As if on cue, the door down the hall opens, and Vin sticks his head out from behind it, looking half asleep. "Where's the party?" he demands. His gaze goes to the woman still in my grasp, and he raises an eyebrow. "Though it looks like you've been having more than enough fun on your own—"

"Get your shit," I tell him, peering into his suite. The curtains are drawn shut, obscuring the view of any would-be shooter positioned outside. "We need to go now."

"What are you…?" Finally, he seems to notice the hole in my door. And the blood on my shirt.

"Holy shit!" He ducks into his room, presumably getting dressed.

"Sir," Javier says. "I have a team scouting the perimeter, and Lionel will bring around the car to the garage."

"Who do you think it could be?" Vin demands, staggering from the room while wrestling his foot into a shoe. "The Salvatores?"

"Could be," I say with a nod. "The sniper, at least." I turn to the woman and tighten my grip on her arm just as she tries to slip from my grasp. From the corner of my eye, I catch Vin staring at her, but there's no conspiratorial glance shared between them. Vin has a shit poker face, but in his expression, I see nothing but genuine interest as he scans the woman's thin frame.

I grit my teeth, caught off guard by the irritation that flares. Apart from her attempt on my life, I have no claim to her. Though, on second thought, I do. The mystery she presents regarding Safiya's memory is mine alone to explore.

In whatever way I chose. By coming to me, she sealed her fate. I'm entitled to her—at least to making her talk. And I fully intend to.

"So, what now? Were you hit?" Vin demands, turning to me. He slips his hand into his suit pocket, and I feel a sense of pride. The boy is already prepared to fight, future doctor or not.

Not that I plan for him to ever pull a trigger.

"I'm fine, but now I need to get you out of here. You—" I incline my head to the other guard. "Take Vincenzo to the countryside villa." One of my new properties purchased after I secured the port. "Javier—" I turn to find the man still issuing orders into a headset. "You come with me. We'll go separate routes in case we're followed—"

"That's stupid," Vin argues, still fastening his pants. "I should be with you."

"The shooter came after me," I point out. "You'll be safer on your own."

"On my own," he says, eyeing the woman pointedly.

But I don't have time to explain. "We need to move. We'll meet up at the villa."

When he hesitates, I approach him and throw my free arm around his shoulders. Lowering my mouth to his ear, I say, "Me getting a bullet through the head isn't the same as you getting one through yours. Trust me on this." This is no time for fucking bravado—I let him hear how my voice breaks. I mean every word. "Do this for me, my boy. Please."

He scoffs, rolling his eyes. "Fine. But next time, I want a companion like yours." He nods to the girl, and for a second, I consider letting her go with him. Then I remember her prowess with a knife.

My grip on her wrist tightens even more, and I sense her tug, attempting to resist. But for whatever reason, she doesn't scream. Doesn't shout. Doesn't kick me or utilize her nails—yet.

Again, that pesky, dangerous suspicion creeps in. Could she be Safiya? Perhaps. Or just a damn good double, hired and armed with a knowledge of the girl's medical history.

Either way, I don't let her go, dragging her down the hall after Javier.

"I have two cars ready, sir," he explains as Vin and the other guard depart in the opposite direction. "The authorities have already been contacted. Those on your payroll will form a perimeter escort."

"Any word on the shooter?"

He shakes his head as we enter the stairwell. "Not yet, sir. But we—damn it." He stops short, his hand on his headset. Wide with alarm, his eyes cut toward me. "I've gotten word that a group of men has entered the hotel. Not Salvatore from what my men can tell. I'm not sure if they are hostile, either."

"Who?" I ask, recognizing the way he's parsing his words. He's beating around the bush for a reason.

"They are Stepanov's men," he says bluntly. "I don't know if it's coincidence or—"

"I just prostrated myself before the bastard and kissed his ring," I say, frowning. "He has no stake in my feud with Salvatore—" At least none that I know of. "Could it be unrelated?"

"I don't know, sir," Javier says, continuing down the steps. "However, I suggest we move. Now."

I start after him and nearly have my arm wrenched out of its socket. I turn to find the girl gripping the banister so tightly her knuckles are white, her heels practically digging into the floor. Again, it's like I can read in her eyes everything she doesn't say out loud.

She's terrified. Is Stepanov who she works for? Though why the man would go through the trouble of digging into my past and taunting me with Safiya's memory, I don't know. Or maybe Mischa is another unwilling bastard on her hit list? He may be somewhat reformed now, but I've been out of the game far longer, though that doesn't seem to matter to her.

I could let her go.

Track her later and cut my losses.

Or I could throw my arm around her waist, catching her off guard and wrench her off her feet. She's so slight, it's almost too easy to throw her over my shoulder. Her fists land harmlessly over my back, but even now, she doesn't scream. Doesn't make a goddam sound apart from the frantic pace of her breathing.

The unwelcome suspicion bites even deeper, but I ignore it, pushing everything from my mind but the need to move.

"Put extra detail on Vin," I command Javier as I draw up to his side. We're nearing an emergency exit, hopefully near the garage. "If all hell breaks loose, he takes priority. I don't care what the fuck happens; you save him over me. Do you understand?"

"Yes, sir," the man replies, though his frown reveals his thoughts on that plan. "Master Vincenzo will take a majority of the detail."

"Good."

I'd rather take a Salvatore bullet myself than risk Vin coming anywhere close to danger. Though hell, I did escort him right into the home of the ultimate devil.

Mischa Stepanov's name has come up tonight more often than not.

And an ominous feeling in my gut warns that I may not like wherever these clues lead.

## WILLOW

’m lost within another waking nightmare, but pinching myself does little to wake me up. Each vicious stabbing of my nails against my wrist just reinforces the grim reality I can't escape.

Over and over, my own brain mocks me with the images— watching Donatello Vanici come within seconds of death— a fitting end he deserves—but rather than let it happen…

I reacted in a way I will never understand.

I should have killed him.

I came so close…

The worst fact to reconcile is that I can't even explain it rationally. Fear wasn't what held me back. Weakness either —and if so, all I had to do was sit back as a telltale red dot appeared over his chest. Ironically, he was the reason I recognized the target for what it was. When Vinny and I would play with water guns in the summer heat, he would affix tiny lasers to our weapons with tape to heighten the fun. I clearly remember turning my firearm on him more than once, aiming my light over his smiling face before pulling the trigger and drenching him.

I could have let him die.

Why didn't I? Rather than come up with an answer, my brain is too busy scouring the past. A million lessons circle my mind, each one uttered in Mischa's gruff baritone. *"Never let your guard down,"* he would insist until his voice grew hoarse. *"Always aim to kill. Focus, Mouse! Focus! Focus!"*

And yet, I failed. My quarry sits unharmed across from me in the back of a black armored car driven by his guard, and all I can do is stare at him.

At his chest.

While covered by his shirt now, the image of the bared, tanned flesh beneath is seared into my memory. Some of the scars I remember him sporting, even back then. The silvery straight line along his collar that he swore resulted from him being stabbed as a teenager. Those ropey, circular patches across his pecs he would always refuse to explain.

He's gotten even more injuries since then—but one new set of scars startled me the most. It was a name, tattooed there in ink so scarlet it could have been blood.

The name of a girl he sold to a monster. His little Safy. His beloved adopted sister. It isn't awe or sentiment that has rendered me speechless since I first glimpsed it. It's rage. Anger so all-encompassing my brain cannot comprehend it.

My mind goes blank as my chest tightens with every breath I take. My eyes burn with the threat of tears that never fall —but I'm beyond sobbing.

The bastard had the nerve to mourn me. To act as if saying my name caused him pain. To act as though he cared. A different woman might be fooled, but I will never forget his face the day he led me to Nicolai Baryshnikov like a lamb to slaughter. I will never forget his steely, ice-cold expression, or the words he said to me before turning his back and leaving me to die.

*"Do what you will with her. I don't care…"*

Years later, armed with the knowledge that living within Mischa's orbit endowed me, I know now how dramatic a statement that was. How pathetic. How cowardly.

And now he mourns me as a martyr, a fallen innocent whose name he bears out of some twisted sense of guilt. But he has no right.

No amount of regret can bring that Safiya back.

And killing him won't avenge what has been done to me. I know that now. He deserves more. A pain worse than death. Pain like that of a child sold to be a slave.

Some aspects of those early days in Nicolai's care are too dark to relive even after all of these years. To survive, I had to suppress those memories and focus everything I had on survival. Time in Mischa's family healed some of those wounds; I can't deny that.

But just by being here, in Donatello's orbit, all of those old injuries feel ripped open and raw. The pain distracts me from everything—like common sense.

Up close, he looks the same, as strange as it is to acknowledge. My imagination has transformed him, distorting his features, and making it easier to picture him as a creature befitting of his sins. However, his hair, though slightly longer, is still thick, neatly trimmed. His skin still clings to hues of gold and his eyes…

They're the same eyes that have haunted me relentlessly all this time. Watchful, quickly shifting from charming to stern, to—whenever Vincenzo's safety is called into question —terrifying.

Losing me didn't change him. Didn't humble or harden him. He just went on, the same old Donatello.

He lived without me.

But I've thrived without him.

*You are a Stepanova*, I tell myself, pinching a sliver of my wrist. *You are the daughter of a lion. You are protected. You are loved...*

"I know who you are," Donatello growls. His sly grin glimpsed in the semi-darkness throws my reassurances into question. "Antonio Salvatore hired you," he declares, his voice smug with conviction. I vaguely recognize the name from our shared past—the one he cursed to hell and back after Olivia died, sounding crazed as he did so. "The bastard dug into my past and told you how to act. How to look.

You are convincing, *tigre*, but I am not fooled. Tell me your real name. Though, trust me when I say I would prefer to pry it out of you."

I shiver, hating the raw note in his voice—stubbornly, my brain instantly defines it—pain and anguish. Like he cares. Like the little girl he referenced matters to him at all. When she doesn't. I didn't.

So, I meet his gaze and do nothing. Eye contact with him is a different animal from years ago, when I had to crane my neck back just to look at him adoringly. I had viewed him only as Don, then. My savior. My protector. In a violent world, neglected by my parents, I knew he would always be there for me. Save me.

Love me.

My love for him was easy to shed after barely a week in Nicolai's custody. But the hate? That remains, festering inside me, coloring the way I sit, hunched away from him. The way I breathe, my nostrils flaring, chest heaving. I think the hate has permeated my entire being so thoroughly he can smell it on me.

He sits forward, inhaling audibly, his eyes narrowing and widening in quick succession. Cocking his head, he furrows his brows. "Are you Safiya?" The question comes in Italian, and I barely manage to keep my expression composed.

How long has it been since someone has spoken to me directly in my mother tongue? Too long to count, though I've studied it as well as I can on my own, narrating old fairy tales to myself in the language. But hearing him speak it is a twisted, callous reminder of everything I've lost.

His punctuation is crisp, musical in delivery. With three words, he taunts me. Three little words.

Still, I give him nothing.

He sighs, sitting back in his seat, crossing and uncrossing his legs. "No," he says, deciding on an answer for himself. "You are not her. Safiya was sweet. *Delicata*. A little dove. You, seem to be a vicious little snake."

I clench my jaw—I can't help it—and by doing so, I fall right into his trap. His eyes gleam in triumph, and he sits forward again, tucking a fist beneath his chin.

"You understand me, don't you?" he murmurs. All along, he's been speaking in our native language, mocking me with this relic of my past. It hurts to realize that I don't understand him fully. My brain struggles with some of his pronunciation. But his expression clearly conveys his meaning, adding context to every word. Every syllable.

"Tell me your name, little *tigre*," he says softly, switching to English. "Say it, and I will let you go. I know Antonio sent you. You reek of his meddling, and I believe you are his type —" He looks me over and chuckles. "Too sexy and probably too damn young."

His tone implies a double meaning to that insinuation, and heat floods my cheeks. Amused, he chuckles.

"What lies did he feed you about me for you to bare your fangs, little *tigre?*" He eyes his side, and I feel a flush of guilt mixed with pride. I stabbed him. But in the process, I lost my knife, breaking another one of Mischa's prized rules— always cherish your weapon.

It's in his pocket, and he brushes his hand over the telltale lump in the fabric as if to taunt me. "He must have told you something horrific enough for you to look at me the way you do. So vicious. Like you want to do more than sink your claws into me."

He's right. I want to kill him. But my original plans for revenge are already growing and expanding. Having a knife in his chest isn't good enough. No. He deserves something far worse.

"Tell me your name," he goads, reaching out to stroke my cheek.

I start to cringe from him, but recognition hits me like a punch, locking me in place. His hands are calloused from years of hard labor, and my traitorous body grows hot, remembering this aspect of him so clearly. He used to tell me stories of the days he would work in his father's repair shop, doing whatever odd jobs he could to help his family stay afloat. That business acumen pushed him to excel in any enterprise he undertook, even the criminal ones.

I'd been so naïve to his true nature back then. To me, Donny was God. The man who sheltered me from my parents' instability, giving me respite, welcoming me into his small, makeshift family. He had a wife then, Olivia, and a little baby boy. To be honest, he transformed into a stranger days before taking me to Nicolai. If I had to pinpoint the moment he changed, it would have been the day his wife and son died.

The light in his eyes vanished overnight, and the warmth in his voice grew cold. In theory, what he did to me should have hardened him more, completing his descent into madness. But here he is, more like the old Donny, the figure in my memories.

But then his eyes darken, scanning my face. "Safiya…" He inhales sharply as if just saying the name pains him, and I sit straighter, steeling myself against whatever he might say.

"She had an illness as a baby," he explains, seemingly oblivious to how I jump. "Afterward, she developed aphasia. She was mute, you see. Never said a damn word in her life. Though your boss must have told you that. But it was more than a coy little silence." He sits forward even more, practically frozen mid lunge. Something in his expression changes, darkening his gaze, making his shadow loom taller. "She couldn't cry out when afraid. She couldn't whimper. She couldn't scream. When in pain, she couldn't even gasp in alarm like you or I can. It is a silence unmaintainable by anyone without her affliction. And when you scream for me, little *tigre*, I will know for sure that your ruse is a hoax. So I suggest you come clean now."

A shudder runs through me. This tone I also recognize from my memories. The voice I used to overhear him utilize during heated conversations with the men in his employ. The voice I heard the day Olivia died.

The voice of the Donatello who struck fear into the hearts of his enemies.

Do I fear him now? The answer comes to me easily. No.

I meet his gaze and hold it until he's the one forced to turn away. Just when I think I've won, those cold eyes return to mine, glinting with a renewed intensity.

"Javier?" he snarls toward the driver's seat. The tinted window in the partition separating the back of the vehicle from the front lowers.

"Yes, sir?" the driver responds, a man with short black hair, olive skin, and a serious expression that renders him the polar opposite of my playful Evgeni.

"Has Vin made it to the villa?"

"Almost, sir. They have so far been unbothered by any attacks."

"Good." Returning his attention to me, Donatello raises an eyebrow in a way that makes my breathing hitch. "Send word to them not to wait. We'll be taking a detour."

"Oh?"

"I'm in the mood for a drive. Take us to Havienna."

My eyes widen, and he nods, stroking his chin.

"You recognize that name, eh *tigre*?" He reaches for me again, fingering a lock of my hair. "I'm sure your employer told you all about that. But how much will his money be worth when I'm through with you?" Switching effortlessly to Italian, he murmurs, "Tell me your name, little hellcat. I don't think you'll like what lies in store for you if you don't."

He fits the part of intimidating captor; I will give him that. His body is practically balanced on his knees, his eyes boring into my own, his tone a lethal whisper. At the back of my mind, I think I should feel some ounce of alarm.

But I don't. I feel nothing.

Donatello Vanici cannot hurt me any more than he already has.

I'd bet my life on that.

# 11

# WILLOW

Within minutes, he grows bored of me and returns to his previous position, slumped against his seat, his gaze focused on the window. Alarm makes me stiffen, and I cut my eyes to the door, wishing I had the energy to wrench it open and leave. I prefer the anger. The threatening side of him is easier to withstand.

Because when his eyes soften… Something in his expression now recalls those old, peaceful days when I would curl up by his side with a book while he pored over ledgers or business documents. Little had I known what his true work entailed.

In my ignorance, I only knew that I enjoyed being beside him, sneaking glances at his stern, focused face while he'd been too distracted to notice. No matter how lost in the details of his empire he became, he would always humor my presence. Always.

His large hand would absently stroke through my hair in acknowledgment, and I can still recall the feeling of calm that used to come over me. A feeling I haven't been able to ever achieve since.

God, I used to live in such awe of this man.

Now, without the lens of childhood to distort him, all I see is a cruel bastard no different than any other in this twisted war of men. But Mischa doesn't clothe himself in the blood of dead children by way of armor.

"It must be exhausting to be so angry with me," he taunts, leaning his head back against his seat. He lets his eyes fall shut, an act that betrays just how little he fears me.

A smart woman would lunge for the knife. Instead, I lower my gaze to the strip of flesh bared by his ruined shirt and can't seem to do anything more than stare. My fingers twitch, my teeth grinding together as I imagine his reasoning for having that name tattooed there. For sympathy? Pity?

It certainly can't be out of guilt. He had weeks to find me before Mischa Stepanov entered Nicolai's that fateful day— but he never came.

I don't even realize I'm moving until it's too late. My fingers twitch in the still air, reaching across the distance between us, grappling for the lapel of his tailored suit jacket. It's expensive judging from the fabric's softness—a world apart from the simplistic clothing he used to wear.

But he still smells like tobacco. Like old, expensive cigars and musk. Like fresh air and rain. My lungs greedily fill with his scent, comparing it to those old dangerous memories. My throat tightens at the threat of them, and I wrench my hand away just as he stirs, opening his eyes.

Rather than react in alarm, he snatches my wrist, running his thumb along the back of my hand as if testing the flesh for any hint of my identity. These smooth, manicured hands obscure so much of who I really am. His frown deepens.

"You are not Safiya," he says coldly. But then he raises his free hand, tugging his shirt aside, revealing the planes of his chest and the letters scrawled across it in scarlet ink. Tightening his grip on me, he forces me to touch the curve of the S. The A next, which curves around the outline of his pec. The f…

"Do you want to hear what I did to her?" he asks, though there is no pride in his voice. Just exhaustion that matches the wrinkles etched into the flesh around his eyes. "I lied to her," he tells me, forcing my fingers to trace the path of the I. "I told her I would always protect her, though I knew then that I couldn't. I wouldn't. I sacrificed her love to my hate, and at the time… I didn't regret it. You know what they call me, *tigre*? The men who hired you and the others. *Il Mostro*." He switches to Italian, using his free hand to stroke my cheek. I don't know why I let him. Why I'm so riveted by the flesh beneath my fingertips. Up close, it's easy to tell that this tattoo wasn't done carefully like Mischa's many adornments. With every new child, he has their name added to a tally on his back, his way of marking his growing family.

Those carefully inked designs are nothing like this. Raw, jagged lines. Smeared ink as though something other than a professional instrument made the initial incision. And I can picture exactly what from my own experience with the weapon—a knife. A small one, wickedly sharp, utilized crudely to form the final creation inch by inch. To stain the skin, the creator had to use raw ink, rubbing it into the open wounds for no other reason than to cause pain. Agony. Horrified, I realize that this isn't a tattoo.

It's a punishment.

"You're disgusted," he murmurs, dragging the pad of his thumb to the corner of my mouth. My reaction doesn't seem to bother him. If anything, he relishes in my discomfort, swiping his tongue along his lower lip in satisfaction. "Aren't you, little *tigre*? Horrified by what I've done. Your boss fed you a lie, didn't he? That you could stick your little knife through my chest. Kill me. Avenge whatever wrong you think I've done against you. But he was wrong." He laughs and presses down on my lip to expose my clenched teeth. "You couldn't kill me, even if you wanted to. I've been dead for a long damn time. You really want to hurt me? Tell me your name. End this game for good. Kill any hope I may have that you could be…"

His hand falls from my face, but his grip on my wrist doesn't relent, forcing me to feel where a crudely shaped letter y ends, roughly over his heart.

"You are not Safiya," he tells me, applying so much pressure my nail is driven into his skin. "Say one little word and prove that to me. That will do the job better than any knife, *tigre*. Because Safiya? I didn't kill her with my own two hands—that would have been too easy. No. I had to see the look on her face when I delivered her into the arms of a twisted, sick son of a bitch. I had to watch her cry for me, unable to make a sound. She couldn't scream even if she wanted."

He shoves me back so hard I slam against the leather seat cushions. Hunched over, he tears at his hair with both hands, but his expression is anything but anguished. He smiles, teeth bared, eyes flashing with a maniacal gleam.

And for the first time, I feel my heart clench in a way that could be out of fear.

"I knew what would happen to her," he says, laughing softly more to himself than to me. "I knew. And I told myself it was worth it, *tigre*. Her pain, her death, her lost innocence would all be worth it. Because if I could do that to her—" He breaks off, his eyes on his hands as he lowers them before him. "I could do anything. I could survive anything, and I have. I've survived. But if you are Safiya… Everything I've suffered would have been for nothing. So, tell me your name."

I jump at the growl concealed in those final words. It's not a command, but a plea. A poor man begging to be put out of his misery.

When I don't grant his wish, his nostrils flare, cheeks flushing red. "What is your name—"

The mechanical whir of the partition lowering renders him silent, and the driver calls from the front seat. "Sir?"

"What is it?"

"We've arrived."

Dread forms a rock, sinking to the pit of my stomach. Arrived. That word has more connotations to it than I think the poor driver is aware of. Even before I sneak a glimpse from the window, I know he made good on his threat.

To bring me here. The place that had been my haven long before Mischa's manor. The place where my life was ripped apart by the very man seated across from me.

"Welcome home, imposter Safiya," he tells me, wrenching open the door to the back seat, ushering in a burst of cold air, damp with a drizzle of rain. "Get out."

I can't move. My gaze is riveted on the looming manor house. It's been over seven years since I saw it last, but in so many ways, it seems like I've never left. The darkness obscures any signs of age that might mar the stone structure, but the faint moonlight enhances its old beauty to a painful degree. The lawns have since become overgrown and wild, though the same curved stone path leads to the main entrance—a large double door, painted red, nearly swallowed by a swath of creeping vines.

"Come," Donatello commands, exiting the car first. Before I can react, his hand lashes out, snagging my wrist, dragging me after him.

I dig my heels in, twisting to free myself from his grasp—but he's persistent, snatching me by my waist and lifting me off my feet entirely.

"Don't tell me you aren't enjoying your homecoming," he snarls, ruthlessly mounting the front entrance to the house.

Memories come in a flood, drowning me in remnants of the past. Living here with him. My old room, adorned with pretty pink wallpaper. The study where he used to work. The spacious backyard and the fountain I used to play in. The hallways where Vin and I would waste hours over games of hide and seek.

My eyes burn, and no amount of blinking can keep the tears at bay. They descend in a torrent, and I lash out at the only target within reach. Him. I kick wildly, hoping to strike his chest. My fists hammer at his back before I try clawing at his forearms instead.

Unperturbed, he adjusts his grip on me to kick open the front door, stepping inside.

And in a mocking twist of fate, I'm home again, in the arms of the man who threw me away. His laugh forms a haunting bridge to the past as he sets me down and drags me further inside.

It's dark, and a cloying layer of dust drifts on the air, making me cough. Despite the thick shadows, it's obvious that some level of care has gone into maintaining the property. Donatello grapples at the wall, and scattered lights come to life, bathing everything in an orange glow.

I go numb, struck by agonizing recognition.

The hallway—though less furnished—looks the same. Still, emerald green, accenting the wooden staircase leading to the upper level. I can make out the doorway to his study from here, bathed in the glow of moonlight.

And whatever my expression reveals makes Donatello release me as if stung. Swallowing hard, he backs away, blinking rapidly. Anguish washes over his face for a heartbeat before something cold hardens his expression, darkening his eyes and tightening the line of his mouth.

He grabs my arm again, this time brutally enough to hurt. Whirling on his heel, he tears toward the study almost too quickly for me to follow. I trip in his wake, forced to brace my free hand against the wall for balance. On my way through the doorway, a series of marks catch at my fingertips. Tiny little cuts etched into the wood.

I don't have to look to imagine the small handwriting accompanying each one. Names. Don. Olivia. Vinny. Safy.

"Look at me." Wrenching me forward, Donatello shoves me into a leather chair positioned before a massive oak desk. His desk, coated in a layer of dust. His bookshelves remain, as do the paintings he'd had hanging even back then.

One, in particular, greets me now, looming on the wall behind him. The self-portrait of a little girl, painstakingly crafted with a mixture of finger paints and crayons. I'd insisted on him putting it right there.

So he would never be alone.

I would always be with him.

"Look at me, little *tigre*." He crouches before me, bracing his hands on either armrest, trapping me in place. "You are not her." He scoffs at the prospect even as his trembling fingers find the ball of my chin. He touches me. Snatches his hand away. Grips me tightly, shoving my head back against the leather.

His eyes rake over me mercilessly. From my scalp, down to my heaving chest. His jaw twitches, his breathing audibly unsteady. Heavy. Rasping.

"You can't be her…" To prove it, he grinds his thumb down the length of my cheek as if the bone structure alone is evidence enough. A dangerous possibility creeps into my thoughts. Did he ever stop to picture how his Safiya might look seven years after his betrayal? Did he imagine some weak, broken, mournful creature?

Anyone but me. I am not broken, holding his gaze even as tears blur my vision. I am not some sniffling little victim.

But he is still that man. That brooding, expressive Donatello. Even now, the look on his face robs me of the anger I've held onto. He should be shocked at the sight of me. Alarmed. Repentant. Fearful.

This man…

He's hateful, his eyes blazing as his nail catches the corner of my mouth with a searing sting.

"Tell me your name," he bellows. "Now. Tell me your fucking name!"

His eyes are unfocused, cutting lower to my throat. Without warning, he hooks his fingers beneath the thin straps of my dress, wrenching them down my shoulders before I even have the sense to stop him. I'm at the mercy of the cool air and his unyielding gaze, assaulted by both at once. My hands jerk in a vain attempt to shield myself, but the look in his eyes freezes me in place.

He shows me no mercy, eyeing my womanly body smugly as though the curves prove his next words true.

"You cannot be Safiya."

Not the little stick of a girl he knew. His *cucciola*, his puppy, lovesick with devotion. In his mind, she never grew up.

His trembling finger continues his inspection, tracing my collarbone, and I flinch, my thoughts colliding. This isn't how it's supposed to go.

"You can't be Safiya," he says, laughing coldly to himself. "I wouldn't want to fuck you if you were."

To him, it's perfect logic, emboldening him to cup my breast in the palm of his hand. Callously, he drags his thumb across my nipple, laughing harder as I stiffen.

"Ah, no, little *tigre*… Your game is up," he declares, his smile breathtaking, wide with relief. "That girl meant the world to me. I'd know her…"

And yet he condemned her to a fate worse than death. He swallows hard at the realization, and his next stroke is harsher, making me jump. I can't take my eyes off of him as he boldly gropes a part of me no other man has touched.

My brain tortures me with flashbacks of the man he used to be. Of us. Back when I was a useful toy to him. A silent little spy. No man has ever looked at me the way he does now.

Like I'm prey.

"No," he growls, clenching his fingers around the globe of flesh in his grasp. "Tell me your name. Now. Tell me." He lowers his mouth to my ear, letting his gruff rasp drip against the lobe. "Though it's too late. I've already seen through your ruse. My little Safiya wouldn't endure this treatment. Not from me."

From him. The man she loved so innocently. Her protector. Her Donatello.

His touch would make her cringe. Resist. Fight. It would be wrong to endure the heat of his palm. To inhale his scent and remain still.

Still enough for him to press forward, muscling his bulk between my thighs, utilizing his weight like a battering ram.

"No, little *tigre*," he murmurs, letting his lips graze my jaw. "You almost had me fooled." He repeats it ceaselessly, as if hearing it out loud reassures him where his eyes do not. He doesn't take them off me, peering into me with increasing confusion.

My lips part as his thumb rasps over my nipple. Again. Harder. Harsher. A sharp inhalation catches in my throat, the sound alarmingly loud in the quiet.

"Don't tell me this arouses you, *tigre*," he scolds. His opposite fingers sink into my hair, fisting a handful to lock me in place. "You like it rough?" He flexes his fingers, teasing me with the tips of each nail.

My heart races, surging, pounding against my ribcage. That faint taste of fear grows more potent. Run, a part of me warns. My brain issues a string of commands to my paralyzed limbs, but they don't budge.

"Your employer must have paid well to acquire someone so determined. You have grit; I will tell you that," he says, withdrawing his hand to stroke my other breast. The light touch proceeds the moment he catches the entire globe in a grip so tight my teeth chatter. "What was the deal, huh? You seduce me if you couldn't kill me?" He chuckles and withdraws his hand, using the tip of a finger to caress over my nipple so intimately my cheeks flush.

It's the surrealness that addles my senses, sending my thoughts into turmoil. Before my eyes, this man melds into an amalgamation of the caring figure who used to tuck me in at night. And a creature eyeing me with an emotion that makes my breathing hitch. It's the way Mischa looks at his wife in the shelter of darkness when he thinks they're alone and concern for the children no longer tempers his actions.

Hunger. Fire. Lust.

"You're blushing, *tigre*," Donatello warns, tilting his head so he can better observe my mouth. "Tell me your name. You've excelled at your act until now. Give me your name."

He clamps down on my breast and tugs, pulling me toward him. Heat floods my belly. Disgust…

"Perhaps you don't want our game to end?" he suggests, running his tongue along his lower lip. Switching to Italian, he says, "Tell me your name. I'd fuck you senseless if that's what you want. Just give me your name."

Anger flashes through his gaze at my silence. He palms the armrests again, and the furniture creaks as he leans forward, bringing his nose within a hair's width of mine.

"Perhaps your aim is to drive me insane?" he wonders, letting his breath baste my cheek. "Fuck. It breaks my heart to tell you this, *tigre*, but I'm already there. I lost my mind years ago. You think to torment me? I live in torment."

His large hands move to my waist, grasping at the skirt of my dress. Grunting, he tugs. Cold air assaults the flesh of my stomach before I even process what he's done—rip my dress open, baring my front fully to him.

His irises look blacker in the dim lighting, adding a harshness to his features the man in my memories lacked.

He's a stranger, hunched over me. A stranger who smells like home and feels so familiar my body is a slave to the contours of his fingers, unable to sense the danger in them my brain is all too aware of.

His hands find my hips, so large they nearly overlap as he lifts me from the chair and shoves me onto the desk nearby. Limp, I fall back, forced to stare up at him, still trying to reconcile this man with the specter who has haunted me all this time.

Donatello, the man whose face I used to fall asleep picturing while imagining all the ways I'd kill him. Get my revenge. Make him regret leaving me. Forgetting me. Erasing me.

In this moment, those childish fantasies die. The little girl who conjured them is forced to grow up, faced with the ravages of time.

"Now, this is a skill I'm sure your employer won't approve of," he scolds, fanning out his fingers over my waist. The touch distracts me from his words, and I shiver as his thumbs toy with the waistband of my panties, threatening to slip beneath the thin lace.

"Pity," he continues in a harsh tone that doesn't match the unsteadiness apparent in his trembling fingertips. "How can someone like you feel pity for a poor bastard like me? Don't deny it. It's written all over your face. You may hold your tongue, but your eyes…" He inhales sharply as if tasting the word, relishing the flavor of it. My eyes. He might as well be drooling over my soul. "Those eyes give you away. I see you clearly. In every way, I see you."

He sounds so earnest. He truly believes that, every word… While the truth's twisted irony grows the longer he lets his touch linger over me. The more he looks. I think it's the inherent wrongness that leaves me so riveted despite the indecency.

He sees me, his Safiya, right beneath his nose. Maybe he never really knew me. Never really cared.

Something in his gaze shifts as if he's reading my mind, and he shakes his head.

"No. No! You don't look at me like that." He curls his fingers around the waistband of my panties in cruel retaliation for insulting him. "Like I'm the one toying with you, when you… You provoke me in the worst way. A lesser man would kill you for desecrating what you've tried to."

He brings one hand to my throat, toying with the thrum of my pulse. His thumb finds a spot Mischa taught me to recognize— a vital artery. He presses down directly over it, hard. Harder…

"Would anyone even care if I killed you?" he wonders in a cruel whisper. I brace myself as he lowers his weight over me, hovers his mouth above where his thumb still lies. "You are at my mercy. Tell me your name, and I'll let you go. Or gasp. Whimper. Anything to prove it. I'm begging you. I'll get on my knees if that's what you fucking want." He chuckles madly at the thought of it. He sounds mad.

Earnest. A man at his wits' end with nothing to lose. "Prove to me you are not Safiya. Or… Prove to me you are her."

He frowns as if he doesn't even understand the question leaving his mouth. He tilts his head, his breath hot on my cheek, his hips pressed hard against mine, dominating the space between my legs.

"My Safiya wasn't a fighter," he says near the hollow of my throat, still pressing so hard I feel lightheaded. "She loved me like… She loved me—" His voice breaks, triggering an unexpected pain lancing through my chest. It builds and builds, spreading up my spine, setting my eyes on fire.

"She loved me," he insists. "And do you know what I did to her? What I let happen to her? My Safiya? My sweet girl…"

Lace rasps against my hips, ruthlessly dragged over the tops of my thighs. I remember how to move, lurching against him, swatting at his hands.

"I sold her." His eyes are unfocused, staring into space beyond me as his strength easily overpowers what little resistance I muster. He cinches a fistful of my panties and tugs. Fabric tears, making my stomach lurch before cool air replaces the thin barrier, and there's nothing to shield me as his touch roams. He palms my thigh, and I go rigid again, my thoughts spiraling.

"I offered her on a silver platter to men who would tear her apart." His voice goes hoarse with dread. Guilt. Agony. "I let them hurt her. God knows what they did to her." His mouth finds the crook of my shoulder as his hand inches higher. Higher.

I pummel him, trying to clamp my thighs against the intrusion.

He doesn't even flinch, so lost inside his own memories, I doubt he can feel anything. "I killed her in so many ways, *tigre*," he whispers into my flesh, sounding like a broken man, a world apart from the ruthless finger prodding between my legs.

My lips part, my breathing harsh on the air. It's an impulse I haven't done in years. Try to scream…

My nails dig into the flesh of his forearm as he brushes his thumb against me. Soft. Harder, forcing my flesh to conform to the pressure. Fire ignites my cheeks. I know what happens between a man and a woman. I am well aware of the physical act my parents so obviously enjoy.

But rumors, or my classmates, or what snippets of romance I glimpsed in books made it sound so blasé. So simple.

This is punishing. Relinquishing your body to another. Feeling them force their way inside despite the sheer limitations screaming that it's unnatural. They could never fit. Even a finger is too much. Too big.

"Ah… *Sì*," Donatello declares in triumph. "You may hold your tongue, for you are not Safiya," he states, drawing back so suddenly my head swims. "Count your blessings on that. I may be a fool. I may harbor pathetic hopes of her bestowing her forgiveness upon me from beyond the grave

—but I am not that naïve." He steps back, adjusting his askew suit jacket. Cold, his eyes sweep over me. "Go back to your employer, whoever he may be. Tell him that you failed. But know this…"

He starts for the door and pauses over the threshold, his back to me.

"Come after me again, and I won't show the same restraint. Believe whatever lies your master fed you about me, but understand one thing, *tigre*. I am still *Il Mostro*. Attack me all you want, but if you ever insult the memory of my family again? I will kill you. With my bare hands, I will kill you. Slowly. Sloppily. I'll have you praying to the devil himself for mercy before I'm through."

He leaves, shutting off the light as he goes.

# 12

## DON

By the time Javier and I reach the villa, it's mid-morning, and Vin has the nerve to come skipping down the main staircase as I stagger into the foyer.

"You look like shit," he declares while looking sufficiently bright-eyed and fucking bushy-tailed. "Where is your little friend?" He cranes his neck to peer beyond me, as if expecting the blond to come in through the front door.

I push past him in search of a couch to lie on, ignoring the question.

Where is the puzzling little *tigre*? Hopefully, on her way back to her master, sufficiently convinced to leave me in peace.

Peace…

That's the name I've given to this hollowed state of being. Peace. *Peace.* I scoff out loud, feeling my upper lip quirk as I slump onto a leather chaise in the drawing room. As a relatively new property, it's sparsely furnished with whatever the previous owners left behind.

"Looks like someone didn't get any sleep last night," Vin remarks from the doorway. I can practically hear his smirk. But, like always, he's too kind-hearted for his own good. Already, he's crossing to the large windows, drawing the curtains shut to block out the sunlight. "I wouldn't either," he adds from over his shoulder. "Because of sex, hopefully. Or the pain—there's blood on your shirt, Don, and your cheek is scratched. You sure you're okay?"

"I'm fine, smartass," I grumble, letting my eyes shut. Behind them is a wealth of misery, waiting to follow me into my dreams. Safiya, her face blurred by years of neglect, her memory faded and worn. And an older, beautiful blond, her dark eyes taunting me with the threat of a reality too painful to imagine.

Too tempting to resist.

My Safiya back from the grave, willing to put me out of my misery for good. I'd suffer whatever revenge she'd bring my way. Anything. I'd suffer anything for her.

But as my little virgin *tigre* proved, my hopes are futile, as fragile as a hymen straining against my fingertip. I will admit that it was a shock, a welcome bitch slap to my senses. I'd almost fallen for her scheme…

She wasn't Safiya.

But she was different. I can't stop myself from flexing the finger I'd had inside her, recalling that tight warmth. My brain is a sick fucking thing, conjuring dangerous realities where they shouldn't exist. Like that, my would-be assassin was a virgin, so tight I doubt she'd had a man touch her before, let alone fuck her. And her smell…

My forefinger is in my mouth before I know it, and I groan at the remnants of her taste. Sweet. Ripe. My cock stirs, and I regret leaving her there, though perhaps it's for the best. I've kept Havienna in my possession for too damn long. Soiled by the memory of the imposter Safiya, it's about damn time I burned it to the ground and let those ashes fade into dust.

I need to let her memory do the same.

Finally, I need to let my sweet girl go.

"I'll leave you alone to relive your night," Vin taunts, his footsteps tracking his retreat into the hall. "That cut looks nasty, though. When you wake up, hopefully, you'll be in a good enough mood to let me apply some First Aid—"

"Vincenzo." I lift my head as much as I can, straining my eyes to make him out through the dark. My side does sting like a bitch, but any treatment will have to wait. "I want you to pack your things. I'm sending you back to London."

"Why?"

"I've changed my mind. A gangster's daughter is not good enough for you. You deserve to struggle through medical school a lowly bachelor and find some sweet nurse to marry," I rasp, letting my head fall back against the cushions. As I stare up at the ceiling, I think I'm trying to convince myself of this course of action more than him. "Who needs a Stepanov name when you have mine?"

And I'll do whatever it takes to forge enough of a reputation that the mere whisper of the name Vanici will guard him well enough even in the afterlife. God himself wouldn't dare touch him. I owe him that much.

"I've thought about transferring here," he says, catching me off guard. *Here,* where the schools aren't anywhere near as prestigious as the one he attends. And damn it, the boy is so damn sensitive I suspect that's his real motive without having to hear his explanation. He thinks I can't afford his shiny new future.

Either that, or he's more concerned by my burgeoning vice than he's let on.

"No," I growl. "You're getting your ass back to London even if I have to kick you there myself."

"I'm not a little boy, Don."

"You're not," I agree. "But you are my boy. Mine to protect, even if my love is overbearing in nature. You are all I have. So, let me spoil you to my heart's content as any good Papa should. You're staying at that fucking school."

"I know, I know," he says in a tone that betrays he's rolling his eyes. "I'm your sole heir, burdened with the weight of redeeming your fearsome, gruesome reputation, dear uncle."

"And you will," I say in agreement. "I have no doubt about that."

I may have failed Safiya, but Vincenzo will salvage this sordid legacy. He'll live well into old age, find a good loyal wife, and spawn multiple children. He will know the peace denied to me.

So help me, God, he will know it.

"Goodnight, Don," he says, closing the door to the room after him. "Try to get some sleep, and we'll discuss this when you're sane and less fixated on mulling over your eternal torment."

I choke out a laugh. "Smartass."

In the silence he leaves behind, the specters return. Olivia. Little Nico. Safiya…

"I'm sorry," I tell her, reaching out for her ghostly figure. "I'm so sorry, my little Safy."

She fades without an ounce of mercy.

Not that I deserve it.

For what I did to her, I deserve the pitiful conclusion no doubt awaiting me at the end of this miserable life.

And I'm ready for it.

*A* commotion of noise and chaos snaps me awake. Alarmed, I reach into my jacket for a weapon before I realize several defining realities. One, I didn't think to arm myself before sleeping—a testament to just how badly the little *tigre* assassin has shaken my resolve.

Two, if the figure storming into the room I'm in now were my enemy, I'd most likely already be dead—and their first course of business wouldn't be to wrench open the blinds, ushering in a painful stream of white-hot daylight.

"Son of a bitch." I shield my eyes with the back of my hand, struggling to regain my bearings. Judging from the headache pounding through my skull, I'm long overdue for my morning shot of whiskey. "What the hell—"

"Have you lost your goddamn mind?"

"Fabio?" I lower my hand and strain my burning eyes through a sea of white light. Sure enough, the accountant is the one glaring down on me from the center of the room. One look at his face, and I know the brutal wake-up call is the least of my worries. "What's wrong?"

"You tell me," he croaks. His hands are shaking, tearing at his graying hair as he starts to pace. "What the fuck, Donatello? What the actual hell? I put my life on the line. For you! My literal neck on the chopping block, and you do something like this—"

"If you care to explain what it is that I've done, I'd be more than happy to apologize," I grouse. It takes nearly everything I have in me just to get the words out.

Damn, I feel beyond hungover. Beaten. Wrecked. I could chalk it up to a near-death experience, but that only touches the surface of what truly ails me. Sleep was a poor refuge from her. That face. Those eyes. Not quite wide and innocent like little Safy's. Colder. Harder, shaped by unmistakable hatred and rage.

She couldn't be Safiya…

But she haunted me nonetheless. I see her still, daring me to make her talk. Taunting me with her silence as Fabio rants and raves around her.

"…know you have a suicidal, self-destructive streak," the man growls, and I reluctantly attempt to focus on his ramblings. "But this? Even the mere thought of it is so insane I knew I had to ask you directly. You wouldn't be that foolish. Not with this."

I incline my head toward him, wincing as pain stabs through my skull. "With what?"

He stops short, frowning as he realizes he never exactly told me what it is I'm accused of. It must be bad, I suspect.

So bad that the calm, collected Fabio has lost his cool.

"Willow Stepanova," he says, scanning my face intently as if to see how I'll react to the name. "Her family is in an uproar."

He pauses as if expecting a reaction from me. Groaning, I swipe at my jaw and shrug. "Let me guess. She didn't enjoy her party?"

"No," he rasps. "She went missing last night. Mischa has his whole damn entourage out looking for her."

Alarm cuts through the fog in my brain, and I sit forward, trying to picture who would dare rip away the man's daughter right from under his nose.

"Do they know for sure that she was taken?"

"Not yet," Fabio says, still eyeing me sternly. "But there are rumors, Don. Rumors that claim you were seen at your hotel with a woman who suspiciously matches the girl's description."

I scoff. "I never even met the woman! You were there when I was unceremoniously thrown out on my ass."

"Yes." He nods, his eyes wide. "I was there, Don, when Mischa Stepanov insulted you. I was there when you left. But I wasn't there when you supposedly dragged an unwilling blond from your hotel room in the middle of the night. I wasn't there for that."

My brow furrows. "That's a rather interesting retelling of it. Especially considering a sniper tried to kill me in said hotel room and I was 'dragging' said woman to safety."

"My God." His face falls. "Are you serious?"

"Dead serious. I want intel run on Antonio Salvatore," I say, curling a fist. "If the bastard came after me directly, he won't get to make the same mistake twice. He's always been a jealous son of a bitch. I bet he's pissed that I won the port deal over him. I've heard he's been trying to buy a share for years—"

"Noted," Fabio says over me. "But first things first, tell me more about that woman. Like why you were with her in the first place. A whore? A fling? What did she look like?"

"She looked…" Blond and slender with haunting cat-like eyes. "She looked like a woman who waved a knife in my face; that's what she looked like."

Fabio strokes his chin. "You and your entanglements."

As though I'm accosted by murderous women daily.

"This… This was personal," I say. "I took the woman so we could have a nice long discussion about why it is unpolite to dredge up someone's past."

"So, you spoke to her?" Fabio sighs and staggers to a nearby chair, collapsing onto it. "Thank God. If you had a conversation with her, then that settles it. It wasn't her."

I raise an eyebrow, confused by the leap in logic. "How so?"

He shoots me a strange look. "It's not common knowledge, but Mischa's daughter is mute. Can't say a damn word. Some kind of trauma from when she was young and… Don?"

"Describe her," I croak, sensing the blood drain from my face. "His daughter. What does she look like?"

"Blond. Pretty. Smaller than you'd expect for a girl of nineteen. God, don't look at me like that. Tell me it wasn't her."

"She tried to kill me," I croak, lurching to my feet. "She tried… With a knife!"

And if, by some horrible twist of fate, the little *tigre* had been Willow Stepanova, why would she want me dead?

"Don't look at me like that," I snap. "I never even met the girl!"

"You need to fix this," Fabio demands. "Where is she now?" He scans the room as if expecting a woman to come jumping out of the closet.

"I left her," I say.

"Where?"

"Havien—a property I own in the countryside." There's no need to bring up Safiya or my old home and the suspicions that might arise in him. I taught the girl a lesson, nothing more.

He nods, raking his fingers through his hair. "Okay. You were attacked. You took her to safety and left her in a countryside villa safe and sound. Right? Tell me you didn't touch her."

The look on my face makes him hunch over, cupping his hand against his mouth. "I'm going to be fucking sick—"

"It has to be a misunderstanding," I insist. "Why would Mischa's daughter want to kill me?"

"Forget his daughter! What about the man himself? If I heard the rumors about you, then I'm sure he already has as well. It doesn't look good for you, Donatello, even if what you say is true."

His tone sends an ominous sense of dread through my stomach. Turning to the doorway, I call out, "Javier?"

The bodyguard appears there within seconds. "Yes, sir?"

"Where is Vin?"

The man frowns at my tone. "He went into the city—"

"Bring him back and get him on a plane," I say, pushing past him. "Now. And get me into contact with Mischa's people. Offer whatever assistance he needs to find the girl."

"While you get your ass to that villa and make sure your little knife girl isn't the daughter of the most powerful man in the city," Fabio snarls. "And if she is, you get on your knees and do whatever it takes to fix this. Whatever it takes."

"It wasn't her," I snap. But I was more convinced in the case of her being Safiya. As for Willow? *She's mute*, Fabio said. *Can't say a damn word...*

But Willow's birthday was supposedly just the other day—Safiya's was several months ago. I try to cling to that small shred of reinforcement, but it surprisingly doesn't soothe the unease brewing in my gut any.

"Let's pray she's hiding out with some lover, and her father will find her decently scandalized like any rich, well-bred girl," Fabio warns, coming up to my shoulder. "Because if she isn't…"

The answer doesn't need to be voiced out loud.

If the girl was Willow Stepanova, I might have signed my own death warrant.

And Vin's.

# WILLOW

He left me once to a much worse fate…

And I survived. I endured. I went on to thrive in a new world he could only dream of me living. His betrayal hurt me, but I stayed standing.

Watching him leave this time shatters the pathetic barrier I spent seven years building. Those lies I told myself. The scenario I fed myself, the fantasy promising that I'd find him again as I am now, and put a knife through his chest. As he lay gasping, I'd stare into those glinting eyes until they went dark for good. He would see my face in his dying moments and realize with a cold sense of finality who I am. What he did.

I'd finally be able to let him go.

The man in that fantasy was cruel and heartless but resigned to his fate. He'd always see me coming.

In reality, this Donatello is a stranger—an unpredictable one at that. Tormented, haunted, anguished. He keeps the name of a dead girl slashed into his chest as a constant reminder. He mourns her jealously. He's martyred her.

But when faced with her specter, he crumbles into denial. More than that. He was so damn convinced I wasn't her. Because his perfect, precious Safiya was a saint. Someone he loved enough to threaten murder at anyone who dares challenge her memory.

He loved her.

And he let her die.

Why?

Why?

It's the confusion that barrels into me in a brutal, relentless assault. It leaves me gasping, clawing at the dusty wooden floor in search of stability. An answer. Clarity.

Why?

The walls of this place laugh at me and all those childish whims I've clung to. Reality is as cruel as a searching hand, prodding into one's deepest depths. There is no hiding from it. No escape.

Donatello didn't even recognize me—not because he had forgotten his Safiya. I just don't match the horror he conjured for her. His innocent little Safy's suffering isn't comparable to my own. Even after he threw me away, my pain isn't good enough to impress him.

He can't even recognize the scars of the wounds he inflicted.

Because in his mind? They aren't gruesome enough.

I'd laugh if I had the voice to. Scream. Find a new knife and stab him again, and again and again until he saw me. Really saw me.

I am his monster.

Mischa's grace changes nothing. Donatello ruined me far beyond any physical violation. He teased me with what love could be and ripped it away.

But Mischa and Ellen have shown me what love is. It is brutal, violent affection. The tears fall as I recall all the ways they've protected me without question.

How do I repay them?

I can't even be their perfect, accomplished Willow Stepanova.

I will always be Safiya Mangenello. Unwanted, rejected, repulsive little Safiya, undeserving of Don's love even then. And now, I can't even live up to his memory of her.

I don't know how long I lie here. Minutes? Hours?

As if from miles away, I hear the sound of approaching footsteps, but I can't move. I can't even lift my head to see just who is rushing toward me.

Because I know in my heart that whoever they are isn't him. He left me again, truly left me. The little girl in Nicolai's manor at least got an explanation. *I don't care...*

This time, I get nothing but comparisons to a dead girl who no longer exists.

Even now, I'm not good enough for him.

I never was.

"I think it's her," a voice calls, distinctly male but unfamiliar. His steps race toward me, and warm fingers brush the hair from my face. "God, it is her. Send word to Mischa. Fuck..."

The horror in his voice triggers a wave of confusion until I realize I'm curled on the floor beside the desk, my face coated in dust. I don't have my knife anymore, just a crumpled business card clenched in my fist though I don't even remember grabbing it. My dress hangs off of me, my panties discarded nearby, my knees clamped together, my face damp with tears, eyes squeezed shut.

And the blood. *His* blood—I can feel every smeared drop, drying on my skin.

"She doesn't seem injured," the man nearby says, his voice wavering with relief. "From what I can tell, at least."

I can't move to reassure him, or the other worried voices that erupt nearby.

I can't move at all.

"Here," another man demands, "put this on her. Cover her up now, you idiot!"

Soft fabric drapes me. A coat?

"Are you okay, Ms. Stepanova?" the first man asks. "Can you hear me?"

"She's in shock," someone else declares. "We need to get her home."

I'm a little doll again, callously thrown away, but I lack the rage that infected Safiya in the aftermath of Donatello's betrayal. I don't fight the man who bundles me into his arms and rushes me into a waiting van. I don't bite at the fingers that gently wipe the grime from my face. I can't even process the voice urging assurances into my ear.

"You'll be okay, Ms. Willow. You're safe."

Without Donatello, I have never felt safe. If anything, I've rebelled against any feeling of stability or peace. I always held out hope for him, even out of hatred. He would see me. Acknowledge me. Let Safiya finally die avenged.

But Donatello never loved that girl I used to be. He couldn't even see her shadow standing before him years later.

Only one man has ever upheld his promise to keep me. Protect me.

I don't feel anything until I finally open my eyes and see him, standing on the steps of our family home. The van barely comes to a stop before I lunge for the door and scramble out of it. I run to him, but he's already halfway to me, wrapping me in his arms so fiercely he takes me off my feet.

I break. The tears I've kept in until now spill down my cheeks. My shoulders shake, wracked with sobs I can't voice.

But Mischa holds me tight, crushed against his chest.

"I've got you," he says, his mouth buried in my hair. "I've got you. You're home now. You're home. I've got you..."

## DON

The girl isn't at Havienna when I arrive, Fabio in tow—but someone was. Someone strong enough to break through the front door. In the dust, several sets of footsteps allude to the presence of more than one person. All men, judging from the size. They primarily lead into the study with individual groups advancing further into the house. But fairly quickly, they must have left.

Taking the girl with them.

"She might have called her employer," I suggest out loud.

Fabio doesn't seem convinced. "There are at least five sets of tracks here," he deduces. "That's more than enough for a private team. Like one of the many Mischa has in his employ. I need to confer with my contacts, but if he's miraculously found his daughter within the past few hours, then we know."

Know what? That the little *tigre* who tried to kill me was really the daughter of a Russian mobster. *The* Russian mobster. A literal princess in her own right with no reason to want me dead.

At least none I dare entertain. Swallowing hard, I direct a question toward Fabio, "You said she's a mute?"

He nods absently, manipulating his cell phone. "Much isn't known about why. The man isn't exactly known for his openness when it comes to his family. She is a musician, so I guess she can hear."

Like Safiya, stricken as an infant with an infection that left her hearing intact but prevented her from ever speaking. In all other aspects, she was no different than any other girl. She could read. Write. Draw. Play.

It was easy to forget her silence, when she was more than boisterous enough to make up for her lack of speech. The barrier was never a hindrance between us—I only had to look at her face and know exactly what was on her mischievous little mind.

And her final expression is all I see whenever I close my eyes. The features have faded with time, but that tormented stare remains. The pain. The anguish. The betrayal.

"I can't get a signal out in this fucking godforsaken..." Hissing, Fabio heads for the foyer. "I'm going to go see if I can get better service out by the car. Though honestly, we should be heading back. Even if you didn't take the Stepanova girl, someone did. And someone tried to kill you as well." Wincing, he stoops to stroke his thigh and sighs.

"My knee is acting up the way it does before shit hits the fan."

He storms from the house, and I should follow him. I don't know what keeps me here, standing motionless in the center of this study.

I left this place the day I sold Safiya. I couldn't bear to step one foot through the door and wander these halls without hearing her echoing footsteps. I couldn't imagine sitting at this desk without having her sneak in to curl onto the floor beside me. Living here without her was out of the question.

After all this time, it's still the damn same, stocked with what furniture I didn't bother to salvage or sell. Books still line the shelves, old business tomes mainly, but even now, a few titles catch my eye. Her old favorites.

I'm drawn to one in particular, and my hand shakes as I wrench it from a thick layer of dust and observe the cover in the fading daylight.

Pollyanna. It was her favorite. I think she strove to fashion herself in the same way, hopeful and optimistic in the face of strife. My happy girl.

The pain of her memory feels sharper now more than ever. A constant throbbing in my gut, made worse by the marks I spy scraped into the dust on the floor. The rough outline of a small body is visible over by the chair. Someone bigger than Safiya but still diminutive and slight.

A woman too feisty, too fierce to be even a *mafiya Pahkan's* daughter.

"Donatello."

I turn to find Fabio standing in the doorway once more. One look at his face and my heart stops.

"Willow Stepanova was returned to her family earlier today," he says hoarsely.

"Thank god," I say, laughing with genuine relief.

But Fab isn't smiling.

"What's wrong?"

"She was found half-naked, covered in blood," he croaks, his expression a cross between disbelief and horror. "Her clothes ripped from her body. Her underwear in pieces. I shouldn't have to tell you where, should I?"

"Son of a bitch…" The room spins, and I collapse into the leather chair, rubbing at my temples. "She couldn't be—"

"Correction, she is," Fabio hisses, crossing toward me, his face red. "You kidnapped Mischa Stepanov's daughter. You dragged her away from the city and raped her in your derelict family home—"

"I did not!" I bellow. "I barely touched her."

He shrugs with a callousness I've rarely seen in him. "That's what it looks like. And who do you think Mischa is likely to believe? You? The bastard he can't even be bothered to grant an audience with despite you pining for it for years? Or his daughter's torn clothing. His men found her, you think he won't believe them? You've been waiting for death for a long time, Donatello. I think you're about to get your wish."

"Let him come for me," I growl, still rubbing at my throbbing temples. Reality tempers my bravado a bit, and desperate hope is all I have to cling to. This is a dream. A nightmare. Any minute I'll wake up to Vin taunting me about having hidden my whiskey. Still, I play along, scoffing at Fabio's insinuation. "I can handle Mischa."

It's a lie, but only in the context of loss vs. gain. Mischa has far more at stake than I do—but what I do have worth protecting is too great to risk.

"Vincenzo!" I lurch into motion at the thought of him, rising to my feet. "I need him safe—"

"I've already suggested your men move him to another location," Fabio says, and I sway with relief. I'd hug him if the man didn't look liable to slap me. "But this is deep shit, Don. I can't help you. Fuck, I shouldn't even be seen with you."

"So enduring your friendship and loyalty is, Fabio."

"Don't give me that shit," he snarls, digging through his breast pocket for an item that makes my eyes widen in shock. "Don't look at me like that, either."

He proceeds to prop a cigarette between his two fingers. He withdraws a gold lighter as well and ignites the end, inhaling deeply. It's been over a decade since I've seen him reduced to this.

"It will take more than your alcoholism to explain this shit away," he adds, starting to pace. "You're lucky I'm still standing here. And if you want to fix this, I can help you. But I want honesty. You mentioned that she tried to kill you, if I believe your little story. So what did you do after, huh? Enact your revenge?"

"No!" Gritting my teeth, I storm away from him and brace my hands against the desk. Contrary to his snide remark, I remember every fucking second of last night. All of it. "I'm telling you, I didn't fuck her. I barely touched her."

"So, what did happen, then?"

"I…" After sleep and in a somewhat clearer mental state, I know how crazy the truth sounds. Insanity. A madman's paranoia.

"Now isn't the time to play coy, Donatello. For the love of God!"

"Alright! I thought… I thought she was pretending to be Safiya."

"Shit," Fabio says as understanding dawns over his expression. "She's mute. And the girl was… I didn't even stop to think of that."

I nod, scowling. "I thought Salvatore or some other twisted cunt hired her to get to me. If she couldn't kill me, then her aim was to torment me. Make me relive that guilt—"

"When in reality, she was the poor daughter of a fucking psychopath. For all we know, she could be simpleminded."

In horror, Fabio hunches over again. His face pales, and he truly looks on the verge of vomiting. To console himself, he takes another hit of nicotine and exhales harshly.

As dramatic a display as it is, I can't blame him. I've worked so damn hard to cultivate peace for Vin's sake. In one cruel twist of fate, have I fucked up everything?

Or was that her aim all along? The sneaky blond with the fiery eyes. What the hell did I do to her?

"I think your best chance is to request a meeting," Fabio says, rising to his full height. "Now. As soon as possible. Request a meeting with Mischa. Explain your past. Prove you didn't harm the girl."

"And what?" I demand. "He'll take me at my word and send me on my way with a kiss? I couldn't even get an audience with a bastard to form a truce over the fucking harbor."

"But that was a formality," Fabio warns, his tone cold. "This? This is life or death, Donatello. This is no game. For Vin's sake, I suggest you prostrate yourself before the man and plead for mercy. Trust me, you do not want a war with Stepanov. The man is ruthless, and he has enough money to not only kill you—but ruin your name and anyone associated with it forever. The only doctor Vincenzo will ever be is the kind who uses his fancy degree to keep him warm at night while begging on the street for spare change."

I flinch at the imagery and slam my fist against the desk so hard my knuckles crack.

"You know I'm right," Fabio says.

And he is. Mischa is a force to be reckoned with.

But so was I. Once.

I know the heartlessness required to build a name attached to a fearsome reputation. I know what it takes for a man to cut off his humanity. I know the lengths such a man must go through to purge his soul.

Even now, Mischa does not frighten me.

But if the man takes it in his head that I did harm his family and decides to retaliate, Vincenzo won't be spared regardless of my guilt. It's the thought of him that makes me sigh, resigned.

"Do it," I say, spinning to face Fabio. I lift my hands in defeat like a child accepting his punishment. "Call a meeting. Whatever the terms, I'll uphold them. I only ask that the man hold his fire until we can speak face to face. Secure Vincenzo's safety in the meantime. As for Mischa? I'll meet him anywhere as long as he keeps this between the two of us."

"Good," Fabio says, already racing from the house. "Very good."

So is the price of a future. For Vincenzo, I'd pay anything. Give anything.

I've already failed Safiya.

I won't fail my son.

# WILLOW

Death has been a permanent fixture in my life, the one constant that even Mischa's carefully constructed haven can't fully eradicate. When Ivan—Mischa's long-term mentor and the grandfather of his children—died suddenly of a heart attack, a pall had fallen over the house unlike any other sadness to come before it. Time seemed to stop, and this cheerful, private world was forced to accommodate the harsh, grim reality if only for a moment.

The child's laughter had quieted. The bright, cheery colors had been slowly replaced with black accents of mourning, and a picture of Ivan dominated a space in the drawing room where it still resides.

For all his protectiveness, there is only so much Mischa can shelter his family from.

And to anyone who might not know better, the house reeks of mourning. Hushed voices sound muffled from behind my bedroom door. Gone are the typical shrieks and laughter of the children playing. Any movement throughout the manor now is done softly enough so as not to disturb even the mice hiding in the rafters.

Or the one in this bed. Lying here, I eye the ceiling, recalling the past seven years I've spent in this home as Willow and the playful Mouse. I used to pine for Havienna and its sturdy walls, but this place is my true home, even if I've only ever felt like a stranger. An outcast struggling to fit in where I don't belong.

My spacious room holds so many more memories than the tiny, modest one I left behind. I picked out the wooden bed frame myself under Ellen's direction. Eli and I used to take turns squeezing under this sturdy piece of furniture to hide during our games of hide and seek. Mischa himself helped me paint the walls a soft shade of beige to make the space my own.

There wasn't a day I spent away at school when I didn't wish I could be back in this very spot.

But now a shadow looms above me, casting a pall that even the bright colors of my room can't overcome. It stretches across the ceiling, growing darker with every minute to pass by. Soon, I see a face lurking within the darkness, his eyes cold and watchful, eyeing me dismissively.

*You are not Safiya...*

"Willow?" A quiet knock on the door ushers in a slight figure who crosses my room with soft, cautious footsteps. I sense her approach my nightstand, and a dull thud alludes to her placing something there. The smell of food tickles my nose, though I don't bother to lift my head and see the meal for myself. "Darling?"

The mattress barely dips beneath Ellen's weight as she presumably sits beside me. Soft, her fingers run through my hair, parting the strands. At the back of my mind, I know the silence is cruel. I can't imagine what she and Mischa might be thinking after the state I returned to them in.

I know it's wrong to give them not even an ounce of reassurance.

And yet…

I can't move.

"You need to eat," she says gently. "I've brought your favorites. I even managed to get a hold of that jam you like. The one with the strawberries. Willow?"

She sits with me in silence for a while, continuously petting my hair before finally, with a sigh, she stands.

"I'll just leave it here," she says.

She's barely left before a heavier set of footsteps advance toward my room, resonating determination. This visitor doesn't knock, boldly opening my door and approaching my bed without waiting for an invitation. I can recognize him by the sound of his heavy breathing alone.

The mattress sinks beneath his weight, and I expect a loud, bellowing command to follow.

Anything but a sigh, deeper than Ellen's.

A small commotion of tinkling silverware draws my notice. I don't turn to see what he does, but a minute later, something appears before me, dangled inches from my nose. It's square, beige, and slathered in a red, jelly-like substance.

"Take a bite," Mischa urges tiredly. "Just one. You can give me that much."

His tone tugs at some inner part of me I can't resist.

"That's it," he praises as I raise my hand, accepting a piece of toast slathered with jam. I sample a pathetically small bite, barely registering the taste.

"Another while you're at it," he says, refusing to take the bread when I offer it back. "If I could bribe you to eat the whole damn thing, I would."

Despite everything, a smile tugs on my mouth. I try to resist it, but Mischa's thumb appears from above to softly brush my nose.

"A few dollars could get you to do anything," he taunts. "God, help me the day I can no longer goad the girls with treats."

And I remember. Money was the language to bond us. When I was younger, he used to slip me coins in exchange for chores or favors. If only a bribe were enough to change things now—but no amount of currency can erase the crushing pain lingering in my chest. Donatello's return was just the final straw to compound a deeper question that's haunted me for longer than I care to admit.

Mischa knows me only as Willow, his little Mouse.

But who is that woman, really?

"Look at me," Mischa demands, his voice a shadow of its usual baritone.

I pull myself upright, registering the details I hadn't before. It's late in the day, my second being back. Or is it the third?

"That's it," Mischa murmurs as I finally turn to face him.

He props his thumb beneath my chin, lifting it.

I've never seen him look so…old. Wrinkles enhance the haggardness of his appearance. Bloodshot eyes reveal that he hasn't slept, and dark blond stubble coats his chin, marking days without shaving.

But as he watches me swallow, some of the tension in his expression loosens. He sighs again.

"I think I will bribe you," he says, drawing his hand away. "Whatever you want, it's yours. Just eat for me."

He lifts the tray Ellen left for me and settles it over my lap. I scan the items, desiring nothing. More bread, vegetable soup, and a ham sandwich carefully constructed with extra tomatoes and no crusts.

He watches me sample each item, and when I finish, he ruffles my hair. The shape of his mouth could be called a smile if it weren't so tormented.

"I have tried never to coddled you," he says, his voice gruff. "You deserve this honesty, even if it hurts."

But he struggles to voice it, and full minutes pass before he finally cups my cheek, urging me to face him again.

Fathomlessly dark, his eyes scour mine, seeing into my skull without requiring the aid of any sign language. "Did he hurt you?" he demands. I sense the tension in his fingers that he struggled to keep from his voice. They shake. His throat twitches around a hard swallow.

For me, I sense. He's tempering his anger, his rage, all for me.

I reach out, brushing my finger along the blond stubble on his jaw. It clenches against me, and he sighs in relief.

"He asked to meet with me," he says. No name, but none is required. Only one man might make him glare so icily.

Donatello.

"If you don't allow it, I won't." His expression makes me shiver despite his obvious restraint. A man like Mischa can only suppress his fury for so long before it seeps into his gaze, promising vengeance. "You say the word, and I will rain hell down on him. You say the word, and I will kill him. Do you understand me?"

I do. Much as I used to fantasize as a scorned little girl, Donatello Vanici's life is in the palm of my hand.

All it would take is one frown. One nod. One nuanced reaction he could interpret as permission.

In pursuit of such a thing, he tilts my face against his palm, inspecting my expression. Whatever he sees in my face makes him nod and swipe his hand across his mouth as if he has to physically remove the fearsome scowl forming. Gradually, his lips flatten into a hard line, and he nods.

"Alright." He smooths the hair from my face and reaches for a glass cup filled with water resting on the meal tray. "For you, I will show this restraint. Only for you. Now drink."

He brings the cup to my mouth without giving me the chance to refuse. Dutifully, I down every last drop of liquid, and he ruffles my hair, cracking another faint smile. But then it fades, replaced by a more serious expression.

"Your mother wants me to convince you to let the doctor examine you."

When I shake my head, he grabs my hand, bringing it to his chest.

"Please," he says in a tone I've never heard from him. "Do this for me, please. If he hurt you… Let me protect you, Willow. Give me this one thing."

Let a doctor examine me. He'll find nothing, but maybe that's the point. I've been so wrapped in myself; I haven't stopped to think about what my parents must be feeling. Their pain.

Their fear.

Extending it any longer would be cruel.

So I nod.

"Good girl." I'm in his arms before I know it, crushed against his chest as he shoves the tray aside. I don't resist the embrace. He feels so different from Donatello even as he had back then.

Don was warm and light, his laughter infectious.

Mischa is solid, rigid, but unyielding. A brick wall that won't crumble easily. A permanent fixture I'm not afraid to trust, relaxing into his grip.

"I know he hurt you," he says, smoothing his hand over my hair. "I do not know how, but I will make him pay. You say the word, and I will."

He tilts my face to meet him, inspecting my expression.

Slowly, he nods again. "Fine. You let the doctor examine you, and I will hear what the motherfucker has to say for himself. Deal?"

I nod, but I find myself leaning into him again, pressing my cheek against his shoulder.

And he doesn't let me go.

# 16

## DON

Meeting Mischa Stepanov, unarmed and on his terms, is one thing.

Looking the part of a fucking sycophantic patsy while doing so is another. I couldn't stand to face myself in the mirror before leaving the house, but I'm sure I look every bit as ridiculous as I feel. This emerald, piece of shit jacket was Fabio's idea, and already I'm tugging at the collar, feeling my body strain against the confines of the cotton. To be fair, I figure no designer in the world constructed a suit specifically with this type of meeting in mind. Groveling before a *mafiya* leader in the hopes of convincing him that I didn't violate his daughter. *Fuck,* what a mess.

A glass of whiskey couldn't soothe my nerves.

Deep down, I'm partly convinced it's all a trap. I'll walk into this neutral territory and find a bullet lodged in my skull before I can even utter a greeting. Hell, I'd deserve it for being stupid enough to fall for it.

That fate would be a fitting end, all things considered. Once again, little Safiya is smirking at me from the grave. Once again, because of her, I've stumbled, jeopardizing everything I've strived to create for myself. I will never outlast her memory.

I feel her presence now more than ever, haunting me down the narrow hall of Fabio's downtown offices in the heart of the city. Its location makes it difficult to ambush. With Fabio's connections to the governor, no man would dare mount an attack on him directly.

It's as figuratively safe as a mother's bosom, but I'm not naïve enough to trust in it completely. Mischa isn't known for his strict adherence to the typical rules of engagement, be them explicit or otherwise. The man made his mark by clawing at every bit of his sizeable empire that wasn't handed to him out of fear. He waged a bloody war against an oil magnate he believed wronged his family, and as the rumors go, his own wife was once his captive, brutalized and scarred for his amusement.

As cold a thought as it is, I have to wonder if the man truly even cares about his daughter's supposed predicament out of love? Or just anger at what it looks like on the surface? Another man dared to defile what is his, leveling a slight no true leader could ever let go unchallenged.

Though, even I can admit another man wouldn't show this level of restraint. Antonio Salvatore would have already tried to tear me to pieces were one of his daughters found in the same state.

And what a state it was. The blond, fiery-eyed *tigre* who just so happens to be mute. What grudge could she have against me?

My brain dances around the answer. It could be the whiskey in my system, or sheer twisted logic, but the more I mull over her, the more solutions come to mind. Like the fact that Mischa Stepanov is the type of man to run in the same circles as Nicolai Baryshnikov, a well-known money lender to the Russian mob. Could Mischa have a fetish for children and procured a girl for himself? My Safiya, raised as his own?

*No.* I shake my head, laughing at the possibility. My black heart might get some peace from the ending, but it's too much like a fairy tale to ever be real.

Isn't it?

Lost in thought, I tug on my tie, and I barely register a man's voice, addressing me from up ahead.

"You're properly dressed at least," Fabio remarks from the doorway of his private office. As agreed, a Stepanov agent lurks at the other end of the corridor, while my men, including Javier, have to wait outside of the building.

"You play this right, and you can smooth this over," Fabio warns, opening the door. "You can wait in here."

His office is empty apart from two leather chairs placed directly across from each other, out of range from any of the large windows showcasing a view of the city.

"At least my kennel is well furnished," I grouse halfheartedly. As agreed, I'm expected to wait on the man like a naughty child called to a headmaster's office. Patiently, I must anticipate my punishment.

"Don't fuck this up, Donatello," Fabio warns. "But I know you won't. If there is one thing you care about, it's family."

He's right.

And he's wrong. Safiya Mangenello is proof alone as to the opposite. I'm a selfish fuck, and I always have been. But Vin isn't like me.

"How long until he shows up?" I ask Fabio as I enter the office and take a seat facing him.

He shrugs, smoothing his hands down the front of his own suit. In a crisp navy blue, he cuts a stern figure befitting any neutral party. "Whenever he fucking feels like it. You're lucky he even agreed to this."

"And his daughter? How is she?"

"You probably have a better idea of that than I do," he says ominously. "Seeing as how you claim you didn't touch her."

"I said I didn't rape her," I clarify. "And I didn't drag her kicking and screaming into my room either. She came at me. Besides, I'm still not even convinced the girl I was with is Willow Stepanova. Attacking an unarmed man with a knife doesn't sound like the actions of some innocent, sweet little pianist, daughter of a *mafiya* lord or not."

But it's starting to sound more and more like the actions of a spurned daughter, alright—just not Mischa's. Gritting my teeth, I glower from the window and try to refocus on what matters. Making it through this meeting with my hide intact, for one. Doing whatever it takes to keep Vin out of any potential feud.

In short—be on my best goddamn behavior.

"Well, let's be sure before the man comes, why don't we?" Fabio reaches into his pocket and withdraws a folded slip of paper. A photograph.

And the woman staring up from the glossy surface renders me silent.

"So, it *was* her, you son of a bitch," Fabio snarls, shoving the picture into my hand. "God damn it, Don! I got that picture from her fucking school files. Look innocent and sweet enough for you?"

And by God, she does. Pale as snow, hair like spun gold, eyes that soul-sucking shade of brown. She cleans up nice, the little *tigre*, her hair in a neat bun and a starched white blouse in lieu of a low-cut dress—but even as she smiles, I'd recognize that stern tilt to her mouth anywhere.

"I don't understand," I blurt out loud, swiping my finger across that beautiful face.

Fabio laughs. "You fucked up, Don," he says, fishing yet another cigarette from his pocket. He lights it up and inhales deeply, flicking the ash into the base of a nearby potted plant. "To be honest, you were probably drunk. I wouldn't blame you if you were, but now you need to make this right. Wait for Mischa; I don't care if it takes him a fucking week to show. You wait for him, and you make this right. Understood?"

I hiss out a sigh of agreement. "Yes, Mama. I'll be a good boy."

Fabio jabs the lit butt of his cigarette toward me and nods. "I'm going to hold you to that, Don. As for addressing Mischa, do you remember what terms to use?"

Now I really feel like a scolded schoolboy. "That outfit of his likes to refer to their leaders as *Pakhan.*"

"Good," Fabio says. "I suggest you practice your pronunciation as we wait."

Trailing a cloud of smoke in his wake, he leaves the room, slamming the door behind him.

I slump into the chair, still eyeing the picture in my grasp. With the pad of my thumb, I trace the pouty line of the woman's mouth, imagining it curled into a snarl, those eyes filled with hate.

"What the hell did I do to you, little *tigre?*" I murmur.

But the potential answer is too insane to consider seriously. I swat it away for as long as I can before it unfurls in my mind regardless.

Safiya Mangenello, all grown up, somehow rescued from her fate by a man with a reputation fearsome enough to strike terror into the devil himself. It sounds too surreal.

Too much of a fantasy. Not to mention that even if Safiya did survive, her birthday would have been months ago, not days.

And if Mischa *did* get a hold of the girl, then it was probably with an aim in mind more sinister than adoption. Nicolai Brayshnikov certainly isn't known for fostering a nurturing environment for children or women.

Regardless, Mischa bought her, and despite how impossible it seems to believe…

His Willow could be my Safiya.

After seven years, the tables have finally turned. With Mischa on her side, my girl has the power to destroy me.

And Hell…I can't blame her if she did.

# 17

# DON

Nearly three hours pass before I sense the mood in the entire building shift. The place falls silent as if someone flipped a switch. Any chatter drifting from the hallway dies instantly. Hell, no one so much as coughs.

Footsteps approach next, and Fabio opens the door, followed by another man who needs no introduction.

Mischa Stepanov has been a boogeyman for so damn long that meeting him in person, I'm struck by the fact that he is just another man. A tall one, his blond hair hanging loose around his shoulders, his dark eyes cold.

He wears a pair of faded green combat fatigues, eschewing the suit and tie dress code Fabio insisted on. With a sweep of his gaze, he sizes me up without extending his hand in a customary greeting.

"*Pakhan*," I say, rising to my feet. Hands in my pockets, I don't know what to do other than incline my head in respect. "Thank you for meeting me like this—"

"The only reason my boot isn't on your throat is because my daughter asked me not to kill you," he says, his accent so thick the pronunciation gives his words an ominous twist.

I grit my teeth just to trap a stupid question in my throat where it belongs. *Did she ask verbally?* That alone would disprove the theory of her being Safiya.

And assuage my guilt.

I still can't reconcile the obvious. The way she reacted to the girl's name. The mere fact that she seemed very intent on driving a knife through my chest. No other reason fits unless I drunkenly laid with the man's daughter at some party within the past year—and given that she's been supposedly sequestered at a prestigious conservatory, I doubt that.

Not to mention I know for a fact she's a virgin.

"I figured you would be begging by now," Mischa remarks with a scoff. He takes a step, and Fabio lurches as if he means to throw himself between us.

"Shall we sit?" he asks, ever the stickler for protocol. "Please, allow me to—"

"On your knees," Mischa says over him, his gaze boring into mine. "Rushing to explain why my daughter was found on your fucking property. Naked. Alone. Covered in blood."

Fabio cringes at the mental image. So do I.

"It was my blood," I clarify, swiping my finger across my cheek. Days later, the scratch left by *tigre* has scabbed over into a thin, scarlet slash. "She attacked me." Though I don't have a right to be fucking defensive. Given how Fabio glances at me sharply, I suspect he's thinking along the same lines. "What happened was a misunderstanding," I add more softly. "I didn't touch her."

Mischa's eyes narrow, but devoid from them is the rage I figure most fathers would show if they truly believed another man violated their daughter.

"You know that," I suspect out loud. "I didn't force myself on her."

"We both know that there are other ways to force yourself on a woman other than with your cock," he growls, his upper lip curling from his teeth. "If that is your excuse, I'm unimpressed. And I heard that you were supposed to be the wordsmith."

It's a low blow—a dig to my past that dredges up old memories. Like the creative ways I used to describe the many methods I might use to kill a man.

Before enacting them out one by one.

To his face.

With Fabio in the corner of my eye, it's easier than expected to choke down the insult and keep calm. "There isn't a poetic way to describe one's innocence," I say. "Maybe you should question why your daughter came into my room alone?"

It's the wrong thing to say.

He starts forward, his hands in fists, a muscle in his jaw prominent. "Are you implying what I think you are?"

"I'm only stating the truth," I say. But for some reason, the rest won't leave my throat—*that she came at me with a knife. That she might be Safiya. That I sold her as a child and left her for dead.*

"You know what I think would clear up this misunderstanding?" Mischa suggests. "You prove your sincerity."

I swallow hard at his tone. Whatever the man may be thinking is obscured by his stoic expression. To find out his aims, I have to use my balls and ask. "How so?"

He smiles cruelly, and I doubt a simple verbal plea is what he has in mind. "You forfeit your holdings on the harbor to me—"

"That sounds like blackmail," I snap, unable to restrain my tone this time. Anger rips through me, and I have to breathe in through my nose just to keep my vision clear. Vin, I think, curling my fists so hard my nails dig into my palms. Think of Vin. Think of Vin...

"We should put this in writing," Fabio suggests, moving toward his desk. His tone is businesslike, but he grimaces as he fishes out a pen. Even in his rush to please both sides, he knows an unreasonable ask when he hears it.

"Why would you even want the harbor?" I demand, facing Mischa. "Considering you've spurned my every attempt to form an alliance when it comes to securing it."

"An alliance?" he questions, palming his chin. "Or a mercy to prop up what little holdings you have left? When it comes to doing business, I only enter agreements with men I trust. Not only will you forfeit your holdings. Afterward, you leave the city, and you stay away. If you ever come near my daughter again, I have every right to kill you. We both know why."

It's a blunt insinuation. One that makes me wonder just how much he knows of his supposed daughter's past. Going off the look in his eye? Everything.

And it all makes sense.

"You've been hostile to me for some time, Mischa," I say. "I've always wondered why. Most men who show me such avoidance aren't shy about their reasons."

"Most men have a code," he counters. "Lines they refuse to cross."

Like selling little girls to men like Nicolai Baryshnikov. He doesn't say it out loud.

He doesn't have to.

"From what I've heard, some men might consider your code looser than most," I snap. "For instance, I don't think most men meet their wives the way you met yours."

I certainly didn't. I would have gladly run a knife through my chest before ever laying a hand on Olivia. Mischa's wife was not so lucky, it seems.

An eyebrow raised, the man laughs. "And most men don't discard the children in their care the way I heard some chose to."

There is no mistaking it now. He knows. Just how much?

"Whatever happened between your daughter and me is in the past," I say. "I didn't hurt her."

"And yet here you are, aiming to make amends," he points out, gesturing to the space around us. "Or do you wish to compound your insult?"

By rubbing it in his face.

By spurning his gross extortion.

By spitting on the hand of the man who sees himself as the king of this shadow empire.

I want to. I do.

But I would be condemning Vin to a lifetime of fighting.

"Take the harbor," I say, dropping all pretense. I turn to the window, eyeing the glistening waters of the bay in the distance. I let the sight ground me, picturing Vin superimposed over the image. His life is worth more than property. More than anything.

"You leave my family alone," I add. "I'll keep my distance from yours. I don't want a war with you."

"If you ever come near my daughter again, I will kill you myself. You leave me the harbor, you leave the city by the week's end, and I'll be expecting a generous donation to my daughter's conservatory in Vienna to cement your contrition. Of your own volition, of course. You have a week to make the necessary arrangements, as well as to vacate any property you have within twenty miles—"

"And leave it to you?" I hiss, whirling to face him.

His eyes gleam. "Out of the kindness of your heart for any trouble you may have caused. I'm glad we cleared up this misunderstanding."

"I don't need a week," I snap to Fabio, who's hunched over his desk, pen in hand. "Give me until tomorrow. I'll be out of this fucking city. I hope your daughter enjoys the peace."

"She will," Mischa growls. "And you will never see her again."

He turns on his heel and storms from the room.

"That was…better than expected," Fabio says faintly, his eyes on the doorway.

"Fuck me. Just get it over with," I snarl. "Do it. I cede my hold on the harbor. Have my things removed from the hotel. And get Vincenzo on a goddamn plane."

I turn to the nearest section of the wall and form a fist, slamming it knuckles first mere inches from a painting of a scenic landscape only Fabio would find soothing. To me, it's a fucking taunt. I've spent so long clawing at pieces of land for myself only to see it ripped away in an instant.

"I'll overlook that," Fabio says. "But trust me, Don. You're doing the right thing."

"By rolling over like a whipped dog?" I hiss, inspecting my throbbing, reddened knuckles. The hand isn't broken, not that I care. I curl it again, landing another blow. Another.

"By choosing peace," he corrects calmly over the racket. "By choosing Vincenzo. Don't worry. I'll make all of the arrangements. You go cool off—preferably without another blond of questionable heritage."

I push past him, leaving the building in time to catch Mischa entering a car out front, flanked by his retinue.

As angry as I am, I know Fabio is right. I dodged a bullet.

And whether she truly is alive or not, Safiya got her pound of flesh.

May she finally rest in fucking peace.

# 18

## DON

*I* leave Fabio's office and head to my own across town with the enthusiasm of a spanked child. So much for my grand, triumphant homecoming—it's already become an unceremonious exile.

I've barely owned the property for six months, and already it's out of my control. I might as well clean it out myself while Mama Fab tidies up my bad boy messes. *Fuck.* With every passing second, the reality sinks in—and damn, is it grim.

I've just given away almost everything I own to Mischa Stepanov without so much as a fight to show for it. The harbor. My holdings. My pride.

The last thing is the hardest loss to reconcile. That icy impulse deep within me stirs to life, aching to be indulged more than ever. The man I used to be would never tolerate that bullshit treatment from anyone.

Least of all, a man cocky enough to twist the knife when he

has a rival cornered with his back against the wall. Not that I would have shown any more mercy.

All because of her. Even if the little bitch was Safiya... *Is* Safiya...

My thoughts trail off as I slump against the back seat of my car, my head in my hands. Rubbing at my temples, I drop the anger and taste the guilt lurking underneath. It's a bitter pill to swallow.

If Willow is Safiya, she could demand so much more from me. So much more.

I'm too much of a coward to try and imagine what she's been through. What she's seen. Though, isn't it obvious? The kind of pain and horror so intense that seven years later, she comes after me with a knife.

"Sir?" Javier calls from the driver's seat.

I lift my head and find that we're pulling into the parking lot by my office—but that isn't what has Javier so alarmed. Another car is already here, parked in the space beside mine. I don't recognize the model, but only two types of bastards would drive something so goddamn flashy—a blood-red sports car with gaudy gold trim.

The first being a blind, tasteless fucker with too much money to spend.

Or Antonio Salvatore.

"Call for backup," I snarl to Javier. At the same time, I stoop to reach under the seat and drag a black case from beneath it. With a grim shudder, I can only appreciate the fact that the little *tigre* didn't notice this cache while she sat in this very spot. I open the latch and withdraw a handgun. It's already loaded, and I tuck the weapon into my pocket, returning the case to its spot.

"Should we leave, sir?" Javier questions.

"Hell no," I call back. I'm already shoving my door open, climbing from the car. "Just keep the engine running and get another team over here."

"You think he's here for an ambush?" he questions, fiddling with the headset affixed to his ear.

I laugh. "I don't fucking care if he is. But if I kill him, I'll need the body disposed of quick, *so get another team over here.*"

I slam the door and start forward, finding my office already unlocked. It's a small building, staffed by a lone janitor I haven't gotten the chance to know too well. From what I recall of the man—older with a limp on his right side—he might be the type capable of being threatened into opening up the place. Sure enough, I enter the small lobby where a secretary would sit on a normal business day and find it empty.

Inside my office proper, a man lounges in the chair behind my desk, reclined to its fullest position. Dressed in a cream suit every bit as tacky as his car, he has his feet propped on top of the polished surface, leaving a trail of mud inches from my nameplate.

"I hear you've been naughty, Donny," he says, steepling his fingers. So many gold rings are stacked on each one that I'm surprised the sunlight glinting off the bling doesn't blind him. "Very naughty indeed." His eyes gleam, staring from a face that's seen the end of a fist too many damn times—mine especially. His crooked nose disrupts the polished, rich aura he desperately tries to exude. While his black hair may be coifed and his fancy jewelry 18 carats, at his core, he's still the same punk ass he's always been. Once I even called him a friend.

Antonio Salvatore.

"You have five seconds." I don't bother explaining any more than that. I reach into my pocket and grab my gun, withdrawing it.

Salvatore chuckles. "Relax, Donny. I'm here on business." He nods to the view beyond my window—a postcard-perfect snapshot of the waterfront. From here, a man could easily position himself to control the flow of goods that keep the world running smoothly—or this city at least. "Nice position here you've carved out for yourself," Antonio remarks with undisguised greed. "It would be a damn shame to give it all away. Especially to a cunt like Mischa Stepanov."

"I don't do 'business,' with men who try to have me killed," I snarl, hunting his expression for any hint of a reaction. The bastard was always good at his poker face, despite failing at everything else. He doesn't even flinch.

"Don't tell me you've had a hard time, Donatello," he simpers, raising a black eyebrow.

I grit my teeth. I could always kick him out, but he's here for a reason. Rat's like Salvatore do nothing without putting their own self-interest first. So why come to me and risk pissing off someone way higher on the totem pole?

"If I'm not mistaken, you were at the home of said cunt just a few days ago, sniffing around his daughter," I point out.

He smiles and shrugs. "A man's gotta eat. As much as it pains me to admit, Mischa runs this fucking city—and with the harbor, no one will be able to stand in his way. That just doesn't sound fair, does it?"

"Spare me the dramatics," I hiss, feeling my eyes narrow. At a glance, the fucker appears to be alone—but I doubt that. Given my recent brush with a certain sniper, I make sure to take a step back, putting myself beyond the window's range. "Tell me why I shouldn't shoot you. Don't doubt me when I say I've been dreaming about it."

God knows I have. If I were still the sort of man who kept a hit list in his back pocket, Antonio would be at the top of the list.

"Still so paranoid," he remarks. "You were always looking for enemies among friends. Though after what happened to your wife...any man would be rattled. Olivia was a beautiful woman."

I grit my teeth, recognizing the bait for what it is. With his lip quirked, the man watches me for an ounce of a reaction he can pounce on.

I meet his gaze instead and question—not for the first time—how I ever once called this bastard a brother.

"Olivia was beautiful, and she loved me," I say coldly. "No matter how many jealous bastards sniffed after her, she never strayed. Few men can say the same about their wives."

Salvatore's smirk flattens. "It's a shame what happened to her."

He doesn't even try to conceal the verbal knife this time. What happened? Someone gunned her and my newborn son down in our own fucking home. Various excuses had floated around then to explain the attack, but I know the real reason—someone wanted to hurt me. Killing Olivia was the best way to do that. The bastards thought I would crumble.

But I didn't, did I?

Facing Salvatore, I say, "Only a pussy would target a helpless woman and her child."

"Then it's a damn good thing you punished her murderers," he replies, returning his gaze to the window. "What a shame about Gino, though. You treated the man like family. Especially his little girl—it's a shame about what happened to her as well. What was her name again? Sofia? To die so young."

I flinch, and like any snake, Salvatore stirs at the reaction, flicking his tongue along his lower lip as if tasting the blood in the air.

"What the fuck do you want?" I demand.

With a sigh, he sets his feet on the floor and sits forward, leaning over my desk as if he owns it. "I want you to give your share of the harbor to me. I will deal with Mischa. The bastard cannot contest it as long as you make a legal trade. If he tries to draw blood over it, I have the *famiglia* at my back, and our allies are numerous. He wouldn't dare challenge it."

"No," I say. "But funnily enough, my safety doesn't seem to be included in that little plan."

I have to laugh, though, am I surprised by the half-baked scheme? No. Salvatore was always a covetous piece of shit, wanting what he couldn't have—namely everything I did. My position. My influence. My wife.

But to come here and ask me directly to piss off the *mafiya* on his say so? The man must have grown quite the pair of balls since our time under the elder Giovanni Rossi.

"Of course, you would be protected, old friend," he insists. "I'd love to welcome you back into the fold."

And have me groveling at his feet instead of at Mischa's.

"Get the fuck out," I snarl, dropping all pretense. I lift the gun and finger the trigger, wishing more than anything that

I had the impulse to pull it. Maybe without my morning shot of whiskey…

As it stands, I need a reason to, not that I'd have to look too far. "Now. House rules say you're trespassing. I'd have every right to kill you."

"No need for threats." He stands, dusting off his slacks. "I will leave. But I wouldn't be surprised if Mischa finds himself unable to uphold his end of your little bargain— don't look so surprised, Donatello. The entire world knows of how you violated his daughter like the pig you are. But I suggest you think carefully—" He snickers as I take a step toward him, curling a fist. "Join me now, transfer the harbor rights to me, and you may see the glory you once achieved again. The offer won't last forever."

My trigger finger twitches with alarming resolve. Maybe that whiskey wasn't enough, after all? I can feel the icy coldness at the back of my skull, urging me to give in. Teach this sick fuck a lesson…

Shaking my head, I ignore it. "Leave."

He does.

And I slump into my chair, wondering just what the smug son of a bitch was hinting at.

Something well beyond my trouble with Mischa. Could Salvatore be planning to make his own play? If he were behind the attempt on my life, I wouldn't put it past the fucker to aim a little higher.

The only reason I haven't killed him—despite having no proof that he was behind the attack on Olivia—is because though nowhere near the height of their power, the *famiglia* is still a force to contend with this side of Hell's Gambit.

And if Salvatore is making a play for Mischa's throne, then even I can admit that a hell of a war is in store.

Should I do the good thing and warn Stepanov of what danger might be headed his way? After all, Salvatore is one to play dirty, preferring to break his target from within. Sounding the alarm would be the good, neighborly course of action.

Fuck that. I lean into my seat, prop my feet on my desk, and fish through a drawer for a cigar.

I may not trust my intuition much, but what is it telling me to do now?

Sit back and watch the fucking world burn.

As long as Vin is safe, I really don't give a damn who wins either way.

# 19

## WILLOW

*M*ischa may have left me alone for the rest of yesterday, but his visit seems to serve as a signal to the others. It's barely dawn, but already a commotion outside of my door breaks the heavy silence I've been living in for at least three days—a tiny, girlish cry followed by a louder, boyish shushing.

"Be quiet," said boy declares, most likely Ivan, utilizing his bossiest tone. "You'll wake up Mama and Papa."

"She stepped on my foot!" a girl declares indignantly. "I'm telling Mama."

"Not uh, Jona," another girl counters. "You're such a baby."

"Uh-oh," Ivan mutters as louder, sterner footsteps approach. "Here comes Mama—"

"I told you, my darlings," Ellen says gently. "Willow needs rest. Leave her be. Why don't you play outside?"

"Is she sick?" one of the girls asks.

"Jona said Willow is dying!"

"She's not dying, my sweet," Ellen replies. "She just needs rest. Out to play. All of you."

As the children scamper off, whining their disapproval, a knock gently sounds on my door.

"Willow?" The door opens, and Ellen pokes her head from behind it. Her tense expression softens once she sees me sitting up, facing her this time. Warily, she takes a step forward. She's already dressed, her hair swept back into a neat braid draped over her shoulder. "How are you feeling?"

I shrug, and she advances with more confidence. The second she's close enough, she strokes her hand through my hair, tilting my face toward hers. A beautiful grin shapes her mouth, obscuring the concern visible in her gaze. I don't know what Mischa has told her; all I sense from her in this moment is genuine warmth. "Eli and I are going into town for some of those flowers you like. Do you want to come?"

I suck in a breath at the invitation. While their relationship may be far different from that of most mothers and sons, they do have their small traditions that have carried on even while I've been gone. Once a week, they go to the market, just the two of them. For her to invite me means more than a simple outing.

Heart in my throat, I scan her beautiful features, and guilt strikes me with unexpected force. All this time, I think I've been resisting it—her simple affection. But like Mischa's, I know it's genuine.

I shake my head but brush my fingers over hers reassuringly. Her smile widens.

"Get some rest, darling." After placing a kiss on my forehead, she withdraws, cradling her swollen belly with the flat of her hand. "Enjoy the quiet while you can. It won't be long now."

I smile in return and watch her go. It seems like my door barely has the chance to close before a smaller figure appears in the gap, watching me with huge, guarded eyes.

He says nothing, but I can sense why. My heart constricts as I remember the state I left him in—one he obviously hasn't forgotten. He may be able to read me better than anyone, but I can read him just as well.

I lift my fingers, watching them shake in the air before I find the nerve to finally sign, *I'm sorry.*

He blinks and turns away, shrugging his small shoulders. Like Ellen, he's dressed, ready to go.

Cautiously I stand and cross over to him. He doesn't move an inch, not even as I sink to my knees and pull him into my arms. This position makes it painfully apparent that we're almost the same height. He has to lean down just to return the embrace.

"I didn't want to tell," he confesses against my shoulder in a voice I've never heard him use before, faint and hoarse. My eyes burn, but I let the tears fall. He deserves that much.

"I didn't," he insists. "But Papa was so mad… Where did you go?"

I cradle his cheek against my palm and shake my head. One day I'll tell him, I swear it to myself. As it stands, all I can do is squeeze him, appreciating his love more than ever. I was so selfish to take him for granted—to take them all for granted.

Donatello can only damage what I'm willing to let him desecrate.

And he will have no more of me.

"Are you okay?" Eli asks once I finally loosen my hold enough for him to pull away. He scans my face intently but whatever he finds makes him press his lips together, unconvinced.

*I'm fine,* I sign. *Now go get me my flowers. I want the best ones.*

A wary smile alights his face, wrinkling his cherub nose. "I'll bring you some candy, too," he declares.

I nod and sign, *My favorite, of course.*

He beams. "You got it. A chocolate chunk bar."

"Eli, darling?" Ellen calls from down the hall. "Are you ready?"

"Coming!"

As he scampers off, I cross to my wardrobe and withdraw a simple shirt and jeans. I shower, get dressed, brush my hair, and when I leave my room, the hallway is surprisingly empty.

It doesn't take me long to sense where the other occupants are. Boisterous noises drift from below; excited murmurs and girlish shrieks draw me into the drawing room. I hover near the doorway, peering at the scene taking place within.

"And then what, Papa?" Aljona demands, bouncing on Mischa's lap as he sits on a leather chair positioned by the fireplace.

Marnie stands behind him, somehow having wedged herself between his back and the chair. Her position makes for the perfect perch from which to studiously braid pieces of his long hair. Across the room, Ivan lounges on the couch, his nose seemingly buried in one of his books. More often than not, his attention drifts to the tale Mischa is telling.

"And then, the prince found his princess," the man declares, his voice deep and booming. "She had already escaped the villain on her own, rescuing another princess while she was at it."

The girls exclaim in awe, clamoring for more.

"And then what happened, Papa? Did they get married? Huh?"

In disgust, Ivan mutters from under his breath, "That would be boring."

Chuckling, Mischa rushes to appease his audience. "And then…" He trails off, his dark eyes cutting in my direction. "It seems we have another listener who wants to join in. Should we let her?"

The girls turn toward me in confusion and squeal with delight.

"Willow!" In a flurry of flying pigtails and pink skirts, they rush to me, each one claiming a side of my waist.

"We thought you were dead," Marnie declares solemnly, her amber eyes wide.

"Are you feeling better?" Aljona asks, prodding my hip with a tiny finger.

I place my hands on their heads and nod, allowing them to drag me over to where Mischa is.

"Come sit!" they command.

Obediently, I claim a seat beside Ivan, drawing my knees up to my chin. Taking his eyes from his book, he meets my gaze with a rare, impish grin.

"Now, where was I?" Mischa asks, folding his hands over his lap.

"The princess!" Marnie declares, reclaiming her perch behind him.

Aljona crawls onto an armrest and cups his jaw in both hands. "Tell it right this time," she warns sternly. "It has to have a happy ending. And no monsters—" she glares at Ivan, who I assume from his innocent shrug was the culprit of what apparently derailed their last story time.

"Alright," Mischa concedes with a nod. "Now, the princess—"

"Sir?" The stern voice cuts the cheerful mood like a knife. Sporting an expression no less serious, Evgeni appears in the doorway. One look at his posture—and the telltale bulging in the pocket of his suit where his hand rests—sends alarm surging down my spine. Instantly, the girls fall silent, and even Ivan sits up, his expression puzzled.

Mischa's eyes narrow before he quashes the expression beneath a blank mask. "What is it?" he demands. I know firsthand how hard he's strived to maintain the boundary between the sheltered safety his children appreciate and the world beyond them.

With his jaw clenched in determination, Evgeni shatters that façade by crossing to him, his head lowered in respect. Going off his pained grimace, I suspect he is well aware of the norms he's breaking with every step. Whatever he has to say must be well worth risking his employer's ire.

"I apologize, sir. But…" Near Mischa's ear, he murmurs something the makes Mischa lurch upright so suddenly, he dislodges Marnie and nearly knocks Aljona off the chair altogether.

He spins to catch her a heartbeat before disaster, but brings her to me, lowering her into my arms.

"Papa? What's wrong?" She tries tugging at his hand, but he gently pulls away.

"You stay here." The order is as bracing as a slap in comparison to his previous playful baritone. Without another word, he turns, leaving the room with Evgeni on his heels.

I rise to my feet, thoroughly shaken. In all my years of knowing him, I can't name a single time he's ever shown this side of himself to his children. Not the caring father, but the cold *mafiya* leader striding with purpose. If I had to guess, only a handful of subjects would ever be the cause of this disruption.

The safety of his family being paramount among them.

I start after him, but Aljona grips me tight. "Don't go!"

"It's okay," Ivan says. Dutifully, he sets his book aside and takes Aljona's hand. Marnie races to him, and he wraps his free arm around her shoulders, holding both of his sisters protectively.

"I'll watch them," he declares with a brave nod. "I can do it."

Reluctantly, I leave them there, approaching the foyer. Dread pools in the pit of my stomach with every step I take. A cruel flashback taunts me—a moment seven years ago, when another man left a similar play session in horror. We had been at the beach, and I can still remember the day so clearly.

Vin and I were frolicking in the water while Don watched protectively from the shore. Suddenly, he received a call that made him take off, leaving us to the care of a bodyguard. It was only hours later that we learned the tragic reason as to why.

I have to blink back the memory, returning to the present. I'm in the foyer, facing the front of the house. The main doors are wide open, swinging aimlessly in a slight wind. At the base of the front steps, Mischa stands, watching the road, Evgeni beside him.

"They're approaching now, sir," the bodyguard warns.

I can hear the metallic clang of the gates opening in the distance, followed by shouting. The alarmed cries only seem to grow louder. More men stream from various corners of the property as if in some eerie, coordinated display.

They stop short near the road, and at the end of the driveway, a van appears, speeding toward the house. I vaguely recognize it as one of the family vehicles, but it's instantly apparent that something is wrong. A jagged crack slashes through the windshield, and shards of glass glitter over the lawn, falling at random from all four main windows. In a violent spray of dirt and gravel, it sways on and off the road before skidding to a stop in a bed of roses. The door to the front seat opens, and the driver staggers out.

Her slender shape sets her apart from the usual men Mischa employs. Horrified, I recognize her pale face, contorted in pain. Ellen.

I don't even register moving before I'm already running across the lawn on bare feet.

With a roar, Mischa barrels past me, gathering her into his arms. She resists the embrace, reaching for the mangled body of the van.

"Eli…" Her voice is a faint shadow of its usual cadence as if it's taking everything in her just to speak. Blood paints a startling bright path from her forehead down to her shoulder, staining her yellow dress.

Whatever pain she's in doesn't deter her from her sole focus. Persistent, she reaches for him, oblivious to Mischa. "Eli," she murmurs, her eyelids fluttering. "Eli…"

One of the men wrenches open the door to the back seat, and my knees buckle at the scene awaiting within. Blood paints the tanned leather in a vicious spray. Amid the carnage, slumped on his side is a figure so small, so pale…

I barely recognize him.

My mouth opens for a soundless scream. I can't hear. My pulse surges through my eardrums too fiercely, drowning out everything else. I reach for him, swaying on my feet. Only when Evgeni climbs in beside him and feels along his neck can I breathe again.

"He's alive," the man says. Easily, he lifts the boy into his arms and carries him out onto the lawn. What the light reveals churns my stomach even more. He may be alive, but his right arm is twisted at an unnatural angle, drenched in blood from the shoulder down.

"Fuck," Mischa rasps. His eyes dart helplessly from his wife to his son. I've never seen him like this—paralyzed.

"We need to get him to a hospital," Evgeni deduces. Turning to another man, he snarls, "Bring another car around! Now!"

"Is he alright?" Ellen demands, clawing desperately at Mischa's forearm. She's too weak to lift her head enough to see the boy for herself, no matter how hard she tries. "Please, is he alright?"

Even as she speaks, Mischa swears and drops to his knees, cradling her against him. He snatches a handful of her skirt, and I realize why. Ellen's whiter than snow in his arms—I've never seen the color drain from anyone's face so quickly. Not all of the blood staining the fabric comes from her forehead. A glaring amount streaks her legs, and a growing stain paints the fabric near her waist.

"Stay with me, Rose," Mischa pleads, stroking her cheeks as her eyes finally shut.

"The car is arriving, sir," Evgeni calls.

In a coordinated effort, at least six guards carefully arrange Ellen and Eli into the back of a different van, and Mischa takes the front seat.

"They were attacked on the road," I hear Evgeni explain, scrambling into the driver's seat. "Adamo was killed trying to drive them to safety. It was an ambush."

"Who?" Mischa demands, his voice nearly drowned by a sea of guards shouting out various positions and directions.

Evgeni looks at me as if noticing my presence for the first time. "Stay inside, Ms. Stepanova. Victor!" He nods to another man who comes up behind me, placing a hand on my shoulder. "Get her inside. Secure the property while we're gone."

The van starts to move, heading from the property with alarming speed. Even so, a cruel gust of wind throws Evgeni's parting words in my face, uttered in a tone I'm not intended to hear.

"My men are on the scene," he declares. "But you won't like what they've found…"

# 20

## WILLOW

Night has already fallen when a commotion erupts from below, and I startle to awareness in a leather recliner positioned in between two small beds draped in pink sheets. A distant thud rattles the house to its very foundation—that of a door slamming. Even from here, I can sense the tension crackling in the air. Uneasy, I glance around the nursery, from the girls beside me, to Ivan asleep on the other side of the room. Marnie stirs, mumbling in her sleep, but as the seconds pass, neither child wakes up.

Gingerly, I untangle myself from the girls, gently interlocking their grasping hands together. As I slip from their room, my footsteps echo throughout the deserted hall, disconcertingly loud. Among them, I catch a series of muttering voices drifting from the direction of Mischa's study, but this time he isn't alone.

"It isn't proof," Evgeni warns, his tone neutral. I advance toward the doorway and find him standing before Mischa's desk, his back to me. My father sits slumped in his customary chair, his face in his hands. My heart aches as I take in what little of his haggard features are visible. In little under a day, he's aged an eternity.

"But my men were able to identify one of the attackers found near the market," Evgeni says. "He was already dead, but they are almost certain that he worked for—"

"The bastard taunted me," Mischa says over him with a cold laugh. Incredulously, he shakes his head, still laughing. The sound grows louder and louder, so booming that I'm sure it could wake the children. Suddenly, he stops, his gaze fixed ahead, beyond this room, I suspect, at something Evgeni and I cannot see. "That son of a bitch. Right to my face… he taunted me."

"I must insist upon caution, sir," Evgeni insists. "I don't have any right to advise calm after what happened today, but I—"

"Mouse," Mischa growls, his eyes cutting toward me. Before I can move, he crooks a finger, beckoning me closer. "Come."

The bodyguard clears his throat. "I will leave you two, sir—"

"Don't," Mischa says, letting his hand fall. "You talk. She deserves to hear this."

"I'd rather be sure, sir," Evgeni insists, displaying a rare hesitation. "My men will not stop until you have your answers."

"Answers," Mischa says with a scoff. He meets my gaze, his eyes so bloodshot that at a glance, they seem scarlet. Ablaze.

But I know him—if his wife or son were dead, he would be nowhere near this composed.

"They are alive," he says as if reading my mind.

An overwhelming wave of relief nearly brings me to my knees. Evgeni approaches me, grabbing my arm to steady me. As he guides me to a chair, Mischa continues. "I won't spare you the truth," he says hoarsely. "Not this time. Eli was badly hurt. He'll live, but they don't know yet what the long-term damage might be. His arm was shattered…" He groans, rubbing at his temples. After a second's pause, he says, "He's conscious at least. Anna is there with him. Your mother isn't so lucky. She is alive, but they had to take the baby early. Both survived the surgery, but for her own good, they had to keep Ellen sedated. She lost a lot of blood."

Despair clenches my lungs in a fist, but dread builds the longer I meet his gaze. He's telling me this for a reason, warning me to steel myself.

Because as painful as this is to hear, it's not the worst of it.

Not by far.

"They were attacked," he says. "And I could lie to you. Hide this from you. But I won't."

He slams his fist onto the table, knocking a pile of documents to the floor. As his eyes cut back up to mine, they burn fiercely, in a way I've never seen them. At least not in years.

Not since the day he acquired me as little more than a fearsome stranger.

"Tell her," he barks to Evgeni. "Tell her what you've found."

The bodyguard stiffens, his jaw clenched. "Sir—"

"Fine. I will tell her. They were attacked by Donatello Vanici's men," Mischa says. "And I love you, but this time… I won't show mercy."

He stands, pushing past his desk. My mind goes blank as my body reacts on sheer instinct. I scramble to my feet, reaching for his hand.

Turmoil rips through my thoughts, displacing any sense of logic.

All I can see is Eli and Ellen, covered in blood.

I see Donatello, the man who left me for dead.

And now I see Mischa, shrugging me off so violently I trip and land on my knees. Watching him go, I can't reconcile the fear constricting my chest, crushing the air from my lungs.

I can't breathe.

Can't move.

All I can do is try to scream.

# DON

It's a good fucking day. Despite the rain pouring down and the fact that Vin is glaring at me from the top of the hallway steps, I'm determined to make it so.

"A good damn day," I say out loud, slamming my hand against the banister for emphasis. We've already packed our things, and between the two of us, the villa's foyer is a maze of suitcases. Admittedly most are mine rather than Vin's; his consist of just a few bags though the heaviest of the bunch. The boy likes his books.

"Good for who?" Vin grumbles. Shouldering a duffle, he descends the staircase to meet me. Without a fancy party to attend, he's exchanged the suit for a sweater and jeans. From behind his glasses, he looks every bit the doctor in training —one who is scowling at the fact that, while dressing half-asleep, I managed to put on the same pants from said fancy party, speckled with my own blood.

As well as judging me for the minor crime of oversleeping, causing us to run late and miss my morning whiskey.

But, I suspect he's pouting for another reason. Sure enough, he declares, "You're not the one being shipped off like some unwanted stepchild."

"Correction," I say, stepping forward to cup his jaw in both hands. I squeeze his cheeks and coo like a mother hen. As he wrenches out of my reach, I'm lucky he doesn't punch me. "You're being shipped off like my only child. My cherished baby boy. Be glad you don't have a mother here to pinch your cheeks. Though I may get teary-eyed when you finally leave, so take that as fair warning. Now give me a goodbye kiss."

"Knock it off, old man!" He winces, dodging my hand as I reach for him again. "You do enough fussing over me for ten mothers."

"Damn right. Now be a good lad and gather your stuff. By this time tomorrow, you'll be back in your dorm, crying with homesickness."

And I'll be somewhere outside of the city, crying over a shot of whiskey at the state of my finances.

"Whatever you say, Don." Rolling his eyes, Vin marches past me for the front door. A car is already waiting outside to take us to the airport, and with an exaggerated sigh, he heads toward it. From over his shoulder, he quips, "Since I'm your cherished boy, you should carry most of the bags, right?"

"Think again, smartass," I call after him.

The second he's out of view, the smile I've been sporting for his benefit falls. Fuck. Heavy with dread, I approach the room off the main hall that I've been using as a makeshift study. For the first time, I scan the pile of documents lying on the desk in a neat stack, left by Fabio, who worked all night to compile them. I look them over, hissing through my teeth. In a sense, they serve the same purpose as a white flag, ceding my control of the docks—and much of my income.

After Mischa's suggested "donation" to his daughter's conservatory, my disposal accounts will be all but drained. The rumors weren't exaggerating about the bastard's malicious streak.

God only knows how I'll scrape together enough to continue to cover Vin's tuition. He still has his trust fund, separate from any other accounts, but I'll find more. Even if I have to sell the rest of my assets piece by piece. I'll fucking find every last cent.

I form a fist at the thought of Mischa's ultimatum and smash it against the wooden surface of the desk.

"Everything okay, Don?" Vin calls out.

"I'm fine," I rasp back.

I'm not.

My knuckles smart like a bitch, but a grim truth dulls any pain I might feel—it could have been worse. Much worse.

No matter the damage done to my pride, I'd be a fool to challenge these terms.

I would be an even bigger fool to waste any time. Turning tail and running now is the best course of action for everyone involved—regardless of whether or not I feel like a whipped dog in the process.

"Don?" Vin calls from the hallway, but the inflection in his tone catches my attention. He's alarmed. "Are you expecting a meeting or something?"

"A meeting?" I call back. Then I groan at the thought of Fabio dropping by to issue yet more stern mothering and fucking paperwork—I turned my phone off just to avoid his calls for a reason. The man is well known for his tendency toward overkill. Forcing another smile for Vin's sake, I head for the foyer. "Coming."

I've barely gone a step before I realize what he means—a sudden commotion erupts from the front lawn, but Fabio's arrival never draws this kind of fanfare. Or chaos. I break into a run, shouting for Javier as the piercing sound of squealing tires is followed by a sharper crack that chills me to the core.

As I near the doorway, I see the cause for myself—a black car crashing through the gate, speeding toward the house.

I know instantly the driver isn't Fabio, and my blood goes cold. On the list of potential suspects, one stands out, and I take a step toward the gun safe I've yet to clear out in the living room. Apparently, Salvatore decided to stop playing coy with his attempts on my life and try a more direct course of action. But no...

The second I see the car's model—a practical kind, not flashy and expensive—I know I'm off base. Only a professional would ride like this.

And not to discuss financial terms, either.

"Vin, get inside!" I demand.

He's standing on the front steps, watching the car approach. I barely manage to shove him behind me as the vehicle careens up the front path, swerving to a stop before the steps.

The door to the back seat flies open, and a man lunges onto the pavement without so much as a warning. Confusion roots me to the spot the second I see his face—this man doesn't work for Salvatore. Long blond hair streams down his shoulders, his expression cold, his identity chilling.

Mischa.

One look at his face, and I know he's not here to gloat over my capitulation. Recognition gives me a cruel taste of déjà vu. In his eyes, I see a blind rage I know all too well—the same look I saw in the mirror seven years ago.

It happens in slow motion. I see the gun he pulls from the pocket of his gray fatigues. See his hand aiming. Hear the shot...

The booming sound rips through my eardrums, and my mind goes blank.

Blood rushes to my head, deafening me to any sound.

I've been shot before—more than once. I know the fiery agony to expect. It hits like a crushing blow, taking even the strongest man off his feet.

I grit my teeth in anticipation of it, but as the seconds sluggishly tick by, I stay standing.

Snippets of action unfold before me, but I'm powerless to move.

Mischa jumps back into his car and drives off. Even in the brutal aftermath of uncertainty, I know I should be taking after him. Or preparing for another attack—no one takes one shot and walks away.

Unless I'm hit.

Gradually, sensation returns to my limbs. I run my hand across my chest, surprised when I feel no sputtering warmth of fresh blood. No fire.

Last time a bullet hit my collar, fracturing the bone, and I nearly blacked out from the agony.

This time...I don't feel anything other than an emotion I hate to acknowledge, resonating in my gut—fear.

Across the lawn, a man lies sprawled in the dirt. His dark suit warns that he's one of mine, and I dread knowing his identity. Javier? Another guard?

I can't be sure before I catch sight of someone else racing from the other end of the property, their lips moving, eyes wide. Javier. He sprints up the front steps, weapon drawn, but his eyes aren't on me—and whatever has his attention must be bad.

So bad the man pales, his throat cording around a shout.

Confused, I turn around…

And the next thing I know, I'm on my knees. Mischa shot me after all—I'm in a coma, hallucinating the unthinkable.

That's the only reason to explain this.

Because what I'm seeing isn't real. It can't be him. Not Vin, lying on his side, a puddle of scarlet seeping from his ear. He's too pale. Too red. Too red.

I call his name, hearing nothing but the surging pulse of my own heartbeat in response.

They say grief has stages to it, that there's a perfect name for every emotion. While it sounds nice in theory, it's all bullshit some doctor came up with while in his nice, neat office. Someone who never truly experienced the depths of that despair. Or known the brutal, violent kind of loss…

There are no fucking steps to follow, no pretty ways to quantify it. The shit hollows you.

There is only pain to judge the passage of time. One day, you can almost barely live with it. That's coming to terms with it, I guess. Or what you say to stay out of the fucking shrink's office at least.

The truth is that nothing will ever lessen it. Ever. Time merely soothes the sting, and alcohol may dull the ache, but the wound is always there, always smarting at the slightest touch. No amount of mourning ever eases it. You just linger there in the pit of that sadness, always waiting for it to consume you again—or you cling to the few people whose presence can distract from the pain.

I don't mourn Vin.

I don't weep and writhe in sadness. There is no point.

Throwing my head back, I just laugh. And laugh. Seeing my hands coated in his blood has me chuckling so hard I wind up clutching at my chest. Moisture spills from my eyes—an unavoidable, biological reaction. But they burn. Every fucking drop sears rivulets into my cheeks, branding me with the proof of my own goddamn weakness.

He's dead only because I failed him.

What a goddamn riot.

I laugh harder and harder until I'm on my fucking knees, braying at nothing.

But then it sinks in. I'm not in a coma. This isn't a hallucination. I never wake up. From the corner of my eye, I can see him, unmoving. So pale, his beautiful eyes closed, his nose—that signature Vanici nose—draining a trail of blood.

There's no way to quantify the loss—everything I've worked toward dies with him.

But some part of me must find that so fucking hilarious. I'm still laughing as I stagger to my feet. There's no aim in mind—just a need to keep moving. Breathing. I'll suffocate if I stay still. So, I pace the length of the room, watching the blood spread across the floor. I can smell it, salt, and copper. Taste it on my fucking tongue.

And Vin...

I can't look at him fully. Not yet.

I can't fucking look. All I can do is just register the silence. That looming, oppressive goddamn silence. The absence of his voice—I'll never hear it again. It's the same quiet that filled the air when I found Olivia and Nico.

And no matter how hard or how loudly I laugh...it never ends. So I shout. Scream. Yell until I can't hear a damn thing but the rushing of my own heartbeat surging through my ears like a fucking taunt. He's gone. He's gone. He's gone...

But then it's like my mind clears all at once, and I remember the culprit.

The animal who did this.

Mischa.

I lunge for the safe in the living room, rip it open, and practically teleport to the front door, a gun in my hand. I'm aiming it blindly, hunting for a target.

But he's already gone. All that's left are tire tracks ripping across the lawn and my own men scattered about. Some look wounded, but I don't even have the sense of mind to stop. Acknowledge them. Breathe.

I keep running, chasing a specter down to the end of the driveway. A noise finally pierces the fog encasing me—a gunshot. My finger throbs, cranking on the trigger, firing at nothing.

Again.

Again.

Again.

Doggedly, I'm racing toward the boundaries of the house. A car appears in the distance, and I aim for it, feeling my heart hammer against my chest. As it comes into view, I recognize the model—one of Fabio's.

It slows beside me, and the driver's side window lowers.

"God, Don…" His eyes take me in, widening in horror over my hands. My fucking hands…

I don't know what I say to him, but whatever it is makes him curse under his breath. "Let me see him," he says in a cautious tone. Then he drives, heading toward the house.

His reaction makes the reality even more real. Inescapable. Vin.

I'm frozen solid, gun still raised, chest pounding, heart on goddamn fire. I can't even look at the house. I can't…

But I can't leave Vin there, unguarded and alone. In a daze, I return to the villa, staggering into the living room to find Fabio there crouched beside the body.

I surge toward him, swatting his hands away. "Get away from him—"

"He has a pulse," the man says gently, rising to his feet. "We need to get him to a hospital."

"What..." He might as well have punched me. Struck dumb, I shake my head to clear it and croak, "What did you say?"

"He has a pulse," Fabio insists. He already has a cell phone in hand, rattling off a series of orders. "Bring a van around! We don't have time to wait for an ambulance. Now!" Turning to me, he gestures toward my chest. "Take off your shirt and apply pressure to the wound."

Apply pressure. While I'm not a doctor, I know that pressure won't help a gunshot to the head. It won't...

God knows I tried with Olivia. Even if it meant holding her skull together with my bare hands, I tried. Finally, I look over and groan aloud. Blood pools around him, clashing with the color of his skin. He's so damn pale.

"Fab..." My voice breaks several times before I finally get a coherent word out. "His head..."

"Don." Fabio grabs me by the collar, his eyes boring into mine. "Take a walk! Take a walk, brother. I've got this. I'll take care of Vin. You take care of yourself. Keep your head, Donatello!"

Keep my head. A task easier said than done. It's spinning as more men stream into the room, led by Javier, who clutches at his shoulder. Was he hit?

Meeting my gaze, he shakes his head before I can even ask him.

"A van is out front," he says.

"Good." Fabio strips his suit jacket and gently wads it around Vin's head.

I choke down the part of me wanting to demand he let him go. Leave him in peace.

As if reading my mind, Fabio meets my gaze directly. "We have to move him quickly. We can't take him to any hospital in the area. Not with the *mafiya*—" He breaks off and gestures Javier over. Together they lift Vin between them. "I know a man who owes me a favor," Fabio says as they head for the door. "He'll get the best care, Don. I will see to that."

He'll see…

I can't. The world goes dark, and I feel a bitter sense of dread. The same darkness that came over me when Olivia died.

When Safiya…

That thick, hopeless black.

The only way out is to breathe.

Suppress.

Feel nothing…

But rage.

In this moment, anger is the only cure.

Retribution—by any means necessary.

## DON

"He's alive." It's the first thing Fabio says the second he steps foot into the villa, and it doesn't even register.

Alive.

That word lacks the connotation he thinks it has. After hours of silence, I've come to terms with what to expect. Hell, I've lived through this before. Seen the aftermath. Suffered this hell. You don't come out of a gunshot wound to the head alive. If anything, you exist—a shell fed by a series of tubes and machinery. Breathing, but not much more than that.

So no, I can tell from his face alone that even if he has a heartbeat, Vincenzo isn't alive.

Hope is a cruel fucking thing, gnawing away at my psyche regardless, daring me to believe—but I can't.

I won't.

"Donatello?"

Fabio steps closer. I haven't moved from the position he left me in, seated on the floor of the entryway. His jaw clenches as he realizes, horror flashing in his eyes. I look down and discover why. Fuck, my hands are sticky, covered in red. So much goddamn red.

The amount only proves my point. He's dead.

"He's alive," Fabio repeats, crouching to meet my gaze directly. I've known him for too damn long not to see the fear written across his face, contradicting the words leaving his mouth.

"Tell me the truth," I demand. God, I don't even recognize the sound of my voice. This cold, lifeless man. He's a phantom I thought I'd left in the past.

"I won't lie," Fabio warns. "He's in a coma. His condition is serious. There is no real prognosis."

"Where is he?" I start to stand, but Fabio sighs.

"Someplace safe with a doctor I know. One of the best in the world. But…" He grimaces before he says, "I think it's best if you don't visit him for now. Not with Mischa—"

"Why the fuck not?" I snarl, gritting my teeth.

He blinks. "Because Mischa Stepanov put a hit out on you." I have to give it to him. Somehow, he manages to sound gentle—like it's not the exact opposite of everything I've done my goddamn best to ensure.

"Why?" I demand, unable to keep the rage from my voice. The confusion. The hate. I'm too damn sober.

And at the same time, I'm numb.

"I gave him everything he asked for—"

"You tell me what happened, Don," Fabio demands with an exasperated sigh. "Did you call off the deal?"

"No," I croak, swiping my hand through my hair. Nothing makes sense. This could still be a dream if it weren't for the dull, throbbing ache in my chest, intensifying with every beat of my heart. No nightmare could ever feel this real. Meeting Fabio's stare, I say, "I did everything you told me. Every fucking thing."

Because like a fucking idiot, I expected the man to have some shred of honor.

Uphold his word.

One would think I would have learned by now—you can't expect mercy from an animal.

"What you need to do now is come with me. This is bad, Don," Fabio says bluntly. Moonlight from the windows ghosts over his pale face, enhancing the wrinkles exaggerating the corners of his mouth. "Very bad. I'm not an official part of the *mafiya*, but I've never been shut out like this before. Hell, I barely got any fucking warning. And... Did you do it?" He meets my gaze so reluctantly that even in this state, I'd feel some shred of guilt.

If I knew what to feel it for.

"Do what? Sell my soul to that motherfucker only to be betrayed?" The more I say it, the more real it sounds. I laugh again at the insanity of it. To work so hard to be a good man…

All to have it end like this.

"Mischa's family was attacked yesterday," Fabio says. His tone is comparable to a bucket of ice water being dumped over my head. Abruptly, he stands, putting his back to me. Both of his hands tear through his hair, his breathing heavy and labored. This isn't like him, the antithesis of the calm he tries to maintain. He's frantic. "His wife is in a coma—they don't know if she'll even live," he says. "His baby girl was born too soon. His son… The poor kid may be crippled for life. From what I heard, they were ambushed on the road and barely got away with their lives. Donatello… Tell me you didn't do it. Don?"

His voice echoes ceaselessly, but I stop hearing him.

In his place, I see another man, gloating over his own power. His smug, satisfied smirk should have alarmed me even then.

And guilt rips through me.

If I'd used my fucking head, I could have stopped him.

I could have stopped this.

"Donatello!" Fabio stands over me, his voice reverberating down to the house's very foundation. "I know you're not in the best mindset right now. But you need to trust me. You shouldn't even be here. I have a property out of the city where you can—"

"Salvatore." The name rips from me as I rise to my feet, heading for the door. Red paints my vision, and too many thoughts crowd my head. The dark, twisted shit I've spent years suppressing—the need to find the bastard. Make him pay. Make him bleed. "That son of a bitch."

"Don!" Fabio appears in front of me, placing his hand on my chest. "Where are you going? At least give me the gun."

I still have it, I realize, looking down. But I can't seem to relinquish my grip on the handle.

"Don," Fabio warns as I push past him. If I reply, I don't even know what I say. I just keep seeing that smug bastard. Hearing his voice.

"Wait! I have a car waiting," Fabio says, grabbing my arm as I approach the front steps. "I need you to get inside of it, Donatello. Get somewhere safe. I'll give you regular updates on Vincenzo's status, and we can figure out a plan later. Your safety is my first concern—"

"Vin…" As much as I love him, the pain is harder to process than the anger. My steps falter as I see him again, my poor boy. The blood. His fucking head…

Blown apart because of me.

No, because of Antonio Salvatore.

"I won't pretend like his condition isn't serious," Fabio warns, raising his voice until I look at him. "But he's alive.

That's all that matters, and Donatello? He needs you to stay the same. Okay? Come with me and get in the car."

He tugs on my arm until I follow him. Nearby, a black car idles in the driveway, too expensive to be one of mine.

"Get in," Fabio says, opening the door to the back seat. "My driver Oliver here will take us someplace safe."

Oliver is a balding man who looks every bit the dutiful, professional type Fabio would hire. He barely even blinks when I raise the gun in my grasp and aim it squarely at his head.

From the corner of my eye, I see Fabio take a step back. "Donatello…"

"Out," I tell the driver.

With a glance at Fabio, the man complies.

"Don't do this, Donatello," Fabio begs, his hands raised. Even he knows better than to approach me. "Just let me handle this!"

I ignore him, claiming the driver's seat for myself. Before he can try to climb in, I put the engine in drive and step on the gas.

# 23

# DON

*I* don't see the road. I have no idea which force is even in control of the fucking steering wheel. I'm not. My body may inhabit this vehicle, but my brain is somewhere else.

All I can visualize is Antonio Salvatore. Mocking me. Taunting me.

Over and over again.

My jaw aches from how tightly I'm gritting my teeth—but I bite down harder. The pain is the only thing I have to cling to. That and the rage.

Like an old friend, the icy, cold mindset of my past self takes over, and I let it.

I let the hatred narrow my focus, and breathing becomes easier. Thinking is suddenly more direct. My thoughts have meaning again, and the plan they spell out is so fucking simple.

If Salvatore wants to play politics by pitting me against Mischa, I will level the playing field. He won't get to declare checkmate with my foot up his ass.

The first step? Find him.

The potential options are too many to consider. Logic is a luxury I don't care to indulge in. Raking through my memories, I settle on one at random—he had a house, years ago, when I dared to call him "friend." I remember it clearly, some pussy fucking mansion in the hills where he could pretend to be a big man. I'm headed there now, watching the landmarks and street signs pass in a blur. It's like I'm possessing another man's body. A reckless asshole who speeds without a damn given for anyone else on the road.

A monster.

Eventually, that house appears up ahead, perched on an overlook that gives the bastard a clear view of anyone coming. I should slow. Park somewhere secluded and case the property for any weakness.

I only have one gun and hardly a full clip left. No extra ammo. No backup.

In a sense? No sane course of action.

I know from experience that Salvatore keeps at least a handful of *famiglia* goons around him at all times. He's always been a cowardly son of a bitch. Approaching him on my own is pure suicide. So, I keep driving, pressing on the gas as hard as I can.

Up ahead, a set of metal gates loom, barring the entrance.

But I don't slow.

Instead, I brace for the impact and catch myself laughing out loud as the front of the car careens into the barricade. At the back of my mind, I know that reinforced steel meeting the body of this car should be the equivalent of a tin can being crushed against concrete—but good old Fab. He invests only in the best.

My head rears back with the force of the collision, but the airbags don't even deploy. One side of the barrier gives way in a flurry of sparks and squealing metal, bent completely off its axis. The headlights illuminate the twisted chaos, but I wrench open the door and climb out, barely feeling anything.

Movement comes from my left. A guard? A Salvatore cunt? The gun is in my hand, and I aim and fire without a second thought. No restraint.

At the back of my mind, the new Donatello cringes, warning of the potential consequences.

So I aim and fire again until any other noise falls silent—in my head or otherwise.

Circling the car, I observe the gnarled wreckage of the gate. It's almost overly easy to wrench the twisted portion from its frame and shove it aside. Apart from a busted headlight, the car looks none too worse for wear. It's still running. My brain goes a mile a minute as I climb back inside behind the wheel. I continue forward up the winding driveway lined in fucking statues that cast shadows in the dark at full speed. They flicker like a chorus of devils urging me on.

Mama used to claim the road to hell is paved with good intentions. So I must be headed somewhere far worse.

There's nothing good in my soul now.

Just pain and bitter fucking amusement.

While I've scrounged for every penny, Salvatore's done well for himself. If male compensation for a tiny dick was personified by the number of acres, fancy hedges, and white marble a man owns, then Salvatore has a lot to make up for. It feels like it takes ten full minutes before I reach the house itself. A sprawling mansion, the place is ablaze with light that reflects off the parade of luxury cars parked on display in a circular driveway. A fountain bubbles in a small courtyard, and already two more guards come running.

I park in a bed of flowers and step out before they can fire. It's been years since I've shot at anything other than a stationary target at the range. For a second, I hesitate, recalling that promise I made all those years ago. On Olivia's grave, I swore it—I would change. Become a new man.

Repent for those old sins.

But that new Donatello? He didn't have his nephew's blood all over his fucking hands, or those images of Vin in his skull.

Ignoring him is as simple as giving in to the icy darkness creeping across my consciousness. I surrender to it gladly, letting it smother any regret. Any doubt. Inhaling deeply, I feel my grip tighten, trigger finger flex…

And it's too easy. Like slipping into an old piece of clothing, you thought you'd outgrown. Lo' and behold, it fits like a glove, ushering in a wave of memories. Paramount among them? How good it felt wearing it.

My brain doesn't even make the mental connection of aiming and shooting before both men go down. I keep moving, passing through the main courtyard.

It's a weak man's idea of luxury, as is the fucking row of marble steps leading to the entrance. I take them two at a time and kick open the front door before entering a spacious hall decorated in black marble and enough gaudy ornaments to stock some cheap-ass roadshow. The man likes animals. The place is a fucking safari of various creatures made of solid gold.

It's a world apart from Havienna's modest hallway, that's for damn sure. Especially on that day just over seven years ago. There were no golden figurines of tigers to gape at when someone entered my house then. My home.

There were only scattered toys and photographs. Safiya's dolls and Vin's books. Little Nico's burping cloths and his tiny blankets.

Not one damn item held them back. Made them rethink their course of action.

Like monsters, the bastards found my wife in the drawing room unprotected. As she shielded her newborn son, they shot her twice in the head at point-blank range and left her there.

And my fighter, my Olivia…she held on. For longer than any doctor was willing to give her credit for, she held on.

Stinging tears blur my vision as I blink, returning to the present. I'm the bastard now, advancing through a house that lacks any of the familial touches mine did—and my target is a lot harder to find. Antonio Salvatore isn't in the huge-ass living room that overlooks a swimming pool. Neither is he in a dining room with a glass table and a crystal chandelier.

I have to hunt for the motherfucker, letting instinct guide me.

Up a circular staircase where even more windows display the property. I can see headlights in the distance, and I laugh out loud. He must have a panic button, rigged to call for backup.

Good.

Panic is a drug more potent than alcohol. My nostrils flare as I breathe it in and round the corner of a wide hallway. I could aim to sneak up on the bastard, catching him off guard.

Or I can make him piss himself.

"Where the fuck are you hiding?" I call out.

A sudden noise draws my attention a few doors down. A glance through the doorway reveals what seems to be a master suite. Cautiously, I advance, spotting a large bed with silk sheets on one end, positioned near a row of mirrors. Vanity was always one of Antonio's many flaws. There's even a portrait of the man hanging above the polished mantel of a marble fireplace in the far corner.

I know even before I see him, that he's here—the stench of his cologne gives him away.

"You've lost your mind," Antonio Salvatore himself declares from the mouth of a doorway. Naked save for a towel slung around his waist, it seems that I caught him at a bad time.

Nonetheless, he has a gun in his hand, aimed squarely at me. But Salvatore was always a coward when it came to finishing a job. He preferred to have others do his dirty work.

So rather than shoot him, I meet his gaze squarely.

"You attacked Mischa's family," I say, surprised by how calm my voice sounds. Cordial, even.

His eyes narrow, and he sputters. "You've lost your damn—"

"Mind," I finish for him in a growl. "And you bet your ass I have."

My finger twitches. An explosion of sound rips through my eardrums as blood sprays across the glass door behind Salvatore. He falls back, his eyes wide, lips hollowed around a startled o-shape. Whether I've shot him in the chest or the arm, I don't care. I just know he's not dead.

Yet.

"Admit it." I move to stand over him, watching him cough and clutch at his side as I kick his gun out of reach. Wide, his eyes find mine, but while a coward, it appears he is still a smug son of a bitch. He spits at me.

Blood mixed with saliva lands against my pant leg, joining the stains already there. I'm wearing navy, and it's mottled with a million shades of a darker substance.

Fuck…

I sway. The room blurs around me as I paw at my side, spotting a splotch of scarlet there I'd missed. Hell, there's even more on my shirt.

Blood.

Vincenzo's blood.

"Ass…asshole," Salvatore croaks, drawing my attention back to him.

My nostrils flare, catching the scent of blood in the air— and the stench works on my brain better than any shot of whiskey. My vision clears again. All of a sudden, everything is so fucking clear.

Raising the gun, I fire again, aiming for his knee.

He squeals, and it's music to my ears. A melody so sweet it blocks everything else for the moment, and I'll do anything to make it last.

Crouching to my knees, I prod Salvatore's chest with a finger, narrowly missing his wound.

"Confess," I tell him. "To everything. Vin. Olivia. I should have killed you then."

"You don't have the balls to kill me," he rasps. "I'll have all of the *famiglia* on your ass. You'll be strung up just like that dumb bitch—"

I drag my finger over until it hits fleshy, warm wetness. Then I dig in with the tip of my nail so that beautiful song grows richer. I'm intoxicated by that tune. Laughing, I inspect my finger and swipe it across Salvatore's chin, painting him with the color.

"Red looks good on you, Antonio," I tell him. "And you don't want to confess your sins? The fuck if I care. Because I don't. Not really." Aiming the gun near his head, I watch his eyes widen, and the color drain from his cheeks.

It's a look I've waited seven fucking years to witness.

And…to be honest?

I don't feel a damn thing. Revenge is an itch reminiscent of hunger. Thirst. You can only satiate it for so long, but at the end of the day, it's in your fucking nature to. No reason to celebrate.

No reason to mourn.

Denying yourself is a game of control that only hurts you in the long run.

So I don't celebrate as I turn my pistol handle-first and whip the bastard across the face. He grunts, blood spraying from his jaw as a crack issues from the bone.

I still feel nothing.

Just a cramp in my hand as a grim curiosity sneaks into my skull.

"I wonder what your brains would look like, huh?" I ask him, gesturing to the pristine white, marble flooring. "Sprayed all over this wall. You've got some fancy digs here; I'll give you that."

I cock my head back to take it all in. A nice fucking place. Vaulted ceilings and black walls lined in gold crown molding and baseboards. Great acoustics, too.

I hit him again to experience the full effect, and he jerks onto his side, coughing up even more blood.

"Beautiful," I breathe, grinning in appreciation. "I think the place looks nice with a little red, don't you think?"

He doesn't answer.

Sighing, I smack his chin until he faces me.

"I said, what do you think—"

"Daddy?" That sound.

It's ice water to my senses. A gut punch.

I lurch to my feet, and for a second, the world shifts as reality descends. Where I am. What I'm doing.

"Kisa," Salvatore croaks, his voice thick, eyes fixated behind me.

Numb with dread, I turn as well and clench my jaw around a groan. A tiny girl stands near the doorway of the room. Curling dark hair, wide blue eyes. She looks young. Six or seven, dressed in a white nightgown, a fucking teddy bear clutched under her arm.

That look on her face is one I'll never forget. I saw a similar expression seven years ago.

But that girl came back to haunt me.

I see her again, my Safiya, laughing as movement flickers from the corner of my eye. I barely manage to avoid the kick Salvatore aims my way as he scrambles for his gun.

Before he can reach it, I pivot and hit him again. The blow lands so hard his eyes roll as blood splatters down his chin. Whining like an animal, he falls back, still alive.

A good man would leave now.

Let him live in the presence of his little girl.

That good man would pat himself on the back and call himself reformed.

Then that good man would lose every fucking thing despite that good deed. He'd never even see it coming.

Everything I've done has been for Vin.

And even if he's still alive…

I don't deserve him. I failed him once. If to protect him, I have to become someone else, so be it.

I advance so quickly my hand is around the girl's neck before I realize. She goes rigid, her eyes staring blankly. Still, she moves as I urge her forward and crouch down beside her.

"You have a beautiful little girl," I tell Salvatore in a voice so guttural I barely recognize it. "Kisa, is it?" I finger a lock of her dark hair and feel my stomach lurch. Damn… Looking in her eyes, the old Don rails, still there inside me.

But he's getting harder to hear.

"Don't…" Salvatore croaks, and I release the girl, turning back to him.

Propping my fist beneath my chin, I observe him skeptically. "Don't tell me you have a heart, Antonio? After what you did to my family? One would think you had no soul at all."

He grunts, and I lean closer only to realize that the gasping sounds he's making are laughter.

"Don't think I give a shit if you threaten her," he boasts, cackling maniacally. "Do it. Kill the little bitch. Her mother was a Saleri—the *famiglia* will just take it as an insult."

And I could. It's not like I hadn't done it before—used a child to prove a point. The Saleris are a powerful family, but so were the Vanicis once. Power didn't prevent an attack on us. As for punishing Salvatore in this way?

Gino Mangenello reacted similarly when it came to his daughter's life, smug and pompous, so convinced I wouldn't stoop to his level.

"Close your eyes, Kisa," I tell the girl.

She doesn't, her body trembling, tears glistening on her cheeks. With my hand on her shoulder, I manually spin her to face the wall before turning back to Salvatore.

"I could make you beg," I tell him, raising my voice to drown out his gurgling breathing. "Make you squeal and squirm. But you know what? Frankly, I'm too damn tired. All I want is proof. A name. An account. Whatever mercenary you used to carry out your plan. Tell me."

"Fuck off!" He spits again, this time, narrowly missing my cheek.

I don't even realize my hand is in my pocket until I feel it— the handle of a weapon I don't even remember putting there. All this time, I must have carried it with me in these fucking pants. Slowly, I withdraw it, watching the light play off the silvery surface of the tiny blade. *Tigre's* dagger. Safiya's dagger.

"I'm not going to kill you," I tell Salvatore as his eyes twitch toward the blade and back. "You 'kill' animals, like all those fucking toys you have around the place. There's mercy in that word. But what happened to Olivia? That was a slaughter. To Vincenzo?" My voice breaks. I can barely say his name. "That? That was murder."

Salvatore chuckles, and what I mistake for a grimace at first I suspect is another reaction entirely—he's raising an eyebrow. "Don't tell me that whelp is who got his brains blown out? I heard Mischa launched an attack... He just got the wrong man—"

An impulse seizes control of my limbs, and I'm too sober to even try to suppress it. I slam my hand down, driving the knife blade first into his chest. That glorious smell grows more pungent, that song rising to a crescendo. Howling, Salvatore jerks, his eyes rolling, but the wound won't kill him outright. Oh no...

"A name," I demand in a voice that resonates an octave deeper.

Salvatore falls silent as his eyes flicker in recognition. Despite everything, I have to laugh. That wasn't the voice of the good old Donatello I've spent the past few years pretending to be. It's a tone that feels more natural to me than breathing. The guttural cadence of *Il Mostro*.

"A name," I say, relishing in the resulting echo.

All this time, Salvatore's mouth has been wide open. He's trying to scream—he just can't find enough air. Poor bastard.

"Cat got your tongue?" I ask. Then, I rip the blade out to see if that helps.

And it does. He makes a sound this time, sharp and piercing enough to echo in a beautiful song. And that song…

I hum along to the melody—it's music to my fucking ears.

"Give me a name," I command a second time.

He gurgles. Croaks.

But not once does he look at his little girl, shaking with silent tears. Not once does he hold my gaze. Not for one damn second, does he show an ounce of regret.

"You won't tell," I deduce in disgust, rising to my feet. "You always were a secretive little cunt. You're just buying time until your backup arrives. But if you think I'll play your game? Think again. Blowing your brains out is a death far too good for you. But I'll spare your daughter the horror of watching you die. I won't give you the satisfaction."

Turning, I grab the girl by her arm and approach a set of doors on the other end of the room. Time is ticking, and I'd prefer not to waste a second. Still…

As her frightened whimpers reach my ears, some impulse makes me hunt for somewhere to put her. The new Donatello deserves that ounce of mercy. As suspected, the doors open onto a closet—but one so damn big I whistle in approval.

"Nice. Who knew there was so much money in being a lying cunt, huh?" I look back, but Salvatore seems too busy groaning to answer me.

The girl, I leave beside a hanging series of multi-colored suits, tailored finely enough to suit Fabio's most fashionable wet dream. She curls in on herself, her eyes so damn wide. I turn away, clenching my jaw so tight it throbs. As I do, I discover a promising weapon dangling from a custom rack —ties, all of them silk. Grinning, I grab one, a deep crimson which seems fitting for the occasion.

I return to Salvatore, winding the material between my fingers as I scan the room itself. It's an old habit—how I loved to ingrain every moment in my memory. I wasn't the kind of man to shy from his crimes.

I reminisce over them.

Salvatore's bedroom is admittedly one of the most boring places I've killed in. Apart from the king-sized bed, the bastard has a marble fireplace overlooking a view of the property. Not too far from where he lies is a doorway leading to a large bathroom with a sunken tub and gold fixtures.

And there, resting on a gleaming countertop, is an object that renders Salvatore himself nothing more than a liability —a cell phone. I approach the counter and grab it, stroking the smooth surface as I turn to face him.

"You always did like your devices," I say with my own chuckle. I swipe at the screen, unsurprised to find it locked by a passcode. "Laptops. Journals. With your shit for brains, you always had to write shit down to remember it later. Giovanni used to rip you a new one for that." I toss the phone into the air and catch it one-handed. "I suspect this will tell me everything I need to know, won't it?"

His expression alone is my answer—*hell, yes*. And if it's nothing more than a dead-end?

At the moment, I don't fucking care.

"I could say a speech, I suppose," I tell him, stooping back to his level as I slip the phone into the breast pocket of my shirt. "Draw it out. Make it dramatic. But I've realized one thing since we last worked under old Giovanni, old friend. You aren't worth the fucking effort."

Carefully, I raise the tie and watch understanding dawn across his face. The gun would be too quick. Quicker than Olivia suffered.

For him? I make it slow, taking my time to loop the length of silk around his neck. Taking both ends in my hands, I twist them together and tug, carefully controlling the pressure, watching every second.

How his eyes bulge.

How he flails.

How his face reddens before turning blue as he sputters for air.

I once told myself that revenge wasn't worth the damage it inflicted in the long run. A man can only sow so much evil in the world before it comes back to him tenfold. I wasn't much of a saint before Olivia died. Hell, to tell the truth?

I deserved to lose her.

I deserve to die.

But Vin didn't.

Even as Salvatore finally goes still, his eyes bug wide; it doesn't feel good enough. Grisly enough. Brutal enough. Hissing through my teeth, I kick the son of a bitch, hearing bone crack in response.

Apart from a slight throbbing of my big toe, I don't feel a damn thing.

No relief.

No satisfaction.

Just pain.

Swaying on my feet, I scan the room and find a wooden series of cabinets near the fireplace. My hands shake as I wrench open the doors of one. Sure enough, inside one is a fully stocked minibar. Antonio was almost as bad of a drunk as I am. I grab a bottle at random and down half of it before a sudden sound makes me drop the damn thing.

It shatters in a spray of scarlet liquid as I look over to the closet. The doors are open, and a tiny figure stands there watching me, her eyes so wide, just like Safiya's.

*Safiya…*

I traumatized her in much the same way, though I let that girl live even if in hell. But now? This dark, twisted impulse warns me not to make the same mistake twice.

"Kisa?" I ask her gruffly. "Is that your name?"

She doesn't answer.

"I could let you go," I tell her, advancing on her position. "But in seven years, you might come back…"

I crouch beside her and look into those eyes…

And even the icy mindset I crave can't break this last bastion of the new Donatello.

Hissing, I grab her, throwing her over my shoulder.

Unlike Safy, she screams. Pummels me with tiny little fists. Each blow lands harmlessly as I cross to the bar and shove a bottle of clear liquor into my pocket.

Grunting with the effort, I carry her down the stairs and out of the mansion where what I assume are *famiglia* reinforcements fan out across the lawn, guns drawn.

My, how the mighty have fallen.

In my day? Three times as many men would have been already stationed on the property in fucking uniform. These men wear jeans and shirts as if scrambled here from a night at the bar.

"Get down, you son of a bitch!" A man calls from a group of at least four.

One look at the girl, and they fall back.

Aware of that, I shift her tiny body, holding her in front of me, my arm around her waist while I keep the gun trained in my free hand.

I'm not fool enough to think it will stop them—hell, would it even stop me? Regardless, I keep moving, carrying her right to the car. One of the men steps toward me, and I fire without thinking. He goes down with a howl, clutching at his leg.

"Salvatore's dead," I say coldly, preempting any other threat.

Against me, the girl stiffens, and my steps falter…

I didn't even have the balls to tell Safiya as much back then. I couldn't even give her a reason to her face. Why I sold her. Why I needed to hate her in that moment.

Because her father betrayed me.

But the truth is more twisted than that. Crueler.

By hurting Safiya, I wasn't hurting Gino.

I hurt myself—and God, I *needed* to hurt.

"Don… Donatello?" one of the men calls. I brace for a shot, but none comes. In the dark, I vaguely recognize his face as a *famiglia* lieutenant. Luciano.

"Come after me if you want," I declare, approaching the car as they watch. I head to the driver's seat and find a lever to pop the trunk. Still keeping the girl within view of the men, I move toward the rear of the vehicle and drop her inside.

She's fallen silent, curling onto the floor of the compartment.

For a second, guilt almost levels me, slicing through the haze of rage.

Before it can take hold, I slam the lid and turn around. All this time, my back has been to the men, but they haven't moved, even as their comrade groans on the ground.

And deep down, I think I know why.

That name I've struggled to outrun. That reputation I've tried to redeem.

An identity I know now I can never fully shake.

Under *Il Mostro*, the *famiglia* was untouchable, an outfit unrivaled. Even now, it seems some men still remember those days.

"If you want to see the *famiglia* respected again, then wait for me to call," I say, letting my voice ring out.

As I return to the driver's seat, no one fires a single round.

Even as I drive away.

# 24

# WILLOW

The Donatello I knew was a man who, at his core, embodied everything I grew up admiring. Strength. Wisdom. Most important? Kindness.

I still remember the first day I met him, hiding behind my biological father's pant leg as he paraded me before his boss.

The memory hurts to relive, and I've resisted it so bitterly until now.

Gino Mangenello was the type of man who saw those in his orbit merely as tools. Even me. At my young age, I knew my worth—to him, I was more of a doll than a daughter. A toy he could use to curry favor.

Or a pawn he could leave on a shelf in the meantime.

That day, his friend "Don" had stared down on me from behind a massive desk at the old complex he and my father "worked" at, a sprawling mansion outside of the city. What they did exactly? I didn't know, only that Donatello was a man that even Gino—a brutal drunk who raged at everyone weaker—deferred to.

Fully aware of that reputation, I'd been so shy in his presence. So curious of this man, my father so respected.

I remember inspecting every inch of his loose-fitting gray dress shirt with the sleeves rolled up to his elbows. It was ugly. The first two buttons had been left undone, revealing a sliver of his chest and a tiny gold cross he wore back then. Cautiously, I'd observed the bold features that shaped his face, and the pink lips pressed studiously in concentration as he inspected a set of documents. The second he looked up, I didn't feel that strange disconnect I did when most people observed me, knowing that I was different.

*"Dumb as a fucking rock,"* Gino used to gripe. *"Retarded."*

He growled at me, using his fist when he couldn't understand me as easily as he wanted. Honestly, the reactions of others were far worse to endure. They would exaggerate their features and speak too loudly as though the dramatics made up for the fact that I couldn't talk back.

Maybe it made them feel better. They could project onto me their own intentions as though I were a pretty, smiling little puppet.

Donatello Vanici didn't. He eyed me as though he knew exactly what I was thinking. With a dark eyebrow raised and his head quirked, he could see every thought and feeling written clearly across my face.

"Your father told me about you, Safiya," he'd said to me sternly that very first day. "He said you were a quiet, mindful little girl. I can take one look at you and see that he was wrong."

Gino had stiffened, laughing nervously while I'd gone still in horror, my tiny cheeks flushing. It was a directness that no one had ever presented me with, and I was sure he would use it against me.

Already, I could sense the beating brewing if this meeting went poorly.

But with a booming laugh, Donatello surprised me again. His face transformed in an instant, and he withdrew a handful of sweets from nowhere, presenting them to me on his massive palm. "You look like you enjoy fun, eh? And even silent, you aren't shy about what you're thinking. Is my shirt really that ugly?"

Instantly I knew that he was different, a man apart from my father or the others he associated with.

Perhaps, I remember hoping, a man I could trust...

And even though he left me. Forgot me. Couldn't even recognize my face as I stood before him; I know one truth in the pit of my soul, despite how hard it stings to acknowledge—the man I knew would never send his thugs to attack a woman and her child.

Much like he dragged me into Nicolai Baryshnikov's lair himself, he would mount such an assault. If he wanted to harm Mischa, he would do it himself. No one else.

In a way, Mischa is the same, and his absence chills me to my core, distracting me all morning though I do my best to put on a smile for the children.

They're worried.

Marnie and Aljona cling to each other, barely touching their toys while Ivan lurks in the corner of the nursery, a book under his arm. By bedtime, Mischa still hasn't returned.

Tension poisons the air, and I suspect even the children can pick up on it, though they don't mention their father, or Ellen, or Eli once.

At least until I tuck Aljona beneath her blankets and she demands, "Where is Mama?"

"She's sick," Ivan says matter-of-factly, already having crawled beneath his own blankets.

Marnie whimpers. "Sick?"

I shake my head, smoothing back her curls as she ignores her own bed and crawls in beside her sister. Holding each of their hands, I remain beside them until they finally drift off.

"I don't need to be tucked in," Ivan says as I stand and inch my way toward his corner of the room. Nonetheless, he submits to a kiss on the forehead.

Beyond the nursery, moonlight illuminates the darkened hallways, casting shadows that sway like phantoms. One looms over me as I enter the wing of the house overlooking the front entrance. My imagination runs wild, transforming the swaying shape into a solid figure, one so tall I have to crane my neck back to take him in. Fathomless, his eyes meet mine accusingly.

He's not real. I know that.

Still, I hear him in my head. *You wanted your revenge, Safiya?* he taunts. *Well, you've gotten it. How will Mischa enact it for you? A shot to the head? A knife to the throat? Either way, he won't fail like you did.*

His rich laughter haunts me as I advance toward a row of windows with a view of the main driveway. I have a clear look at the road from them, and at a glance, I can tell that Mischa hasn't returned yet.

*He's probably washing the blood from his hands,* the specter of Donatello murmurs near my ear. *Don't pout. It's what you wanted, isn't it? Me dead—though you can't even be honest with yourself as to the real reason why?*

I shake my head, fighting to ignore the thoughts.

But they persist, feeding on the unease building in my stomach with every second that Mischa remains gone.

*You were jealous,* that voice hisses, impossible to escape. *It wasn't that I threw you away that hurt you so much, Safiya. It's that I kept Vincenzo. I always loved him more than you. Always. You knew from the day I took you in that you were nothing more than a burden, always on borrowed time.*

I can see that very day unfolding before me. My father had made me pack a bag, telling me that I was going on a "vacation" for a little while.

But we never went on vacation.

And, given his lack of a suitcase, he wasn't coming.

On our way from our small, cramped house, we'd passed by mother lying on the couch, too drunk to acknowledge my leaving.

Even now, my heart flutters as I recall that very first day that I saw Havienna, that big beautiful house in the countryside. A pair of oak trees had shielded the front path, perfectly framing the stone cottage with its big red door.

Donatello himself met us on the front steps. As he descended them to greet me, he tripped over a cracked piece of stone and cursed. "This damn place. It's falling apart."

But to me?

Then and there, I knew one certainty—it was paradise.

Laughing, his wife Olivia had scolded him from the doorway, "Language in front of your little guest, Donatello." Her laugh was infectious, sending him into his own raucous bout of mirth.

And I just remember standing still, watching him. Dappled by morning sunlight, he was a figure unlike any I'd ever known, and as our gazes met, he smiled in that reassuring way. Even the memory makes me shiver. One quirk of his upper lip, and I would feel so safe…

As my father drove off, he crouched to my level, taking my small suitcase in his hand.

"I won't lie to you," he warned. "I can take one look at your face and realize that you understand what's really going on. You aren't here on 'vacation.' You are my guest. For as long as you need to stay here, you are welcome."

And looking back, I realize something the little girl I used to be had been too naïve to understand. Even then, he always left a route for him to rescind his offer whenever the urge struck him.

*But you can admit that day didn't come out of the blue,* the phantom of him hisses. *Did it?*

No.

The day Olivia died was the day the Don I knew changed forever. He'd been colder after, more prone to isolating himself in his study rather than spending the evening playing games with Vincenzo and me like he used to. Most telling? He never once looked me in the eye as if avoiding the truth he knew he'd find there.

I had been so worried about him.

Because as well as he could read me, I could interpret him just as adeptly. I knew him. Deciphering every nuance to color his expression came as naturally to me as reading the words in a book. I understood how to read his many smiles. How to scour his face for a hint of softening.

And I knew the way his eyes narrowed when he sensed my presence after Olivia's death—a reaction he never displayed before. How he'd stiffen when I tried to meet his gaze. There was more to his response than grief.

And, even at that age, I knew that few men knew the way to Havienna. Knew that Olivia would be there.

Knew how to truly hurt Donatello Vanici.

And somehow, in my heart, I knew why my Don's love for me turned to something else overnight. Hatred.

Because my father's betrayal led to Olivia's murder.

A flash of bright light snaps me back to the present. Beyond the window, a vehicle approaches, driving slowly up the long winding road leading to the house. My heart pounds against my ribcage as I recognize the shape of the sturdy van —one of Mischa's.

Turning on my heel, I race down to the main entrance just as the massive doors open in tandem. I stop short before I even realize why.

The smell reaches me first—a sharp scent I've never sensed from Mischa before. Alcohol. A lot of it. Shadows drape his form, obscuring his expression, but he stands rigid, moving slowly in a way I barely recognize. I step forward as a million fears race through my mind. Is he injured?

Slowly, he turns in my direction, his head cocked. I wait for him to speak. Acknowledge me. Anything.

But all he does is keep walking, trudging down the hall toward his study without a word.

On his heels is another man who races through the main doors, closing them behind him. Evgeni. He takes one look at me and sighs, shaking his head.

"You should go to bed, Ms. Willow."

He heads after Mischa, leaving me alone in the entryway. Silence falls again, seeming so unnatural in this large house.

The same quiet fell over Havienna the first night Donatello mourned his wife. How he could even manage to stay in that house, I'll never know. I remember how he hugged Vincenzo to him as though God himself couldn't tear the boy away.

As for me…

He didn't make me pack a bag like my father had. He didn't feed me some lie about a "vacation" that would span the better part of two years. Donatello said nothing to me at all until we finally reached our destination, a foreboding, unfamiliar fortress far from what had become my home. I recall clinging to his hand so tightly it hurt, desperate to find the warmth in his touch I usually could.

But he was stone that day, ice-cold as he wrenched his fingers from mine.

Then he left me there.

Tears sting as I blink them back. Swallowing hard, I find myself creeping down the hall in the direction of Mischa's study. Paces down from the room, his voice reaches me, so gruff and hollow, his accent thicker than ever.

"You can hold your mothering," he growls, presumably to Evgeni. "It's already done. Have your men patrol the perimeter tonight. I wouldn't put it past him to retaliate soon."

"Yes, sir," Evgeni replies in a crisp tone that makes my breath catch in my throat. I know him well enough to predict his expression even before I near the doorway and peer inside. He stands beside Mischa's desk, his hands clasped behind his back—but as expected, his expression is constricted, visible in the moonlight streaming in from the window. I don't think I've ever seen the faithful bodyguard so troubled in the presence of his employer.

The two men stand in the dark apart from the silvery glow emanating from outside. Mischa leans over his desk, his hands braced against the surface. Head lowered, his hair falls wildly down his shoulders, obscuring his face.

"You want to say something," he snaps. "So say it."

"Vanici may have been behind the attack, but going after the man directly could start a war that I doubt you truly want."

Mischa scoffs. "It's too late for your scolding—but I'm sure you know that."

My blood runs cold. I turn, bracing my back against the wall for stability as the air sticks to the inside of my lungs.

Donatello…dead? It's a reality I've told myself over and over that I wanted. The only way to move on from him. Forget him.

I try to picture him lying lifeless, those dark eyes closed forever, his laugh silenced—and I don't feel an ounce of joy or satisfaction.

I just feel cold.

"The man will want his revenge," Mischa says, and something in his tone draws my attention back to him. With difficulty, I focus on his voice, trying to decipher the words he says. "And he can come after it if he wants. He will lose more than his son."

Confusion rips through me as my brain tries to identify the unnamed figures. *He* as in Donatello. And as for his son…

*Vincenzo.*

Maybe I've always known, the same way I know Mischa and how he responds to his enemies—violently and callously, rarely striking them head-on at first. He prefers to make them suffer. The same way he kidnapped Ellen to prove a point to her first husband. He wouldn't attack Donatello directly.

He'd do the next best thing and attack the one person whose loss would hurt him the most.

I barely register wandering down the hall on trembling legs. My fingers flex against the icy wall as I brace myself in some distant corridor.

Left in turmoil, my thoughts are a tangled mess of fear and doubt. Donatello gave me away without a second thought.

Then he martyred that girl and turned her into some kind of saint. But now?

All I can do is think of him.

His pain.

And his rage.

I know Mischa well. I once knew Donatello even better. If Vin is really gone, nothing will hold him back.

And no one.

*Nicolai Baryshnikov was a tall man with piercing green eyes that seemed to cut through me like a knife. He ruled his domain like a tyrant, one with a vicious streak who preferred for those under his control to *resist* his commands.

Then he could break their will to the point they never questioned him again.

To such a man, even a little girl was nothing more than a tool to be utilized as he saw fit. And yet…

Looking back, I can admit that much of his brutality might have been for show. Those first few weeks in his custody, I was beaten and put to work around what little of his complex I was allowed in—just a few rooms and the kitchens. But as an adult with the knowledge of the true horrors this world has to offer, I know it could have been worse.

And Donatello expected as much. He didn't give a damn about what might happen to me.

He wanted me broken.

Brutalized.

He wanted me dead.

I shouldn't shed a single tear for him—and I'm startled to realize that I'm not. I don't sob or weep even while my steps carry me into another wing of the house. All the same, my body rebels against my mind.

I'm in my room, crossing to my bed without understanding why. At least not until I sink down and feel underneath the frame for a crumbled item I vaguely remember dropping here the day I was brought home from Havienna. My fingers curl around it and, trembling, I lift it, straining my eyes to view it in the dark—a business card with a number printed on it.

A number that's entirely useless considering that I don't have a cell phone—according to Mischa, I don't require one. While at school, I'm rarely alone. Any communication between us was always done with the aid of a bodyguard's device.

Still, I stand, moving toward the servant's entrance, my mind racing.

Mischa owns several vehicles for various purposes. Most are kept in a large garage several yards from the main house. The second I creep down the narrow hall before the back exit, murmuring voices catch my ears.

"I'll take the first shift on the perimeter," a man says, "then I'll switch to the gate. New rules say that everyone takes double shifts. No inch of the property goes unpatrolled, so cut your break short, so I can charge my battery, lazy ass."

"I'm guarding this entrance," a man replies with a yawn. "I've been outside all damn day."

"Alexi is watching this side of the house," the other man snaps. "So, you'll be on the south lawn."

A heavy sigh echoes in the wake of the warning. "Let me at least take a shit first," the second man replies. "Don't touch my phone, either. You can wait to charge your own. Your little girlfriend can wait five damn minutes for you to reply to her sexy little photos, eh?"

"Asshole."

Both men storm off, their steps echoing in the opposite direction. Cautiously, I creep forward and spy the narrow room off the entrance where the servants sometimes take their breaks. Attached to a cord in the wall is a plain, black cell phone. Without thinking through the consequences, I dart forward and grab it.

Silently, I backtrack and retrace my steps to the main hall. Apart from the servant's entrance, there's a side door on the other end of the house for deliveries. Sometimes, Eli and I would play here, dashing down the halls.

A sturdy lock on the door complete with a passcode always left it less patrolled than the other entrances. Eli, as smart as he is, figured it out by the time he was eight and spied on a servant accessing it.

Even years later, that same code works, and the door opens with a musical ping. Cautiously, I creep out into the west side of the property. Flashing headlights betray a passing van. Another in the distance reinforces the previous guard's observation. Mischa's set the entire security on high alert.

To evade them, I have to rely on the skills I haven't used since childhood. The three of us used to play hide and seek on every stretch of this vast property—me, Mischa, and Eli. My favorite hiding spot was an oak tree near the very edge of the property. If I climbed it high enough, I had a clear view above the stone wall lining the perimeter.

I find my way there in the dark, treading over the damp earth of the west lawn. I'm barefoot, wearing nothing but a pale sundress Ellen bought me two summers ago. Why I chose it now, I don't know.

I don't even know why I'm trying to find a way out at all.

Or what I plan to do afterward. Finding Donatello now would be insanity. Reckless. Suicidal. Besides, he could be anywhere.

And yet…

I'm running through the shadows, trying to evade detection.

Maybe it's a grim need to see his face. To gloat?

Or to grieve.

After everything he's done to me. Everything I've been through since his return.

I deserve to see him now, no matter the reasons.

Or so I tell myself.

And there is one place he would go—the one structure haunting us both.

# DON

Havienna laughs as I approach, the place where everything began. Once my haven, these old stone walls were the last place I experienced my family intact—and the hell where I watched it fall apart. And now? This house is the very purgatory where my Safiya returned with a vengeance.

It's an irony even someone as twisted as Antonio Salvatore couldn't devise. The little cub grew into a tiger, and she got the revenge her parents could only dream of.

Damn her.

*Damn...*

As the moon rises high in the sky, I park near the abandoned garage behind the house and climb out, staggering toward the old structure. All it contains now are canisters of lighter fluid and dust-covered wood for the fireplace.

With the liquor bottle from Salvatore's in hand, I head for the house, leaving the car behind without even looking at the trunk.

This damn house. It mocks me as I enter through the kitchen in utter darkness. Even after seven years, I know the floor plan by heart. This modest room with its old appliances was where Olivia spent more time burning our meals than preparing them. Still, it was in her nature to try something over and over until she succeeded.

Safiya was the same way. She excelled at proving wrong anyone foolish enough to doubt her. And yet, at her core, she was sweet. Kind. A girl who strived for peace above all else. Vin, as good as he was, could be stubborn, prone to grudges from time to time.

But never her. Not Safiya.

At least, until now.

I don't think I've fully let myself process it. I haven't pored over the mental image of her all grown up, trying to compare it to the little girl I knew.

With the speed of an old man, I move to the staircase and climb it, wincing at the memories. Her room was the last on the left, beside Vin's.

My heavy breathing echoes in the air as I curl my hand around the doorknob. Turn it. Push it open.

A cloud of dust swirls to lift, illuminated by a stream of moonlight. I don't bother to switch on a lamp. Even in the darkness, I can tell it's the same. Her pink walls. The wooden bed frame pushed against the wall. Her nightstand —even her old bell is there, something Vin devised for if she needed help, and no one was in view.

But that's all that remains of her. Everything else I had packed up. I had been too much of a coward to do it myself, assigning Fabio to the task.

All of her books, her toys, her little dresses. Gone.

And, like the pathetic son of a bitch that I am, I wish I had them now. Something to tie me to that lost little girl, my Safiya.

Something tangible to torture myself over.

As it stands, I only have my own fucking memories. With a sigh, I raise the bottle I took from Salvatore's. Crouching on the edge of the tiny bed frame, I drink.

And drink.

Intoxication isn't the aim this time—just relief. Numbing myself numbs those memories of her, if only for a second.

But this place persists, driving the past into my skull despite my blurring vision and fractured thoughts.

My girl. My sweet, innocent Safy.

I will never forget the look on her face the day I left her behind.

But another expression creeps into my skull, supplanting it. A beautiful woman with haunting dark eyes who, in every sense of the word, is a stranger. A woman with a face so enchanting that I hate myself for the thoughts that crept into my skull as I saw her. That body. That supple mouth.

In some ways, Safiya's supposed future self is a fitting punishment. I threw her away, but she survived, finding a man who could protect her better than I ever could. A man who could give her a world she would never have access to as a Vanici.

A man who protected her. Cherished her.

Killed for her.

It should be Mischa's blood speckling my chin right now, not Antonio Salvatore's. Mischa, whose demise dominates my fantasies. Mischa, with his perfect, cherished family hidden safely behind their high walls.

I could show him how easily such a fortress can be breached. How it would only take a few bullets to shatter his carefully cultivated paradise.

And how that pain could drive any man insane.

The loss of sanity is something you don't realize at first. Not until the day you're guzzling whiskey just to keep your thoughts clear.

But what's the point?

I could hurt Mischa. Hate him.

But my head is spinning, throbbing badly enough to outweigh the rage. To rectify it, I grab the clear bottle resting at my feet and drain it. Then I stand and leave this room, trudging back down the hall without any clear destination in mind.

I'm outside again, observing the house in the moonlight. I used to dream of torching it. Setting the entire damn thing ablaze and watching it burn.

But Vincenzo loved it. I kept it, hoping to give it to him one day when he could do as he wished with it. Maybe raise a family here. Salvage the darkness that tainted our once beloved home.

But now?

Those dreams die with him, and there's nothing left to hope for. This goddamn house should go the same way.

I march to the garage and grab the red bottle of old lighter fluid along with an old book of matches. At the back of my mind, I doubt I even have the balls to go through with it. Still, I carry it back into the house, moving blindly from room to room. Eventually, numbness sets in, turning my limbs to lead. I find myself slumping into a chair, my gaze unfocused.

I'm in the study of all places, sitting in the same chair I left the little imposter Safiya in. If I breathe in deeply enough, I can still smell her. Fresh. Like a field of fucking roses.

It's so real.

And then I see her, pale and slim, she hovers near the doorway. A plain dress makes her the most innocent apparition. A hauntingly beautiful one as well. I snarl at her. Then I sigh.

"I knew you'd come," I tell her, pointing the tip of the bottle at her face. It's a cruel twist of irony that she's beautiful.

She blinks, shock painting her delicate cheeks pink.

I stand, approaching her unsteadily. My hand finds that cheek, cradling it against my palm. Her lips part beneath the pressure of my thumb, and I can't silence a groan. So pink. So pretty.

She could be real…

"Come to laugh at me from hell, Safiya?" I ask her, brushing my lips along her jaw. My brain is a cruel fuck. I can smell her more clearly, how I think she'd smell anyway. Fresh. Sweet. Her warmth is an echo biting through my numb fingers.

It's the goddamn alcohol that does this to me. Makes me imagine her so damn clearly. Makes me notice things a man like me never should about a woman so young. My Safy…

I cup her chin with one hand and rake the other through her hair—though it's not like she could run away. She's paralyzed, this apparition. Her eyes meet mine, so wide. So goddamn bright.

Another groan rips from me as I press my forehead to hers, sensing the small body trembling against mine. She's afraid of me, this phantom Safiya.

And she should be.

I fist my fingers brutally through the thick strands, drawing her closer. I can hear the air entering her nostrils and leaving her chest in little pants, but even in my head, she doesn't scream.

Good.

I press her against the wall, inhaling at the way she feels. Small breasts, narrow hips. I cup one against my hand and hiss in amusement. It's disgusting how slight she is. How delicate.

"You are a sick son of a bitch, Donatello," I tell myself.

But I can pay for my sins in hell—I'm already on my way there.

"You came to watch me die, Safy?" I open my eyes to find her staring back, but again my own imagination surprises me. Wetness glistens on her cheek, and I swipe my finger against it, marveling at the glistening residue.

Something in my chest clenches, but I force whatever emotion it might be away.

"No!" I growl against the hollow of her throat. "You don't get to haunt me like this, Safy. I want you to laugh. Smile." I close my eyes and open them again, expecting it to happen like magic.

Her tortured frown would be replaced by a ghoulish grin. She'd laugh somehow. It's all in my fucking head; what does logic matter?

But she can't even give me that. She watches me in horror, her eyes so damn wide, her chest heaving, lips trembling.

And I'm too weak. Too drunk. Too tired.

"You know what is worse than knowing you're alive?" I ask her, following that sweet scent to the crook of her shoulder. Shamelessly I inhale, keeping her pinned in place—though she doesn't fight. "Do you?" I laugh, but the sound echoes back like a mongrel's howl, pathetic and wild. "It's that you're so damn beautiful. I wanted to fuck you, Safy. How sick is that?"

It's a reaction fit for a degenerate. A pathetic fool who failed anyone foolish enough to love him. Over and over again.

"Do you want to know why I did it?" I tell her, a confession admissible only now. Here in Havienna. "Do you?" I murmur against her ear. But she won't answer even in this form. "Because you would hurt. Losing you would hurt so bad, and that pain would be enough, Safy. Enough to keep me going. Make me fight and kill those bastards where they stood. I would have crumbled without that pain."

I stroke her delicate jaw and search those eyes for any hint of understanding. More tears fall silently, each one more disarming than the last.

"I loved you so much," I confess, my throat tight. "So much. You were my little *principessa*. I would have done anything in the world for you. Anything… But I needed to hate you, Safy. Because if I could lose you, I could survive anything."

But I was wrong. I didn't survive what I did to her. All this time, I haven't been living, just crawling through time, barely coherent enough to witness it passing.

And now with Vin gone…

"I'll join you soon, the real you." The little girl who doesn't belong to Mischa Stepanov. "I'm sorry, Safy. I'm so sorry."

But, as always, she doesn't do a damn thing other than watch me, tears streaming from those beautiful eyes. I swipe at them, again startled by how real they feel. How wet.

"It's the alcohol," I murmur to myself, laughing.

But curiosity is a twisted fucking thing. I press against her and hiss through my teeth. She feels real, so small that even touching her like this feels dangerous. Like I might break her. Crush her.

And she would deserve it.

"You did it, Safy," I say. My fingers twitch for that slender neck, but I stop myself, only to laugh. Even against a shadow of her, I hold back, cringing in guilt.

No more. Gritting my teeth, I encircle that column in both hands, forcing her to meet my gaze. Slowly, I squeeze, watching those eyes go bug wide. Her hands fly to mine, clawing weakly, but she doesn't fight like the real girl would.

She just watches me, sobbing silently, and I realize just what emotion she's conveying. No hatred.

Just pity.

"You took it all away, didn't you, Safy?"

I let her go and return to the desk. Grabbing the bottle of lighter fluid, I wrench off the cap and nearly choke at the goddamn smell. I fumble for the matches in my other hand. When I turn around, she's still watching, her eyes even wider, and God damn me for the observation that crosses my mind—horror on her is so lovely. I hate myself for appreciating that. How perfectly my brain can represent this grown figment of her when I've spent years banishing her memory.

"Here's to you, Safy—" I lift the bottle in a mock salute. Then I upturn it over my head. The liquid clings to me, dribbling over my nostrils and down my lips. I smell nothing anymore. Feel nothing. Laughing, I inspect the book of matches and hunt for the best one, and I find it; a defective strip smaller than the rest.

It will be a bitch to light, and I deserve the struggle. I rip it from the packet and prepare to strike it.

The force that slams into me is so slight I barely notice it. Regardless, the matchbook slips from my grasp, tugged free by slender fingers that shouldn't have the strength to do so. I take them back, but that insistent touch persists.

I'm insane. Laughter rips from me so violently I clutch my stomach. After all these years, I've finally lost it. But of all things for my brain to conjure, this one is beyond belief even for a desperate man—Safy, stopping me from ending my miserable life.

She claws at the matches, wrenching them away. But it's even easier to snatch them back. Her warmth comes as a greater shock this time, as does the solidness of her limbs. Her touch. Those eyes.

"If you want to watch, just watch," I growl, readjusting my grip on the match. "Enjoy the show—"

She lunges at me; this time, her weight knocks me back against the desk. Tiny nails gouge at my forearm as she tries to steal the matches again. I lash out with the back of my hand, and she goes flying.

But she doesn't vanish. Curled on her side, she stares up at me, blood dribbling down her chin. Real, red blood…

I clutch my skull and blink just to clear my vision. This is too damn much. Too surreal. But when I return to that spot on the floor, she's still there.

"Fine." I crouch and snatch the bottle of fluid, crossing to her. I overturn it, dousing her in what little liquid is left. She gapes in shock, her damp hair clinging to her slender shoulders.

"We both can die if that's how you want it." I rip a new match free and aim the tip against the back of the matchbook, but I never move to strike it.

She grabs at my knee, straining the fabric of my pants. I can feel her nails. Her trembling. *Fuck,* I can feel the pulse surging beneath her skin.

"Damn you..." I sink to my knees, cradling my head in my hands. "What the fuck do you want from me? Tell me!"

She's silent, of course.

So goddamn silent.

"You want me to suffer, is that it? I can't even die. You want me to stay here and suffer for what I did to you."

Softness flutters against my cheek. It's not real, but I react to it anyway, opening my eyes to find an endless pair staring back. I reach out, brushing my fingers along that beautiful cheek, down to her throat. I encircle my fingers around it, gripping tight, so hard her eyes bulge.

"Is this what you want?" I ask her.

She bats at me, but I shove her down, pinning the specter to the floor. With both hands, I squeeze so hard... I could break her neck if she were real.

"If I kill you, Safy, will you finally go away?"

Her limbs jerk beneath me, her pink cheeks losing their color, her lips parting wordlessly. But even now, railing against the shadows, I can't hurt her. My hands slip from her skin, and I sink against her, even more alarmed by how real she feels. Air wheezes in and out of her throat, her body limp, eyes still staring.

I seek out refuge against her shoulder, pulling her against me so that she can't turn away. My sick brain makes her react to me how she never would in reality. Her fingers fist through my hair, her breathing heavy.

And even though she's a phantom, her nearness has an effect on me it shouldn't—a calmness deeper than what a joke from Vin could instill.

A grotesque amalgam of peace.

Horrible, mind-numbing peace.

## WILLOW

*I*'m in a dream. A nightmare. In it, I leave the safe protection of my family home and venture into a world of darkness.

Draped beneath the shadows, I walk right into the lair of a monster—a tormented beast who seems determined to destroy me.

But somehow, I wind up lying in his arms, tasting blood on my tongue, suffering his scent in my lungs, unable to move. I'd consoled myself with the lie that I was here to gloat over him. To relish in my triumph and watch him suffer as I once suffered.

But as his breath fans my throat, the tears falling from my eyes won't cease. The silent sobs wracking my chest only grow in intensity, each one threatening to launch my heart from my ribcage.

But the physical pain is a welcome distraction from the agony clawing through my mind, scrambling any coherent thought. Horrified, I can only lie here and bear the onslaught.

Watching Donatello Vanici in the throes of madness should draw laughter from me. Not sobs. Not guilt.

His pain shouldn't hurt this much.

Closing my eyes against him, I try to examine my emotions. This man betrayed me. Abandoned me. Hurt me in ways I never thought possible to hurt.

Until now.

I could always comfort myself with the idea that what I'm feeling is jealousy. In the end, Mischa wrought this revenge, not me.

My pounding heartbeat resonates through my eardrums as if to counter that lie. For the same reason, I didn't kill him at the hotel, and the reason why I came here in the middle of the night…

I'm here because he always had a hold over me.

And now… I'm at his mercy.

Shivers wrack my body as he stirs, groaning. My cheeks flame as the masculine sound ripples through me, raising goosebumps over my skin. The only other man I've ever been this close to is, well him.

His knee is between my legs, his hands clasped behind my back, locking me to him, chest to chest with his mouth against my throat.

He mumbles something unintelligible, and I jump as sturdy warmth brushes my shoulder.

"You," he croaks in a tone I barely recognize.

Shock startles me into opening my eyes, and I tremble at the sight that meets them. A nightmare would be preferable to this—Donatello so close. He's awake, his eyes unfocused and wild, his breath tinged with a sickening amount of alcohol.

And lighter fluid. We both reek of the cloying substance.

"You can't be here," he tells me, his voice hoarse. "You aren't real…"

He sounds so convinced. So…angry—at himself for daring to envision me, this corrupted version of his precious Safy. Frowning, he runs his thumb beneath my nose and frowns. Red paints the tip, and he shakes his head with a hollow laugh. "This blood isn't real." But confusion shatters the confidence in his voice.

I'm hurt, marred with the physical injuries inflicted by him. My throat aches, bruised by his touch. My nose smarts, and I can taste the hint of blood on my tongue. Fear should embolden me to resist him now. Fight.

Not stare.

Like a man utterly lost, he shakes his head, his nostrils flaring as he looks down, eyeing our close, entwined bodies. Something dark crosses his gaze, tightening the line of his mouth, exaggerating the wrinkles crinkling the skin. My breath catches, watching the nuances of his expression shift and change.

Gone is the wild pain that made my heart ache in the face of it.

Bit by bit, the focus returns to those piercing eyes, honing them into narrowed slits. Abruptly, he withdraws from me and stands. Without his heat, I'm freezing, my teeth chattering.

"You're not real," he says, breathing heavily.

But with every breath of air to enter his lungs, I know that he can sense the same pungent odors that I can—things far too real to exist in a dream.

Or a nightmare.

Blood.

Tears.

Lighter fluid.

Something in my belly unfurls, urging me to move. *Run!*

I barely twitch a muscle before his hand flies out, latching onto a fistful of my hair. Grunting, he drags me to him, heedless of the pain blazing across my skull. Tears sting my eyes, but I'm alarmed to realize that they never stopped falling.

Blurred, his shape looms above me, his lips a pinkish smear moving, his voice a growl.

"You aren't real," he insists. "But if you are..." He tugs me to my feet so swiftly stars dance across my vision. I stagger, desperate to find any traction over the cold wood beneath my feet.

He's unmoving, but as my vision clears, I'm more confused than ever.

Why am I here, facing this man?

Because, whoever he is...

He is not Donatello Vanici.

Bloodshot dark eyes glare into my own, slicing through me with the ease of a knife. That mouth, composed of lips I used to easily goad into a smile, flatten against me, and I suppose he lets me go more out of shock than mercy.

"Safiya."

Hearing that name stings—again, there's so much reverence in it.

Lowering his gaze to the floor, he sighs. "Willow Stepanova. But no," he says, shaking his head. Turning his back to me, he laughs, and the sound is chilling.

It's a madman's wail.

"Willow Stepanova wouldn't come to me, no. Unless it's to gloat. Your father got your revenge, didn't he? Didn't he?"

I flinch in the face of his shout—that brutal baritone I've only heard once before as he bellowed at a man who made a mistake that cost him money.

"Is Mischa waiting for me, outside, huh?" He grabs my arm and storms into the foyer so quickly I have to stumble to keep up. Still laughing, he throws open the front door, glowering into the pale dawn light.

"Come out, come out, Mischa!" He shouts, hauling me after him down the front steps.

It's a twisted reversal of our first meeting. That day he helped me up these very steps, his touch comforting.

Not restraining. Now, his nails dig in uncaringly, no doubt drawing blood as he hunts for enemies among the trees swaying in the morning breeze.

"Come out!"

Despite how loudly he demands as much, no one comes to meet him.

He wrenches me around to face him. "Where is he? Waiting to take his shot?" Shoving me back, he steps forward, his arms outstretched. "Take your fucking shot, you son of a bitch! I'm ready."

My pulse surges—I'm terrified. But not for the reasons I should be. I can hear the honesty in his voice. The desperation.

He's not cockily boasting.

He's begging.

One touch—I don't even realize I'm doing it, swiping my fingers along his forearm.

He jumps violently, whirling to face me. His constricted expression reveals that he would prefer to take a bullet from a gun. Anything but have me touch him like that.

Like I don't hate him.

He snatches my arm, pulling me against him. Our chests slam together as he forces eye contact, staring me down. Whatever he finds in my gaze makes him scoff. Then utter a cry in between a groan and something more primal. Guttural.

His free hand ghosts my cheek, his thumb tracing the curve of my mouth. Each stroke of his thumb applies more pressure as understanding shapes his exhausted features. It's like watching a corpse come back to life.

Fire ignites in those fathomless irises. Color returns to his cheeks, giving his golden skin more definition, and finally…

His finger quivers against my skin, and he releases me.

Before I can think to move, he grabs me again, capturing my waist in both hands. In a quick motion, he hauls me over his shoulder, marching across the property.

I'm too stunned to react the way I should. My hand curls into a fist that lands harmlessly against his back, but by then, he's already approaching a car parked alongside the old garage.

The front is horribly dented, the windshield cracked, but he opens the driver's side door without hesitation and finds the release for the trunk. He carries me toward it, and I struggle, but when I see what lies in the bed of the compartment, I go limp, my lips parted around a gasp I can't voice.

Huge blue eyes meet mine, glazed with fear. They stare from a small face, shrouded by tousled black curls.

It's like looking into a mirror. One that reflects the worst-case scenario and taunts me with it.

A girl. Donatello has a child in the trunk of his car. A girl wearing only a nightgown, her trauma apparent.

Grunting with the effort, he shoves me in beside her, and I barely have time to curl in on myself before he slams the lid down, drenching us both in darkness.

Through inches of metal, I hear his voice, gruff with burgeoning rage.

"Safiya. Willow—whoever you are. You should have stayed safe in your cage," he says, sounding more monster than man. "Your father took my son from me. My heir. But you? You will give me another."

The way he says those words, along with their implication, roils my belly. He can't mean it. He can't…

A thud slams against the lid of the trunk as though he slapped it. "I'm going to break your wings, little bird," he promises, distorted by the barrier between us. Nonetheless, the malice in his tone is crystal clear. "I'm going to take pleasure in ripping them off."

His footsteps echo in ominous tandem before I feel the car jolt as a door opens and slams shut. Around me, the engine roars to life, punctuating the silence along with a muffled whimper near my ear.

And then the car itself moves, taking me to only God knows where.

As the captive of a man I no longer recognize.

# QUEEN OF THORNS

# ACKNOWLEDGMENTS

Thanks so much to everyone who supported this draft along the way, including the many beta readers who provided encouragement! Please keep in mind that this story includes dark, graphic, and explicit content matter that is not suitable for readers under the age of 18—or for readers who are uncomfortable with the following subject matter: age gap relationships, explicit sex, mentions of sexual abuse, and graphic depictions of violence.

# 1

## DON

 was fourteen the first time I ever killed someone. It was a sloppy hit, done at point-blank range with a stolen 9mm. Later on, I found out that was intentional on the part of the man who put me up to it— throw off suspicion by making it seem like a reckless, random robbery.

I'd merely been a pawn in a game I'd been too damn young to even guess the scope of. Such is the way of the world.

*Everyone* is a fucking pawn.

I don't recall much of that day, though I sure as hell remember the messy aftermath. Namely, the blood splattered all over the pavement and the pile of puke I left alongside it. Shaking from head to toe, I could barely grip the gun in my hand. Rather than dispose of it like a seasoned hitman would, I turned tail and ran, leaving both the body and the weapon there out in the open, a rookie mistake.

I don't even remember the poor bastard's name. As far as I knew, he had been an enemy of Mr. Rossi, a mobster I'd pledged my loyalty to, and that was all that mattered.

Loyalty.

It was my one talent, and what I thought would cement my status as a member of the *famiglia,* age be damned. Until I learned a lesson they don't bother to teach in schools, that is. A boy doesn't become a man the second he commits murder.

No, my old boss and leader of the *famiglia,* Giovanni Rossi himself, told me the truth from across his desk that night. Later, as I washed the blood from my hands, I realized that some lucky bastards never learn it.

Becoming a man relies on knowing one universal certainty. Understand it, and even the poorest, dumbest son of a bitch can become whatever the hell he wants, be it a doctor, a teacher, or a fucking crime lord.

So what is it? This—*all* men have the same capacity for evil. No matter what he does. No matter what he wears or says. No matter how good his upbringing is, or how much money he has in the bank…

*Everyone* is the same underneath.

The true question of morality is whether they choose to embrace the darkness or suppress it—though the Bible tries its damn hardest to muddy the waters. I grew up with the lies, reading every classic moral lesson, which typically ended with all sin leading neatly back to the devil.

A good, God-fearing Catholic woman, my mother abided by every warning and did her best to teach me the same. The only problem? I knew early on that it was all bullshit.

The devil isn't real. Greed is. At his core, every man is little more than a creature born of sheer *greed*. A priest and a mobster are both one and the same—a snarling, vicious animal out to satisfy the most basic urges. Strip him down to the bone, and he'll do whatever it takes to eat. To fuck. To shit. And...if necessary, kill.

God rest my mother's soul; I wish things were different, though. I wish a simple prayer could cure every act of evil.

The death.

The violence.

The blood.

I wish I could still blame my sins on the devil—though maybe I can. Just one of flesh and blood who goes by another name.

Mischa Stepanov.

*He's* the reason I'm here—driving up the west end of Hell's Gambit in a stolen car with a kidnapped woman in the trunk. I barely remember the how and why. My skull throbs as I pick through the scattered memories, each one as blurred as the last.

Mischa let himself be played by faulty information. He came after me. Vin got attacked...

I left the villa, I think, though I didn't go see the man I should have.

No, I went right to the source of the lies. The man who tried to have me killed and then framed me for an attack on the Stepanovs. Antonio Salvatore.

I broke into his fancy manor and tried beating any information I could out of him. After that, I strangled him with my bare hands and used his own daughter as a human shield to evade the remnants of the *famiglia*.

Then I went back to Havienna and…

Groaning, I take one hand from the wheel to rub at my temples, but the grainy images don't get any clearer. At least one fact is answered—if all of what happened was real, then there are *two* bodies in the trunk—one being just a child, kidnapped from her own home.

*Fuck.* I laugh out loud and meet my gaze in the rearview mirror. Ironically, I look like hell. Bloodshot eyes. Hair mussed to shit and dripping with a substance that sure as hell ain't water. One hard sniff and I can peg the acidic stench—lighter fluid.

That's right. I doused myself in it.

Maybe *I'm* the devil in this tale?

If only reality were as neat as the Bible. I'd confess my sins and accept the punishment. God knows, I've been down this road before, and the good Donatello, the man I've strived to be… He would turn around. Do the noble thing and bend the knee to those who wronged him.

Fall on his sword like a repentant bastard.

I can't say the idea isn't tempting. I'm so damn tired. Breathing is a struggle, let alone driving. The car veers from lane to lane as the steering wheel bucks against my grip. My lungs ache with every breath I take, and even blinking hurts. I just want to sleep. I'm so weary of running, and scraping, and suffering. I'm so exhausted of hiding from the past.

From Safiya.

Why not surrender to both in one fell swoop? Let the past have my pathetic soul and allow Safiya Mangenello her pound of flesh. As it stands, I should have died seven years ago, anyway.

Or…

I could say "fuck that" to mercy. I tried the good boy routine once, and it cost me the only damn thing in the world I care about. The only person whose life truly mattered. Vincenzo…

Every time I think of him, it feels like I'm the one taking a bullet to the skull. Over and over again.

I see his face everywhere I look, hovering before me, my smiling boy—only he isn't smiling now. His dark eyes blaze, his lips moving wordlessly, demanding an answer to just one question—*how could you fail me, Don? How?*

I swear I see him right now, standing in the middle of the road.

"Vin!" I wrench on the wheel just to avoid him, sending the car into an arc. Mud flies up, speckling the windshield as the tires squeal in protest. Deep down, I know I'm being insane, but the second the car screeches to a halt, I scan the landscape for any sign of life.

Predictably, he's gone. In his place is just an endless fucking road and a swath of trees looming beyond.

I'm drunk. In my right mind, I'd never be driving, especially not here. It's what the city natives deem the no-man's-land —a swath of hills on the outskirts, hugging the bay. There are no guardrails this far out, and my heart races as I glance over to where the shoulder ends—at a cliff. Somehow, I'd managed to hit the brake without driving right off the edge. Though fuck, I should.

A sigh rips from my throat as my toes twitch over the pedal, easing up, bit by bit. Bouncing over the uneven terrain, the car lurches into motion, barreling toward the edge of the drop. Slowly. Faster. Faster…

Right when the momentum picks up, *one* thing has me slamming my foot on the brake again—self-pity.

A death dashed on the rocks below is too good for me. In my soul, I sense I'm destined for something far worse, an end worthy of a monster.

Giovanni Rossi met his via a heart attack on the eve of his daughter's wedding. Imagine that. A week before, he pulled me aside, as if he'd seen it coming. In his typical gruff baritone, he imparted one last piece of advice to me, his heir primed to take over.

*Life, for all its pretentious bullshit, is just a game, sonny,* he said. *You can be a coward and cringe from battle. Or you declare fucking checkmate. At all costs, you go for the checkmate. You pound your fist on the damn game board if you have to. Don't you ever give up. The second you do, someone's already beaten you. It's game over.*

To him, everything was just a round in an unending game with every player fighting his way to the top.

Thanks to Mischa Stepanov, my time playing is nearing its end. Giving up now would be forfeiting everything to him, the ultimate checkmate.

Though, what else could I do?

As if Giovanni himself sent me a reminder from the grave, I sense something around my right hand and hold it up to the light. It takes several blinks before I can focus on it—delicate strands of golden hair looped around my fingers. I bring them beneath my nose, inhaling the scent I swear they still carry.

Roses and hatred.

I can clearly picture the source—a head of golden hair, framing a face crowned by watchful dark eyes. Wrapped around my fingers, their presence alludes to the violence that resulted in them being there. Fighting her off. Shoving her aside. Putting her in the trunk...

I catch myself eyeing the direction of it in the rearview mirror. When I lower my hand, a new emotion takes hold, and I gladly let it. *Rage.* Along with it comes a new perspective. Mischa may have won the last round, but as Giovanni used to say at the *famiglia's* lowest moments, *the war is far from over.* Especially when I have in my possession one of my enemy's very own pawns.

Willow Stepanova herself could be the perfect tool to ensure that no one wins in the end.

And there are a million ways I could wreak my vengeance through her. Brutal, sick fucking shit I would have never thought myself capable of doing, even at my darkest. My fingers twitch against the steering wheel as the possibilities cross my mind.

I could rip her apart limb from limb.

Tear that beautiful body to pieces.

Torture her. Torment her. Then send the aftermath to her father, wrapped with a bow.

The truly sick part? My hand is already inching into my pocket, closing over the handle of a dagger I don't remember carrying. It's hers, small enough to fit her grasp with the word *Mouse* etched into the hilt. I run my thumb over the metal's edge, surprised by how sharp it really is.

Sharp enough to slit a throat.

Slowly, I reach for the door handle next, but my fingers shake too badly to grip it. Out of guilt? That's right. I made a vow once. Hell, I swore it over Olivia's grave. To redeem the Vanici name. To never return to my old ways. To set a good example for Vincenzo and leave a legacy they both could be proud of.

I've failed two of those vows, but I can still fulfill one final pledge. I can make the Vanici name worth speaking again— even if feared.

Mischa Stepanov will pay for what he's done.

Wrestling my hands into submission, I finally push the door open and yank the lever alongside my seat that unlocks the trunk. Slowly, I climb to my feet, bracing one hand against the car while the other returns the knife to my pocket.

It's slick as shit out, with nothing but gravel and mud underfoot. Even now, a spitting rain speckles my skin, coating everything in a slippery, silvery layer of frost. On top of that, my balance is shit. As I try to take a step, the world rocks beneath me, and I vaguely remember drinking from a bottle stolen right from Antonio Salvatore's minibar.

This whole thing could be some booze-induced hallucination. Still, I start forward.

As I round the back end of the car, a faint rustle draws my notice, and I freeze mid-step in grim anticipation. Will she jump out to meet me? Try to fight? My knuckles twitch, until both of my hands form fists so tight my own nails cut into my palms.

I wait, but the top of the trunk doesn't budge.

The booze still in my system might be to blame for the feeling that comes over me next. Weightlessness. I stagger forward, but it's like I'm watching a stranger curl his fingers beneath the rim of the lid, wrenching it up in one go.

Thick cloud cover obscures the sun, leaving only a faint bit of light to see by. Even so, I have no trouble making her out, curled on her side at one end of the compartment, the Salvatore girl on the other. Golden hair fans out around her, shrouding the pale limbs bared by a thin yellow dress. If I had to imagine how she'd appear, I'd assume afraid, trembling fearfully in anticipation of what I'd do next.

One look at her shatters that fantasy. Her dark eyes meet mine head-on, fiery in the grayish daylight. In them, I see a challenge portrayed so brazenly it might as well be branded across her forehead—*What will you do, Donatello?*

The answer is as elusive to me as it is to her. Her knife is still in my pocket, but all I seem capable of doing is staring. Remembering.

*Her...*

More obscure images from last night flash across my mind. Us, together in my old study, her body struggling against my grasp. A groan revs in my throat as I recall why—I'd been ready to set the entire house on fire, myself along with it.

Only one force had been able to stop me.

Her.

I remember her wrestling the matches from me, and my broken psyche adorned her with a million different embellishments then—that of a vengeful angel clothed in gold, condemning me to live another day out of spite.

In broad daylight, there is no hiding from reality.

She isn't flawless like a soldier of divine mercy would be. No. She's battered and pale, her yellow dress askew, her eyes as bloodshot as mine are. Liquid slicks her hair to her skull, reeking suspiciously of accelerant. That's not all. A necklace of dark bruises encircles her fucking neck. Irrational anger flares at the sight of them, and I'm already wracking my brain for the identity of who could have possibly hurt her.

Only a monster…

Not even a heartbeat later, I catch sight of my wrist, and I realize that I don't have to look far for the culprit—*me*. I did this to her.

My hands shake, outstretched before me, bruised and bloodied. In contrast, she looks so small.

And so dangerous.

"Is this what you wanted?" I direct the question toward her, still inspecting my fingers. An assortment of cuts and bruises mar each digit, but not enough to cause the amount of rust-colored liquid encrusted beneath each fingernail. There's no shying from what the substance really is. Blood.

Mine.

Antonio Salvatore's.

And Vincenzo's.

"Why?" The shout echoes throughout the narrow clearing this part of the road runs through, bellowed and broken.

But how does she react?

When I finally look at her again, she's just staring.

And staring, and staring…

There's no answer reflected in those dark irises. No hate. No fucking emotion.

Not even when I lunge for her, grasping at whatever I catch. Warm flesh trembles beneath my palm as I find myself tearing back through the trees, dragging her with me.

"You wanted to punish me, is that it?" I say in between pants. "Well, now we can both find our retribution."

Giovanni was right. Why give up when you can ruin the game? And what better way to circumvent Mischa's inevitable win than to aim straight for his heart?

I'll do more than pound the damn game board. I'll break it.

The woman resists, digging her bare heels into the earth with every step—not that there's much she can do. I'm heading for the edge of a sheer drop, overlooking a section of gray water churning beneath. A fall from here would be deadly. If the height alone doesn't do the trick, then the rocks down below should.

Two birds with one stone—a fitting end for Donatello Vanici, and a fitting punishment for Mischa Stepanov.

I take another step, and the woman by my side goes still, her gaze fixated on the drop.

Watching her triggers another memory, but one that occurred years ago rather than hours. Someone younger had been in her place, her dark eyes just as fearful, though the drop, in that case, had been the edge of a pool.

She couldn't speak, but I had no trouble reading her mind. Her face was so expressive; she couldn't keep anything secret from me even if she tried.

*"You're afraid," I told her with a smile. "Don't be. As long as I'm here, you've got nothing to be afraid of. Just close your eyes and jump. I've got you…"*

*No!* I bare my teeth against the past, forcing myself back to the present. The woman struggling in my grip bears resemblances to that little girl—but it doesn't matter. She should have no other identity than who she is now. An enemy. A means to an end. Willow Stepanova, daughter of the man who took everything from me. Everything…

And yet for someone so consequential, she doesn't look it, so small she barely comes up to my shoulder when I shove her forward.

My grip on her arm is the only force keeping her upright. With every twitch and gust of the wind, she staggers, her feet scrambling for balance on the uneven ground. Beneath that tattered yellow sundress, she's so slight that one strong breeze could blow her away.

All I'd have to do is let go.

So I do.

Alarm flits across her face for an instant, widening her eyes and parting those pink lips. Her impending death is a slow, morbid dance of slender limbs against relentless gravity. Her right foot loses contact with the ground first, followed quickly by the second. Left with no stability, her entire body jolts backward, that hair swaying in the wind.

Even as she starts to fall, her eyes shoot up to mine, and her brave façade cracks. Beneath it, I see her fear. The grim realization that I'll let her die.

She knows I will…

"Fuck!" The curse slips from me, as my hand shoots out before my brain can fully process the motion, gripping the neckline of her dress. Grunting, I yank on the material, hauling her back over the edge. As I let go, her fingers fly to the rocky outcropping, using it for stability to drag herself up.

She falls to her knees as a monstrous sound rips through the silence. Booming and guttural, it's seconds before I realize it's coming from me. Laughter. Manic, unstable laughter.

The emotion tearing through my chest isn't amusement, though—far from it. Just sheer, dizzying confusion.

"Why are you here? Did you come to distract me so your father or one of his men can finish the job?" I demand, spinning around as if expecting another car to appear on the road at any moment. "Where are they? Don't tell me he's watching from the shadows, pleased with the show? Because he sent you, didn't he? He sent you here…"

It's the only explanation that makes sense. Either that, or she wanted him to save me for herself, so she could be the one to drive the knife into my chest.

But then why stop me?

Her eyes flicker toward me and away, giving me the answer.

"You came on your own." I sound as incredulous as I feel. It seems insane to even consider—that she snuck from Mischa's fortress of a home. Made her way to Havienna alone. Made her way to me.

For what?

Voice rasping, I propose the obvious answer, "Did you come to watch me die, Safiya?"

She should sneer in confirmation. Instead, a muscle in her jaw twitches, and I imagine her clenching her teeth behind those pink lips. In anger? I hunt her gaze for an answer, reminded of another moment from the past. Those same eyes in another lifetime. So dark, they'd seem to touch on red whenever their owner felt enraged.

The day I left her behind, they blazed…

Now? They're too dark to interpret clearly. I just see defiance. *You don't control me,* they declare. *You lost that right.*

"You're mine now," I snap, turning away from her. Fuck the past. *This* is all that matters. Who she is now and what she's done…

She's mine.

And I don't have to kill her to enact my revenge.

I grab her arm, dragging her back to the road. The second we near the car, I shove her in the trunk beside another figure I've almost forgotten. She's curled in a ball, staring from behind a curtain of black curls. Antonio Salvatore's little girl, her eyes glazed over.

Both figures watch as I slam the trunk closed over them. Shaking, I reclaim the driver's seat, moving on autopilot as I put the car back into drive. A U-turn later, I'm speeding toward Hell's Gambit. I don't know where I'm heading at first. My brain churns sluggishly, fighting to catch up with my body's impulse.

Then it comes to me—I'm going home. How does that saying go? Things have a way of coming full circle. When I've hit rock bottom, what better place to complete that descent than the very location I rose from at the start of it all?

I still remember the whirlwind of those early days after I'd freshly joined the *famiglia*. Old Giovanni Rossi kept a public front in the heart of the city—a casino that Antonio Salvatore took over after ascending to the top of the outfit. Apart from that, the old man mainly did business in a small restaurant, but his pride and the true heart of his operation was located about an hour outside of the city proper.

Only his most trusted lieutenants knew of it, and even fewer were allowed to set foot there. From that old complex, Giovanni conducted his true business, using the place as a headquarters for the real source of his money—cocaine. A hell of a lot of cocaine, sourced directly from the most vicious Colombian cartels. I doubt Salvatore dumped that part of the operation. Given the lavishness of his mansion, the fucker has been enjoying the benefits of such an enterprise.

Who knows how much of that fortune remains. But even if Antonio spent every last penny, I know a way to garner more.

Enough to rebuild an empire all my own and destroy any hold Mischa Stepanov has on Hell's Gambit. I think we're more alike than either of us would admit. I valued the life of my son more than anything, enough to forfeit it all…

How far will Mischa go for his own daughter?

I'm willing to find out.

2

WILLOW

*A*rt glorifies even the most grotesque aspects of human nature and perpetuates a devious lie.

That it can be controlled. Harnessed. Made beautiful. Those of us who study music are especially vulnerable to that belief. Under the spell of a particular concerto, or haunting song, we become naïve to whatever tragedy inspired it, so entranced by every note.

And we sometimes fail to question the mindset of the man who wrote it.

One of my professors used a certain term to describe only the most complex pieces and the eccentric composers who crafted them. *Depraved.*

To him, those men were so lost and consumed by emotion they embodied it in every piece they created—though he didn't make it sound like a bad thing. In his opinion, true madness could craft the most esteemed works of art.

Maybe that beautifying of humanity's darkest aspects is what drew me to music in the first place. I could find a reprieve from my past as I played, drowning my reality in dazzling noise. As a pianist, I could appreciate those works both as a caution and something to aspire to.

Now, I know the innocent folly of that admiration—madness isn't beautiful.

It's terrifying.

The men capable of honing such insanity are arsonists with no aim in mind other than to burn. To watch the world burn. To them, pain is a tool.

It's fuel.

It's fire.

Donatello Vanici is *depraved*; no other word describes him. Instead of music—pain, agony, and hate form the notes of his own horrifying melody. His symphony is one of vengeance and terror, and only God knows how it ends.

And in this case? *I'm* the instrument being ruthlessly played.

My neck throbs with the imprint of his fingers, and I can't stop myself from tracing each mark in the dark. Neither one hurts per se. They merely sting, but the intent behind them is more alarming than any physical pain.

Tears burn behind my eyes as a sudden thought bites deep. Seven years of hating him never left me prepared to feel anything else. I've replayed the moment of him leaving me behind over and over. His retreating back. His parting words.

But never—not once—could I see him doing anything more than that.

Until now. My legs smart from scraping against the ground, as my heart still pounds with residual fear. I've never felt that terror before, so potent I could taste it.

Still can—copper like blood.

I will never forget the look on his face. One devoid of any shred of recognition. No hate. No anger. In that moment, I knew in my soul he would do it.

Let me fall.

Watch me die.

He betrayed me once, but for some naïve, childish reason, I always explained the act away as selfish cruelty.

Not hate. As pitiful as it sounds…I never expected him to hate me.

*Ignore him,* a part of my brain hisses. *Focus on where you are. Form a plan.* If Mischa were here, his advice would be simple—*run. Escape. Don't give in to fear.*

If only it were that easy.

Mischa, for all of his experience, couldn't imagine a moment quite like this one. Shrouded in darkness, I have every reason to be terrified. The most prominent example?

I'm still in danger. My eyes burn as my lungs contract to expel the stench of the accelerant dripping from my hair. The acrid smell fills the confined space of the trunk and beside me, a tiny figure coughs, overwhelmed by it.

Her presence presents another horrifying reality I can't acknowledge just yet.

So I put everything I have into the only task that matters —*escape*. Blindly, I extend my hands, feeling along the smooth interior of the compartment beneath me. It rumbles with the motion of the vehicle—the only clue I have as to the driver's intent.

To be as reckless as possible.

He's driving erratically, making it hard to get my bearings. Every jolt of the car, rams me against the narrow body beside mine. She whimpers, recoiling as much as she can while I try to create a mental map of the space.

It's small. My fingers tremble so badly it's hard to tell the softer material coating the inside of the trunk from the metal of the car's frame. Clenching my jaw is the only way I can keep my teeth from chattering, not that it matters much in the end. I'm shaking all over. I could blame the chill seeping in from outside, or acknowledge the unease gnawing at my resolve.

I'm panicking.

No matter how hard I try, my thoughts keep returning to the man in the driver's seat. Namely, his final threat to me, uttered in a voice gruff with malice. *I'm going to break your wings, little bird...*

And after that? His threat became even more specific.

That I would give him an heir to replace Vincenzo...

Something hard brushes my palm, snapping me back to the present. Cautiously, I curl my fingers around it. Something round and firm that gives slightly with a bit of pressure. An emergency release?

Any triumph I may feel, however, goes to war with common sense. I know better than to pull it now. We're moving quickly. Too fast. Way too fast. My heart lurches up my throat as I try to picture where he's heading in this state. Unfortunately, only one destination comes to mind—him speeding toward one of the cliffs overlooking the harbor—but I shut my eyes against it.

*Focus!* Instead of Donatello, I channel Mischa and the stoic mindset he drilled into me since childhood. *Focus, Mouse!*

Obeying the mental plea, I go still, breathing in through my nose and out through my mouth. With every breath, some of the fear gives way to logic.

If running is out of the question now, then the only course of action left is…

*To fight.* I curl my fingers into fists and wrack my brain for any available weapon. Apart from the girl beside me, the trunk seems to be empty. For the first time, I turn to her, straining my eyes through the darkness to make out what I can.

She's young, and my heart clenches with terror at that realization. She is so young. Dark curls glimmer in the absence of light, the only detail I can make out. Her soft breaths scrape on the air, adding a chilling backdrop to the engine's constant hum and the roar of rushing air rebounding off the vehicle's exterior.

God, he's driving even faster now. Suddenly, the car lurches, shaking violently as if the road switched from the smooth pavement of a main highway to a rougher texture. Stone? Gravel? Whatever the surface, it's uneven. Hissing traction comes from the wheels, making me suspect that we're traveling steeply up an incline.

That vision of the cliff returns, sharper in clarity.

Would he really do it? The answer terrifies me—I know nothing about this Donatello.

Nothing at all.

Fortunately, the only things a musician needs to play any piece, are their hands and an instrument.

All I need to kill Donatello is a weapon.

And this time, if I get the chance…

I won't falter.

# 3

# EVGENI

A man in my line of work abides by a simple code—if he wants to keep living, anyway. Loyalty should be his most prized asset. Only survival gets second priority. Leave the political games to politicians, and finally, never get too close.

To your employer. To anyone.

After a decade without dying yet, I've never questioned that creed once.

Until the moment I'm faced with an empty bedroom and a missing charge, that is. For a second, I consider a nice retirement somewhere far away from murderous employers and their sheltered daughters. The thought is a warning sign —I've failed the last bastion of my code already.

The missing daughter, in this instance, isn't some nameless mark. I've watched her grow up from a stoic little girl into an accomplished woman who lacks the spoiled apathy of most with her kind of privilege.

I know firsthand how power can corrupt families, and how the sins of the father can easily infect a child. At least until now, Willow proved to be an exception to that rule. Shunning the violence and brutality of Mischa's realm, she sought shelter in the mundane future of a quiet pianist.

I'd never admit as much out loud, but I always admired that drive in her. Some aren't so lucky as to choose a differing path from the world they grew up in. While it comforts some to separate men in terms of good or bad, morality has nothing to do with it. In a sense, it's only natural, no less tragic than a wolf pup learning the ways of a predator. Darkness begets darkness. Murderers beget murderers.

Monsters go on to sire even more brutal monsters...

Few can break that cycle. By forging her own path, Willow was braver than I could ever hope to be—though Mischa is the kind of man decent enough to allow his children the freedom to grow into their own.

Most aren't, and most children never escape the crushing weight of their forebearer's shadow.

It's a line of thought I try to avoid, and for a good reason. Control is an asset a man like me comes to cherish— namely, because it's so rare and fleeting. I lose my grip on my thoughts for a second, and they scatter. Instead of Willow, I see another face. Just as pretty, her hair darker, eyes rounder. She never got the chance to live out a life following some innocent future endeavor.

Because I failed her too.

The guilt I feel is a knife slicing at my splintering control—but a simple mantra is enough to repair it. *Loyalty first. Survival second. Stay focused on the job at hand and never lose sight of your task…*

I repeat that creed until my mind clears, but I'm no less ashamed by my own failure. Gritting my teeth, I express the irritation the only way I can. "*Fuck.*"

That curse says it all—this is my fault. My responsibility.

"There's been no sighting of her at all since last night?" I demand of the man beside me. The question—as is our presence in this very room—is a mere formality. It's already been hours since the alarm went up, with the mid-morning quickly approaching.

It's not a question of *if* Willow is missing but for how long—and who might be involved if she left willingly?

There aren't many options given the size of her social circle—her family's manor, or her closeted school in Vienna. Two teams of my men are out scouring the nearby road, as well as four key locations, but given their lack of contact, I doubt they've found anything useful yet.

And they might not.

Time is ticking. Who knows how far she's gotten by now. Or what state she's in…

"Yes, sir," one of the men replies, drawing up to my side. Fairly young, he's a new recruit, and I spot his hands fidgeting with the sleeve of his gray uniform jacket. I know how he feels, but just months into the job, he hasn't gotten it yet—our most important work is done in these quiet moments, far from gunfire.

Even if it feels as useless as twiddling thumbs.

"Tell me what you've deduced so far," I command, facing him directly.

He clears his throat. "She's not on the property. Left alone, it seems. No signs of forced entry," he adds. "If you plan on sending out another team, I'm ready."

I ignore the suggestion, though I'm just as anxious to get moving. Do something.

*Damn, Willow.* She's not like the other coddled heiresses I've dealt with. A beautiful girl with a wealth of secrets behind her silence. What in the hell would make her run?

There's always the possibility that someone breached the manor and took her—but I secured the premises myself. Two teams of ten patrol at all times, covering every inch of the property, not to mention the state-of-the-art surveillance. I'm fairly confident that God himself couldn't break into this manor.

But a certain sheltered heiress could find a way to sneak out, if she were so determined.

Before I know it, I'm questioning yet another tenet of my tried and true creed. What use is loyalty to a family wrought with secrets? How can I protect what I can't even begin to understand?

I know the answer—my intuition hasn't failed me yet, and it's telling me that this has everything to do with one man and one man only.

Donatello Vanici.

What is his tie to the Stepanovs beyond the obvious? Mischa rarely gives in to impulse, but he drew first blood against Vanici without even waiting for better intel. Only God knows what can of worms he might have opened as a result.

And I'm the fool left to wrangle the mess with no clue as to the nature of it.

"Sir?" the man beside me questions.

I wave him off. "Give me a moment."

Setting aside any suspicion, I refocus on the room itself. There has to be something here. A clue. Anything. I start with the bed. It's been left fully made, the sheets undisturbed. The only means of exit, other than the door, are the windows, both closed. I test the latch of one, finding it locked. Not to mention it's too high from this floor to climb down unseen.

"She didn't leave from here," I state out loud.

Which makes one possibility all the more likely—though I have enough tact not to say as much. Not until I've left the rookie behind and retraced my steps throughout the house, finally entering a study on the first floor.

Sympathy is an emotion I tend to shun, but if any man deserves it, it's Mischa Stepanov.

I don't think he's slept for days. Seated behind his desk, he could be mistaken for a ghost. Pale skin and windswept blond hair only add to the effect, and I wouldn't put it past him to have patrolled the outskirts of the property himself on foot.

All night.

One look at him, and I feel compelled to bend those boundaries I've steadfastly maintained.

"Mischa…" On second thought, I suppress the urge in favor of doing the one useful thing I can.

Stay professional.

"Sir," I say instead, pausing near the threshold of the room. Spacious, with a view of the west lawn, it's a prime position to spot any traffic in or out of the manor. I can't resist scanning the expanse of road, hoping to see a *mafiya* van on the horizon, Willow in tow.

All I find are the gray sky, fields, and the trees beyond.

"You've rechecked the property as I asked?" Mischa asks without looking up from his clasped hands. The muted response is a world apart from his initial reaction hours earlier—a fact that would terrify anyone who knew the man personally.

His anger may be legendary, but he's at his most dangerous when calm.

"Yes, sir," I say in answer to his question. "There is no sign of forced entry. I have my men in two teams out looking, but Vanici's residences have been cleared out. There's been no sign that he's left the city, and—"

"She couldn't have gotten far on foot," Mischa interjects, turning to stare from one of the windows.

Like me, I suspect he's merely going through the motions, voicing the expected questions when the answer is painfully obvious.

"Yes, sir," I reply anyway.

"She left on her own, didn't she?" There is no despair in his voice. No anguish.

I've never seen a man so drained of everything but pure exhaustion.

Standing at attention, I don't mince words. "My guess is that she left on her own but impulsively." I can't disguise the irritation in my voice.

Willow could be calm and reserved well beyond her nineteen years—but at her core, she's still nineteen. A child.

Mingled among the reports from her detail overseas in Vienna would be anecdotes of her sternly exposing a professor who insulted her or reprimanding anyone who dared to treat her any differently due to her disability.

"She's strong," I say finally.

"She's impulsive," Mischa snaps. "She's stubborn."

He's right—and she has no fucking clue as to the way things really are, or how far some men might go to gain leverage over her father.

Mischa's worked hard to keep his family safe. In the process, he's also kept them sheltered from the reality of their status. Willow never understood one truth. She isn't a normal woman—she's a pawn in a game of power.

"Fuck, I should have known better than to leave her alone," Mischa snarls, curling his hands into fists. "Hell, I should have locked her in her room and thrown away the key. I knew she couldn't leave him—" He breaks off, but I can suspect what he doesn't say. Who.

So I voice it for him. "You mean Donatello Vanici."

He says nothing, but the look he sends my way is a clear warning to tread carefully.

Well, I'm tired of tiptoeing. "If she went after him, I need to know why. What happened between them?"

Still nothing.

"Sir, it's only a matter of time before he retaliates if he isn't already planning an attack," I point out. "We need to stay on guard. Track his allies. Maybe he's contacted someone in the *famiglia*. We need to—"

"Enough." Mischa swipes a hand through the blond stubble speckling his chin. From this position, I have a glimpse of paperwork stacked haphazardly before him. What could be so important he'd pick now of all times to read it? As if aware of my attention, he shoves the stack aside, further from view. "I will handle Vanici."

"Alone?" I raise an eyebrow. "Sir, maybe if I didn't let you go after Vanici *alone*, we might have been able to avoid—"

"Are you challenging me, Evgeni?" His eyes cut in my direction as his raised voice echoes throughout the room.

"I'm just asking a question, sir," I say softly. Though I couldn't disguise the annoyance from my tone if I tried. Mischa went and kicked the proverbial hornet's nest, attacking Vanici's nephew. And for what? All on shitty intel and a reckless whim.

But I know the man. In six years, I've never seen him act without an ironclad cause.

Unless it's personal. Emotional. Only then can his instincts sometimes tend toward…irrational.

"Vanici's left his villa," I add, voicing what little intel I've managed to gather in the aftermath. "His associate, Fabio Botelli, has gone underground. There is no word on the status of his nephew, though we've assumed the worst. Finding Vanici should be our top priority."

Not playing hide and seek with a girl we both know is long gone. And yet, Mischa inclines his head to glower at the grayish sky, stubbornly silent.

It's been a game we've played since Mischa had the man removed from his daughter's ball. A verbal round of tag in which I ask more potent questions about Vanici and his history with the Stepanovs, and Mischa avoids answering every single one.

I can't fathom why. Mischa certainly isn't known for being demure—neither am I—and now isn't the time for coyness when Willow's life may be on the line.

So damn tact. "Can I ask why, sir?" It's a question loaded with a million others left unasked. "Why attack Vanici with little more than hearsay to go off of? Why was Willow found in his home after her first disappearance?"

The questions get more unsavory from there, but I'm not stupid enough to voice them now.

*Why is she drawn to him?*

*Why has Mischa eschewed his usual tact and restraint where Vanici is concerned?*

*Why is he playing so coy with the answers?*

And why is he hampering the efforts to find his own daughter by keeping me in the dark?

"I need you at the hospital," he says tiredly. "I want you stationed near my wife. Only you."

I nod, smothering my irritation. For now. The concern in his tone takes precedence, and I know he wouldn't ask this lightly. "Any improvement in her condition?"

He winces. "Eli is stabilized enough to possibly come home tomorrow," he says, referring to his son. "The baby could be released in a week."

But as for his wife? His silence says for him what he can't. Her condition is unknown, so tenuous the prognosis changes daily.

"Go," he demands, turning his back to me. "Vanici could attack the hospital next."

I nod, starting for the door. As I toe the threshold, however, I hesitate.

"What about Willow?" I ask. "I have my men searching Vanici's known properties as we speak. But if I knew more of their history… Even more about what happened after the debutante ball—"

"I will handle Vanici," Mischa growls.

But what could happen in the meantime?

Especially if the man has Willow. I have no delusions about what he might do to her. I've known men like him. Hell, I've worked for them. Be him a mercenary or a crime lord, the breed is the same. If he doesn't kill her—or worse—then he'll attempt to make contact soon, if only to sell her.

"Sir, time is of the essence," I insist.

"Evgeni…" When I look over my shoulder, his gaze meets mine with an intensity that would make the rookie upstairs piss himself. "Are you refusing a direct order?"

"No," I say—which should end the conversation. My feet twitch against the floor, but I don't move.

Despite my better judgment, I can't let this go. Sending me to the hospital now would be the equivalent of shoving me to the sidelines.

Why?

"I think I could be of more use to you here—"

"Ellen is the one who has *use* of you." He whirls around, bringing both hands hard over the surface of his desk. The resulting thud resonates through the room like a gunshot. A warning.

"I meant no disrespect—"

"Go," he commands, dismissing me with a wave of his hand. "That wasn't a request."

"Sir." I nod, finally reentering the hall, clenching my jaw against another retort.

Or an accusation—is this really the time to withhold information? Especially whatever might prove vital to anticipating Vanici's next move. Though a part of me sneers that the real question is a different one entirely.

How much is Mischa willing to pay for his daughter's life?

I'm sure that will become clear soon enough.

# 4

# DON

West Helm Lumber. An unimpressive facility with an even less impressive name—and by design. No one would ever suspect the seat of the *famiglia's* power rested in this sprawling, nondescript complex in the hills surrounding Hell's Gambit.

Which is the point.

Giovanni loved the juxtaposition of, instead of the casino or the restaurant, the true heart of his establishment residing someplace far different. *In a Podunk hellhole,* as he liked to joke. The man could be poetic when he felt like it.

It's been seven years since I've made this drive, but it still looks the same. Sort of. Leading off the highway, the asphalt road switches to beaten dirt, as old and worn as the day I came here as an eighteen-year-old kid, over four years into my career.

I'd been blindfolded that very first time, herded into the back of a van by the men more senior to me. It was tradition to make a big fucking deal of it all, if only to drill in the importance of what coming here meant—you were trusted. In the fold.

Part of the family…and how did I repay that trust?

By turning my back on the organization entirely—a mortal sin in our world. You don't just leave the *famiglia* and come back.

Still, I can't help but taunt myself with that fucking cliché at the sight of the battered sign appearing up ahead, pointing the way forward.

*Home sweet home.*

It even smells the same, a stench that seeps into the body of the car, despite the windows being rolled up. My nostrils flare to inhale it all. Damp wood, dirt, and musk.

Up ahead, the gate's entrance looms, a simple twisted wire fence outfitted with more security cameras than some military bases. Whoever is manning them has seen me coming for a mile now—but, oddly enough, they haven't mustered the cavalry to meet me.

Yet.

A battered metal speaker is affixed to a pole, easily reached from the driver's seat, and I wrench the window down, craning my neck.

"You know who I am," I say into it as a weak smattering of raindrops pelts my head. "Either let me in or put a bullet in my head now. I don't fucking care."

I mean it, and I close my eyes in grim anticipation of a response. If fate would have it that my story end here, then so be it. What a pathetic finale, but at least I'd have some ounce of peace. I might even see Olivia again on my way to hell…

It isn't long before an answer comes—not a gunshot. Rattling metal and the telltale whine of turning gears cut the silence instead. I open my eyes, resigned to the sight I find.

The gates slowly drift apart, clearing the way—but it's not the greeting one would expect in the old days. No men appear to line the road, and no warning comes from the speaker. Both signs don't bode well at all. Either the *famiglia* has become more welcoming to visitors, or I'm heading straight into a trap.

Though, hell, it's not like I have any other options. Sighing, I grip the wheel and drive.

It could be the fact that I'm viewing everything through a cracked windshield smeared with mud, but the landscape doesn't look quite how I remember it after all. Gone are the meticulously maintained fields and hints of regular patrols. Nature's returned with a vengeance, swallowing every inch of available land in thick weeds, and I don't see a guard or van in sight. Not only that, but the fact that I've made it this close without being met with gunfire speaks for itself.

Trap or not, one thing is apparent. Antonio let the place go to shit.

The overall layout still resembles a large rectangle with the main headquarters residing in the center, three outbuildings on the perimeter, and a lumberyard in between. A layer of grime shrouds the landscape, and if I didn't know better, I'd assume the property was abandoned. Most of the equipment appears rusted with disuse, and the piles of lumber stacked out in the open look suspiciously as though they've been there since the days of Giovanni.

The old man is turning over in his grave. Maintaining the sawmill was one chore he always insisted on, no matter how much money his empire amassed. Everyone, including him, worked at least some part of the business. In his words. *You forget the upkeep; you might as well forget your freedom. All the power in the world can't buy you a good cover.*

Because the sawmill is just a front. *Beneath* the property is where the real business lies—an underground warehouse with direct access to the river.

Though who knows what state the enterprise is in now.

With every inch I gain on the winding road leading to the main building, Antonio's influence becomes more obvious —primarily in the row of luxury vehicles parked amid a yard of overgrown weeds and sparse gravel. Apparently, he and his cohorts have taken the money for themselves rather than use it to maintain the façade.

And it shows.

Only five men stand on the steps of the building up ahead, weapons drawn—a fraction of the men Giovanni kept around at a given time. They look trained enough, despite wearing a mismatched array of jeans and casual shirts, another breach of protocol that would catch Giovanni's ire.

None of them move as I park and climb out. They just stare. As I spot my reflection in the glossy black paint job of Fabio's car, I realize why.

I look like hell. My hair is a fucking rat's nest, my clothes rumpled, drenched in booze, and lighter fluid.

Or maybe it's the blood that has their attention? Reddish smears streak my hands. My wrists. My chin. My clothing is stiff with it, like armor against the judgment of anyone watching. I start to tug on my collar, only to let my hand fall. Instead, I jerk my chin without adjusting a damn thing.

Let them stare. I may look like an animal, but they're no different.

"Keep your hands where I can see them." The man in the center of the pack steps forward, keeping his pistol trained over my chest. A formality, I suspect, given he had every chance to stop me at the gate. I recognize his face. Luciano. Hours earlier, he watched me stroll out of Antonio Salvatore's mansion.

"You have some nerve coming here," he says. His tone gives me nothing to go off of, his expression blank. I'm impressed despite myself—as far as poker faces go, he's damn good.

Which is a bad sign if I intend to navigate this meeting peacefully. Looking at him, it's impossible to guess his motive—mainly why he let me go in the first place. Not to mention why he hasn't shot me now. I could always go the intimidation route to gain answers, but as I spy the blood on my shirt, I lose the urge.

Instead, I drop all pretense, facing him with my arms outstretched and nothing held back. Whatever he sees makes him grimace, though it doesn't take a stretch of the imagination to guess what impression I've made—that of a crazy motherfucker covered in blood.

He'd be better off opening fire—but he hasn't, and as the seconds tick past, he never gives the call to attack. Even his men don't seem to understand why, trading questioning looks between them.

It's easy to conclude that on this battlefield, Luciano is the only one worth confronting, so I turn my full attention to him.

"You haven't shot me yet," I finally point out, but there could be a multitude of reasons why, none of which being a desire to reconnect with an old ally. One real possibility is that he has Mischa already lying in wait inside? Admittedly, I didn't think this far ahead in terms of returning to my old outfit. Coming here at all could be neatly summarized as a suicidal death wish.

As I observe the mouth of the gun, I'm forced to admit that could very well be the reason. Why? I don't feel a shred of fear.

I don't feel a damn thing.

Luciano's expression reveals nothing either way. Without a word, he eyes my hands, and a muscle in his jaw twitches, but I doubt it's the blood alone that has him so wary. Sure enough, his eyes flicker toward the trunk, giving me a clue as to what might be behind his restraint.

Surprisingly, it might be as simple as basic human decency.

His next words leave no doubt. "Where is Kisa?"

Kisa Salvatore. The child I took from her home still dressed in her nightgown after strangling her father before her eyes.

From the man's tone alone, I can tell exactly what he thinks happened to her—I, *the Butcher, Il Mostro* himself, killed her.

Rather than answer him out loud, I circle around to the car.

"Why are you here, Donatello?" Luciano snarls as I run my fingers along the side of the driver's seat, finding the lever for the back. "Come to finish us off the way you did Antonio? Did you hurt Kisa too? Answer me! Don't think I won't fucking put a bullet in your skull—"

"Kisa," her name tastes like blood. I spit and realize that the flavor isn't all in my head—I must have bitten my lip sometime during the trip here. The warm moisture I feel dribbling down my chin must be the reason why Luciano backs up a step as I shoot him a glance over my shoulder. "Is she why you haven't attacked me yet?"

He keeps his face blank. "Did you kill her? I wouldn't put it past you—"

"If you believed I was a threat, you wouldn't have let me through the gates," I point out. "And if you really gave a damn about Antonio, I don't think you'd be interested in chatting to his murderer."

His eyes narrow a fraction—I hit a target, though I'm not sure which one. Maybe the fact that he obviously wasn't as loyal to Antonio as he wants me to think.

But he does care about the girl—and if he truly thought I'd hurt her, he probably wouldn't be so friendly.

"You let me go," I add, raising an eyebrow. "Why? Did you think the *famiglia* needed a change in management?"

"Fuck off." He spits on the ground, his gaze unreadable. "Maybe we didn't think you'd be so fucking dumb as to come here alone. It's five against one, Don. All I have to do is say the word."

"Then say it," I snap to no response.

The silence alone proves my hunch was correct—so much for staging a trap. Despite the show of force, Luciano isn't willing to risk an outright firefight. He's concerned for the Salvatore girl, or maybe that's his excuse. Objectively, he doesn't have much to mount an attack with, assembling barely enough members to form a welcoming committee.

"I'll tell you why you haven't shot me," I declare, thinking out loud. "You can't take the risk. Sure, I killed Antonio, but he wasn't in the running for boss of the year, I'm assuming. The *mafiya* isn't known for being the most welcoming of outfits. Mischa would consume the *famiglia* rather than align with it. Which means that you aren't in a position to be picky when it comes to allies."

How tragic. As stoic as he tries to be, Luciano's narrowed gaze proves I'm right. I'm not the only one who's been diminished in the shadow of the *mafiya*. Without Antonio's leadership, the best the *famiglia* can look forward to is being picked off by a rival faction or making a power play of their own. To do that, they need leverage—something I might have. Either way, another potential ally, even a murderer covered in blood, is better than nothing.

"You need me," I say, to sum it up nicely. I don't know why, but I can't silence a laugh at that realization. It rings out hollow, echoing on the morning chill only to trail off as I approach the trunk and hook my fingers beneath the lid. I lift it slowly, hissing through my teeth as light falls over the two small bodies curled within the compartment, one blond, the other dark-haired.

They're lying side-by-side, the girl whimpering while the blond…

I tense, expecting her to lunge at me, nails drawn, like she had during our first meeting. Instead, she grabs the child's hand, a simple motion that conveys more than any words ever could. She has enough space to jump from the trunk and run if she wanted to. I've seen her in action; she's more than capable of making a decent attempt at escape on her own.

Instead, she's focused on protecting the weaker entity.

From *me.*

I blink as if struck, and it takes a second to dull the guilt slicing through my chest—a long, fucking second. In the end, I banish it with a sharp shake of my head. Then I reach for the smaller girl, grabbing her opposite wrist. She whimpers fearfully, her bottom lip trembling.

As the blond stiffens, I catch myself snapping, "Let go."

Her eyes flit up to mine, and I can practically see the battle taking place beneath her skin. Muscle straining against restraint. Logic warring with instinct. Her lips pull back from her teeth in a feral expression I doubt she's even aware of. She wants to fight.

I know the feeling.

A second ticks by. Then another before she finally lets go.

I tug the girl out without resistance, easily pulling her into the men's line of sight.

"Kisa Salvatore, safe and sound," I snarl, releasing her.

Some of the tension leaves Luciano's jaw, an observation I note for later. Meeting his gaze, I ask, "Are you going to invite us inside?"

Luciano stiffens, an eyebrow raised. "I thought you were an upstanding businessman," he sneers, sarcasm dripping from his tone. "Better than all of us. You stepped down for a reason, correct? Only to return like a prodigal son. And what? We're just supposed to fall into fucking line?"

He has a good point.

Without answering, I turn on my heel, rubbing at the stubble on my chin as I try to decide the truth for myself. The booze is wearing off, making my thoughts clearer. Why am I here? Why now?

Amid the swirling chaos and pain in my brain, one coherent thought tumbles out. Revenge. Retribution. Petty rage. Whatever the fuck it's called, I feel it in the pit of my very soul. I think I always have, but I won't run from it like I have for the past seven years.

God, I want to indulge in it.

I need to.

This, I realize, is the only thing keeping me going —payback.

Taking a glance around the yard, I home in on the rotting, dried-out husks of lumber stacked haphazardly across the place. The more I look, the more painfully obvious the state of disrepair becomes.

If I hadn't already killed Antonio, I'd strangle the bastard a second time. Only an idiot would shoot himself in the foot by neglecting the main financial arm of his operation. To be fair, I'm the bigger dumbass who left him in charge.

Irritation aside, at least he did leave one useful thing behind, something that might help turn the tables on Mischa. I slip my hand into my pocket, finding the small device I managed to salvage from my successor. In it, hopefully, lies the key to finding out who he ordered to put a hit out on the Stepanovs.

And if not?

I haven't thought that far ahead.

"Don't let me interrupt," Luciano snaps. "It's a beautiful fucking day to waste my goddamn time. You've got balls, I'll give you that—"

"Tell me something," I say, directing my voice toward the men behind him. "What has the *famiglia* become under Antonio Salvatore? Don't tell me that four fucking men is all you could muster to guard the very heart of the operation." I don't even have to look at their faces to know I hit the truth on its head.

I only have to inhale. Shame has a certain stench to it, more potent than lighter fluid and blood.

"You've lost your standing," I say, raising my voice. "Your position in the world, forced to kowtow to someone like Mischa Stepanov for a seat at the table. All while Antonio pillaged the coffers and spent your money on his fancy-ass mansion. Pathetic."

"Antonio wasn't the only one pining for a seat at Mischa's table," Luciano points out coldly. "We've all heard the rumors about how you've chased his protection."

I put my back to him, facing the side of the car, and my own reflection once again. He's right—and as I stare into a pair of soulless dark eyes, I realize what a foolish act that had been. To grovel at the foot of a monster and demand mercy.

In this world? There is only violence and power, and it takes both to survive.

The proof of the first is written across my skin in various streaks of blood.

As for power? A symbol of my own appears before me, much like the angel I'd compared her to earlier. She must have climbed from the trunk, clinging to the side of the car for balance. It's the only clue of instability she gives. Otherwise, with her head held high, blond hair streaming down her shoulders, she seems untouchable.

Murmurs of alarm go up from our audience at the sight of her, though. Bravery aside, she looks even worse now than she had before. A divine being marred by bruises and still reeking of lighter fluid.

"What the fuck?" Luciano snarls from behind me. "You couldn't stop at shoving one girl into your trunk? Maybe you should go talk to the Saleris if trafficking is your thing."

"And Antonio wasn't into it?" I counter from over my shoulder. "Don't tell me he drew the line there."

"Antonio was a dumbass," Luciano says. I turn to find him descending the steps, gun still drawn. "He thought he could take on the *mafiya* himself, but what makes you any better? From what I heard, you forfeited everything you have to Mischa without so much as a fucking whimper. Are we supposed to see you as some kind of savior now?"

"No," I rasp, eyeing my battered hands. The blood on them speaks for itself. "I'm no one's savior."

"So, I repeat the question—why are you here?"

"Because I want to be," I say, letting my hands fall to my side. "We used to own this city—*us*. Mischa sits at the head of the table now, but in my opinion? He shouldn't even have a fucking seat."

"So what do you suggest?" Luciano counters, cocking his head skeptically. "We break into the man's house and slaughter him in front of his children like you did Tony?"

I don't even wince at the suggestion.

"No." Sarcasm aside, that would be too easy. Nowhere near punishment enough for what he's done. Mischa deserves so much more than that.

He should know the pain of reaching rock bottom with nothing to show for it. Not only that, but I want him to know that pain on a first name basis—Donatello Vanici.

"I don't want to kill Mischa." As the words leave my mouth, my gaze comes to rest over the slight figure before me, and I can't resist a gnawing suspicion as to what she's thinking. Does knowing that comfort her?

Her dark eyes watch me without a shred of emotion, and I turn away, ignoring her altogether.

"So, what do you want?" Luciano demands, sounding closer. I turn to find him behind me, but his gun is pointed at the ground. For now.

"What do I want?" I echo, tilting my head to eye the gray, colorless sky above. It's only been a few hours, but the loss of Vin has already changed everything so damn much. The grief is like putting on glasses that rob the world of its beauty. Its laughter. Its joy.

Without it, the world reverts back to the game board Giovanni always taught me to see it as—territory ripe for exploitation.

"Antonio spoke of having allies," I say, scoffing at the notion. One look at his supposed headquarters, and I doubt he's cultivated much. However… "He would be an idiot to try and frame me without thinking he had an insurance policy. Either that, or he was being used as a puppet by someone with a greater interest. Though, with his track record, I don't think he had many friends to pick from."

Luciano's frown proves it.

"Just the Saleris and the local MC," he admits. "Seeing as how you killed Antonio, I think only one of those options is in play for you."

Or neither. Another plan unfurls in my head. One so twisted, so wrong… I cringe in the face of it. Then I remember Vin and all the things playing on the right side of the law got me—nothing.

"I'll let them come to me," I finally say. "I have a feeling they might anyway once word gets out."

"That doesn't sound arrogant at all," Luciano says with another scoff, but considering he doesn't storm off, I already have his attention. "What are you even talking about? 'Word' about what?"

"That I have Mischa Stepanov's daughter as leverage against the *mafiya*."

I wait, and predictably Luciano swears. "Are you insane—"

"Not to mention that I still own the city's port," I say over him. "I'm willing to divvy up my share to anyone ready to collaborate."

"You own it? I thought—"

"If you plan to kill me, you might as well do it now," I suggest. "But if you boys are tired of playing games and want to win, then we have work to do."

Silence lasts for barely a heartbeat before Luciano sighs. "With Antonio dead, it's not like we have much of a fucking choice. So what is your plan?"

I inhale and exhale slowly before returning my attention to my only real leverage. If I wanted to find her cowering, she denies that fantasy.

She fucking smashes it into pieces, facing me boldly. I hate that her beauty draws my notice, even now. Not in a sexual way, either. The emotion swirling in my gut at the sight of her standing in defiance could be grim admiration. Respect, even.

Grown men have shown less resolve—but that doesn't mean I won't treat her the same way I'd treat anyone else who dared to challenge me.

*But she's not just anyone,* a voice in my skull taunts.

I blink, cutting off any memories that threaten to replay. Shake my head. Blink again. The longer I stare at her, the more unfamiliar she seems.

Just a snake with the face of a ghost.

Someone to crush.

Someone to kill if it comes to that.

She's nothing more than a pawn.

"Use one of your men to get a hold of Fabio Botelli. Now. Tell him to cancel any transfer of any assets to Mischa Stepanov. And inform him that he is no longer on my accounts," I say.

"And then?"

"Then… I have information from Antonio that might come in handy." I can't resist running my hand along my pocket merely to feel the shape of the cell phone there. Hopefully, the son of a bitch was as stupid as he was greedy, and the device holds proof that he was the one behind the attack on the Stepanovs.

"Information?"

Looking up, I meet Luciano's questioning stare with a shrug. "If it proves what I think it does, then we go to Mischa directly."

If only to ask him one question—how much is his daughter's life worth?

It takes a surprising amount of effort to turn off the small bit of my soul that might shy away from this line of thought. What might one woman go for on the black market these days? Add to that listing her hair, and those eyes…

I'd go so far as to assume she'd fetch a nice price, even without the caveat of being Mischa's daughter.

*Though you could always kill her now,* a part of me warns.

My fingers twitch as I size her up. It would be so easy to grab her.

But I don't.

Instead, I face Luciano and head for the front of the building. "Bring them inside."

"And put them where?" the man snaps. "I know you haven't been here in a while, but we don't exactly keep a dungeon on this property."

I stop for a second, running through the various rooms I remember. "The office," I say finally. "Put them in my old office. The one with no windows."

And, more importantly, no obvious escape.

# 5

## WILLOW

You can hate someone so much you create a reflection of them to fixate on. A phantom that takes on a life of its own, dwelling in your head. It mimics the source of the rage, sometimes so perfectly that you confuse the two—until you start to believe that you can predict the actual person. Their every action. Their every move.

You learn them inside out, convinced they'll never be able to hurt you again.

The fantasy merely lulls you into a false sense of security, though. Because the moment you finally meet the real being again in person... Only then do you realize just how unprepared you really are.

Donatello in the flesh is a different animal than who I've spent seven years picturing him as. He ambles toward the nearest building, dressed in a rumpled, bloodstained suit, unsteady on his feet. One good push seems liable to knock him down for good, and yet it's unquestionable the hold he has on those around him who quickly fall into line.

And it's laughable just how wrong my memories have portrayed him—confident, like a cartoon villain, evil, and callous. Someone easily shamed by his past, an opponent I could undoubtedly defeat.

All I had to do was face him once and for all.

The real man, however?

He's broken. Exhausted, disheveled, and battered. With nothing left to lose, he's an even more dangerous foe than the figure who abandoned me all those years ago. It's impossible to confront an opponent who can't even look at you.

*I have Mischa Stepanov's daughter as leverage...*

As he growled those words, his voice conveyed malice that terrifies me if I let myself dwell on it. It was the same tone someone might use when referring to an object. A toy. Someone not even worthy of the attention an enemy would command. Just a pawn.

Though should I be so surprised?

He never saw me as anything else.

"Get them inside," the gruff baritone draws my attention back to him. Head held high, he shoulders open a metal door and enters the building, clearly expecting everyone to follow. Which they do, almost in sync like some eerie, physical concerto.

My first instinct is to resist and do the only smart thing I can in this instance—*run*. Impatient, my feet twitch against the muddied earth as I scan the nearest line of trees, a few yards away.

I could make it…

But after that? I don't even know which direction I'd head in. We could be miles from the city, let alone my family's manor. Without proper clothing, or a weapon, it could be more dangerous to wander alone. Though, for all I know, Mischa could already be on his way…

"Keep moving," one of the men nearby warns as if reading my mind. He's tall, though I could probably outrun him. Gray eyes enhance his cold expression, however, and with his gun trained on the ground, he's intimidating enough.

Would he shoot an unarmed woman? I can't tell.

Warily, I turn back to the building, weighing the decision to bolt even as I take a step toward it. I shouldn't stay. Every ounce of common sense in me tells me that if I enter beyond those walls, I may never leave.

But my life isn't the only one in danger. A pale figure catches the corner of my eye, putting everything painfully into perspective.

The little girl huddles in the rain, shivering in a white nightgown, her bare feet caked in mud. Among these towering men, she looks even smaller, and a sense of protectiveness finally spurs me into action.

Rather than head for the trees, I inch closer to her and away from any route of escape. Her hand finds mine, and I grip it tight in return. I can't suppress the panic that rises in my chest as the other guards fall into step behind us both. They're silent, watching on with the intensity of dogs herding wayward sheep.

Or wolves.

Staring past them all, I find my attention resolutely drawn back to the figure in the lead. Framed in the doorway, bathed in the glow of fluorescent lighting, he moves like a man apart from the rest of the world, alone on an island unto himself. The slow, deliberate pace of his steps stirs a painful memory.

I used to be so awed by the rare moments when he revealed this side of himself—the leader. The figure my biological father and others deferred to as "boss." Typically, I only saw the playful Donatello who hardly ever raised his voice. One instance, though, sticks out, a time when his subordinate intruded on our game of tag.

My silly Donatello transformed before my eyes, losing the charming grin I knew in favor of a cold, calculating expression. His eyes seemed to darken, revealing a chilling intensity that could reduce the strongest foes to their knees.

In the years since, I used to placate myself with the idea that his wrath couldn't affect me anymore. I could face that piercing stare and never flinch.

I was wrong. His stare wasn't the worst aspect of him to contend with. It's this—watching him walk away, unable to make a sound. Do a thing. Hit him. Fight him. Scream.

It's the second time I've been faced with his retreating back, and my thoughts feel no different than they had years ago. Childish.

The reason? It's even more pathetic. I've been silent my whole life, but no one has ever made me feel invisible. Ignored.

Insignificant.

*Focus!* I bite my lower lip until I taste copper, desperate to adhere to the mantra Mischa taught me. *Escape.* Nothing more.

I replay his words over and over, but it's as if the child in me is screaming in a way I never could out loud, demanding to be seen. Heard. Acknowledged.

By him.

I dig my nails into my palm in a desperate attempt to stay calm. Regardless, rage infects my entire body until I'm shaking, almost too badly to do the one thing I should in this situation—pay attention.

Beyond Donatello expands a sprawling two-story building with blurred windows, some cracked, and gray metal siding rusted in places. It looks industrial—not a building someone might live in. A warehouse?

Two metal doors guard the entrance, opening onto a wide lobby painted gray with utilitarian tile flooring and fluorescent lights above. The windows are large, but too high up to reach unassisted, and at a glance, no other doors seem to lead outside. Still, I scan every inch of the interior, making a mental map as I go.

Up ahead, two hallways branch off the main space, presumably heading deeper into the building proper. Donatello goes left, but one of the men meets my gaze and inclines his head, indicating the opposite direction.

My fingers throb, crushed by the grip of the little girl. I can't even look at her, but to her credit, she's still standing, smothering her whimpers. When I move, she falls into step beside me as I scour the hallway for anything that could assist during an escape.

The further down the corridor we travel, the more I feel a sense of *déjà vu*. I think I've been here before, maybe as a child. Something about the water-stained ceiling above triggers a memory. Sitting in a corner, counting the square tiles over and over to pass the time…

"This way." This dark-haired man stands further down the hall beside an open doorway. "You'll stay in here."

The room is a small office devoid of windows. A desk cluttered with paperwork dominates the center of the space, illuminated only by the light from the hall. At a glance, there are no exits other than the door.

Warily, I step inside, sensing the girl on my heels. Mischa's advice echoes clearly through my skull—*Lay low. Devise a plan. Keep your head.*

But my head is spinning, filled with mistrustful thoughts. Of Mischa himself. Of *him.*

I still see his expression, mocking me. Taunting me.

Those eyes. That voice.

*I'm going to break your wings, little bird…*

The thud of the door slamming snaps me back to the present. I hear a lock engage, and the light vanishes, robbing me of the chance to gain a better idea of the layout. In the resulting silence, all I can hear are the soft, smothered whimpers of the girl.

Painful recognition hits like a lance, and I try to resist the memories triggered. Cowering in the presence of Nicolai, knowing that Donatello had left me there. Abandoned me.

My sole consolation is that I'm not bound this time. I can walk. Move.

And I can fully plot my escape.

# 6

## DON

Giovanni thrived on power. I've never met anyone more calculating. You gotta be born with a head for business like that, though he did his best to teach me how to think as he did. Coldly and methodically.

Whether that meant retaliating against a rival by slaughtering their prized thoroughbred, or by showering allies in lavish gifts, each method relied on one detail to succeed—optics. Why get your hands bloody when you could put on a show and get the same point across?

The office he kept here is a case in point testimony to his preferred style. The layout is designed specifically so that whoever steps foot through the door would see themselves first, sweating and nervous, reflected in a huge ass mirror hanging on the wall. To cap off the experience, their next sight would always be the old boss himself, seated behind his desk like a king on a throne.

Talk about fucking *optics*. From that position, he could survey his prey while they grappled with having their own fear thrown back in their face. You couldn't buy a better setup than that.

The mirror is still here all these years later. It's antique, I think, about as old as this entire damn building. Dust coats the surface, blurring the glass, as I approach.

For a second, in my place, I see Giovanni. *A man should do nothing that he can't face himself in the mirror afterward*, the old boss used to boast.

Suffice to say, it didn't temper his cruelty any. In his heyday, he was known to sign a death warrant in the morning, kill a man in the evening, greet his children with a smile and check his teeth without flinching, all before this same mirror.

Every now and again, he'd call a man into his office and quiz them on who they thought they saw in their reflection. *Do you see what I see, Donatello?* he once asked me. *I see a leader. A man who can lead these sons of bitches to greatness if he wants to...*

I look on the surface of the glass now, and I see a shadow of that younger man, covered in blood. My hands shake as I swipe a finger through the grime, bringing the image into clearer focus. It's funny... Giovanni always looked the same to me, no matter what brutal deed he'd just committed. The man I see now, though?

He's a monster.

"So let's see it," a voice prompts from behind me. Luciano, absent his gun. He swaggers through the doorway, but I don't doubt for a second that he's still a threat. The fact that he hasn't shot me is due entirely to what Giovanni praised above all—power.

I don't have much left—but I have enough.

"What's this leverage, *besides* the kidnapped woman?" he demands. "I'm going to pretend you never said her name, by the way. Though, fuck. We're dead anyway. What's pissing off the entire *mafiya* but the cherry on top?"

"Here." I reach into my pocket and deposit the item I took from Antonio on the desk. As I do so, a mirrored version of myself copies the motion. Our eyes meet, but it's like staring at a ghost. Nothing at all is going on behind those dark irises. He's a creature moving solely on impulse, no better than a snake.

"A phone?" Luciano remarks, advancing with an eyebrow raised. His tone draws me back to the present, putting everything into perspective.

Revenge aside, I need a plan. Willow Stepanova is a fitting bit of leverage—but only if I can clear my name first. Doing so relies on finding proof that Antonio ordered the hit. Even if that means trudging through the bastard's cell phone.

Sighing, I take the leather seat behind the desk, leaning my head back.

Fuck, it's been a long damn time since I've sat here. This room was the most spacious of them all, with a view of the lumberyard. Surprisingly, Antonio kept much of the original furniture, down to this desk. I swear, Giovanni's coffee stains still mar the old wood. Mine too. As I run my fingers over them, I spot a name plaque encased in gold. I spin it to reveal the initials A.S. engraved on the front.

Guilt could be the name of the emotion lancing through my skull. Either that or I'm sobering up. Either way, I don't think it's really sunk in until now. Antonio Salvatore, the dumb bastard who couldn't find his ass with a map, was in charge of the *famiglia*. I left him in charge.

Giovanni would rise from the grave if he knew, just to kill me himself.

"Do you hear me, Donatello?" Luciano snarls.

"Huh?" With a wave of my hand, I knock the plaque from the desk and into the wastebasket on the floor beside it. Only then can I look up.

"Your ace in the hole," Luciano continues, nodding toward the device placed before me. "Your secret weapon to get us back on the map is a cell phone?"

"Antonio Salvatore's phone," I correct.

Lowering my gaze, I spot the topmost drawer, and I pull it open. Fucking predictable. A few loose cigars roll across the compartment, and I grab one along with the gold lighter resting nearby.

"It's password-protected," I add before popping the end of the cigar into my mouth, lighting it with a flick of my thumb. It's the good shit, and I drag on the damn thing so hard I nearly suck it down. When I finally exhale, Luciano's watching me, waiting.

"Might have the number of whoever he contacted to target the Stepanovs on it," I say. "Can you find a man to crack it?"

He blinks as if torn between bitching some more or getting down to business. Finally, he shrugs and steps forward, his frown still skeptical. "Antonio wasn't exactly Fort Knox. He tended to use the same password for everything. Let me see…"

He grabs the phone, and it turns on, revealing it's still on its last few bars of battery. After he taps a few keys on the screen, it unlocks with a musical chime. Scoffing, he turns it my way, revealing what the bastard had on the home screen —his own fucking picture.

"I thought so. The passcode was his birthday," Luciano says in disgust. "But I don't see how it helps. Trust me, if Tony had something he could use to get back in anyone's good graces, he would have used it—"

"Can it be tracked?" I ask. If Mischa's already put the pieces together about Antonio's death, it's only a matter of time before he settles on a prime suspect.

Luciano fiddles with the screen. "Not anymore. Blocked the GPS signal. It's still pinging with the cell tower, though as far as I know, you need a warrant to access that kind of shit—"

"Hand it over."

He slaps the phone onto my outstretched palm. "So what now?"

"These contacts," I say over him as I scan the most recent calls. "Any of these sound familiar?"

I hold up the screen to him. Squinting, he reads the first few names, and his eyes narrow.

"Paulie Vanetti," he says. "But… He's a fixer but crazy as fuck. Tony rarely used him. He could be sloppy, and expensive as hell—"

"Sloppy enough to cripple a child and attempt to murder a pregnant woman?" I ask.

"Shit!" His eyes widen, and he shakes his head, whistling through his teeth. "He didn't…"

"So you can see why I paid Tony a visit last night," I say, flicking the cigar to knock the ash on the floor. "The fucker tried to frame me. Did frame me."

He nods. "But I wasn't kidding about expensive. Likes to be paid upfront too. If you can't tell, Tony liked to play the big shot, but he couldn't amass that kind of cash on a whim. If he was working with Paulie, you can bet your ass someone else was footing the bill."

"Makes sense," I say.

It isn't unheard of for a bigger player to cover his tracks behind a patsy. If Antonio needed cash, how badly? Badly enough to play the role of a puppet. The real question is, who would have the balls to put him up to it…

I've been out of the game for a long damn time, but I doubt either the Saleris or any of the local gangs would have the capital to pull something like this off. An outside player?

"This Paulie," I say. "You know where to find him?"

He shrugs, crossing his arms. "No, but you have his number. Call him."

I weigh the benefits of doing so now. "Any other day, that might sound like a setup. Think he might be expecting my call?"

"Fuck me." Luciano laughs, raising his hands in mock defeat. "I doubt he knows Tony's dead, if that's what you mean. We've kept it under wraps, so far. Kept the staff from his house. Covered for any meetings he had today. Just until we can come to…an arrangement."

"You've bought time," I say, impressed despite myself. Maybe they all aren't as dumb as Antonio.

"At least a day, maybe two tops," he says, nodding. "The boys know to stick around. No one comes in. No one goes out."

I know what he has the tact not to say—he's done it for morale. To keep what little is left of the *famiglia* from scattering and to stave off any vultures who might come sniffing around whatever Antonio left behind.

If I were a gloating man, I'd state the obvious. As fate would have it, my old outfit needs me just as much as I need it.

"Call him," I suggest. "On Antonio's behalf. See if you can lure him here. Discreetly. And do what you can to keep the tragic news from breaking a while longer."

"And what will you do?" he demands. "I can only buy us another day at most. Someone will notice when Antonio isn't swaggering around town, throwing money left and right. And I'm sure he kept me out of the loop on many of his dealings."

"Me?" I turn my head just enough to see myself in that damn mirror. The longer I stare, the less I recognize the figure looking back. If Vin could see me now, he'd make some dumbass quip. *"You look like hell, Uncle Don. Sober isn't a good look on you. I'd stick to the booze…"*

God, that kid would have never made it past Giovanni's doorstep. The old man would have smelled the goodness on him. Rather than fight, Vin's primary instinct in any situation was to crack a joke. Aim for a laugh. Where some men saw only power and control, Vin saw a world in need of saving.

But when it came down to it, I couldn't even save him. Hell, I can't even face knowing if he's still alive...

"Don?" Luciano waves his hand in front of my face. "You with me, here?"

While dragging on the cigar, I stare down at my own hands, flexing them in and out of fists. These fingers can kill. Maim. Bleed. Yet, when it came down to it, they couldn't even feel Vin's neck for a fucking pulse.

I reach over and fish Antonio's name plaque from the trash and use it as a makeshift ashtray, setting the cigar on top of it.

"Don?" Luciano prods.

"Give me a minute," I say, flattening my palms over the armrests of the chair.

He scoffs. "Because we have all the time in the fucking world to just sit around and—"

"That wasn't a request. A minute."

He holds my gaze for only a second before turning on his heel. "You've got it. Take your minute. I'll go feed our 'guests,' and then contemplate if I've just cosigned the entire *famiglia* to the whims of a fucking madman."

He slams the door while I lift the cell phone and type out a number by heart. Like a fucking coward, I still hesitate before finally starting the call.

Unsurprisingly, it's answered after only one ring. "Botelli."

I suck in a breath at the sound of that voice. He sounds so fucking old. Not only that, but I can tell he's been chain-smoking from the hoarseness. I feel like I'm channeling Vin as I say, "You need a drink, Fab."

"Don?" He curses, and a wave of commotion comes from the other end as if he just knocked something over. "Fuck! Mary Mother of God. Where are you? Do you know how fucking worried I've been? What the hell were you thinking, sending some punk ass to inform me I'm off your accounts. You owe me more than that—"

"I know. I know," I snap. Still, I can't escape the shame I feel like a bitch slap. I've never heard him this fucking frantic. "Just, please… Tell me how Vin is."

"Vin… He's still alive," he says hoarsely. "But I won't lie to you, Donatello. He needs more care than I can provide him. He needs *you*."

"More care?" My head is spinning. "I thought you had a doctor."

"I do," he says. "But he needs a safe facility to operate in, and a skilled staff—more people than I can easily blackmail. Mischa and his allies are on red alert. I know they're tracking me. Hell, I'm surprised they haven't dragged me before him by now, thinking I know your whereabouts."

"Fuck! Have they tried an attack?" I ask, already rising to my feet. What the hell could I do from here? I don't know. But there has to be something. Anything.

"Not yet," he says cautiously. "But he's commandeered the best hospital in the city for his own family. My doctor can keep him alive, but it will be hard to get Vin the care he needs otherwise."

"The hospital…" There's only one nearby worth going to. Mercy, I think, is the name. If Mischa has it on lockdown, there's no way in hell they'd admit a Vanici. Not to mention it's in the heart of Saleri territory. Even as the cons mount up, I know there isn't another option. "I'll find a way to get him there."

"Fine," Fabio says absently. "But you know what he requires the most? An uncle who isn't riling up the *mafiya*, doing God knows what else… Don—" His tone shifts as if he suddenly realized something. "This isn't your number. Where are you calling from—"

"If I can get you a better facility. Would it change anything?"

I know deep down it won't. I'm torturing myself, playing with hope. Fuck, it's all I can do.

"Don… I… It might," he admits. "But where are you? If the worst does come to pass, he needs you here."

"You'll be hearing from me as to when you can move him," I say, barely able to keep up with the plan forming in my head. If I can convince Mischa to allow Vin into the hospital, fuck anything else. I'll beg the man on my knees if I have to.

But I don't. Not if I can leverage a worthwhile bargaining chip.

"Wait for my call, Fab. Until then, you lay low. Put an extra security detail on yourself. I mean it. I'll be in touch when I can." I don't realize I'm setting the phone down until I hear Fab's voice, distorted from the other end of it. "Don, wait!"

I hang up and wind up hunched over the desk, my face in my hands. The terms of the game have changed again.

If I can save Vin's life…

I'll do whatever it takes.

Even if it means making a deal with the devil himself.

Eyeing the door, I call out, "Luciano?"

He reenters the room not even a second later, giving credibility to the idea he might have been listening in this whole fucking time.

Ignoring the suspicion, I ask, "Is the old apartment still available?"

He nods. "Tony didn't use it much, though."

Because unlike Giovanni, Antonio didn't give a shit about the energy and forethought it takes to truly run the *famiglia*. Giovanni warned me before I even took over, the toll such a mantle could take on a man.

*"This fucking apartment? Get used to it. You'll see these sheets more than any other property you own. They'll start to feel more familiar than your own wife's body does at night."*

And he was right. The title as the leader—and the responsibility that came with it—took me from Olivia well before she died.

"Don? Where are you going?" Luciano demands as I stand, circling the desk with my back to my reflection.

I shrug. "I need to shower."

He laughs, watching me with an incredulous expression. "You're on the verge of war with the *mafiya* who, by the way, outnumber us three to one. You've murdered Antonio, who, while a dick, still controlled more men than you have on your own. All of that and you just decide to—"

"Shower? Yes." I rake my hand through my hair and grimace as my fingers come away slick. "See if you can find me some clothes."

"Should I order you some coffee while I'm at it? Some donuts for the boys? We might as well be well refreshed, right? Can I get you anything else this fine evening?"

I nod. "I want that fixer. Now. If not tonight, then by tomorrow."

He sighs, stroking his chin. "The man's hard to get a hold of—"

"Is that too difficult for you?"

He shakes his head. "I'll send a message through Tony's phone. That might lure him here, if he thinks his payment might be in question. What is another fucking piss poor decision to cap off my life? But first, I need to know your plan. Ransom the girl to Mischa? He'd send an army on your head before you could finish naming your price.

Besides, what's to stop me from killing you now and trying that idiotic plan myself?"

He has a point. Though Giovanni liked his mirror for more than one reason. From this position, you had a clear view of the man standing before you. Namely when they're shuffling nervously from foot to foot despite the bravado in their voice.

"You don't have the balls," I point out. "Besides, I have a better idea than that. Do you want me to say the customary words? Fine," I tell him. "Trust me. But before you go off, I need you to do one last thing."

He hesitates for seconds before finally answering. "What?"

"Make sure no one else so much as looks at the girl. She's mine." My voice breaks over that fucking word. I'm disgusted to hear it out loud—and not for the first time either.

She's mine in the only sense that matters. *My* stolen toy to barter with. Mine to break.

A shower can wait. I should see her first.

"Should I be alarmed by your plans for her?" Luciano wonders, his eyes on my face.

I'm startled by the chuckle that escapes my throat. It almost sounds genuinely amused. When I picture my "plans" for the woman secured somewhere within this very building…

They're anything but humorous.

"Not if you don't want to end up like Antonio," I tell Luciano.

His laugh sounds more strained this time. "Just don't make a mess. You hurt her; you deal with her. I told Antonio the same damn thing with his little flings. We aren't the Saleris."

"You can sleep free of nightmares," I assure him. "Put the word out to the rest of your men—only I can touch her. See her. Smell her. Breathe the same air. No one else. No one else so much as enters the room she's in. Are we understood?"

"Very," he says tersely. "They've been fed for now. As for *your* woman…she's beautiful," he adds on his way out of the office. "But I've learned that the beautiful ones bring the most trouble."

He doesn't even know half of the trouble this woman could bring.

On the other hand, if I could trade her life for Vin's, I'd crawl on my knees to do so—nothing else should matter. A smart man would keep her hidden and bide his time to make a deal.

There's no point in seeing her face to face. Watching her squirm. Wanting to know why the hell she came back at all.

Only a fool would confront her now.

But the truth as it's kept, I've done worse. Once, years ago…I had to convince myself to do the unthinkable. Feed myself lies. Wallow in the horrific aftermath with the hopes that one day I might atone for it.

There is no prayer for atonement now.

No expectation of forgiveness.

After these long, cold years, I've made peace with who I am.

Whatever her reason for coming back, this woman should face that man.

If only to learn once and for all, never to challenge him again.

# 7

# EVGENI

Mercs aren't known for being picky when it comes to employment—that being said, few would work for Mischa Stepanov willingly. Ignoring our little spat from this morning, I can see why some might hesitate.

The pay is decent enough. While fearsome, I've had employers with a far worse reputation. Even the *mafiya's* dubious line of business would give few pause. Regardless, any guard worth his salt would avoid the Stepanovs for one reason, and one reason only.

Self-preservation.

A good job should be as uncomplicated as possible. Most are. No amount of money is worth more than that. You study the target. You study your employer even more. You get the money and come out on top always.

Mischa Stepanov, however, guards his secrets as closely as his family. In a word? The man is the definition of *complicated.*

In six years, I've never understood him, nor his past fully. Even the murky origins of his seemingly happy family are shrouded in secrecy—like the paternity of his firstborn son, and that of Willow, his adopted daughter. Logic dictates that those details shouldn't matter as long as I can do my job and do it well.

And they haven't.

Until now.

I suppose I can only blame myself for staying, though, to be fair, the job has been relatively boring prior to a week ago.

Donatello Vanici has brought an avalanche of drama upon the normally quiet household.

The aftermath of his attack on the Stepanovs has repercussions reaching far beyond the manor's limits. With Willow's disappearance thrown into the mix, our already strained resources have been pushed to their breaking point. Assigning me here could be interpreted as Mischa aiming to get me out of his hair, my expertise aside—but I'm not so petty as to ignore the bigger picture.

Protecting his wife is just as big a priority to him. The fact that he would station me here is a sign of trust, especially considering the job itself is no easy task. A squat four-story complex on the city's outskirts, Mercy hospital is a challenge within itself to secure—including the private wing and dedicated team of staff commandeered by the Stepanovs.

Nearly an hour from the manor, the location isn't ideal—in the heart of Saleri territory—and there is always a possibility that anyone with money and power can buy a guard or doctor to their side. All it takes is one faulty piece to topple a house of cards.

With that in mind, I take my time circling the building's perimeter as the evening progresses, scanning the outside for any potential areas of breach. This armored van is one of four, each patrolling a different section of the parking lot. It's mind-numbing work in comparison to the frantic search taking place for Willow. I don't doubt they'll find her; it's only a matter of when.

And how much of her will be left when they finally do…

The thought gnaws at my focus, distracting me from the monotonous task at hand. While uneventful, it's important given the week's recent events. The last thing the Stepanovs need is another attack to go unnoticed.

Blinking, I force my attention through the passenger window of the patrol van, inspecting the horizon. A light rain drenches the landscape, rendering the outer complex virtually deserted—though even a torrential storm wouldn't stop anyone determined enough to mount an attack.

"All clear, sir," the man in the driver's seat says. Mario, one of my best, hand-recruited after joining the manor's retinue. He was a damn good informant in a previous life, capable of finding dirt on anyone with only a name to go off and little else.

Given Donatello Vanici's pervasive reputation, I suspect finding information on him would be child's play. If I had the time, I'd delve into the mystery myself. As it stands, there's only so much I can do on my own.

"Ev?" Mario prompts. "Did you want to go around again before heading in?"

I wrestle with indecision for only a heartbeat. His primary focus should be Mrs. Stepanova—nothing else. Still, no one can garner better intel.

Willow's life is well worth the risk.

Placing my hand on his shoulder, I incline my head, prompting him to switch off the headset affixed to his ear, linking our position with the other six guards spread throughout the perimeter.

"Sir?" he asks, his expression unreadable in the dark.

Sighing, I cut right to the point. "I need you to do something for me, but we keep this between us. Understood?"

He nods. "I hear you."

"Here—" I reach into my pocket, retrieving a handful of rolled bills that I place in his hand. "I want everything you can get me on Donatello Vanici and the *famiglia*. Skip the basics. I know the surface level information, but there has to be more."

"Such as…?"

I exhale in a rush. Fuck it. "I want to know if he ordered the hit on the Stepanovs, or if someone else did."

"Shit." Mario whistles through his teeth, cagily eyeing the money. "Ev, if you're asking what I think you are, though I have to ask… Why go through me?"

"Mr. Stepanov has enough to worry about," I say, opening the door to the van. A cool wind throws the rain in my face like a bracing slap. In the end, the shock only helps solidify my decision. "I'll take the risk if anything comes of it. Think of it as nothing more than classic intel."

He nods, but I can tell from his raised eyebrow alone that he doesn't buy the explanation. "Anything else? The more specific, the better."

I grit my teeth, again weighing the risks. Willow's face appears in my mind, quashing any remaining doubt. Mischa may have barred me from the search party, but there are other ways I can assist. After all, it's better to ask for forgiveness than for permission.

"I especially want to know if Vanici ever had any dealings with a young girl," I say.

He grunts in surprise but hides it well. As long as we've both been in the business, nothing should shock us when it comes to the proclivities of men with power.

"How young we talking?"

"Any age. Any type of relationship. Give me whatever you can. I'll pay the price."

In more ways than one, if Mischa takes offense to my little quest for intel—a barrier I'll deal with later.

"On it," Mario says, nodding. "Otherwise, the birdcage is secure. The dove is resting. No update from the doctors as of yet. Kristoph is on watch. Nothing else to report from my end."

"Good," I reply, switching to a normal tone. "What about from base?"

He shakes his head with a sigh. "I've heard nothing from the Wolf—" our codename for Mischa. "But if anything major goes down, I'll phone you from here."

"Right." I step out, drawing my hood low, though I'm sure Mario caught my expression anyway. I can't shake the irritation that I've been shoved to the sidelines for a reason. Mischa's private security is composed of some of the best men I know—many of them hand-picked by my recommendations. Even so, I'd go so far as to say that none of them care for Willow more than me. Why? It's an entirely selfish reason—I'm the only one with a personal investment in her future.

Once she's safe and sound, living out her sheltered life as a pianist, mine will finally mean something. What's the word for it? Redemption.

I refuse to stand by as another innocent life is destroyed. Not this time.

"You okay, Ev?"

I blink to find Mario staring at me. "Yeah," I say. "I'm fine."

"Well, take care, then." He rolls his window up, and I watch him drive off, presumably to repeat the same route until I return.

Alone, I enter the building through a locked stairwell that leads directly to Mrs. Stepanova's wing. A key card gives me access, one of a few assigned to this wing. Even the hospital's regular staff can't enter these halls unaccompanied.

It's a strict level of security well warranted by the number of *mafiya* enemies who might be looking to make their mark. Suspects who come to mind include Vanici and the *famiglia* or their associates.

All outfits not necessarily helmed by a woman.

The second I enter the hallway, my nostrils twitch, catching a whiff of floral fragrance. Alarm shoots down my spine, setting every nerve on alert as I inhale again. This smell…

It violates the hospital's strict ban on perfume, for one. Not only that, but this fragrance is rich, definitely expensive, reminding me of the high class escorts an old client of mine used to cycle in and out of his home regularly.

The telltale scent of a viper.

Warily, I palm my weapon as I ascend the stairs. A pair of double doors open onto a narrow hall, accessible by only the medical staff assigned to Mrs. Stepanova and her security detail. As expected, only one man stands positioned near the entrance, his stance alert.

"Did you let anyone past?" I ask as I approach.

He shoots me an odd look, alarmed by my tone. "No one. I mean… Just a doctor."

"A doctor? I thought the last update was earlier this morning," I say. "Which one?"

He eyes his clipboard. "Uh… Rachel Main."

The OBGYN assigned to Mrs. Stepanova's case. A woman in her forties who usually visits in the morning. Never have I heard of her making an evening visit.

And I definitely don't recall her wearing perfume.

"You didn't call to confirm the visit with anyone?" I ask as the man sputters. "Has there been a change in Mrs. Stepanova's condition?"

"No… But—"

"Describe this doctor."

He squints before licking his lips thoughtfully. "Blond. Mid-thirties, I think. Attractive."

"Shit." I push past him, sensing the unease in my gut fester.

"She had a badge, sir." His voice chases me down the hallway. "Her name was on the list—"

"Stay back," I snap over my shoulder. "Get ready to call for backup if I shout for it." Without looking to see if he obeys,

I round the doorway of Mrs. Stepanova's room and instantly feel my eyes narrow.

The woman sitting beside the lone hospital bed lacks the stoic demeanor of the other medical professionals I've interacted with. With her back to me, she leans over the bedside, her golden hair falling freely down her shoulders. She doesn't seem to notice or care as I approach the foot of the bed. A glance at the head of the bed reveals Mrs. Stepanova resting, seemingly unharmed apart from the tubes and medical equipment attached to her at all ends.

As for her visitor, other than a white lab coat, the woman's resemblance to Dr. Main is tentative at best.

"Turn around," I demand. "Keep your hands where I can see them and tell me your name."

Her laugh catches me off guard. Warm and icy at the same time.

"Now," I insist, pulling my gun from the holster at my hip. "Slowly."

Another laugh teases the air as she swivels to face me, her head cocked.

I don't recognize her.

As relayed, she's attractive, with bright blue eyes and delicate features—but it's those features that alarm me. Confuse. Those eyes and that mouth don't belong to her, but the woman lying in the bed behind her. It's an uncanny resemblance, and I have to eye Mrs. Stepanova again, just to make sure they aren't one and the same.

"Who are you?" I ask the stranger.

She shrugs. "Just a visitor."

Her voice is nothing like Mrs. Stepanova's, lacking any hint of sweetness. It's a low, husky purr like that of a cat. The accent is crisper, reminding me again of those pricey escorts. They sounded the same way, tailored to mimic the posh lilt of the aristocratic.

Either way, she definitely doesn't belong here. A decoy, perhaps, sent by Vanici? A round of questioning should give me my answer.

I reach for my headset, aiming to contact Mario. To the woman, I say, "I'm going to have to escort you out."

She smiles, but something in the expression makes my finger still, poised to strike the call button. Those curled red lips portray confidence at a glance—at least to anyone not skilled enough to see her throat quivering in the same motion.

Not exactly the response of a trained assassin or even an escort. Before I can pursue the thought further, she stands and stalks forward. Were she anyone else, I'd have my gun trained on her in seconds.

For whatever reason, I don't move. Perhaps it's the tilt to her head, desperate to convey bravado—but her hand shakes, though she runs it along her hip to disguise the motion. Up close, it's apparent that she stole the lab coat. It's large on her, drawn partially closed over a red dress that pairs with her heels. She's as slight as Mrs. Stepanova, and I think I can pinpoint why my usual reflexes are slow to deploy.

Fuck, they could be twins.

"I'm leaving," she says in that husky purr, slipping past me unchallenged. "Though what has the world come to when a woman can't even see her own sister?"

"Sister?" I demand, spinning to keep her in view.

She doesn't head for—what should be—the sole entrance to the suite. Instead, she heads for a service staircase, opening it quickly.

"Who the hell are you?"

She laughs, but light on her feet, she darts through the doorway, slamming it shut before I can reach her. Through the metal comes a muffled taunt, "My name is Briar Winthorp."

I tug the handle, hissing to find it locked. She must have found some way to circumvent the security—a deficit on my part. I reach for the headset again, prepared to send up the alarm and alert the rest of the team about the breach.

My finger twitches against the call button, prepared to strike it. Instead, I find myself returning to Mrs. Stepanova's room. She's breathing, her vital signs seemingly stabilized, not a hair out of place.

I could raise the alarm and only heighten Mischa's paranoia.

Or do my job and handle the situation for now.

It takes just seconds to decide. I make a mental note to switch the guard, but I leave to take my post without calling anyone else.

Whoever the stranger is, I'm sure I can handle her alone.

In any way necessary.

# 8

## WILLOW

*I* never realized how disorienting darkness alone can be. It's endless. Impenetrable. Terrifying. Without a clock or even a view of the sky, I'm all but blind. Very few sounds reach this room to give me any clue otherwise. There are no footsteps. No voices, either.

No way to track the passage of time. Apart from the gray-eyed man appearing briefly to deliver a tray of food—sandwiches we ate in the dark—we haven't been disturbed by anyone.

Forget the relief I felt before. I'd rather be bound if only to have *some* connection to the outside world. My only sense of direction comes from running my palms along whatever I can reach. A smooth wall. Gritty floor. Over and over, I retrace my steps from this narrow corner to the sole door.

There's no use trying to escape this way. The material is too solid to kick through or dent, and the lock too sturdy to pick. Though getting it open would only solve half of the equation.

The real key to winning any battle is to anticipate your enemy—and therein lies the problem—I know nothing about this Donatello. I can't predict him. Can't anticipate him.

So instead, I aimlessly wander through the dark as my mind races. Mischa would snarl in anger if he saw me now. I can clearly envision what he'd say—*Don't sit quietly waiting for your throat to be cut! Find a way. Any way.*

Guilt stabs through my chest whenever I try to imagine what he might be doing. I'm sure they've discovered my absence by now. Does he know how to find me? Does he even want to?

My knee strikes something hard enough to knock me off my feet, interrupting the chain of thought. Flailing, I scramble for something sturdy enough to break my fall. I find it in a firm material that feels flat. Immovable. Like wood.

The desk, I think. It's large, overflowing with paperwork. Letters. Stacks of documents. In the absence of light, they have no purpose. Still, I feel through the various materials, searching for a lamp. My fingers brush something rigid instead, partially hidden beneath a sheet of paper. Whatever it is, it's hard. Metal. Thin. A letter opener?

Hopeful, I swipe my finger along the edge. It's not sharp, but pointed enough to serve as a weapon anyway. Tucking it against my palm, I retreat to my previous position.

A soft cough breaks the heavy silence, and I stiffen, heart in my throat. That's right…

I'm not alone. The girl is on the opposite end of the room, huddled against the wall, only discernable by her stark white nightgown. Another cough and a muffled whimper consist of the few sounds she's made since we came here.

My throat aches with the weight of my silence. I've never been so acutely aware of my own limitations until now. I wish I could say anything, if only to comfort her. Instead, I head in her direction, reaching out until my fingertips hit warm skin. Almost instantly, a small hand finds mine, gripping tightly, and I sink down beside her.

She seems so young. Too young.

Much like another little girl who, if she had a voice, might have cried in a moment like this. Robbed of sound, all she could do was wait in the dark at the hands of a stranger as a million different thoughts crossed her mind.

Fear of what might happen next.

Disbelief.

Hate for the man who ruined her innocence and plunged her into chaos.

In the end, that little girl was spared the worst fate imaginable, rescued by an unlikely source, Mischa Stepanov.

For all I know, that same man could be on his way here now. God, I hope he is.

Straining my ears, I wait for any sound. Any sign of hope.

When none comes, my thoughts turn darker. I think I've stopped myself from reliving that moment until now—when Eli and Ellen returned to the manor in a bloodstained van, barely conscious. Despair is a noose around my neck at the thought that they could have died then. Still might…

And I wouldn't even know, because I decided to run right to the very man who might have hurt them. Mischa thought as much. A good, loyal daughter would trust his judgment. Trust him.

Not the memory of a man who no longer exists. A figure who, even at his worst, could never commit that kind of crime.

Though the girl beside me is proof enough of how very wrong I could be.

I don't know how long we sit like this before footsteps finally pierce the quiet, advancing toward this room. That fragile hope floods my chest, only to quickly die at the cadence of the figure's walk—slow. Unsteady. Heavy—not Mischa's.

Paces from the room, the steps stall, and my heart stutters. Tension teases the air, enhancing every passing second until…

A sharp sound breaks the quiet, alarmingly close. The doorknob? I crane my neck, blinking until I swear I can see it. Turning. Slowly, slowly…

The door itself opens without warning, ushering in a sliver of blinding light.

I blink rapidly, fighting to take in whatever I can. A blurred shape. A person?

"You," he says, dispelling the mystery. That gruff voice is unmistakable. "Come."

He walks away, but I don't budge from my seated position. The light from the hall is enough to illuminate this small corner. Beside me, the girl watches on, her eyes wide as her tiny fingers grip mine tighter.

Our visitor is already gone from what I can tell, his steps advancing away. For a second, I contemplate running, taking my chance now. Cautiously, I rise to my feet, pulling the girl with me, gripping the letter opener in my free hand. We creep forward, but with one look past the doorway, I realize the folly of running. The hallway beyond this room forks into two, but both exits are dominated by one man standing with his back to me.

My heart pangs at the sight of him. He hasn't changed, even though it must be hours since he brought us here. He's still wearing the same filthy suit, his appearance even more haggard. Disheveled. Going off the slow, heavy way he moves, I bet I could outrun him, even with the girl in tow.

Before I can go as much as a step, he inclines his head, the warning clear. *Don't even try it.* As if confident I won't, he continues down the left-hand hallway at that deliberate pace.

I grit my teeth, torn between logic and impulse. The further away he moves, the clearer my way becomes. From what I remember, the main entrance is through the right, and I flick my gaze in that direction.

"Don't." His voice is so soft, not even a shout, barely audible.

I go still regardless.

"Don't run. You wouldn't make it far," he adds.

I swallow hard. The threat isn't what makes me stop short. It's his tone, as chilling as a smattering of off notes on a piano. There was no inflection. No passion—just malice. The way I figure a shark would taunt a bobbing, bleeding fish in its orbit.

He's all but daring me to run, if only so he can give chase.

Because *that's* what he really wants.

Despite knowing that, it takes everything I have not to bolt anyway. It's painful, achievable only by digging my bare heels into the cool tile flooring as hard as I can. Then I loosen my grip on the girl and guide her back into the room, shutting the door behind her.

"Come," Donatello warns, still paces away. Patiently, he waited until now merely to drive one point home.

We're alone. My throat goes dry at the realization. Even with the distance between us, I notice the small details I hadn't been aware of before. Like the fact that I'm wearing only a thin cotton dress. My hair feels slick, and the stench of lighter fluid itches my nostrils with every breath. As much as I want to deny the fear seeping through my veins, I can't.

All I have against him is a dull secretary's tool.

He has…time. It looms, as threatening as any weapon whenever I look at him. That face, the catalyst of so many memories. His hands. Even his steps trigger a painful recollection.

Luckily, pride is a bitter antidote to his poison, potent enough that I can hold my head high and take a step toward him, unaffected. Another. Another.

I can't tell if he's moving too slowly or I'm just gaining on him too quickly, leaving myself little time to take notice of our surroundings like I should.

Breathing deeply, I try to focus, eyeing the length of the corridor. There are no exits within easy distance of the room we're being kept in. Still no windows, either. The only markers we pass are the fluorescent lightbulbs mounted in the ceiling above, casting swaths of darkness that swallow Donatello the further he goes.

Whether due to his intent or mine, the distance between us lengthens, putting me well beyond his reach. Again, the urge to run rises up. I could always fight. Overpower him.

The letter opener is still in my grasp. My pulse surges as I glance down, spotting the delicate strip of silver peeking between my fingers. It could be a useful weapon.

Even so, I don't move to brandish it. Yet. Sweat drips down my spine as I keep walking, tucking the weapon against my skirt.

I almost miss the moment he stops, disappearing through a doorway.

I have a second to glance inside before my toes brush the threshold after him. It's small. Narrow. We're even more secluded from the others, judging from how little sound reaches here—just the buzzing of electricity feeding the lights above.

The room itself doesn't contain much, obscuring his reason for bringing me here. There is a couch in the corner, composed of battered brown leather. A small table is across from it, positioned before a sight that makes fresh hope rise up my throat—dust-streaked windows overlooking a sea of trees. *Finally.* It's dusk, I think. Early evening? Apart from the glimpse of moonlight, the windows themselves look wide enough to break or escape from.

I only need a chance…

"Look at me."

His voice casts a spell over my body, banishing any thought of escape. My limbs jerk, maneuvering without input from my brain. Against my own will, my head swivels, bringing into focus the lone figure standing near the center of the room.

Up this close, it's even more stark how different he is from the man in my memories. Different from the figure I faced just a few days ago, even—a rival who barged into my family home under the pretense of attending my debutante ball.

This Donatello does nothing to disguise who he is at his core. A tortured man. A bleeding man. An empty soul.

"I want to hear you say it…" He trails off, laughing to himself.

The coldness of the wall against my back is a shock before I even register backing away—but I didn't move toward the doorway like I should. A few feet of space separate me from it, more than enough for him to cover in a single stride. I'm trapped as he moves to block my only path.

"I want to see it on your face for myself," he says, amending his request. "The happiness. The satisfaction. After all, this is what you wanted, isn't it?"

His stress on that word paints a morbid picture. *This.* Vincenzo dead, and my father at his throat.

Is it?

The question is so callous I can't even decide how I feel. Insulted? Though if I had to ask myself a better question, I doubt I could answer it either—why did I leave my home in the middle of the night to find him? Why did I go to Havienna alone? Why?

My head hurts, so rather than think, I watch him. It's surprisingly easy to meet his gaze without flinching, as long as there's a sizable distance between us. Every yard brings clarity. Bravado. I can comfort myself with the lie that he won't touch me.

He won't…

"You hate me, fine. I deserve it," he admits in a growl. "But Vincenzo? Did he deserve what your father did to him? A bullet to the fucking head. Did he deserve that?"

I look away, my face on fire. It's a cruel line of attack, but I humor it with an honest answer, anyway, at least to myself. *No.* Vin didn't deserve what happened to him.

While my captor has been vague as to the details, I can guess. Mischa, assuming Donatello was behind the assault on Ellen and Eli, attacked him out of revenge. Sweet Vincenzo with the crooked glasses and wry smile…

It's hard to even fathom that he might be dead. Donatello's betrayal darkened some memories of my past, but not all of them. The ones starring Vin still stand out, filled with mirth and warmth, untouched by hate. Tears prickle my eyes at the thought of them. My old birthday parties. Our petty squabbles that always ended amicably in the end. All of those years we spent together, playing as closely as any real siblings…

It kills me that Mischa could have been responsible for what happened to him—but another emotion quickly seeps into my chest, dulling the pain. Anger. It's a soothing balm that eases my own guilt, directed solely at the man before me.

Vincenzo's death or otherwise isn't my fault.

And only a coward would use that to negate everything else.

"Ah, little hellcat…" Donatello cocks his head as a low, gravelly sound resonates through his throat. A laugh? Or a pained groan. "You think I'm pathetic for mentioning him." He nods as if I spoke out loud, and I can't help it. My eyes swivel toward him narrowed with alarm.

The knowing tilt to his head is the same way he used to look years ago, while accusing me of ignoring a chore or stealing a treat with no other shred of evidence. He only had to see my face and know. To him, I always was an open book.

"Oh yes." He laughs again. "You're brave, I'll give you that. But while you may be silent, your face alone is enough to —" He breaks off, as his expression shifts too quickly for me to track. Horrified? He staggers as if struck, his eyes widening and narrowing in quick succession. When I finally peg the emotion twisting his mouth into a snarl, it's already too late.

Rage.

The next second, he's across the room, his outstretched fingers aiming for my throat. I go rigid. The air in my lungs escapes in a single gasp, and all I can do is watch him.

And wait.

His anger is a wild, ravaging thing, almost musical in nature. The creeping crescendo of a haunting melody that comes from nowhere, as much as a surprise to the person performing the piece as it is to the listener. There is no rhyme or reason to it.

Just pure violent emotion.

"Your face…" His chest heaves as he flicks my chin with the pad of his thumb. I flinch, but he does it again, sloppily, scraping delicate flesh with his nail. And again, applying more and more pressure until I finally meet his gaze.

His eyes flicker as if he's reading my thoughts word for word. I'm *that* vulnerable to him.

"Fuck…" He inhales through his teeth as a realization dawns over his face, transforming the frown into a gaping, formless shape. "I thought you might have done it out of hate. Implicated me on purpose. All for revenge. Revenge. Revenge!" His voice grows more bellicose with every word, bellowing throughout the room untamed. The look in his eyes is what sends ice through my veins, though. Wide, staring, angry, flashing irises, and dilated pupils. It's like he's demanding something from me. Pleading for it.

But I can't give it. Even worse, my own eyes water in response, confusing me further. I don't know what he wants.

"But it wasn't that, was it?" The pad of his finger shakes, grazing over my mouth. He presses hard against my bottom lip, bringing his taste against my tongue. Blood, and violence, and accelerant. A cough rips up my throat, silenced as he slams his palm against my mouth entirely, sealing it shut.

"You don't want revenge," he croaks, seemingly alarmed by the fact. "No. No… You don't even know what you want, do you? You're just a child. You're just a fucking child. *Fuck*!"

He lets me go, bracing himself against the nearest wall. His shoulders heave, his body shaking, a low sound ripping from his throat. At first…

I think it's sobbing—until I catch that telltale wavering note that identifies it for what it really is. Laughing. Uncontrolled, hysterical laughing.

"You're a little girl in a world of wolves," he grates in between the unstable notes. "Fuck. You probably don't even know why you came to me, do you? For a pat on the head? A goodnight kiss? I fucking sold you!"

He whirls around, brandishing a fist, his face so wet I assume he's found more lighter fluid at first, dousing himself in it. But no…

The longer I stare, the more the harsh fluorescents reflect off the signature droplets. Tears. They mirror my own. Burning, hot, painful tears that rake down my cheeks unchecked like slashing claws.

"Fuck, what did you expect from me?" he demands, slamming a fist against the wall. His knuckles leave scarlet smears on the white paint, a vibrant illustration of what he's capable of. "What? The truth? Fine."

The look in his eye warns that it's the last thing I want. An irrational sensation washes over me. Like I'd scream if I could. Slam my hands over my ears. Anything to make him stop.

I can't hear this.

Regardless, he says it. "I sold you for ten thousand dollars. Did you know that?"

I didn't, and I'm sure my expression reveals as much. He could have punched me, and I doubt my reaction would be any different. Lips parting, breathing heavy and broken. The amount stings, thrown in my face as though it were pennies. Change. A worthless sum that mattered little in the end.

Because it didn't.

"I didn't fucking care how much," he adds to twist the knife. "I didn't. I think I spent it on a horse race or some shit. *That* was your worth to me. It could have been ten dollars, and I still would have done it. You meant that little to me."

And it's the truth. His cold stare proves it even before he says the words, "I just wanted you gone. But you were lucky… Mischa," he spits out the name. "He gave you the life I never could." His red eyes sweep over me, and he sighs, swaying on his feet. "He kept you sheltered, Safiya. Sheltered and innocent with no fucking clue as to the way the world works. You thought you could see me again and what?"

He throws his arms out as if expecting the answer to fall from the sky.

"That everything would magically right itself? You'd get your revenge and ease the hole in your fucking heart? No. No…" He shakes his head with pity—but the worst realization creeps in as he sighs again. It's genuine. Eyes downcast, he says, "No, Safiya. The world doesn't work like that. You need to go home. Go back to your pretty little life and forget that you ever left that cage. You belong there."

*There,* safe in Mischa's beautiful family, where I only ever felt out of place. A misfit dove in a world of swans. I try to bat the thought away—the same way I have for seven damn years. But I can't. The truth claws at my chest until I finally acknowledge it—I only ever felt safe with him. Only felt like I ever belonged at Havienna.

And he knows that.

He's relishing in it, denying me the home I never really had.

Sending me away now isn't mercy. It's a pathetic way to assuage his guilt. Mischa's manor is far enough away from him where I can safely be ignored. Thrown away a second time. Branded with a word that stings worse than *tigre,* or *hellcat,* or even a *bitch* he could hate.

Child.

Someone too pitiful to fit in his world.

An innocent too stupid for him to acknowledge.

A ghost.

"I'm sending you back. I'll call Mischa. Take you there now." He runs a hand through his hair, and I realize he means it. With no fanfare. No ransom. He'll send me back with a slap on the wrist. The worst part? He thinks of it as a mercy. "You don't belong here…"

His voice trails off, distorted as if someone turned the volume down. I see him heading for the door, and I don't know what possesses me to move. I gain on him. Step, by step, by step…

Alarmed, he inclines his head toward me at the same time my hand lands against his exposed cheek with a sound so startling I flinch. Vicious, slapping noise. He grunts, and belatedly, I see the letter opener in my fist, glinting in the light. See a flash of crimson splatter the floor next.

And then I see Donatello, frozen mid-lunge. He blinks, struck dumb—only for a second. The next, my wrists are in his grasp, and he's herding me back against the wall with a brutality that snaps everything into motion again.

Confusion on him is torment. He sways, another agonized grunt slipping loose—but it's his eyes that disturb me the most. For once, they meet mine openly with none of the rage. No pity. Just sheer puzzlement that knocks years from his age.

He's just a broken man unsure of what the screeching little girl tugging at his pantleg wants. I'm that much of a mystery to him.

"You hate that I could ignore you," he says. "Are you that fucking childish? You are…" He scoffs at the idea of it. "What? You want me to grovel and beg for your mercy? I won't."

Anger rips through me so fiercely I'm shocked by the force of it. Because he's right.

He *should* be begging.

My teeth clatter together as I fight his grasp, but he's too strong, easily bending my arm behind my back.

"Do you think I won't hurt you?" he demands, his breath hot on my neck. "Is that what you fucking want? To drill it home? You only ever were a goddamn pawn! Haven't you realized that yet?"

I think I haven't stopped asking myself the same question since our uncanny reunion. Could he uphold the twisted boast he made? Sell his precious Safiya a second time? Break her wings?

Doubt circles my skull like an itch I can't scratch, growing all the more irritating by his nearness. Yes? No? Yes…

*Yes, yesyesyesyes!*

His eyes convey the true answer, glaring deep into my own. I can't escape them. My only defense is to rear back while holding his cold, lifeless stare and inhale.

Then I breathe out, my cheeks hollowing as spit flies from my mouth to splatter against that stern jaw. Triumph rips through me, but it's short-lived. Sparks that die in reality's cold chill.

He reacts like a man stuck in slow motion. His fingers brush at the liquid as he swivels toward me. The next second, his hand is in my hair, latching onto my scalp. Wrenching. He uses the leverage to draw me against him so quickly he doesn't even seem to realize he's done it.

"You were always so damn stubborn—" Once more, he breaks off, stopping himself from committing what seems to be the ultimate sin.

Acknowledging my existence.

Admitting the truth.

Seeing me for who I am.

Because this pathetic, stubborn, childish part of me wants to hear him say it.

He hurt me. He hurt me. He hurt me.

And that matters.

The tattoo on his chest implies that it does. I saw it once, etched in red ink as sloppy as if he did it himself. Carved every letter. Every twist and curve.

Safiya Mangenello meant *something* to him. But only as a lie he could comfort himself with. The real girl? She means nothing.

I see that now; his fuzzy, hazy expression blurred by tears is the only evidence I need.

"I'm done with your mind games," he says, dismissive once again. Releasing me, he starts to turn on his heel, but my hand flies out, snatching a fistful of his collar before he can.

It's still damp, a shock that reinforces our present circumstances.

We both smell like lighter fluid. His eyes are bloodshot, his hair a tousled mess.

The evidence of who we really are is all around us—the dust from Havienna on our clothing. The haunting memories of the past. The fact that he can take one look at me and know my thoughts so easily.

"You thought I was bluffing, did you?" He shoves me back, using his bulk as a battering ram to pin me flat against the wall. Air escapes my chest in a rush, as his hands find my waist, so large his fingers almost meet across my stomach.

A million different adjectives flood my mind in a rush to describe how he feels—*warm. Big. Too big. Heavy. Infallible.*

Strong.

So strong…

Once, these hands used to hold me. Comfort me whenever I felt alone or afraid. Never would they creep over me with a boldness that takes my breath away. His thumbs rasp over my belly button as his gaze lowers, and I'm riveted to his every reaction.

Dilated pupils. Flared nostrils. Wrong. The way his tongue flits across his lower lip almost too quickly to track is *wrong*.

And I can't stop it…

For the first time, I feel something itching through my skin I've never felt before. Ever. At least when it came to him. Still, I recognize it instinctively the way any woman would.

Fear.

The kind of fear you can only feel when a layer of fabric is the lone barrier shielding you from a man with nothing left to lose…

"Donatello?" The voice shatters the tense silence. Male? A face appears in the doorway, his gray eyes familiar. The man with the gun, only he's unarmed now.

Donatello shoves me aside so suddenly I go down hard, tasting copper as my teeth catch my lower lip.

"What is it?" he demands, his breathing heavy. "Fuck! What is it?"

"You have a visitor," the man replies, inclining his head. "I doubt you want to keep him waiting."

# 9

# DON

For seven years, Safiya Mangenello has haunted me, a specter dwelling inside my goddamn head. I let her live there. I fed into the lie that as long as I continued to do good, it might somehow make up for my crime against her. Hell, I think I even believed it.

There are no lies to hide behind now.

She's dead, and nothing will ever change that. Whoever Mischa saved, she's someone else. A little girl howling that I atone for the sins of the past as though we're all living in some fucking fairy tale where wrongs can be righted with the wave of a wand.

But this is no fairy tale.

And I'm done fucking atoning.

"Don?" The voice hooks into my thoughts, tugging me back to the present.

"W-What?" I croak, turning to face Luciano. He's gaping at me, mouth wide open, like I'm insane—not that I can blame him. Fuck, I feel like it, shaking my head as though I'm resurfacing from minutes spent submerged underwater. I'm breathing just as heavily as if I were drowning.

Or, in this case, lost in a pair of dark fucking eyes ten times deeper than any ocean. With every glance, they suck me in, demanding something I don't know how to fucking give. An answer? But there isn't one good enough to satisfy that curiosity.

So they'll suck my lungs dry instead.

*She'll* drain me of every-fucking-thing...

"Don? I said he's here."

"Who?" I say, staggering toward him, fighting to stay standing. The figure I leave behind doesn't move, still on her knees, huddled against the wall. Blinking, I keep going. As long as I don't look at her, I can think. *Focus.*

The man observing the show raises an eyebrow but has the sense to keep his fucking mouth shut. Pushing past him, I brace one hand against the doorway and suck in a lungful of air. Exhale it slowly. Try to refocus. He came here for a reason.

A visitor...

"The man Antonio spoke with?" I ask, craning my neck in his direction.

He nods. The fact that he's wearing a different shirt and jeans betrays how late it is. How long did I sit in that damn study, gathering the nerve to see her?

"That's why I'm here. He should be passing through the gates any minute now—"

"Have your men detain him," I say, standing upright. I take a step, and my thoughts get clearer. Another and I can breathe normally again. The further I get from her, the better I feel. In control.

"Wait." Luciano raises a hand before I can leave the room behind entirely. "First… I think you need to explain what the hell you were doing." He inclines his head in a direction I refuse to look, his eyes blazing. "Assaulting the daughter of the *mafiya* head? Are you suicidal? Is that it? Fuck, man! Feel free to take yourself out in a rain of hellfire, but leave the *famiglia* out of it—"

"Are you done?" I ask, raising an eyebrow.

He blinks in shock rather than answer, as if he can't decide whether I'm truly insane or just foolish.

Maybe it's a bit of both.

Reentering the room, I spot a leather couch and collapse onto it. It's uncomfortable as fuck, but it provides enough support for me to ignore the rest of the world and think. My fingers find my chin, stroking the stubble there as I do so.

My first priority is finding proof that Antonio set me up. Though why would he even go through the trouble? Sure, he was a selfish fuck, but seeing the state of the *famiglia* for myself, I doubt control of the harbor would be enough to change their fortunes around. There had to be more to it.

I don't know exactly how much time passes before Luciano loudly clears his throat.

"I'd hate to interrupt," he snarls. "But I don't know, maybe you can relax another time? When we aren't on the verge of fucking Armageddon."

"You don't trust me," I point out, tilting my head to face him directly.

"Frankly, I'm wondering if you're any different from Tony," he warns, cutting his eyes away from me. "You two seem to have a lot in common."

In my peripheral vision lurks a figure clothed in yellow, still hunched on the floor. *Fuck...*

Gritting my teeth, I ignore her.

"And yet you're still here," I say to the man before me. "Don't pretend like you wouldn't be cutting and running like hell if you really thought I was crazy. You're still here, which means you're smarter than you pretend to be."

"Or I could be just as fucking crazy as you are," he retorts. "Perhaps it's the allure of it. I've heard the stories. The big bad Donatello who singlehandedly fought the Hortega Cartel and made off like a bandit with the spoils of war. You were a legend. Though, hell, they could have been just stories."

"Stories," I scoff. "Because Antonio's done so much better than I did—"

"Antonio was a dick, but he wasn't stupid. We always keep an ear to the ground, and you, Donatello? Mischa's been gunning for you like hell. It's all over the fucking city. The real question is, what do you plan to do next?"

I lean my head back as I contemplate that very problem. The good Don? He wants to wallow in his agony and pretend this isn't happening. Forget. Ignore. Repent.

As for the other part of me that isn't drenched in misery?

It only craves power. Revenge, the pettier, the better…

Above that? Vin's safety. If there's any chance of him staying alive, I'll crawl over glass if I have to. Whatever it takes. Luckily—or not—for me, every motive circles back to my captive little Stepanova. Funny, given only a few minutes ago, I'd been ready to let her go.

"I wanted to sell the girl," I admit, ignoring the fact that she's here in this room, listening to every word. "Use the money to challenge Mischa, or barter the threat to make him back down."

Luciano whistles through his teeth, but when I look over, he has his head inclined thoughtfully. "She's pretty enough to catch a nice price, but I don't think you're doing it for the money."

"No." I brace my hands against my knees, surprised by the laugh that rips from my chest. "Not for the money."

But he's right. Her youth and face alone would fetch a hefty amount, even before her identity came into account. Some crime lord would take her, eager to feel like a big man by breaking someone so seemingly innocent.

*Though,* a part of me scoffs, *what makes you any different?*

I try to envision it—her at the mercy of someone else. Their hands mauling that pale skin. Their fingers imparting new bruises around her neck. Another monster forcing his way inside her... The hot sensation flooding my skin isn't glee at the prospect.

"In that case, you should try the Saleris," Luciano suggests, oblivious. "They may not give you what she's worth, but if you want her to suffer… They'll ensure that. The boss' son, Mateo, is a sick son of a bitch. The shit I've heard he's into would make even your skin crawl. As far as I know, they have no ties to Mischa. I tend to avoid the crazy motherfuckers, but Antonio had a contact he used when he got in the mood for an exotic girl."

I can't tell if he's being serious or playing along. I look over, spotting my reflection in the glass of the nearest window. The frown I find shocks the hell out of me. It can't be remorse at the thought of selling her. No. It must be greed. She'd fetch a pretty penny on the market, but why let someone else have the privilege?

Doing the deed myself would be the sickest jab at Mischa. Cold hard revenge. A truly evil act that would kill any hope of redemption for good.

"Or maybe you just plan to sit here and wait for Mischa Stepanov to track you down," Luciano taunts. "I don't think it will take him that long to figure it out. It's not like you have an abundance of allies."

"Ah, but that is exactly why the *famiglia* will be the last place he'll think to check," I counter. "Men like Mischa are all about pride and honor. It takes pride to walk away. In his mind, he wouldn't envision a scenario in which I'd come crawling back."

But I'm not crawling now.

"Take me to this Vanetti," I say, rising to my feet. "Have one of your men record everything he says. You got that?"

Luciano doesn't respond, his attention elsewhere. When I clear my throat, he jerks his chin toward the corner. "What about your guest?"

I can sense her, lurking just beyond my line of sight, those eyes staring fiercely in anticipation of what I might do next. My gaze finds her without permission from my brain, riveted to that body with a magnetic focus.

Gone is the angry little girl. It's the way she holds herself that transforms her. Stoically facing forward, her lips pursed, hands gently smoothing her dress back into place.

Even Luciano's wary scowl fades in the face of her.

I'm too damn tired for jealousy. Too old. Too bitter. But if I could still feel it, the sensation might resemble the pinprick of fire in my gut, searing the longer his eyes trace her shape.

"Let's go." I head for the door, but I can't escape the reality of her presence. I should tie her up, lock her in a cage.

Reinforce her only identity that matters to me—that as a prisoner.

Instead, I exit the room without even looking at her—but I'm sure she'll follow. Even if she doesn't, I may not need her after all. Throwing proof of his stupidity in Mischa's face could be payback enough, sweeter than dangling his daughter's life over his head. With that in mind, I pause to direct just one request at Luciano.

"Get me a knife."

# 10

# WILLOW

A good captive would play her role and hide. Better yet, I'd use Donatello's absence as an excuse to scour the area for any weakness to exploit. Or escape while his back is turned. A smarter woman would run.

I walk instead, following him and another down a narrow hall that opens onto a set of stairs leading to a lower level. Donatello stalks down them with purpose, the other man on his heels. Neither seems to notice me, but I never do the smart thing and take advantage of the moment.

I can't even take my eyes off him.

It's the way he moves. Assuredly, emboldened with confidence that the man I found on the floor of Havienna lacked. I don't know where he's headed—the other man mentioned a visitor—but I doubt joy, or happiness is the factor driving him. Not, I suspect, even revenge.

No... Whatever sustains him now is something I recognize. I feel it too. Desperation. Despair. Hate. A need to rage against everything and everyone, feeding an internal flame. The hotter the fire, the easier it is to ignore the rest. The pain.

If only for a little while. But few things can feed that blaze for long—like sustaining any fire, you need fuel.

My heart pounds with unease as I try to imagine what source he might choose to utilize in this instance. Me? His request for a knife echoes loudly in my mind. He's already bruised my throat. What next?

There are other ways a man can harm a woman…

My body still burns from his touch, that feeling, the look in his eyes—all of it so different from any memory I can call upon of him. The old him. Maybe the only feeling akin to it was the crippling heat that assaulted me when he stripped me in Havienna. When his finger slid inside me, and I knew, if only for that moment, that any past importance I had to him ceased to matter. In that moment, I was a stranger.

At his mercy.

I shake my head to banish the memory as my foot strikes drastically different flooring from the tile before. Concrete? All this time, I've still been following him.

The room we're in now is unfamiliar. A cavernous space with metal siding, naked floors, and a vaulted ceiling. A massive opening at one end of the building allows moonlight and fresh air into the area, but otherwise, there are no windows, and a single door connects it to the hallway we came from.

Four other men stand in a semi-circle nearby. In the center, a man is on his knees wearing a navy suit, his dark hair slicked back to his skull. He was handsome once, with a stern jaw sporting a burgeoning bruise and a straight nose gushing blood. What seems to be a tie has been shoved into his mouth as a makeshift gag, and at the sight of Donatello, he issues a stream of muffled noise.

"This is him," the man walking behind Donatello says. "Paulie Vanetti."

The name isn't familiar, though I doubt he's a friend given Donatello's cold glance in his direction.

Both men draw even with the crouching figure, and I suck in a breath, recognizing the way Donatello cocks his head. Exactly how a hawk might when sizing up a promising prey item. Calculatingly.

He steps forward, drawing all attention to him. "So this is the man Antonio contracted?"

"It's him," the other man says. "He's been cagey on the work he did. I don't think he'll tell us freely."

"There is no need for threats." Sighing, Donatello crouches on one knee and looks the bound man in the eye. They're quite the pair, and one would think the man caked in blood wearing a rumpled suit would look worse in comparison. He doesn't. From this angle, I can only see the periphery of his expression. Those eyes. That wry mouth twisted in concentration.

Still, his posture leaves no mistake. He is the one in control here.

"Was it you?" he asks softly, flicking his thumb along the other man's cheek. "The Stepanovs. Were you the man Antonio hired to do his fucking dirty work?"

Dirty work. The attack on Ellen and Eli? Curiosity has me inching forward before I can realize my mistake. Dark eyes cut in my direction, and I'm sure he knows exactly what's on my mind.

Is this man responsible for what happened to my family? For the chaos that came after, resulting in Donatello stowing a little girl in his trunk before trying to set himself on fire? Is this figure the source of the blood and violence? That pain.

Watching him, I don't know how I feel. What to feel. A million different emotions swarm my body all at once, and it's like my heart is too exhausted to decide which one to internalize. It just aches. Throbs. Swells in my chest until every thump of my pulse wracks my entire body.

The only way I can seem to dull it? Watch. Stare. Listen to the cold, stern baritone that cuts through the confusion, alarmingly clear...

"Were you?" Donatello prods.

"Ah!" the man mumbles, his reply distorted by the gag, but Donatello nods as though he understood every word.

"Oh? It wasn't you? You mean you weren't the sick son of a bitch who nearly killed a pregnant woman and her child?"

His cruel narration triggers a wave of memories. Ellen bleeding and pale. Eli, limp and lifeless…

"I hope the money was worth it," Donatello warns. The anger in his voice reverberates through the open space, and those nearby tense in response. It's too raw. Too intense. A shudder rips through me as I instinctively take a step back. Could this man be responsible for the attack?

*Of course,* a part of me hisses. *It wasn't Donatello. But you've known that all along…*

"Let's hear it," Donatello demands. He grabs one end of the gag and cruelly yanks it free. "Speak. Were you the lapdog Tony sent to do his bidding?"

Sputtering, the man croaks, "Go. To hell. Where the fuck is Tony? I'll teach that son of a bitch to—"

"Tony's dead." Rising to his feet, Donatello flicks the discarded gag aside and clasps his hands behind his back. That simple motion unnerves me for reasons I can't explain. Maybe the dark intent behind his eyes is what has me swallowing hard. It's another layer of cruelty, further separating this man from the figure in my memories.

He could be lying, but the blood painting swaths of his body from head to toe speaks for him. He's killed someone.

He takes *pride* in having killed them.

"You answer to me," he says, towering over the captive man. "Did he hire you to do it?"

"The fuck is this?" The man's eyes continue to dart warily around the room. "What the fuck is going on, Luciano?" he snarls, referring to the gray-eyed man beside Donatello.

"Answer the man." Luciano shrugs. "I don't think he's in the mood for an argument. Did you do it or not, Paulie?"

Paulie's shifty eyes twitch from Donatello to the men nearby and back again. "Tony paid me over a hundred grand for it, but I just did as I was told, okay? It wasn't nothing fucking personal."

"Personal." Donatello's laughter churns my stomach. It's as beautiful as it is disturbing, rivaling the most heart-rending crescendo. "Oh, but this *was* personal. If you won't take my word for it, then take hers."

He inclines his head to me. "This is the man who attacked your mother. The reason why your father tried to kill my son. Did you know that?"

He waits as if for the magnitude of his statement to strike me. When I don't react how he seems to expect, he assumes why out loud. "You knew. Didn't you? Is that really why you came running to me, little *principessa*? Guilt?" Genuine curiosity leeches into his tone. "Let us not forget... I didn't drag you here as my captive. You came to me."

His eyes blaze, betraying just how angry that makes him. Enrages him. In his thinking, I came crawling back, if only to see the mess left behind for myself. Like he said, it was childish.

But the truth goes beyond that, itching away at the back of my skull the more I try to deny it. Leaving the manor is all a blur—but one emotion sticks out. Fear.

Given the way he's scouring my expression, he should see that—but he's already returning his attention to the man kneeling before him.

"You may have been doing Antonio's bidding," he says coldly, "but in the process, you implicated me. My name. Donatello Vanici took the blame. Do you understand that?"

"Look, man," the bound figure says with a nervous laugh. He squirms but can barely keep himself upright, wavering on his knees. "I was just doing what I was told, okay? It was all Tony. He called me up—"

"Do you have proof of that?" Donatello demands.

"Check my accounts, for fuck's sake! Tony wired me the money personally."

"Can you do that?" Donatello asks Luciano.

"Already on it," he replies, fishing a cell phone from his pocket. "Tony only ever used one accountant for any transfers."

"There. Proof," the bound man says. "Now you gonna let me fucking go?"

"No." Donatello's voice rings out so softly I have to strain to hear it. The note resembles the ominous moment nearing the chorus of a thrilling piece of music. The pivotal point on which the entire melody turns on its head. "I'm not going to fucking *let you go.*"

He turns around, and I shiver instinctively even before his gaze falls over me. I feel exposed. Like there's only air between us, and I'm without anything to shield myself behind. This thin fabric means nothing—he can see all of me regardless.

Every thought and fear to flicker across my mind.

Even the dark ones.

"But you knew that," Donatello continues. The corner of his lip quirks, but it's the furthest thing from a smile. More like the grimace of a man so far gone he no longer remembers what humor is. All he can do is relish the few things that bring him joy in its absence—power.

"I want to kill you," he declares, and my heart stops cold. Only the slight tilt of his head implies that he's still talking to the man. Not me. "I want to gut you like a fucking pig—after I make you squeal what you've done on the record so there can be no mistake. I'd string you up, let you die slowly. That would be a start. No, a mere drop in the bucket to atone for the damage you've caused me."

The pain in his tone is unfaked and undeniable. I'd have to be made of stone not to feel something in response. My breathing catches, my throat on fire. Any tears that may be building are kept at bay, though.

I'm too distracted to let them fall.

The musical comparisons return in full force, and I'm reminded of one of my most favorite compositions. It starts off innocently with a beautiful array of delicate notes before the tempo changes, becoming increasingly erratic until the final booming finale.

His rage is like that, a symphony composed of the most devastating instruments—a voice like thunder perfectly accompanied by eyes like fire.

He turns to me again, and I don't know what to expect. Not for him to crack a slow, lopsided smile.

"You feel it too," he declares, his head cocked, an eyebrow raised. He takes a step, and even with him a few inches closer, the effect resonates throughout my whole body. Goosebumps come to life, prickling my skin. I lurch back on my heels.

He advances another step.

"Hate," he continues mid-stride, even closer than before. "That sick need for revenge—and not mere 'justice,' either… You want pain. You want him to suffer, just as you suffered. Am I wrong?"

The men around him stare amongst themselves, obviously confused. Whether he cares or even notices, Donatello doesn't turn his attention from me for one second.

"I can see it written all over your face," he says with a knowing nod. "The hate—and not just for me, either—" he flicks his gaze toward the man at his feet. "How should we punish him?"

My stomach lurches at his choice of words. *We.* A deliberate shift in culpability. Almost as if he's proposing a game, like the many we used to play in what feels like another life.

His version of hide and seek involved water guns, and every board game always had small pots of money at stake.

But something in the pit of my soul warns me that this "prize" won't be so innocent.

And no matter what, no matter what he says or does…

I cannot play.

"Don't deny that you want to," Donatello scolds, advancing another step on me. "So what will it be? A slit throat? A beheading? Name your choice, *principessa*. You wanted to play in our world, so play."

He's serious. His low, stern tone conveys as much. So I don't leave it to chance, emphatically shaking my head so there can be no mistake. I don't want him to do anything.

"No." His nostrils flare, eyes flashing. "You don't have the option to abstain from this little vote. He threatened your family, your mother, your brother. You want more than just his pain. You want more than justice, don't you?"

My heart pounds ominously as images sneak into my skull unbidden. This man, just as broken as Ellen. As terrified as Eli.

*No.* I close my eyes, fighting them back. *Focus!*

"Look at me," Donatello warns. His voice is inescapable, rebounding off the inside of my skull until I finally open my eyes again.

The look on his face… I've seen it before. The most notable instance? The day he left me to die.

He wears it proudly, standing tall, his head held high as he extends his hand. Harsh, his voice rings out, "I asked for a knife."

"Here." One of the other men watching steps forward, presenting a gleaming weapon on his palm. It's small, about the same size Mischa trained me to use. Reverently, Donatello draws his thumb across the edge, and I swear I see blood streak it after.

Nothing in his expression or posture reveals any hint of pain. His back is rigid as his hand assuredly manipulates the weapon, brandishing it in the air.

Alarm grips my spine, rendering me paralyzed—I know the stern tilt to his jaw. The confident stance of a man in complete control. But as he sinks to his knees and presses the knife against the man's throat, one thing is painfully apparent.

I don't know this Donatello.

And he doesn't know me. If he did, he wouldn't play this game. He'd read my fear. Back down. Anything but smile conspiratorially as if our thoughts are one and the same.

"You're going to tell me how to kill him," he says to me. "Every cut. Every scream. It will be all on you. Your face tells me everything I need to know. Your eyes... I see the hate in them. You want this—Don't!"

He lashes out with an outstretched hand, pointing a finger at me accusatorially. "No. You watch me. You watch all of it. Now..." He crouches down again, but there's a predatory grace in the movement. His muscles ripple, creating patterns against his skin. Despite everything in me warning me to turn away, I'm riveted.

"Where should we begin? Ah, of course. We need a name," he suggests, toying with the blade. "Should we start with his tongue?"

His quarry comes to life, squirming so badly he nearly falls onto his side. "What the hell?" His breathing quickens, his eyes so wide I see myself reflected in them. A shockingly small figure gaping on in silence.

"Look at me," Donatello warns the second my attention drifts. I obey, but his eyes gleam so brightly, I turn away again.

"Look at me." His tone raises the hair on the back of my neck. Guttural and raw, but one note, in particular, unsettles me. It's a hallmark of the very last emotion someone should feel in a situation like this. Glee.

Excitement. It lurks beneath the deep baritone, adding a musical tilt to the words.

"I said watch me, Safiya." His eyes are narrowed, daring me to look lower. See what he's doing.

Something responsible for the sharp, inhuman shriek coloring the air next.

"This is your game, after all. Tell me where to cut him. Play your role. Look at me!"

The act is futile, but I purse my lips anyway as if preventing any sound from escaping. I'm sure that every move, every breath, doesn't go unnoticed by him.

I can't think. Not about revenge—like the man writhing in the agony he inflicted on my family. A missing tongue would be nothing. A pittance. A mercy...

*No,* I banish the thought, aware of the gaze piercing through my own.

Regardless, Donatello nods, raising his weapon menacingly. "His tongue, then—"

"Wait!" the man gasps. "Fucking... Wait! You want a name, okay! I never saw the motherfucker, but I know he was working with Tony. I think the hit was his idea."

Donatello blinks like a man waking from a dream. "Who?"

"The bastard just went by J.W. That's it! That's all I know. I swear to fucking God—"

"How did they contact you? How did you know where to stage the hit?"

"Tony fed me all the information. I never spoke with the man directly. I just knew he was footing the cash. Tony didn't have that kind of dough to throw around."

"So you attacked a woman and her child based on the say-so of a bastard like Antonio Salvatore and someone you never met?" Donatello roars. "What did they promise you? It had to be more than money. No amount in the world would be worth pissing off the *mafiya*."

"They talked a big game," the man says, his eyes on the knife dangling precariously above his head.

"Like what?"

"Like taking over all of Hell's Gambit for one. Divvying up the city on a platter to anyone who took part. They said…" His eyes flicker nervously in my direction. "They said they'd cut Mischa down to size. Rip control right from his hands."

"Sounds familiar," Luciano remarks snidely. "I guess you aren't so fucking crazy after all, Donatello."

The man in question doesn't answer, his gaze turned inward, triggering another chilling instance of *déjà vu*. It's an expression I remember from the days of crouching beneath his desk watching him work. It could be beautiful seeing him mull over a dilemma or problem. He would stroke his jaw much like he is now, until finally, he'd nod only to himself, seeing a solution where no one else could.

"Mischa was the target," he deduces finally. "They wanted him out. Why?"

"I don't know! Jesus! Just let me go." The man again tries to wriggle free of his bonds, but the heel of a boot slams against his chest, knocking him backward.

"Why the hell would I do that?" Donatello demands, aiming his foot to deliver another kick. He moves so fast. All I see is a spray of blood before a gash appears across the man's face.

He howls, spitting crimson onto the floor as he struggles to move. His attacker is ruthless, crouching over him, the knife poised above.

"Why frame me?" Donatello bellows. "If he wanted to take on Mischa himself, he had every right to. Why get me involved?"

"The harbor. Needed… Had to import something."

"Import?" the man behind Donatello interjects, his head cocked. "What the hell could they need to import that would require the use of the entire harbor?"

Paulie issues a stream of wailed curses. "I didn't ask fucking questions!"

"No, you didn't," Donatello growls. "You shot at a pregnant woman and a child. You got my son shot in his fucking head. You set me up to take the fall."

"It's just fucking money! I didn't give a shit who they were."

I can't control it. I see them—Ellen and Eli. The blood. The pain. The fear.

"You feel it, don't you?" Donatello rises to his feet as if sensing my rage before I even feel it creeping beneath my skin. He crosses to me, his victim forgotten. Once close enough, he captures my chin against his palm.

"You're angry." His eyes narrow further as he tilts my head toward him. "You have every fucking right to be. But you're suppressing it. Bottling it up nice and neat. Why?" He leans closer, bringing his mouth near my ear. Every movement of his lips sends a jolt through my earlobe, dizzying. "Your father isn't here."

I jump, but he grabs my wrist, locking me in place.

"You've played the role of a good girl for so damn long you don't know how to operate outside of your mask," he snarls, but his tone turns deceptively soft. A mocking perversion of gentle. "What has that gotten you? A life as a pretty doll?"

He steps back, dragging me with him. As we near the center of the throng, he shoves me to my knees. Wincing, I realize I'm kneeling right before the man bleeding all over the floor. Up close, he's pitiful, his fancy suit stained red, his face mutilated.

"You think he deserves your mercy? Why? Because it's the 'right thing' to do? Was it the *right* thing for your father to shoot Vincenzo? Should I show you that same mercy?"

I see his shadow move across the floor before I feel it—fiery pain teasing the base of my throat. Careful, deliberately applied pressure, hard enough to slice flesh, but not enough to bleed.

"He deserves to be punished. You know that as well as I do. So where should we start?"

The blade withdraws from my skin, and I exhale the breath I didn't realize I'd been holding—only to inhale sharply as a firm object presses against my fingers next. I glance down, alarmed to find the handle of a blood-covered blade. He slams it against my palm, forcing my fingers to curl around it.

He's too strong, easily overpowering my attempts to resist. With force, he snatches my hand. Then he makes me press the knife against the man's collar. Hard. Harder.

I can feel his heartbeat through the blade. His eyes bulge, his lips frothing with spit as he bites back a scream. My body takes over, bucking against the man controlling my movements. Fighting.

I'm sweating with the effort, but he doesn't even loosen his grip.

"I could make you fillet him," he warns, his palm shifting over the back of my hand to guide my hold on the handle. "I'd make you gut him. You'd be the one holding the knife. I could…"

To prove it, he makes the knife dance inches from the man's skin. I recoil, wrenching against him until my shoulder throbs.

"You're not a little girl. *Look* at what you're doing. Feel through your fingertips. Do it." His voice sneaks into my skull unbidden, and I catch myself obeying. I see my fingers entwined with his, squirming against the unfamiliar shape of the weapon. The harder I try to pull away, the more he tightens his grasp.

"Stop," Donatello grates, but for a second, his tone loses the cold edge. He's a teacher trying to reach a stubborn student —though this lesson is far different from any Mischa taught me. In his world, survival was all that mattered. To Donatello? It's inflicting pain.

It's retribution.

"We both know that's what you want," he says, speaking to my thoughts directly. "Revenge. If I let him go… If *we* let him go, do you think he'll learn his lesson?"

The man's wide, fearful eyes speak for him.

"No," Donatello says, lifting our combined fist to let the blade catch the light. "He'll just find another contract. Kill another woman. Another man. Another child. You know it as well as I do."

He taught me that lesson himself—the inherent cruelty of some men. It's a world apart from the simple system of actions and consequences the Stepanovs live by. One of their children may beat another or steal a toy. They are punished. Forgiven. The cycle repeats.

Men like this one operate in the same way, but their actions aren't childish impulses. They're violent. Brutal. They end lives and destroy them.

Over and over again.

"Stop living life in a fairy tale." Donatello's fingers graze the back of my hand, and in horror, I realize he's withdrawing.

But I'm left holding the knife. It shakes, the tip wavering in the air aimlessly before twitching in the direction of the sputtering man's throat.

Only for a second, just one—but in this moment, I know nothing is guiding the blade but me. *My* intent. My will…

To perfectly narrate the moment, Donatello's voice slithers against my ear. "You're no better than I am."

*No!* A heartbeat later, horror kicks in. I force my fingers apart, letting the blade fall to the floor as I recoil, kicking back until I'm well beyond that pool of scarlet.

He lets me go, pushing past me.

"So you choose to be a puppet. Fine. You can watch. Hold her," he snaps to one of the men who grabs my arms. "Don't let her turn away. Not for a fucking second."

He returns to Paulie, picking the knife from where I must have dropped it.

Then he lunges.

And I have no choice.

I watch.

He runs his knife across the man's throat like he's cutting through butter. Blood spurts in a waterfall, bathing the floor.

But all of the macabre details are secondary to *him*—Donatello. Through it all, his eyes never leave mine.

And in them, I see my own reflection gazing back without an ounce of fear.

# EVGENI

*Briar Winthorp...*

That name haunts me well into the morning—even though I know there's no way in hell she was telling the truth.

That name carries the same mystique as the Tooth Fairy or Santa Claus in the Stepanov household, just without the inherent goodwill attached.

She is a rumor, whispered about in passing. The children have never met her from what I know. Even Ellen rarely mentions her, her mysterious sister and remaining member of one of the wealthiest families to exist this side of the continent.

I've heard horror stories about the Winthorps, known for their wealth and international investments. Their fortune bankrolled many a criminal enterprise, including the *mafiya* once upon a time. At least until seven years ago when their empire came crashing down after Mischa killed its head,

Robert. Supposedly the rest of the family scattered to the wind after that.

Even if the woman were lying, why that name? It leaves a sour taste in my mouth as I arrive at the manor.

It's the early afternoon, but the place is already a hive of activity. Armored vans mill in the stone driveway, but I don't recognize the men gathered around them. They're professional, watching warily as I march past.

An unfamiliar vehicle sits at the center of the chaos—a sleek black limo.

A visitor, I suspect, but one not cleared through me. As far as I know, I wasn't given any warning, either, or the typical rundown that prefaces any meeting. Warily, I look at the man standing guard by the main door. The second I draw even with him, he inclines his head but never meets my gaze directly. "Mr. Stepanov is in his office."

His tone alone warns me not to ask questions. Biting back an argument, I enter the manor and head straight for the study. I can smell the stench of cologne before I even near the room. For once, the door is closed, sealing off the space from the rest of the house in a way I haven't seen in years. I knock once.

"Come in."

The second I push the door open, alarm tightens my spine. A man standing in the corner draws my notice first, tall, built of pure muscle—obviously a bodyguard.

Seated across from Mischa must be his employer, a bulky man, his expression caught between a grimace and a frown. Gregori Saleri. I know him only from his reputation. An ally of the *famiglia*, his outfit is known for dealing in only one kind of commodity—women. The kind of women who don't *willingly* choose their profession.

As far as I know, Mischa has no business with them—and his wife certainly would prefer it that way. In Ellen's absence, has he tried to get in on the skin game, even with his daughter in danger?

I doubt that.

Seated behind his desk, Mischa watches me without offering an explanation. His face was always harder to read than most—usually, his eyes held a clue as to what he truly thought. Dark, heavy-lidded, and guarded, they give away nothing now. Who the hell knows what he's thinking? It pisses me off to realize that, in this rare instance, I don't.

"I hope I'm not interrupting something, sir," I say as I move to take my place beside him, spinning to face the seated man.

"Gregori was just leaving," Mischa says, nodding to his visitor who stands. Both he and his bodyguard exit, and I step aside, fingering the headset attached to my ear. "Guests leaving now. Follow them out."

"Already on it, sir," comes a reply. The response just cements what's been painfully obvious from the start. Mischa arranged this meeting without me.

Am I alarmed?

Definitely.

As I approach the desk, I strive to keep a neutral tone. "Was that meeting important, sir?"

"Evgeni…" Mischa sighs, interlacing his fingers over the surface of his desk. He's changed into a pair of black slacks and a shirt, leaving his hair to drape his shoulders. "I was enlightening Gregori as to why it would be in his best interest to avoid the *famiglia* and alert me if Donatello Vanici tries to make contact."

I feel my eyebrow shoot up. "You think he went back to them? The *famiglia*?"

It would make sense. A man on the outs would be desperate for allies. In a bid to outplay the mafia's reach, he could seek to return to the fold of his old organization.

"I know there is no love lost between him and their leader," Mischa admits. "But I'd put nothing past him."

"But that wasn't the only reason why you met with Saleri, was it?"

It's funny how well you can get to know a man just by existing in his orbit for years. I've seen Mischa at the heights of emotion, from the birth of his children to the death of his mentor. I've seen him at his happiest and at his worst, but even I can admit that I've never seen him quite like this—stewing.

It's a quiet emotion, alarming in intensity.

"You're wondering why I met with him without you, is that it?" he questions, leveling me with a piercing gaze.

I don't flinch. "Usually, you like to coordinate security when we have visitors."

"I won't play word games with you," he says. "I *deliberately* didn't tell you."

A muscle in my jaw twitches. Am I alarmed by that? More annoyed.

The man tasks me with protecting his family and assets, yet he goes out of his way to consult with a rival faction and keeps me out of the loop while doing so. He isn't petty, so this stems from more than our previous spats over Vanici. It's calculating, designed to make it clear that, at least for now, I'm being kept at arm's length. I suspect this meeting isn't the only thing he's concealed from me.

"May I ask why?"

He stands, putting his back to me as he glares from the window overlooking the property's western half.

At its core, the manor is a beautiful house, nestled in the countryside, surrounded by rose gardens, rolling fields, and gently sloping stone walls.

At the same time, it is a fortress. I've never worked in a place more fiercely guarded, but I've admittedly never worked for a leader more constrained by his emotions. My last boss was a man so cold I doubt the near-death of his wife and child would interrupt his routine dinner, let alone drive him to the brink of war.

Mischa Stepanov's heart *is* his family. What will he do when the very thing he cherishes most is threatened?

I know the answer—become reckless. Tactless.

Vengeful.

The complete opposite of everything I've trained myself to be. Still, I can admit that I never assumed him capable of intentionally cutting me out of the fold. There has to be a reason…

Though something warns me that I won't like what it is one fucking bit. An image comes to mind, but I banish it before it can unfold in full. I merely see a body. Green eyes. Sweet smile.

A hole where her throat should be. She wasn't the only one. I blink, and behind my eyelids, I see them all—each bloodied, lifeless face my burden to bear.

"You're unnerved," Mischa says, drawing my attention back to him.

I shake my head to clear it. "Sir?"

"By my actions," he reiterates. "I can sense your judgment."

"This isn't like you," I counter, shifting my stance. By uncrossing my arms, maybe I hope to detract from the defensive tone sneaking into my voice? "Sitting here, talking to a slave trader. We should be out looking for Willow—"

"You know damn well where she is!" He lashes out, striking the desk so hard it skids across the floor. The monstrous sound rips through the room, but it's not loud enough to keep him from pacing. Violent enough. His hands form fists as if he has to stop himself from hitting it again.

I clear my throat. "Mischa…"

Blazing like fire, his eyes cut to mine, more piercing than ever. In them, I see something I never thought I would, usually glimpsed in men with far less restraint.

He's breaking.

"She's strong," I say as gently as I can. "There's been no sign of her yet. I suggest we stay focused. Search Vanici's known whereabouts—"

"Fuck, you might be right," he says, pushing away from the desk. His hand tears through his hair, his dark eyes fixed on the scenic view beyond the windows. "But in this moment, I don't want your fucking logic."

His still clenched fists make it obvious what he desires.

Vengeance.

"You really want to start a war with Donatello Vanici?" I ask him quietly.

Donatello, a man who—as of a week ago—was little more than an investor of no particular importance who had one piece of real estate worth having—the city harbor.

Until the day he supposedly kidnapped Willow Stepanova out of the blue.

I didn't buy it then, and I don't buy Mischa's caginess now. There's more to this.

"Tell me what happened between you," I say, as close as I've ever come to an outright demand of him.

"A war?" Mischa questions as if I never spoke. "No. I want safety." He eyes his left hand, where a gold ring adorns the third finger. "I want my wife to live. I want my son to have use of his arm again. I want…" His voice breaks, and all I can do is stare. Emotions don't factor into my skillset. Not pain. Not love. Not agony.

I can't face them the way I could an attacker or a logistical problem.

The man sways, overwhelmed by all three at once.

Finally, he regains control, his eyes blazing. "I want my baby girl to have been born without having to fight for her life. I don't want a war, Evgeni. I want *blood*."

"Blood can have a higher cost than you expect," I warn through gritted teeth. "I heard your feud with the Winthorps had a particularly tragic aftermath."

"This is different," Mischa growls. "The Winthorps don't have my daughter, do they? Vanici's gone underground. Only God knows what he's done to her…"

For a second, I can glimpse beneath the rage to the real emotion driving him. Fear. For Willow. For his wife and son.

I'd probably feel sympathy if I had anything in my life worth comparing those relationships to. Luckily, I don't. I am what I'm paid to be—a soldier with no emotional investment, able to stay objective.

"My men are in the process of tracking him down," I say. "He couldn't have gone far."

"You underestimate him," Mischa snarls. "I can assure you that he's not sitting around pining for peace, either."

"So what will you have me do?"

"Go back to the hospital," he says, returning to his desk. "I heard you rearranged the detail on Ellen. Why?"

I swallow hard before answering. It's a switch I hoped would go unnoticed, but one that would hopefully prevent another surprise visitor, Briar Winthorp or otherwise.

"I believe Kristoph will be of better use here on the property. Danil has a better bedside manner."

Mischa's eyes cut to slits. "But you will take the lead," he insists. "I want you there now. Eli can come home tomorrow. He's safer there until Vanici is found."

It's a strain on our detail, but I have enough sense not to say as much now. "How are the children doing?"

A rare softness seeps into Mischa's expression. "As well as can be expected. They miss their mother, and brother, and their sister."

"I should check on Eli while I'm there," I suggest. "Maybe knowing his progress can help lift their spirits a little?"

"I want you there overnight," Mischa says, his head cocked. One look at his face, and I know that this is the real topic of our conversation. He's just waited until now to broach it. "Peter will head my personal detail from now on."

Peter. The rookie, untrained and undisciplined—yet eager to please. He won't ask questions.

"Can I ask why?" I can't disguise my irritation. Disagreements or not, Mischa has never intervened in my staffing before. Not once during all of my employment.

This is personal. I'm sure of that even before he strokes his jaw with a knowing nod.

"I don't want your judgment," he says simply. "You are a good man, Evgeni. But in this world, good men can rarely stomach the actions necessary. And given your history..."

He stops himself from saying more, but he doesn't have to.

So *that* is what this really is about. Trust in the context of "my past." That's his excuse anyway—because he doesn't trust me.

Not anymore.

"Don't coddle me," I snap. My tone slips, harsher than it should be. For a heartbeat, respect isn't a factor. An insult is still an insult, even if coming from an employer. "So you know my background. You've known it for years. That's never interfered with my duties before."

"And I know where you hesitate," he counters, raising his voice to match the volume of mine. "Donatello Vanici will not play by your rules."

My rules.

My creed. A low blow considering I've all but broken them for this family already.

"If we were playing by my *rules*, you wouldn't have gone after Vanici first," I point out. "You would have been honest with me from the start. If I were playing by my 'rules,' Mischa, I wouldn't still be here."

I've gone too far. Despite knowing that, the closest thing to an apology I seem able to muster is clearing my throat.

Mischa's lower jaw twitches, the only warning that I've hit my target. "Is that how you really feel?"

I nod. Even so, quitting isn't even on my mind. "Sir…" I force some semblance of normalcy back into my tone. "This is about *Vanici,* not me. I still think we should figure out his motives. Why would he—"

"You should go," Mischa says over me. Anger ripples through his voice but controlled enough that he doesn't shout. "If Ellen wakes up, I want her to be near a familiar face."

I can't escape the thought. Familiar like her sister's?

I should mention her now. First, an attack on Ellen and her son. Now a Winthorp returning out of the blue. She could have heard of the attack and come out of genuine concern.

But I don't buy it. Last I heard, the woman left the country. Returning in less than seventy-two hours seems a stretch. Unless she was already nearby.

"Evgeni?" Mischa demands.

"I'm on my way out," I say. "Good evening, sir. I'll return to the hospital. I wouldn't want my *past* to affect my judgment."

He says nothing as I storm into the hall.

He knows better.

Some lines you don't cross.

And some events aren't worth dredging up, even to prove a point.

## DON

*I*t's *a big, bad world, sonny boy,* Giovanni told me once. *You're going to do shit that you wouldn't have dreamed of just a day ago. Horrible shit. But if it makes you feel better... Somewhere out there, another man is doing something ten times worse.*

As per usual, the son of a bitch was right.

And he was *wrong.* There can't be anything much worse than goading someone else into doing the unthinkable. Forcing them to watch you do it. Looking into their eyes, seeing only your blood-soaked-self staring back...

And loving every minute of it.

Is that what Giovanni felt? The old man was fucking crazy, but this feels beyond insanity. Twisted. The more I scour those old memories of those days, though, the more obvious it becomes that he never forced me to do a damn thing. I was a willing soldier every step of the way. An enthusiastic one. We were drawn to each other, some might say, speaking the same language of ambitious, selfish men.

Vin never spoke that language—but I should have made him learn it. Pressured him to hold a knife to a man's throat and make him cut. Deep down, I know it would have been pointless.

When he was a kid, barely taller than my knee, he used to wake up every night screaming, convinced a monster was hiding in his closet. I'd never find anything there, but it was real to him. So real, he'd sob until his entire body shook, and it damn near broke my heart. One night I went into his room with a gun, intending to convince him I'd scare the *"monster"* off for good. The show of force was meant to comfort him more than anything.

But good old Vin… He cried even harder at the sight of the weapon and begged me not to hunt his monster down. As tormented as he was, he didn't want vengeance. *Shoot me instead, Uncle Don,* he demanded, his eyes welling with tears. *It's not the monster's fault that he's scary.*

God, he was such a wholesome kid. Never, not once, did I ever see the darkness in him that I always felt lurking inside myself. Even Mischa had his own unique brand of insanity, different from my own. No one's quite meshed with my sick fucking mind, except perhaps Giovanni, and now…

*Her.* It could have been a trick of the light, that spark in her eye. That gleam. But fuck, I felt something stir in my soul like I never have. Curiosity. Maybe a little irritation, too. Of all people, a little blond spoke my language, if only for a fucking second…

And it was music to my ears. Unlike Vin, she didn't want me to shield her monster. Oh no, she wanted me to gut it right at her fucking feet. Those eyes told me how, even if she wasn't aware of it. The way they narrowed as I cut. Widened when the man's screams finally fell silent.

Fuck, she told me exactly how she wanted it done. And it was wrong. Disgusting. Sick.

Because all I wanted to do in that moment was make her keep talking to me…

Cold air hits like a slap, and I blink to find myself stumbling from a side exit, dripping liquid too frigid to be blood. I look up and realize why—it's raining out. The sky above is a lighter gray than it'd been earlier. Hours must have passed, though it feels like an eternity.

Behind me, I hear a door open with a rusty squeal, followed by footsteps hurrying in my direction. "Don?" someone shouts. Luciano? "Where the fuck are you going?"

That's a damn good question. The knife is still in my hand, but I let it fall into the mud as I keep walking without bothering to look back. Soon I'll confront Mischa with what I learned. Make him pay.

At the moment? The only thing that seems to matter is moving. I spot a building up ahead and stagger toward it, with no aim in mind.

In my wake, those trailing steps continue—softer, too soft to belong to a man—but I don't look back.

Giovanni—and I after him—kept an apartment in this outbuilding. We probably slept there more than in our own homes. Days off weren't a factor with the livelihood of the entire *famiglia* at stake, such is the life of a leader. They don't tell any ambitious cuck gunning for the top position the truth—much of it is spent on a hard ass mattress alone.

For that reason, the old man kept the furniture simple. Utilitarian. Years into my tenure, I realized why. The shitty bed and bland furnishings made the few moments we spent away in our own homes with our respective families all the sweeter.

Sweet enough to tide us over as we went back and fought ten times harder. We were men who valued the business above all else.

So, predictably, Antonio Salvatore gutted the place. I know that even before I mount the outdoor steps leading to the entrance and find the door unlocked.

The fucker had the plain white paint replaced with ornate black wallpaper like something out of a sleazy hotel suite. The floors are polished wood, and the sturdy old leather furniture has been replaced with black suede and fur-covered bullshit.

The motherfucker installed a minibar at least, in the same spot where Giovanni would spend hours contemplating the various deals he had with the Colombian cartels. Things were dicey in those days—you got in bed with the wrong associates and could easily wake up with your cock missing, and a blackmail notice shoved down your throat.

Antonio seemed to enjoy having things shoved into his orifices even while at the office. The bedroom is too much of a shitshow to even dissect at the moment. Sex toys lay out in the open near the massive bed, and the dresser across from it is covered in an array of condoms and women's makeup.

Disgusted, I cross over to the closet and find a decent black suit hanging amongst a random assortment of clothing. Judging from the ludicrous level of tailoring, most were Antonio's, but the few dresses—all different sizes—reinforce that he didn't adhere to the "leaders sleep alone" creed.

His renovations of the bathroom were at least more practical, replacing the simple shower with a full bath and a walk-in stall.

I peel my clothing off and stand beneath the spray, letting the water pelt me from above, as hot as I can stand it. In here, there's no one to pretend for. No kingdom to guard, no lies to maintain.

No innocent blond to butcher a man in front of.

I wince at the reminder. If I dissect the emotion swirling in my gut, it could be guilt. Or concern that I'm too tired to feel in full. Logic is telling me to go back. She could have run off for all I fucking know. Good riddance. Let her scurry back to Mischa, having learned one final lesson.

A caged bird should stay in her cage or wind up devoured.

Or…that same bird becomes a predator herself.

Groaning, I brace my hands against the smooth black tile and watch the water pouring off me circle the drain. This shower is as gaudy as the rest of the apartment, too sleek and modern to match the grim seriousness of Giovanni's old hideout. I bet Antonio took glee in erasing any trace of our old boss. In addition to the silver fixtures, he had the base of the stall made of white marble, making it the perfect backdrop to spotlight the rust-colored liquid washing off my skin. So much red.

Too much…

The hue triggers a million twisted images that dance through my skull. I see Vincenzo, my boy, bleeding from his head. Then Antonio, greedily gasping for his last breath. Paulie Vanetti, sliced to pieces.

Last of all, I see her, the beautiful little blond, watching me work without a drop of crimson on her. My chest swells with so much rage it's painful. *Her* blood deserves to paint this shower floor, not Vin's.

And it's not her connection to Mischa that makes her worthy of death. Violence is just the way of this brutal world we live in. I could have accepted her deliberately turning against me. Wanting me dead. Wanting me to suffer.

Knowing her role.

Her real sin?

Rather than let me die in peace, she returned to gloat over the broken pieces. Back to watch me burn…though, when it came down to it, she couldn't even let me strike the match.

So what was her motive?

More images flood my skull to feed the rage boiling beneath my skin. I see her face. Her tiny hands wrenching at mine. Her desperation to keep me from striking a single match, even before I attempted to set her alight as well.

That final look on her face is what does it, though. Enrages me to the point that I plant my fist against the wall of the stall and howl in irritation. That look causes the most pain. The most hate.

Because in that moment…all I saw in those eyes was pity. Concern. As though she didn't want me to die. Not out of sweet, innocent mercy, either.

This life? It's worse than any hell. Only someone especially cruel would force me to live it, and then watch me suffer.

Ironically, if she were here now, she'd get her wish. The water itself feels hot enough to burn me alive more thoroughly than any fire. I hiss through my teeth, surrendering to the assault for what feels like an eternity. When I finally shut the water off, I'm still whole, though. Not ashes.

What a damn shame.

But in the absence of the spray, I finally smell the scent flooding the room, and my body goes rigid with the threat of an entirely different punishment. That smell... I inhale it again, recognizing it instantly. Roses and lighter fluid. *No.* I shake my head, unwilling to trust my own senses. *I've gone crazy...*

But I haven't. Her presence infects the air like poison, impossible to ignore. She's *here*, having followed me across the complex, presumably alone.

"What the fuck do you want?" I demand, wrenching my gaze toward the source of the stench. Even expecting her, the sight of that lithe figure watching from the doorway knocks the air from my lungs. I blink, expecting her to vanish, a figment of my imagination.

She doesn't.

Her face is partially obscured by the steam coating the glass barrier between us—but nothing could ever disguise those eyes. They bore into me as I use my hand to clear a section of the door.

She is here, but I suspect she saw more than she bargained for. Pink spots dot her cheeks, and a quick swallow distorts her throat. For all her bravery, she's still just a woman. A *young* woman, one I know for a fact, has never experienced a man.

Has she even seen one like this before?

The distraction is too tempting, and my tired brain latches onto it greedily. I grip the handle, testing the give of the metal. Slowly, I apply pressure and push the door aside, watching her expression all the while.

"Did you come to wash the blood from your hands, *principessa*?" My taunt falls flat—her hands are pale, utterly clean. Though while that damn stare remains constant, her body…

That body betrays her.

Trembling fingers grip the front of her dress. The bulk of it disguises most of her shape, but what little of it I can see— shapely, pale legs—make me exhale through my teeth.

Shoving the door open wider, I watch her nails dig into the fabric of her dress as if it's armor against me. And it is in her mind—as long as she's wearing it, she's untouchable. Funny, considering she's robbed me of *my* stability, following me even here.

Why should I allow her the same mercy?

"Take it off," I command.

She flinches, her tongue flitting across her lips. Triumphant, I advance, letting the water drip from me freely, slicking the floor with every step. The closer I come, the smaller she seems. The stranger, the less recognizable—and a wave of relief almost knocks me to the ground.

I can dominate this woman. She won't control me.

"The dress," I snap, coming within arm's reach of her. Those eyes are a mirror, and I see myself reflected in them. Every dark, twisted, cruel bit—and it's a relief in a sense. *This* is the Donatello I know.

A monster.

That reflection becomes even clearer as I finger the fabric of the delicate neckline. A quick swallow contorts her throat, and the reaction lights the fuse leading to a part of me I'm desperate to unlock.

Enough wallowing. Enough regret.

I want to feel…

Anything else.

So I keep tugging. Those sharp swallows come even faster, her small chest heaving beneath the cotton. Intoxicated, I feed off every frantic breath, growing bolder with each subsequent pull.

She starts to resist, stiffening her limbs against me, keeping the dress in place the best she can. Even so, a sliver of her breast peeks beneath the neckline, and an answering sound rumbles at the base of my throat. *Enough.* My fingers clench as if of their own accord and pull.

Her eyes cut back to mine, and she's a different person in an instant. A little girl, watching me with raw betrayal etched in her delicate features. A pain that I know in my soul I will never be able to erase no matter how many years pass.

I'm back there all over again, a slave to my own twisted need for revenge. It damn near killed me to do it, but I did.

All I *could* do in that moment was turn my back on her and keep walking.

*No!* Gritting my teeth, I rip my gaze from hers, hunting for any tether to the present I can find. Slim fingers fill my vision instead, and I fixate on them. Long. Slender. Those of a woman at my mercy.

This *body* is at my mercy, like nothing from that memory. Shapely. Slender. Beautiful.

I know that much even before I grip both sleeves of her dress and rip it from her. Split down the middle, the entire garment comes away, and belatedly I realize it's because she didn't put up a fight this time.

I still don't look at her face, choosing to focus on the pale collarbone prominent beneath her skin. The swell of her small breasts, each capped by a dusky nipple. I cup the globe of one and groan through my teeth at the feeling—a sensation I haven't felt in so damn long. Too long.

Something other than drunkenness, or rage, or hate. And it's potent enough to overlook everything else. Everything.

Like her pink lips open and parted. Her pulse surging beneath her skin. The way her body recoils against my touch, trembling and fearful...

"Fucking hell!" I release her and stagger to a row of counters, bracing my hands against them. A mirror hangs above, and I glare at the man watching me from the surface of the glass. Even without the blood, he's a wreck. The sallow wreckage of a fallen soul.

But with her scent in my lungs, it doesn't seem too damn bad to fall.

"Get in the shower," I snap, but I don't turn to see if she obeys me.

I don't have to. Her silence is a weapon, utilized more effectively than any screaming or pleading would be. It rings out, deafeningly loud, until she chooses to break it with a single, soft footstep.

Then another.

Shame sears through my gut before pure greed replaces it. Her body enters the range of the mirror, and the round swell of her ass is a pathetic distraction, but a welcome one.

"No," I warn as she reaches for the sliding glass door.

She freezes, her chin raised, eyes staring straight ahead. In them, I don't find the fear I suspect I should in a woman forced to strip before a stranger.

*Because you aren't a stranger to her, you sick fuck,* a part of me snarls. *And you know it...*

But even the old, guilt-ridden Donatello has no power here. Not anymore.

She isn't Safiya; I know that now.

The little girl is dead. Whoever remains in her place is a phantom, one I have no loyalty to. Owe nothing to.

Can demand everything from.

So, I demand, "Turn on the water."

She cocks her head, and as my voice echoes back to me, I realize why—that growl sounds nothing like me. Old, groveling, whining Donatello. He, too, is dead. My reflection proves it. Glaring at the monster in his place, I bare my teeth and bark, "I said, turn it on."

She reaches for the faucet, flinching as the spray pelts her. It must be cold. Frantic, she twists on the dial.

"Turn it back down," I snap without understanding why. Maybe it's the rare way she displays unease—jerking motions she can't control. It's as addictive as a sip of booze, and I'm sick enough to push her further. Make her squirm. "Keep it cold. As cold as it can go."

Confusion mingles with alarm, contorting her mouth before she bites her lip, squashing it into a firm line. Again, her face does the speaking for her—*Are you really this petty? This cruel?*

I am.

And for the first fucking time, she falters, her fingers frozen over the faucet.

"Did you hear me?" I question.

Her eyes widen a fraction, and it's like I hit a fucking bullseye. That grim satisfaction in me grows. Her unease is a drug ten times finer than the best damn whiskey. Heady and rich, every ounce floods my blood, drowning out the rest of the world.

Just this remains—her and me.

And my cock. It stirs as I turn around and face her directly. Her own reflection doesn't do her justice. Slender and naked, glistening beneath the shower spray, she's…indescribable.

I think I've stopped myself from truly appreciating her body until now, unable to shake that lingering hate. Strip her of that, and she's worlds apart from any other woman.

She's beautiful.

Her body rides the line between too thin, with just enough curves to entice. Her hips narrow into shapely thighs, crowned by a thatch of golden curls. But as beautiful as she is, one feature draws my attention more than any other.

Those eyes. Those rich, deep, incredible fucking eyes. They cast a spell. I stare into them, and the world stares back, or how I see it anyway. Cold, unwelcoming to me. Distant. Unafraid. Uncaring. Cruel.

She stands tall, seemingly unbothered by my presence or the water raining down on her. Until I cross over to her and reach out. She flinches, her lips parting before pursing together as those eyes flicker away from me. Then downward.

And my cock betrays me in every fucking way, twitching. Regaining control is as easy as reaching past her head, gripping the faucet, and wrenching it downward.

The water goes cold damn near instantly. I'm close enough to feel a few stray drops speckle my skin as I withdraw my hand.

But her? She jumps, her eyes widening. That brief break in her mask allows me inside her head as she wrestles with the instinct warning her to move. Her arms twitch as if she has to stop them from shielding her chest, keep her spine from contorting.

Savage pride counters any remorse I might feel. I've won. Her lips press together with the knowledge of her defeat, and I feel mine widen. Break apart. Smile.

So much for her childish little grasp at control. I rake my gaze over her, savoring every sign of unease. I almost miss the moment her eyes flutter, doing the same to me. They find my chest and linger there.

Too late do I realize why.

She's reading, tracing the name forever etched into my skin. Every letter she spies does something to her. She stiffens that spine. Her chin goes back into the air.

She's defiant again.

I swear I can feel her tiny hands, grappling for the upper hand the same way she fought me for the matches. The alarming part? I feel my hand flatten against my pec, obscuring her view. She's damn near winning...

Rage robs me of any mercy. I hear my voice bounce off the interior of the stall before I even register speaking. "Wash yourself."

She blinks again, her eyes gazing past me. The world transforms in the absence of her attention. Those whispers grow louder, the shadows looming nearby loom larger.

Like an addict, I crave another hit.

So I extend my hand, brushing my thumb along her chin, and I receive what I seek tenfold. She quivers against my fingertips, but it isn't enough. I feel the need to push her further. As hard as I can. "Did you hear me, little wife? I told you to wash yourself."

Her eyes fly back to me, and I overdose on the sensation of her fear. What the hell did I even call her? That's right, the promise I made half-drunk, numb with grief. A madman's crazed boast.

Make her give me an heir to replace Vincenzo.

Did I mean it then?

It's not like she'll stay here long enough to find out. As soon as it's feasible, I'll send her back to Mischa. Her life for Vin's…

But fuck it. A part of me loves making her squirm in the meantime. It's the one thing other than booze capable of helping me forget. God, I need to forget.

"Show your future husband what he has to look forward to," I tell her. "Do you even know?"

She doesn't. Good old Mischa kept her sheltered, from the ways of women and men. I can tell just from the color that paints her cheeks. Hell, I felt it for myself days ago in Havienna. That offending finger burns with the memory of her, and I almost can't control the heat surging right between my legs.

This isn't about sex. It's about power—and I have the lion's share merely by toying with her ignorance.

"Do you?" I taunt.

She swallows, her breaths feathering for a reason that I suspect goes well beyond the frigid water she's under. *Now* she's afraid. Horrified.

I press on her pouty lip, hard enough to sense her teeth chattering beneath. "Of all the ways I could use this mouth…"

She inhales, and just as it had in the barn, her face betrays her—*You're insane, Donatello. And I hate you.*

"Good," I tell her out loud, startled by how deep genuine relief resonates through my voice. "Hate me, little wife. Hate me so much you can't fucking stand it. Hate me. Hate me!"

I'm shouting.

She's gritting her teeth, looking past me again. Again, the loss of her gaze stings. Like an itch that doesn't cease itching until I can make her look at me again. Speak to me again.

Her silent fucking lips have conveyed the truest shit I've heard all goddamn day.

"*Willow*," I snap. Like magic, her eyes dart to me, and it's clarity, so sharp I could get high off of it. I already am. Drugged off the rage burning in her eyes. Beautiful, life-giving rage transforms her into this unknowable creature—because the longer I hold her stare…the more I realize that it's not my treatment of her that has her so angry.

It's that I'm not doing it *well* enough. All this time, I've been toeing the line when it comes to her—only someone who knew me well enough would be able to tell.

Restraint.

I'm just playing with her—I haven't *tortured* her.

As insane as it sounds, I think she's furious at me for holding back, because as long as I do…

She isn't fully in control of me.

"You like power, do you, little wife?" I risk submitting my arm beneath the chill of the spray a second time to grip the faucet. I wrench it high, too high. Steam hisses from the spigot, and if she had a voice, I know she would scream at the shock. Instead, her lips part, her throat contorting around a silent gasp. Just as quickly, she wrestles her limbs into control, standing stiffly even as her pretty skin turns an ugly shade of red.

The sick fucker inside me should take pleasure out of this and rejoice at her faltering armor. Instead, I lower the faucet —all the way down.

Biology is a tricky thing. Even if the mind remains strong, the body can't disguise its instinctive reactions quite so well. She lurches to the balls of her feet, sucking in a startled breath as the steam dissipates and the water temperature plummets.

Still, I have to give her credit. Written across her face is a single daring proclamation—*Do you think this will break me?*

"I don't want to break you, little wife," I tell her, meaning every word.

Being this close to her makes it somehow easy to set aside the rage for an instant and think differently. Mischa would love it if I ruined her. Tortured her. Like a hero, he could rescue her and put the broken pieces back together, then use her downfall as an excuse to drive me right into the ground.

That's probably been his plan all along.

And, if I were truly sick, I'd use that arrogance against him. Play into the narrative that her coming here perfectly illustrates—he loves her, protects her.

But I *have* her. I'm in her head, pushing him out. She'll leave his perfect life behind just to follow me. A sick son of a bitch would test just how far she might go...

I won't. Still, I want to hear how it sounds out loud. "I'm going to hone you," I say. "I'm going to bend you to my will, little bird. I'll erase any identity you've had before me. As long as you're here. You're mine…"

She frowns, trying to puzzle the meaning of the words. Hell, I don't understand them my damn self. Inane ramblings of a mad man, but at least I'm still sane enough to recognize as much.

She drives me *mad* with those watchful little eyes. They strip me down to nothing—in them, I'm none of my past selves. Not the fearsome *Il Mostro* or the Butcher. Not Donatello, the family man. Not even the dutiful Don who cared for another man's child out of what little kindness dwelled within his heart.

To this woman, I'm just someone to hate, and there's freedom in that. And damn, she does hate me. With every word, her lips go flatter, thinner. Her gaze turns cutting. She becomes an open book.

"You're fantasizing about killing me now, aren't you, little wife?"

She is. I can see the images flicker in her mind like I'm watching a fucking slideshow. She hates being powerless. She hates how easily I can make her feel that way.

I step back, taking her body in fully. The chill of the water forces a reaction from her I doubt I'd otherwise see. Her skin is so pale the bluish veins peek from beneath, feeding that frantically beating heart. Pink nipples stand erect, bared freely as she lowers her hands to her sides.

If I wanted to mistake the action as out of fear, those eyes would prove me wrong. They cut into me, unafraid, blazing like coals.

I don't look away from them as I cross to the counter and fish a rag from a rack by the sink. Before I fully think the thought through, I throw it at her.

"Wash yourself."

She crouches slowly, grasping the white cloth within her slim fingers. My breath catches—not because of her body. Just her expression. That face is more damning than the mirror, a broad reflection of everything I am. I'm in control of how she sees me, and I want her to gape. To stare open-mouthed as I lean against the countertop behind me and hold her watchful gaze.

Though they aren't true, I want her to believe every word I said.

"Wash yourself, little wife," I say, palming my hip with one hand while the other grabs my cock. I grunt, alarmed to find it already stiff as fuck. My eyes drift down to those breasts; they're shapely enough to explain it. But no. I meet those eyes again and grit my teeth as a wave of fire centers right beneath my fucking hand. Fighting to keep my voice steady, I dare her, "Make it worth my while."

A good captive would cringe and shield herself—that's what she is, after all. My captive. *Mine.* Though one determined to avoid the pretense of being my property.

Holding the cloth securely in one hand, she inches backward just enough to grab the bar of soap from a built-in shelf along the wall. The same soap I used. Laboriously she lathers the rag, taking her time with no hint of fear to quicken her movements. Though she's shivering from head to toe, it's the water doing it to her. Not terror.

If I doubted that, her eyes find mine through the damp strands of blond hair clinging to her forehead. Slowly, she drags the cloth along her body, jumping with every motion of the wet fabric against her skin.

Only a monster would get off on this. Her gentle movements. Her tiny form that makes the stall I just stood in seem massive around her.

Only a monster would want more.

"Turn around."

After a second's hesitation, she does. With her back turned, I can fully enjoy the sight of her. Without her judgment. Without that constant, blank stare.

Unashamed, I lean back, resting my head against the mirror, and let my hand work. Slow strokes. Then harder, gripping my shaft to the point of pain. The longer I watch her, the more I can read her, even with her ass to me.

Stripping her naked and on display for my benefit is one thing, but she hates this. The little witch loathes being out of control. If she can't see me, she can't manipulate me. As if aware of that fact, she inclines her head, and those eyes find mine again. In them, I see her anticipating my next words before I even voice them. Hell, she's taunting me, goading me to say them.

"Turn around—"

"Donatello?"

A knock resonates from the door of the suite, and I hiss through my teeth at the sound of that voice. Luciano. From his tone, I can tell he won't be turned away so easily.

But a flicker of motion from the woman draws my attention back to her. She stiffens, the rag falling from her fingers to slap against the floor of the stall, and I lean forward, my jaw clenched. I can sense her fear even as she turns away from me.

I can see her naked, but she's wary of someone else doing the same.

*As she should be*, a part of me growls. I ignore it. I don't owe her a damn thing.

"Come in," I call, loud enough for Luciano to hear.

In the meantime, I cross over to a larger rack and grab a white towel for myself. Trust Antonio to waste money on a damn good towel. As I wrap it around my waist, I eye her again, my trapped little bird. She doesn't beg me with her eyes this time. She doesn't cower. Not even as Luciano's steps advance swiftly through the suite.

"Where are you?" he calls.

"In here."

He's paces away, his heavy sigh preceding him. With every inch he gains, the woman grows paler. Her hands creep along her ribcage, drifting toward her breasts, and a bitten lip betrays her rage at herself—she hates this weakness.

"Here." Another towel is already in my grasp. I throw it at her, not intending to watch her cover herself with it. I do anyway. She scrambles to wrap the material around her body just as Luciano coldly remarks from the doorway, "At least you finally took a shower."

He hasn't seen her yet—a fact I'm sure of just from his tone alone.

"Wait for me down the hall."

"Will do," he says, already retreating. "I brought you some clothes, and something I found for your…'friend.' I'll leave them by the door."

For me, he left another suit in a hideous shade of gray. Regardless, it fits well enough. As for what he brought for the woman…

The style and cut leave nothing to the imagination as to the kind of women Antonio himself preferred. Black and velvety, it's short with thin straps. Lucky for her, she's small enough that the dress will cover far more than the designer intended.

But is that a good thing?

No, I tell myself, clenching the damn thing in a fist. I should be parading her before these men, humiliating her in any way I can. Because regardless of who she is, only one identity she possesses matters—daughter of Mischa Stepanov, the man who tried to kill my son.

I drop the dress, watching it hit the floor. Then I step over it and head down the hall, joining Luciano in the gaudy entryway.

"I would be lying if I didn't say that I might be doubting this little deal with a devil." He sounds so damn serious. I have to laugh. Then I sigh on my way to the minibar. Liquor is a better vice than any woman. I grab a bottle at random and take a sip without bothering to read the label. It's strong—but it would take the whole bottle at least to get me back to my usual mind state—numb, dumb, dulled to my darker impulses.

I set it down without drinking more. Still, the burning liquid searing down my throat gives my senses enough of a bitch slap to refocus.

"I knew you were a sick bastard," Luciano remarks from behind me. "But damn. I don't think the rumors did you justice."

"Justice," I parrot the word as though it's a foreign term. Maybe it is. I've never felt it for myself. I've chased it.

Waxed poetic about it once upon a time. Dreamt of earning it for myself. Only to come to one brutal realization.

"I don't believe in justice."

"Okay," he says mockingly. "Think I might have figured that after what you did to Paulie. Shit, man. He was a dick, but no one deserves that—"

"Didn't he? Taking a gun to a pregnant woman and child may be a cut above ripping apart said child killer."

"Don't bullshit me, Don. You don't give a flying fuck about the Stepanovs. That was personal. So now that you got off on torture, what the fuck now?"

"Now?" I raise an eyebrow. "Isn't it obvious? You had it recorded like I asked?"

He nods, wincing.

"Good. We send it to Mischa as a little present—along with an ultimatum."

"The girl in exchange for the hospital?" Luciano suggests.

"Eavesdropping prick." I don't even have the energy to scowl. "How much did you hear?"

"Enough to trust your crazy ass plan," he counters, crossing his arms defensively. "You aren't suicidal. You've got something to live for, at least. There's a slim damn chance that you aren't just trying to get us all killed in some last crusade."

I scoff, though hell, he might be right. Something to live for…

But it wouldn't be Vincenzo—I always gave him everything, and it wasn't enough. He deserves far more than me. But Mischa?

*He* is something to live for. I'll fight for every last breath until the moment I can see him suffer. He got cocky, living his life at the top of the food chain. And he'll live long enough to see his own slow crawl right back to the bottom.

"Is everything ready like I asked?" I question, switching back to the task at hand.

Luciano nods. "You mean your little 'present'? It's ready. But first… You might want to see this." He pulls a cell phone from his pocket. It must be his own, a different model from Antonio's, already displaying a video on the screen. It looks like a newsreel from early this morning, and the chyron flashing across the bottom of the picture tells me all I need to know.

**Fire blazes through Hell's Gambit harbor.**

"Fuck." I don't even have enough energy to put shock into my voice. Maybe because it's been a long time fucking coming. Mischa was bound to make a move like this at some point. Better the harbor than Fabio.

"It seems like Mischa didn't take kindly to you reneging on your harbor sale. Don't worry —" he adds as I lurch for the door. "He hasn't struck anywhere else. Yet. But if you aim to put your plan into action, I suggest you do it now."

I sink onto the nearest leather armchair.

My plan.

"Send a copy of the Vanetti recording to Mischa."

"And if he doesn't buy it?" Luciano counters.

"Then we'll send it to every faction with even a sliver of influence in this city," I say, ticking the names off on my fingers. "The Saleris. The Sigerellis. Every fucking MC and every potential ally. I want them all to know that Mischa acted on faulty intel."

"Done." He starts for the door, adding over his shoulder, "Then what?"

"Then… We make the rounds," I say. "If I were Mischa, I'd already be trying to cultivate an army to my side. We need to head him off."

"Anyone particular in mind?"

I swipe at my chin, thinking. "Gregori Saleri," I state out loud. "The hospital is in the heart of his territory. If I were Mischa, I'd already have invited the bastard over for tea."

Luciano skeptically cocks his head. "You think?"

"Hell yes." I rake my hands through my hair and wind up running them over the front of my borrowed suit. It's too small on second thought, constricting my forearms. I feel like a sausage shoved into it, just like I did during that fucking debutante ball, all in a bid to impress and pander. *Fuck it.*

I shed the jacket and throw it on the floor. One by one, I attack the buttons of the dress shirt, ripping them open and leaving my chest bare. Now, I can breathe.

And think.

"There is a reason Mischa isn't setting fire to the entire city looking for me. No…" I approach a window, bracing my hand over the glass. My outstretched fingers slice the view beyond into portions, much like the political layout of the city itself.

"He's biding his time, trying to smoke me out," I say through clenched teeth. "If he can rob me of allies, I'll have nowhere left to hide, in theory. He knows the hospital would be the one place I'd risk trying to infiltrate."

"Because of your nephew," Luciano says softly. "But you have his daughter. I'd personally hunt you down and cut your balls off if I were in his position."

He isn't Mischa Stepanov, a rumored brute, vicious and more than capable of doing a hasty castration—but you don't get to the top by acting primarily on impulse.

"He thinks I won't hurt her," I say, still thinking aloud. "He's counting on that. She'll be traumatized, maybe battered, but alive. He has a bigger goal in mind than merely finding her. I'm guessing he only needs her to hold out another day at most. Then he'll make his final play and come for her."

"Why the delay?"

I exhale, thinking it through. "Why?"

Because old Mischa isn't trying to punish me for these recent events—this is deeper than that. Personal. He wants to save his daughter from her nightmare once and for all as any father would. Drive me from the city. Crush me into dust.

Destroy every trace of all Vanicis.

Me. Vincenzo. He wants us gone.

Much like Vin's imaginary monster haunted him, his precious Willow can't live her life if we're still here.

The sheer cruelty of it hits like a punch to the chest, flipping my stupid hope right on its fucking head. If I go to Mischa now, even with proof that I wasn't behind the attack, it won't matter. He might let Vin be admitted to the hospital, if only to have direct access to kill him later.

It's what I would have done. Hell, I *have* done it. Some crimes can't be punished merely with death, but with brutality.

Gino Mangenello is proof of that.

This war has its roots in what happened seven years ago. I hurt his daughter, and by merely existing, I threw that pain back in her face. In Mischa's thinking, I struck first; therefore, anything is justified.

I could always fight fire with fire and launch a full-out war on the *mafiya*.

Or better yet, I can turn the tables on Mischa and beat him at his own fucking game.

I can make his daughter the perfect weapon.

"Change of plans," I say as the plan begins to unfurl in my mind. "We won't wait for Mischa to come for the girl."

"What do you mean?"

I lick my lips in grim anticipation. I can't even say it out loud. Yet. "You'll find out soon enough. In the meantime, set up a meeting with the Saleris."

"When?"

"As soon as you can. Tonight," I say, heading down the hall. "Just give me an hour."

It's time to drop the pretense of captor and captive. Giovanni had it right from the start—life is all a fucking game.

So I'll let Mischa's daughter decide for herself. To remain a pawn? Or become a more powerful piece...

A queen—one fully under my control.

# 13

## WILLOW

know pain. I know agony. I've seen horrible things in my life, and throughout it all, I've survived. Scarred and battered, but still alive, only there are no wounds as proof of this most recent ordeal. No blood to clean that is my own, at least.

It's all in my head, and that's how he wanted it. Mental scars inflict the most lasting damage—he taught me that.

Fittingly, all there is to mark this moment is my own reflection watching me from a bathroom mirror, my skin pink and tender.

The sight chills me more than any scar would.

This woman is a stranger to me, her brown eyes wide with shock, her lips pursed in a perpetual frown. The ill-fitting dress she's wearing hangs off her lanky frame, highlighting the dichotomy within which she finds herself.

Captive and toy.

Accomplice.

Murderer.

Tears glisten in her eyes, reinforcing the terror written across that face. Inside, however? I feel nothing to match her outward expression. No prickling behind my eyes to herald the moisture falling down my cheeks. Nothing aching in the pit of my soul.

Of everything I've been through in my life, this feeling is the strangest to grapple with.

Numbness.

Emptiness.

Nothing.

But as if to mock me, my ears pick up a distant sound—a footstep—and a million conflicting emotions flood my veins. *Fear. Unease. The building horror that I'm trapped...*

Another heavy footstep echoes off the cavernous walls, creating a cage more binding than this structure itself—but it's invisible, entirely of my own making. The reality is that I could have run from here all along. I didn't have to follow him into this building, this room. Didn't have to submit to his torment, or wear the dress he left for me.

In theory, I don't have to stay here now, and yet with every additional step to break the silence, I'm frozen, unable to move a muscle.

While I may be paralyzed, the face in the mirror isn't. With every step to draw nearer, that pink mouth tightens. Throat quivers. When the footsteps finally stop? Her tongue flits out along her lower lip, and her dark eyes widen as a masculine laugh catches the air.

She can instantly identify the culprit.

His shadow paints the floor beside the doorway, but he doesn't enter. Yet. He wants me to sense him first. For my nostrils to flare with the faint scent of musk that precedes him.

He wants me to remember, every grisly, twisted memory. Not just what happened in the shower, either. My skin is overly sensitive, speckled with throbbing scarlet blotches, but I'd rather be boiled alive than relive the previous moments.

I can barely admit it inside my own head—I watched him kill a man. Butcher him. Take pleasure in doing so…

*But you watched,* a part of me taunts. *You didn't look away.*

Not even when he met my gaze, his fingers dripping blood. For a second, he'd sported that grim, knowing smirk—as if he were seeing inside my head.

And what he found…excited him.

"Look at yourself, *principessa,*" the present Donatello demands, maneuvering to appear in the mirror's view, leaning against the doorway. He isn't fully naked, at least, wearing a pair of black pants, but his chest is exposed, each letter of the tattoo clearly visible. In this moment, I take the time to examine them in a way I couldn't before.

Each sloppily craved letter looks fresh given the coloring. As if he wrote them all in blood.

SAFIYA.

They do the one thing I can't do with my own voice—prove him a liar. The girl he claims meant nothing? The past he's tried to ignore...

It's here. It's *always* been here. My fingers twitch at my sides as if aching to reach out and touch one of those marks. Graze that lopsided A with the tip of my nail and force him to acknowledge me. How would he react? It's not hard to imagine.

With rage. With scorn and hate.

But we'd both know the outcome, in the end…

I'd gain the upper hand.

"Look at that face," he taunts, drawing my attention back to his mouth. Then my own. "Those eyes. In them, you see the same thing I do."

Does he see horror and despair?

He should.

"You know what I see? Nothing," he says, countering that hope. "You don't regret what we did, do you? I can see it all over your face. You enjoyed it."

*Enjoyed.* Is that the emotion to describe my blank expression or the pink cheeks streaked with tears? I shake my head, responding to my own question rather than him.

He laughs again, and those steps echo louder, playing a twisted melody off the walls. As his reflection appears behind mine, I suck in a breath.

Throughout my life, I've witnessed various iterations of Donatello Vanici. The stoic protector. The playful guardian. The vengeful betrayer.

Never before have I faced this specter. His eyes are so dark they gleam like coals, enhancing the hollow planes of his face. Dark stubble coats his chin like an embodiment of the shadows behind him. The most alarming feature of all? Myself, reflected in his gaze, different from the woman in the mirror. Distorted by the hue of his irises, she looks cold. Unbothered. Unafraid.

Just like him.

"Don't," he warns, before I even register looking away. Too late. A span of tile holds my attention now, even as thick fingers harshly grip my chin, wrenching it back to face the mirror's surface.

"You watch," commands the gruff voice dripping into my ear. "You see the truth there, written across those pretty lips. You may not be able to voice it for yourself, but I can tell— you enjoyed this, didn't you, little *principessa*? And I'm not talking about the shower. Telling me where to cut. Hearing him scream—"

My hand flies out, landing flat against the counter, serving as a protest I can't voice—*No!*

"Oh yes," he says amid a low chuckle. His fingers creep along my jawline and graze my throat. In the mirror, two dark eyes watch me mockingly, ablaze with fire. Then little by little…any humor vanishes.

I close my eyes to shut him out. Banish the memories—the blood. The screams. I shove them all as far as I can to the darkest depths of my psyche.

But not far enough.

"We're the same, hellcat. Both sick, pathetic creatures who thrive on pain. Accept that—" What feels like his thumb ghosts the swell of my cheek, lingering near the corner of my mouth. "We are. But you never need to feel guilty around me…"

His voice hitches, touching on an octave deeper than I think he meant to. I reopen my eyes, and even his frown can't disguise the fleeting expression to cross his face. Alarm —as if the words leaving his throat startle him just as much as they unnerve me.

"You can coddle yourself with lies, if you want," he says, raising an eyebrow to become mocking once more. "I won't. You've been sheltered long enough, *Willow*. It's time to face the world."

Before I can recover, he muscles in beside me and turns on the sink faucet. He takes his time wetting his hands before bracing them, still wet, against the countertop. Maybe he did it to draw my attention to them.

They fan out over the dark marble, gleaming like tarnished gold in comparison. Dangerous, thick digits capable of so much violence—the proof of which still smarts along my throat, burning in the heat of his breath.

To counter any self-pity I might feel is a grim satisfaction as my eyes flicker up to his jaw and the two lines sliced there, one a few days old, the other fresh. Both wounds look worse from this angle, even more vicious than the bruises left by his hands. I got my revenge.

"You hate me," Donatello murmurs, but his gaze is distant. Years in the past, I suspect, reliving the very reasons why. Slowly, he nods. "You should hate me. I want you to. Look at me… Look!"

Our gazes meet over the mirror's glass, and the rest of the world fades to a dull hum. His voice alone is powerful enough to rival even thunder. Somehow, his stare is even louder, outlasting the thrum of the still running water and my own frantic breaths. I can't look away.

I can't breathe.

"Hate me," he warns. "If that will make you feel better. Hate me all you want. I'll allow you that much."

*If I want. He'll allow.* I almost can't track the irritation flicking through me until it's too late.

As if he has any right to accept my rage like it's a mercy.

He chuckles in triumph at the response—my lips twitching, eyes narrowing. "You want to learn something, *principessa*? A great, universal truth?" He positions his face near mine, lips inches from my earlobe. "Your hate? It doesn't mean a damn thing. Though, I'm sure you think it does. If you hate me enough, it will somehow matter. Your hate doesn't mean shit. You know what does?" He leans closer, his gaze unreadable. "Power. You need power to get anywhere in this fucking world. Even as a woman, you have what you need."

I stiffen at the reference, but he doesn't sneer to punctuate the punchline. He isn't joking.

"You just never learned to use it," he adds. "You never will. Why? You were always sheltered in the grip of power, never expected to amass your own. What I did to you was *evil*, I'll admit that."

Rare sincerity ripples through his tone, and some part of me cringes in response. It's like a wall gives way, and for a split second, I feel everything...

The pain. The hate. The fear—god, that *fear*. My knees buckle, forcing me to grip the edge of the counter for stability. Back then, I had nothing to rely on as the gravity of what he did to me sunk in. He was gone.

I was alone.

The tears spring to life before I can hold them back, searing the corners of my eyes, unwilling to fall. Yet. Gradually, I get a grip on my emotions—smother them back where they belong, and as I do, I realize something.

His face… If I trusted the honesty in his tone, his eyes are cool enough to suck any warmth from the words.

"It was evil. But it wasn't enough to teach you what you should have learned… Your hate doesn't mean shit in the long run. Real revenge? Real retaliation? You can only garner that from power, and just by being here alone, you've given up any you ever had. Do you understand?"

I grit my teeth and eye the basin of the sink rather than face him. His expression sneaks into my mind anyway. That smug smile. The sly arrogance in his posture betraying that he thinks he's right. He takes pride in being right.

Even now…

I don't mean anything to him.

"Who you are now. Who you used to be…" He trails off. "Truth be told, *principessa*—I can't feel a damn thing. No love. No hate. All I feel?" He brushes his hand over his chest in the vague direction of his heart. "All I feel is pain. Sorrow. Emptiness. So hate me all you want. Maybe one day I'll let you act on it? In the meantime, I've figured out your real use to me."

Fire floods my cheeks, painting them red in the mirror. I can't stop my gaze from darting to his fingers, still braced over the counter, dangerously close.

"You think I aim to fuck you?" I flinch as his lips brush my ear, still moving. "I could. Does that scare you? I *could*."

I wrench away from him, recoiling against the nearest wall. My shoulder throbs with the force of the collision, but I'd propel myself through the barrier if I could. His eyes narrow, tracking my reaction as the words sink in.

He could…

"If you mattered in this game, *principessa*? I'd consider it." He doesn't laugh. Doesn't flinch.

He means it. And I can tell from his low, slow exhale next that he means what he's about to say even more. "But you don't. Hear that now. A smart girl would take comfort in hearing that."

He leans against the counter, examining his curled fist. A muscle in his jaw twitches, undermining his careful, level baritone. "All that matters is Mischa. You heard the truth for yourself. What he did?"

I bite the inside of my mouth so hard I taste blood. I heard. Mischa attacked Vincenzo believing Donatello attacked him first—but he was wrong. Played by faulty information.

*And you knew it all along,* a part of me snarls. *You never questioned it…*

"With you here, there are a million ways I could punish him," Donatello points out, watching me with his head cocked. "You realize that, don't you?"

I do. Yet, I force every muscle in my face to go still rather than show it.

"I could rip you apart. Let every man here take a turn. String you up for the hell of it and send you to him in a box."

He could. Worse things have happened, circling the manor as rumors. Mischa wasn't always a family man. I saw firsthand the way he used to live. Violently. Recklessly.

"He probably expects as much," Donatello admits. "But I know what will punish him more. What he truly deserves."

He lets the seconds pass, ramping up the tension the way a dramatic pause would in a drawn-out sonata. Finally, he moves to capitalize on the moment, advancing to the sink to shut the water off. Facing me from over his shoulder, he says, "I'm going to use *you*. He thinks I dragged you here, but I'll let him know the truth. You came to me willingly. You always came to me. Why? I have a hold over you he never will. Power over his precious little girl. You gave it to me—"

He reacts before I even realize what I'm doing—lunging at him with a fist brandished and no idea of where I'm aiming it. His chest. My knuckles ricochet off the scarlet F carved over his ribcage with a sickening thud—over and over again.

If I had that letter opener, or my knife…I'd use it.

Slice into him just to prove one point—he doesn't control me.

He has *nothing* over me.

"Enough." He grabs my wrist, still chuckling in that insufferable way. "Oh, little hellcat, I'll let you assault me all you want. *After* our wedding night, my body will belong to you after all."

*Wedding night.* The threat hits me like a slap, and I stagger back, tripping over my own feet. A firm grip on my forearm is the only force saving me from a nasty fall. Eyes wide, I gape at the tan fingers coiled against my skin. Like so much of my interactions with him, the sight is familiar, while the sensation—his actual touch—is so *wrong*. Foreign. Unnatural.

Heat radiates from him like fire, burning through my brain's pathetic attempts to remain unaffected.

"Did you hear me?" he goads. This time, he doesn't withdraw—instead, he tightens his grip, drawing me closer with a ruthless flick of his forearm. His opposite arm goes around my waist, setting off a million different reactions.

Air sticks in my throat as shock paralyzes me. Intentionally, I suspect. He wants to unnerve me.

He has.

His nearness assaults me from every direction. His body is an inescapable prison. So hard. Solid. My fingers scramble to find purchase against his chest—to shove him away. Then a sudden shift in his skin texture has me fanning my fingers out, seeking more. Parts of him are so scarred, so rough they hurt to touch. *Here* especially…

Rippling flesh, rugged and jagged.

What the hell happened to him?

I look down and see for myself—I'm grazing the outermost edge of the tattoo. Up close, the scarlet shapes reveal a viciousness you can't see when farther back. This wasn't the typical application—it was violent. Something ripped the skin apart, staining the flesh underneath. It took days to heal, if not weeks, such painful, deliberate marks. I can't resist flicking my tongue along my lower lip as I study them, unsure what I feel. Triumph? He lied—his unimportant SAFIYA left her mark on him, alright.

He immortalized her himself—and he wanted it to hurt.

To bleed.

To scar.

I barely get the chance to track the shudder running through him before he shifts, sinking his free hand into my hair. My reaction is exactly what he wants—I flinch.

But I don't pull away.

"You're not afraid to marry me," he deduces as though I've said as much out loud. But I haven't—I don't even know what my own thoughts convey, let alone enough to portray it.

But somehow, he still claims to know it all. What I'm thinking. What I fear. What I hate.

"Isn't that right, little hellcat?" His finger flits along my lower lip, raising chills in its wake. "No. You're afraid about what that might mean—that you *aren't* afraid. Don't tell me you enjoy playing with danger?" He strokes my jawline as I grit my teeth.

"I could leave you guessing as to what I intend to do to you. I could feed you a million senseless fears. Torment you through vague taunts and threats…"

He fingers a lock of my hair, winding it around and around the width of his finger.

"But I won't. I'm going to marry you. In front of your father and God, I will marry you. You'll consent to every step along the way. I'll become *your* monster to protect. You'll have no choice."

My monster.

I don't know what he means, but his eyes are even darker, his mouth the closest he can come to a smile. Even in obvious madness, he sounds so serious. Too serious. A million thoughts come to mind, each more dangerous than the last.

"Oh, don't look at me like that," he warns, lifting my chin against his calloused palm. "You think I'm going to ravish you, little hellcat? Rip you open over nice, white bedsheets and then display them in the morning for your father to see?"

I can't resist the imagery sneaking into my skull, illustrating his words. The heat in my cheeks turns searing.

"I won't," he says belatedly. "That would be too easy. Too merciful… And if there is one thing I am tired of being, it's merciful. You see, mercy is what got me here."

His tone rings with a double meaning—*here*, standing in an enclosed room with a figure from his past, he thought long dead. Here, proposing insanity with a dangerous smile.

"I am through with mercy," he says, using his grasp on that strand of my hair to climb higher. Soon his fingers scrape against my scalp, guiding the position of my head until I have no choice but to look at him. "I am going to marry you, little hellcat, but do not worry. Our union will not last long."

The way he says those words triggers a wave of unease that rides my spine.

"You're wondering why? Am I threatening you?" He laughs again, but his gaze becomes distant. Colder, if it's even possible. "No, little hellcat. I've decided to warn you—after our wedding night, your fears when it comes to me will be moot."

My dread must show on my face, feeding the slow, ripe smile to shape his mouth. The same emotion I felt when I lashed at his face strikes again. Burning. Blazing. But this time, I don't hit him—my teeth snap instead, barely missing the tip of his thumb.

He frowns, withdrawing his hand. I caught him off guard. Frantic, I realize it's the only way to fight against him.

*React.*

Already he's recovered, fingering a strand of hair a safe distance from my mouth. "Until then, I'm going to become your monster, little hellcat. Lurking in your closet—and you are going to shield me from Mischa. Corrupting you will be his punishment."

He's speaking through me, his gaze distant, even as his fingers work through my damp, tangled hair. "Get dressed."

Abruptly he pulls back, letting me go. His eyes rake over the black dress I'm wearing now. He lumbers into the hall, returning a second later with something he must have already had at the ready—a black case that he throws onto the counter, spilling its contents as a result. Makeup, all different brands, seemingly collected by the various women who might have stayed here at one point.

With him?

"Play your role, hellcat," he cautions, distracting me from the thought. "Good enough, so even I believe it. I won't waste my breath threatening your life, either," he warns, entering the hall. "I don't want a captive bird. But in case you do need some motivation, think of *her*."

The little girl—but his disinterested tone betrays the threat for what it is—hollow. His real tool to motivate me is something far more intangible than another life.

Pride.

Do I have what it takes to play his game?

Or will I cower in wait of rescue like the little girl he thinks
I am…

# 14

## EVGENI

After the way our last meeting ended, I don't expect Mischa to call me back to the manor so soon—and definitely not hours into my shift covering Mrs. Stepanova.

I know the second I see the succinct text—*You're needed at base, now*—something's wrong.

My mind races with potential reasons, Willow first among them. As I park near the front walkway, I sense the mood shift before I even step foot inside the house. Unease tinges the air, affecting everyone on the property.

Case in point? The first man I pass on my way inside has a gun drawn out in the open, a sight so galling, I do a double take.

"What the hell is wrong with you?" I demand, snatching for his wrist. "Have you lost your goddamn mind?"

I glance at the house where the children could be watching through any one of the windows. Mischa may ensure that his property is well patrolled, but the foremost rule is to never reveal the true nature of that presence to his children.

The man before me is well aware of the rules, and yet he shrugs me off, still brandishing his weapon. "New orders from the boss himself," he explains. "We're to stand at the ready. At least until his 'guest' leaves."

"Guest?" The hairs on the back of my neck stand on end. Few "guests" could warrant this kind of vigilance. Donatello Vanici, for one...

Or someone far worse.

"Are they in the study?" I start forward, my shoulders tense.

The man shakes his head. "The main hall."

*Shit.* My alarm only grows, and I have to stop myself from running the entire way there.

The hall is where Mischa holds court only for the most joyous occasions—or the most grave. The man he loved like a father's funeral was here. His wedding took place in the same space. More recently? His daughter's debutante.

And now?

The drastic difference in attendees is one startling change. Instead of well-dressed socialites, Mischa alone dominates the room, flanked on either side by two guards, along with another figure I don't recognize.

Perhaps, because he's in pieces.

Someone delivered them in what once might have been a large blue box delicately wrapped and adorned with a white bow. Hell, it could have been mistaken for one of Willow's debutante presents at first. Instead of the typical necklace or bauble, a severed head lies within on a bed of tissue paper, along with a bloodied hand presumably from the same unfortunate individual.

"Who ordered this open?" I demand, scanning the box intently. I don't see a name or other identifying feature. "Was it even searched properly—"

"I did," Mischa says. One look at his face, and I suspect the delivered body parts are only partly the cause of the tense mood in the air. I can only name one other time he sported this pained grimace, that being when his wife and son arrived at this very home barely alive.

"This came with it," he says, presenting a tablet, sporting a blurred image of several figures in a room. A warehouse? Taking it from Mischa, I press play.

A man's voice rings out from the device next, cold and booming. I recognize it instantly—Donatello Vanici's.

A high-pitched cry answers, and my blood runs cold before I note the low pitch. Not a woman's, at least. Not Willow's.

But then I see her. She's visible for just a second, her back to the camera, blond hair loose. Her dress is filthy, but otherwise, she seems unharmed. As the video continues to play, I start to question for how long. Is this a recording of her death?

That fear only grows when the camera pans over Vanici's face. Despite the video's poor quality, it's easy to read the murderous intent in his eyes. Instead of Willow, he's fixated on another figure, however. Someone out of view.

*"This is him," a man behind Vanici says. "Paulie Vanetti."*

I cut my gaze over to Mischa and find him watching as well, his face stone. I can't tell if that name means anything to him, but it triggers a vague sense of recognition in me. *Vanetti.* I've heard rumors of a mercenary like that, prized for his ruthless skill.

When I return my attention to the video, I can barely make out the figure in question, kneeling on the floor. Bound?

*"So this is the man Antonio contracted?" Vanici asks.*

*"It's him," the first man replies. "He's been cagey on the work he did. I don't think he'll tell us freely."*

*"There is no need for threats." Vanici crouches on one knee, inspecting the man before him. "Was it you?" he asks softly, flicking his thumb along the other man's cheek. "The Stepanovs. Were you the man Antonio hired to do his fucking dirty work?"*

Recognition washes over me, and I almost can't keep myself from blurting my observation out loud—I was right. From the corner of my eye, Mischa remains impossible to read, his eyes fixated on the screen.

*"Let's hear it," Donatello demands, yanking the man's gag free. "Speak. Were you the lapdog Tony sent to do his bidding?"*

*"Go. To hell," Vanetti croaks. "Where the fuck is Tony? I'll teach that son of a bitch to——"*

*"Tony's dead." Rising to his feet, Donatello flicks the discarded gag aside and clasps his hands behind his back.*

*"You answer to me," he says, towering over the captive man. "Did he hire you to do it?"*

*"The fuck is this?" The man's eyes continue to dart warily around the room. "What the fuck is going on, Luciano?"*

"Luciano," I echo. This name I recognize. "*Famiglia* agent."

If that surprises Mischa, his eyes reveal nothing. I get the sense that he's focused on something else entirely. "Keep watching," he says.

*"Tony paid me over a hundred grand for it," Vanetti stammers. "I just did as I was told, okay? It wasn't nothing fucking personal."*

*"Personal," Vanici snaps. "Oh, but this* was *personal. If you won't take my word for it, then take hers."*

*He inclines his head to a figure barely visible behind him.*

*"This is the man who attacked your mother," Vanici tells her. "The reason why your father tried to kill my son. Did you know that? You knew. Didn't you? Is that really why you came running to me, little principessa?——"*

"Son of a bitch," Mischa growls, slamming his hand against the desk.

He's already seen this, I suspect. But despite it all—his daughter captive, standing so close to a madman—this is the part that unnerves him the most. Her, standing toe to toe with Donatello Vanici as he taunts her. But not just any taunt—*principessa*, said with such scorn there's no doubt that he means it as an insult.

*"Let us not forget... I didn't drag you here as my captive. You came to me," Vanici growls.*

I'm so busy watching Mischa, the next parts of the video register only in the broadest terms. Vanici extorts supposed proof from Vanetti that he was responsible for the attack on the Stepanovs. Anger burns hot in my chest, and I'm already planning a full on assault on Antonio Salvatore and his assets—dead or not.

Even as I do, I keep glancing back at Mischa, alarmed to find that he doesn't seem to feel the same. This video proves that he—literally—jumped the gun. He potentially waged war against the wrong man.

But as his teeth pull back from his upper lip, I realize that something more egregious than that is what really has him on edge. A sight that enrages him beyond Vanici's supposed guilt in harming his wife. A crime that outweighs the man's supposed innocence.

*He approaches Willow, speaking to her in a low, unsettling tone. "You feel it too," he murmurs. "Hate. That sick need for revenge—and not mere 'justice,' either… You want pain. You want him to suffer, just as you suffered. Am I wrong? I can see it written all over your face… The hate—and not just for me, either. How should we punish him?"*

Alarm builds in my gut. "What the hell is he doing?"

"Watch," Mischa warns.

*"Don't deny that you want to," Vanici tells her. "So what will it be? A slit throat? A beheading? Name your choice, principessa. You wanted to play in our world, so play.*

Willow's face is barely visible from this angle—a dark brown eye blazing fearlessly, riveted to the man before her.

*"He threatened your family, your mother, your brother. You want more than just his pain. You want more than justice, don't you?"*

*Vanici turns to one of the men nearby. "I asked for a knife."*

"Shit!" I rock on my heels, my jaw clenched to the point of pain. Will he hurt her? Are pieces of that morbid "present" from Willow herself? Again, Mischa's face doesn't give me an answer, but he's more animated than before, his gaze blazing.

Warier than ever, I force myself to keep watching as Vanici is finally given a blade. He raises it…

But I sway with relief when he turns away from her.

*"You're going to tell me how to kill him," he says. "Every cut. Every scream. It will be all on you. Your face tells me everything*

*I need to know. Your eyes... I see the hate in them. You want this—Don't! You watch me. You watch all of it. Now... Where should we begin? Ah, of course. We need a name," he suggests, toying with the blade. "Should we start with his tongue?"*

It's a cruel, sadistic mental game. One I know all too well, and a skill Vanici masters—manipulation. It's all in his tone —a mocking, stern rasp that can make the insane seem logical.

The unconscionable bearable.

The kind of charm that can sway a young, stupid boy to commit the unfathomable.

*"You promised me your loyalty, Geno. Do you want to live up to your father's legacy? Then stop questioning..."* The voice echoes through my brain as if spoken aloud—but not by Vanici. Regardless, I tear my gaze from the screen for a split-second, eyeing the doorway as if expecting someone else to come strolling through, his features untouched by time.

My heart races, and I have to grit my teeth to refocus. Vanici is my current target, and I wrench my gaze back to the video.

*"I said watch me, Safiya."*

A part of me reacts to that name before I realize why. He knows Willow's name. Why call her that? Safiya...

*"This is your game, after all. Tell me where to cut him. Play your role. Look at me!"*

"The son of a bitch," I croak, forming a fist though I know it's a futile gesture. It's all I can do, digging my nails into my palm as he makes her watch. He toys with her. Taunts her while threatening to kill a man.

But it's the familiarity between them that alarms me. An unspoken weight that enhances every glance they share between them, Willow and Vanici. It's uncomfortable, triggering an unease I can't name.

*"You're angry. You have every fucking right to be. But you're suppressing it. Bottling it up nice and neat. Why?" He leans closer, bringing his mouth near her ear...*

Mischa hisses in a way I've never heard, his eyes slits. Still, his restraint is remarkable—especially when Vanici shoves Willow to the ground, placing his knife against her throat.

I grit my teeth, lurching on tip-toe as if I could leap into the recording itself and stop him.

"Wait," Mischa says. "Keep watching."

Watching as Vanici continues his sick game, playing with Willow's head, goading her into cutting the man. Killing him. Until finally, he grows bored enough to do the job alone.

*"So you choose to be a puppet. Fine. You can watch. Hold her," he snaps to one of the men who grabs her arms. "Don't let her turn away. Not for a fucking second."*

By the video's end, several points are painfully clear. The first was that Antonio Salvatore ordered the hit on the Stepanovs, not Vanici, or so this stunt was meant to prove.

That should be a good thing, right? It follows what I've suspected all along, but I don't feel pride in this moment. Disgust rips through me as I glance at the "present." The head is distinctly masculine—not Willow's. Still, the implied threat is obvious.

That bastard's gone insane.

And he's hellbent on taking Willow right along with him. If I didn't suspect as much before, I do now—there is more between them than some silly debutante ball. A history, that Mischa is fully aware of.

An accusation of as much is on my lips. Only prudence holds me back—there are more important things to worry about for the time being.

"Who sent this?" I demand, though the answer is obvious. "How did it get through?"

"I allowed it," Mischa says tiredly. "That's not all that came."

He gestures to a corner of the room I previously overlooked. There a pile of documents lies discarded. Warily I cross to them, and at a glance, I instantly come to a conclusion that has me cursing under my breath.

"You were right," Mischa calls from over my shoulder, narrating what I've been able to read. "Vanici didn't order the attack. Supposedly this is what's left of the man who carried it out at least—" He nods to the grisly box. Presumably, he's the man from the video. "And I already confirmed that Salvatore is dead."

"So you believe it," I suspect. "Salvatore set up the hit along with someone else. Not Vanici."

Which leaves the origins of the attack even murkier than before. The only lead? A figure mentioned briefly, J.W.

"Yes." Mischa nods, hands in fists, teeth bared. "The bastard sent those documents to verify. Bank transfers. Phone records." He inclines his head, stroking his chin thoughtfully. "I hear from my contacts that he's already in the process of contacting the *famiglia's* old allies."

"Fuck," I say. The part I hold back is the kicker—in most men's eyes, Vanici has every right to. Still, I'm in no mood to gloat. I was right. Mischa was reckless.

All that matters now is Willow's safety, and the rest of the family's. "Do you think Vanici will mount an attack on his own?"

This time he'd have more than enough cause—a life in exchange for his nephew's.

Mischa's expression wavers for a split second before his frown becomes a terrifying smile. "Let him try. Attack aside, he still went after Willow. Only God knows what he's done to her."

Real concern breaks through his stoic façade. Despite everything, the man loves his daughter.

And he's right. Only God knows what's been done to her already. I eye the tablet still in my grasp, stroking that faint glimpse of blond hair.

"Do you know where this was taken? If Donatello went to the *famiglia*, maybe—"

"You are needed at the hospital," Mischa says over me. His eyelids lower as if he remembered something. Something he doesn't want me to know.

"Sir, I think I should be here—"

"I want security on my wife tripled," he commands. "Eli is being brought home tomorrow, and he and Anna are to be protected around the clock. I want you to split your best guards between them."

Reluctantly, I nod. "Of course. But…"

He cocks his head, raising an eyebrow. "Is something wrong?"

"Antonio Salvatore ordered the attack? You think he would really mount something like that alone? With no motive other than maybe gaining the harbor?"

"According to Donatello Vanici," Mischa says coldly.

I look over at the so-called evidence again, but see nothing definitive beyond numbers and inferences. Antonio Salvatore ordered the hit, but was he working entirely out of his own interest? Vanici's proof alone suggests he wasn't.

*"The bastard just went by J. W. That's it! That's all I know. I swear to fucking God…"*

"Sir—"

"I thought I told you to handle the arrangements for the hospital?" Mischa snaps.

"Yes, sir. But… The man in the video mentioned someone else. What if there was another motive to the attack, apart from merely harming your family?"

A motive that a certain Winthorp returned from obscurity to hint at.

Mischa hisses. "What? Forcing my hand so that I look like a goddamn fool?"

"No," I say softly. "But what about any other leads? I think your wife was connected to the Winthorps. Could they have a motive?"

One in particular. Her name is on the tip of my tongue, but for whatever reason, I don't voice it. Yet.

"The Winthorps?" His eyes narrow. Does he find such a theory plausible? His expression is nearly impossible to scrutinize.

"Most of them are dead," he says finally. "And those who aren't don't have any claim to any influence, let alone money."

It's a fair point, one that festers as I mull over the potential reasons. All of them, I suspect, lie within the mind of a certain Winthorp.

"What about Ellen?" I ask, still on the man's heels. "Didn't she have a sister? Briar, I think, was her name."

He scoffs. "She ran off with one of my men seven years ago. There's been no word of her since, but I frankly don't give a damn. You know who does have my full concern? My *wife*."

I nod in respect. "Yes, sir."

But I've been in Mischa's employ for too damn long. I know when he's reaching the end of his patience—and I know when he's deliberately provoking someone. He wants me gone, and quickly. Why?

The state of the guards outside might give me a clue.

"You're expecting someone," I say softly. "A visitor?"

Or a potential ally. If Donatello went to the *famiglia* alone, he wouldn't bother with reinforcements—the *mafiya* outnumber the dwindling outfit by more than two to one. But if Donatello managed to sway others to his side, Mischa might be driven to only one person.

Someone he swore to never associate with.

Rather than dance around the suspicion, I voice it outright, "You summoned Nicolai Baryshnikov—"

"I would summon the devil if it meant protecting my daughter," he bellows, his voice booming.

Instinct—and common sense—warn me to pause. Tread carefully.

But I can't. Not when *that* bastard is the topic of conversation. "I think Willow would prefer you work with the devil instead."

"What did you say?" He stiffens, his hand forming a fist. Honestly, I wouldn't be surprised if he did strike me. A part of me braces for the blow. Instead, he turns to me directly, his expression strained.

"I trust you, Evgeni. Above everyone else, your opinion is the one I trust—"

"But not on this," I interject.

"No." He levels me with a piercing stare. "I think your past is clouding your thinking. I've never ordered you to commit a massacre, have I? I'm not ordering you to stay, either."

I blink. It's the first time he's ever directly mentioned it. *I never ordered you to commit a massacre...*

Because one man did—but Mischa doesn't give a damn about the blood that may or may not be on my hands. He references it merely to prove his point. That's why he doubts my resolve. My ability to be trusted. My loyalty.

"If you mean my past when it comes to Nicolai Baryshnikov, then I don't think that is a bad thing." Anger tinges my voice, and I can't even begin to hide it. The memories swarm on the fringes of my psyche. It's harder than ever to push them back. Forget.

"I have always been able to rely on you," Mischa says with a sigh. "Always. But I've learned throughout the years that there are some lines certain men cannot cross. No matter the price, no matter their loyalty, and I am sorry, my friend, but when it comes to protecting my family, I will be cowed by no one."

"Is a war really what you want?" I ask. "Even if it's against the wrong man?"

He places his hand on my shoulder, letting the contact linger before he finally turns away, crossing to the center of the room. "Show me the man who has my daughter in his grasp, and I'll turn my attention to him," he says. When I remain silent, he gestures to the doorway with a violent slash of his hand. "Now go. From now until further notice, the hospital is your main post."

His tone alone makes his motive painfully clear. Whatever he's planning, he doesn't want me anywhere near it.

Because he knows I'd try to stop him.

# 15

# DON

No one spared their praise while I was rising in the ranks of the *famiglia.* I heard it all, from mindless worship to having grown men pledge their lives to me.

Fuck modesty—it felt good to be king.

No one warns you what happens when you fall from that high perch, though. Life isn't the same at the bottom as it is on top—and sure, you thought you knew that from the outset.

But you didn't.

The truth is that hardly anyone experiences what it's like to have it all, and fewer understand the pain of losing it. Not just the money or the prestige—that shit is secondary. It's the stuff you put by the wayside on your ascent that you miss the most. The people you took for granted, the memories you minimized, and the lovers you exploited for your own gain.

Their silence is deafening, and no amount of money or power or booze can fill the void.

All you can do is bury the agony and fixate on useless distractions. Like plotting your ascent back to the top, even if you gotta kiss a few asses on your way there. Or stab them. Butcher.

Bloodied hands are a sight preferable to an empty house and full graves any day.

I lack the foresight of a Giovanni Rossi this time around, though. Forget power and influence. My focus is restricted to one target—*Mischa*. Now that I have his daughter in my grasp, the world is figuratively mine to take all over again via checkmate.

I could always kill her to achieve that aim—or go a step further and bind her to me in a way that humiliates him more than her death would. I could marry her...

A part of me scoffs at the notion, though I'm the one who proposed it, initially as a way to fuck with her head. But now? It's an insane gambit. Only a true madman would actually go through with it—a wedding for my new bride with her father as the honored guest. You can't make that shit up.

*Forget her.* I shove the Stepanovs aside for the moment, returning my focus to Vincenzo. His safety is all that matters tonight, dominating my thoughts as I exit Giovanni's old apartment into the cool night air.

I've wasted enough time already. The "one hour" I promised Luciano unintentionally stretched into several—all spent staring at myself in the closet mirror, pondering the figure staring back. Who was that bastard?

A stranger I barely recognize with the face of an old man and the eyes of a murderer.

I've spent seven years too drunk to function, but sobriety feels more disorienting than the worst hangover. It's like my entire body is a shell that no longer fits, though I could blame the discomfort on my clothing. Antonio's old suits just enhance the feeling of wrongness I haven't been able to shake since losing Vin. I can't even keep the days straight anymore. Or the time.

"You're late," a voice calls disapprovingly. I look down the wooden steps leading below, surprised by the change in the landscape. It's dark out now, and Luciano stands near the railing, his expression barely visible in the absence of sunlight.

"Got caught up," I lie, smoothing my hand over the front of my jacket. "I'm ready."

"It's about damn time," he remarks. He's changed, wearing a suit, his hair slicked to his skull. It's a throwback to the old days and the dress code Giovanni preferred. *Professional,* or so he called it. *You may act like an animal, but you dress like a man.*

Two other men lurk behind him, similarly dressed. Parked a few yards back is a car that looks like it was taken from

Antonio's harem of them. While I've been daydreaming, Luciano's been busy putting the plan into action—it's time to go on a field trip. If I'm going to make headway against the *mafiya,* then I need an audience with the Saleris.

Putting that aside, for now, I refocus my attention on the task at hand—getting there in one piece. "Is everything in place?"

Luciano nods. "This is Ash—" he points to a man beside him with black hair pulled into a ponytail. "And Sanders," he adds, gesturing toward another figure standing further back. "They'll play point on your crazy ass fucking trip."

I feel an eyebrow go up. "You aren't coming?"

He shakes his head. "I'll hold down the fort here. That is if you aren't blown apart by Mischa, in which case, I'll be waiting my turn." He laughs before clearing his throat. "Saleri is at a club he owns on the Strip—"

"*Felicità,*" I say, running my hands over the front of my suit. I swapped the gray for the black, and I prefer the fit. Tucked in the inner pocket is a certain knife, along with a pistol stolen from a stash Antonio kept behind his minibar. The drinks, however, I left untouched. My brain buzzes in the absence of alcohol, my thoughts clearer than ever. Sharp. This has to be the longest I've been sober in...

A long damn time. I inhale, relishing the tension in the air. Much like tonight's unofficial dress code, the mood reminds me of the old days. The perilous calm before preparing to do a job, knowing that the only thing at stake is power.

The one currency every man puts stock in.

"Don?"

"Yeah," I say absently. "I remember the place."

"Then you know security won't be a walk in the park—but it's neutral territory. If you can meet Gregori in person, maybe he *won't* shoot you on the fucking spot. Let's hope he hasn't realized what happened to his granddaughter."

My eyes narrow at the thought of her. *Kisa.*

"She's safe and sound," Luciano says as if reading my mind. "I suggest you use that fact to your advantage."

I raise an eyebrow. "I thought you might be above such a threat."

He shrugs, his expression suddenly serious. "That's the language the Saleris speak, those crazy motherfuckers. Threats. I hope you remember that. Anyway, you'll take this car—" he gestures to the red one. "The men will take the front and the rear. Now, what about your other guest..."

He trails off, presumably for the same reason the hairs on the back of my neck stand up. Said "guest" picks this moment to make her appearance, exiting from the apartment without being called. I don't look back, taking the stairs as if the devil is on my fucking heels.

She could be to blame for why my head feels so damn screwy. Hours in that suite with her and it's like recovering from a hangover to reenter the world again. A world that doesn't smell like roses, untainted by that childish fucking presence.

My reprieve won't last long. Just the time it takes to set off for the Saleris'. There, I'll have no choice but to endure her, *without* the benefit of being in another room.

"Let's go." I snatch the keys Luciano hands to me and enter the car. As the seconds pass, I wind up eyeing the dashboard, forced to wait. For her. Ten seconds. Twenty. A full minute…

It's like she's *intentionally* aiming to piss me off.

Or it could be that I'm not giving her enough credit. She might have run? Just as I start to scan the yard beyond the windshield, a flicker of movement catches my eye. When the passenger's side door finally opens, I say nothing, letting my hands palm the steering wheel. Though fuck, I should throw her in the trunk.

She must have showered again. Her skin carries a freshness that floods the car's interior as she settles onto the seat, closing the door.

Just like that, I relapse on roses. On *her*.

The only acknowledgment of her I allow myself is a single glance in the rearview mirror. Instantly, I regret it. She's ready for me, meeting my gaze without a hint of fear. Those eyes gleam, seemingly larger than usual. *Makeup,* I suspect. Thicker lashes and a line of dark kohl enhance the depth of her irises. They're endless.

Ripping my attention away, I focus on the road and hit the gas, following the van in front as it takes off toward the main gate.

I don't owe her a damn thing, not even an explanation—but if I want to play this right, I have no choice but to gauge her mental state. Did my words from the bathroom truly stick?

"I'm only going to tell you this once," I warn, fighting to keep my tone level. "You wanted to play this game? You play. If you're planning to escape, I suggest you think twice. That little girl…"

I hear rather than see her stiffen; the squeal of leather gives her away.

"Her life is on you," I say to twist the knife. Surprisingly, that's where I let the threat die. Why? Mentioning the Salvatore child at all is merely a formality.

I know that now, just from the stubborn tilt of her chin I catch when I sneak another glance her way. She'll accompany me if only for one reason, and what a childish reason it is. With her this close, I can't ignore her. She's aware of that. Fuck, I know she is—relishing the way I eye the road rather than look at her directly. Even as I do, my nostrils flare, swollen with her scent. Given the state of her, I might be imagining it, floral somehow without the aid of perfume or scented soap.

Roses. Goddamn roses.

I'd rather suffocate than breathe it in.

Unfortunately, dying isn't part of my plan. To outwit the Saleris, I'll need her on my side. We'll have to play the political games I used to hate. To his credit, I'd rather face Mischa than Gregori Saleri.

Mischa at least claims some semblance of honor to live by. The Saleris only understand greed, a philosophy that's allowed them to wrestle control over much of the city's central territory despite the *mafiya*. Aware of their dwindling share of power, they lord over what remains with an iron fist.

I've been to *Felicità* a few times, none remembered fondly. Smack-dab in the heart of the city's wealthy entertainment district, the strip club serves as a notorious front for the Saleris' rumored trafficking operation. The catch? The place is also the preferred haunt of politicians and businessmen alike, leaving no mystery as to why they've gone so long without being raided by the police.

Gregori Saleri must have studied at the same school Giovanni Rossi did when it came to maintaining a façade. No one, short of the *mafiya*, has a better operation.

Or a more tentative grasp on sanity. Known for both his ruthlessness and unpredictability, Gregori is an opponent I can't afford to underestimate. Unlike Antonio, he doesn't surround himself with five toy soldiers and a little girl, either. His men are well funded and expertly trained.

It'll take tact to circumvent them. There's no chance in hell I could fight them one on one. Sneaking in is also out of the question. No point in using blackmail either if my aim is to forge a peaceful conversation—leaving only one entry route.

To go in through the front fucking door and pray that Mischa or his *mafiya* aren't already inside.

On that point, at least, I have one note of reference to rely on—Mischa, the family man, wouldn't be caught dead in a skin bar while his wife is still in the hospital. No, if he met with Gregori, it had to be somewhere far from here, but that within itself presents another obstacle.

How to state my case *without* getting my head blown off, for one, and then there's the small detail of the woman…

Her scent floods my lungs, fighting for attention. It's harder than it should be to block her out. Hell, I'm edgier than I've been in years without a sip of alcohol to numb the anxiety —but the feeling isn't all bad. The adrenaline shooting through my veins recalls my early days in the *famiglia*. Back when Giovanni would throw me into the deep end, unconcerned whether I sank or swam. Survival depended solely on my own instincts back then. On my gut.

And right now? Every ounce of intuition I have tells me that the woman beside me holds the key to everything. Punishing Mischa. Reclaiming my throne.

Staying alive.

If only I can suppress the urge to wrap my hands around her neck.

She's too comfortable here. Despite sitting stiffly in her seat, there's no fight in her. We might as well be on our way to tea, given how she stares dispassionately from the windows.

It unnerves me to think that I might know exactly why she's so calm—for the same reason I am. Beneath the jittery tension fogging my thoughts lurks a chilling, ironclad patience I haven't felt…

Well, since I strangled Antonio Salvatore.

Could the little hellcat feel it too? I've never actually seen her under Mischa's spell or with her family—just a picture, that of a woman who seems worlds apart from the creature near me now. Oddly enough, I have no trouble envisioning how she must have looked.

Tense. Uncomfortable. The way I feel when shoved into a suit, attending some fancy fucking soiree when I know it's not where I belong. A caged bird never acts the way a wild one does—it can't. Life in false security robs it of the one thing it needs to feel alive—danger.

You set a dove loose, and it might fly right into the mouth of a wolf—but was it because life in the cage made it too naïve to the danger? Or was it just *that* damn desperate to feel the fear? The thrill. To tempt the forces, it was born to tempt.

My little bird? She's fluttering just beyond the reach of my mouth, too prideful to admit that's why she's really here— to watch me snap.

"Listen to me," I catch myself growling before I manage to wrestle my tone into some semblance of calm. "I could kill Mischa. Blow his fucking brains out."

She doesn't move a muscle, but I know she's listening.

"Or he can stay alive if you play your part. I could drag you in there, make those men think I ripped you from your safe little bed. I could…"

And she expects as much, her head held defiantly high. I lick my lower lip in anticipation of uttering the typical threat. *If you don't obey, I'll kill you.*

It's the only language anyone else would understand.

Not her… I suspect she's fluent in another tongue. One relying on subtler imagery. Taunts. Games. Hell, after her reaction in the barn—when I killed a man in front of her eyes—I think it's a dialect we share.

"You want to know how this story ends?" Dropping all malice from my voice, I speak to her the same way I'd talk to Vin. No…

I speak to her the way I'd talk to myself.

"You play the captive, Mischa comes for me—and I kill him. God, I want to. You *know* I want to."

From the corner of my eye, I watch her turn to stone. She can hear the honesty in my voice. The excitement too.

"But what would be the point? Your pretty little family gets torn apart," I add. "But mine already has been.

Vincenzo…" God, it stings just to say his name. "You want to help undo the damage Mischa's done? Then help me save his life. He's still alive."

Her sharp inhale triggers a reaction in me I don't expect. Surprise? I swallow hard, forced to admit that she might have some interest in saving him as well. Good. I've been wasting too much time, getting distracted at every fucking turn. He needs a hospital, and by God, I'll get him one.

"If you want to help him, then hear me out," I say. "When we get in there, follow my lead." I grind my teeth as if to stave off the words I wind up hissing anyway, "Want to prove your worth to me? Then save your family. Play the game."

As the words leave my mouth, I park. We're here, but I wrench open my door without giving her further instruction. Deep down, I already doubt this plan. I should make her squirm. Cry. Run.

By making her effectively a partner, I'm giving her a taste of power. And I'm fully aware that she might get addicted…

"So what's your plan?" one of the men calls from the van up ahead. I've parked on a side lot across from the building, forcing them to find their own spaces nearby. As they do, I try to come up with an answer to that very question.

"We go in through the front," I finally say, tugging at the collar of my suit jacket. "One of you comes in. The other stays out. Keep close, don't draw so much as a pair of nail clippers without my say so. Understood?"

The look they share between them speaks volumes—*This fucker is crazy.*

Without giving them the chance to argue, I step forward, jerking my chin toward the club. "Let's go."

"What about her?" one of them, Sanders, nods in the direction of someone behind me.

The soft thud of a door shutting is the only clue I have that she left the car. Her steps punctuate the air next, and I realize that I've yet to look at her fully. Is she wearing heels? She must be, enhancing her height enough to explain the warm breath ghosting the back of my neck.

*What about her?* My thigh twitches, desperate to keep moving without bothering to see if she follows. Let her run into the street. Fly away.

Let the little bird prove my point—that's exactly what she is.

Still, I find myself extending my hand out to no one anyway. A dare, perhaps. Or a test. As only cool air lashes at my palm, I get the response I want. Nothing. "Let's go." Curling a fist, I start walking.

A flurry of motion flashes in my peripheral vision. At the same moment a touch softer than silk brushes my hand— slim fingers boldly intertwining with my own. My first impulse is to jerk back before I come to my senses, snatching that grasping hand in a loose fist. Far from a romantic gesture, but at least my fingers aren't around her throat.

Voice rasping, I repeat my last command, "Let's go."

The men say nothing as I start forward, pulling a smaller body along. There's no need for stealth. I'm sure the second I cross the street that the entire place has already been alerted.

Predictably, the show of Saleri force is visible even from outside the building. Two men stand guard near the front door, with several more no doubt lurking nearby. Despite the intense security, it's telling that this place lacks the long lines that form outside the rest of the clubs on the Strip. One can't just enter *Felicità* uninvited. Only those who run this city have that privilege.

I rarely took advantage of that right. Even so, my reputation must proceed me. As I approach the nearest guard, his eyes narrow, his hand moving toward the inside of his suit jacket, presumably for a weapon.

Shit.

"Your boss is expecting me," I say before he can draw his gun. My tone alone makes him blink, fumbling for his headset. I hear a faint voice come from the other end, muffled and distorted. Barely recovered, he tries to wipe the shock from his face and nods. "You can head in."

His eyes dart from me to the woman by my side. I tighten my grip, hauling her through the glass doors, framed in gold, that make up the entrance. Does he recognize her? I can't tell, and I'm not inclined to find out.

Any second I expect to feel a bullet go through my skull—but at least one thing is on my side.

Optics. Shooting me here wouldn't go over well with the wealthy guests, and the Saleris subscribe to a different brand of extravagance than Antonio Salvatore. One that relies on maintaining a certain image.

Even if a rival barges inside unannounced.

Up ahead, a beautiful redhead stands guard beside a doorway leading to the main floor. She murmurs something worriedly into her headset. In the time it takes to approach her, I finally observe the figure to my right.

*Fuck.* Appreciation swells in my chest. Or shock. I could cruelly describe her image as a good girl obeying my wishes, but I'm not that cocky. Or stupid. She's an opponent, wearing the armor the war demands.

Beauty aside, I can now admit why the others reacted to her as they did. The dress suits her, even if it's too damn big. Paired with black heels, the effect isn't quite so glaring. She managed to dry her hair, letting it tumble freely down her shoulders in wild, loose curls. The makeup from this angle enhances her delicate features, adding an unexpected hardness to them.

She's more hellcat than dove, if only for a second.

A flurry of commotion draws my attention back through the doorway where a man now stands, his suit a deep shade of navy, his green eyes honing in on mine.

Son of a bitch. Rather than alert their security, they've sent out the welcome wagon.

"Donatello Vanici," the man coldly greets, his arms crossed. "You have some damn nerve showing your face here."

I notice he doesn't pair that statement with a threat—yet.

"Mateo Saleri," I reply, matching his icy tone. "Last I saw you, you were still in diapers. Don't tell me your father upgraded you to his doorman. I want to speak to him."

His eyes narrow. "Bold words for a wanted man." As he speaks, his attention flits to the woman, and his tongue traces his lower lip. "You even brought a diversion."

I tug her closer before I realize why. Not out of possessiveness, but prudence. To accompany nearly every rumor about the Saleris and their chosen business, is a horror story or two starring Mateo.

He's a fool, but a dangerous one.

"No time to share tonight," I warn.

"That's a damn shame." His gaze slithers over the woman again, but then he shrugs, turning on his heel. "This way."

He marches through a doorway leading onto the main floor. It's designed like a billiard room, with plush forest green carpeting and gold filigree wallpaper to complete the effect. A mahogany bar lines the back of the room, and positioned on either end of it are raised platforms where two beautiful women gyrate beneath the golden glow of a chandelier. My little guest falters, and I have a suspicion as to why.

"You're blushing," I warn, lowering my mouth near her ear. "Don't tell me. You've never seen much beyond your little school."

Apparently, the women in Stepanov manor don't prance around in tight black G-strings, their tits bared. An amusing suspicion sneaks into my skull—has she seen another *woman* naked, let alone a man?

To her credit, she keeps her face positioned away from me, and I shift my energy toward taking stock of the battlefield.

Apart from the main attraction, the layout of the club floor is nothing special. Men in leather armchairs watch the show from various positions as more women—clothed in black uniforms—circle around with trays of drink.

Giovanni brought me here once. Young as I was, I remember palming the ass of a dancer who jumped so violently she tripped, spilling her tray of drinks. No one ever had to convince me the rumors were true. I only have to remember that woman. Her eyes. I've never seen so much terror in one person.

To credit whatever good remained in my black soul, I kept Gregori and his brood at arm's length during my time at the helm of the *famiglia*. Any man rumored to trade in flesh and bone, isn't one I'd eagerly climb into bed with.

To be fair, he's done well enough without me.

Just as he had over a decade ago, the man himself sits at the very back of the room in the center of a leather booth built into the wall. Like a king, he lords over his domain, stuffed into a navy suit, his graying hair neatly combed. Nearly every fat finger sports a gold ring, his wrists dripping with diamond-encrusted cufflinks. His prized adornment at the moment is a brunette in a red dress lounging across his lap, lighting the cigar sticking from his mouth.

When his eyes settle on me, he undergoes an almost comical transformation. He huffs, his cheeks flushing red, and I spot at least ten men stiffen, instantly at attention.

*Shit.* The back of my neck prickles, and I curl my free hand into a fist to keep from drawing my weapon. Coming here with only two men for backup was a brazen move. Even more brazen? Parading Mischa Stepanov's missing daughter on my arm.

She draws notice from every direction as we cross the room, my own included. There are a million other things that should consume my interest—staying alive for one.

Even in this unfamiliar realm, her eyes blaze with irresistible fire, her red lips pursed in contemplation. Her mind is an open book, mine for the taking. I can read her the same way I did in the barn, crouched over Paulie Vanetti. Like me, she sees the folly of this plan.

*Do you know what you're doing, Donatello?*

I don't. Though I can only blame myself if this backfires. Or *her*—the innocent Stepanova is a factor I haven't seriously assessed until now. A girl who's never ventured inside a club before, let alone seen a man. It's pure insanity to expect she could play along.

"Wait." I release her hand, tracing a path up to her shoulders as I bring my mouth near her ear again. "This is your moment, hellcat. Prove me wrong. You're loving this, aren't you?"

Her answering shiver ripples through my tentative grip. *Yes.* She's excited, though she flattens those red lips in a vain attempt to disguise it. Intrigued, I risk ignoring Gregori and his brood to step closer to her, leveraging my weight against her slight frame.

She shivers again as I swipe my thumb through her hair, tucking a strand behind her ear. On this battlefield, it would only make sense for her to falter, woefully unmatched.

But I swear I catch her inhale. See the muscle rippling in her shoulders as she keeps her head high. Her eyelids flutter, and I can envision the mental commands she must give herself, a list of them—*Focus. Breathe... Fight.* As unmatched as she is, she proves to possess her own weapon in this war with one simple motion. The art of surprise. She leans into my touch, and I'm the one caught off guard.

She looks at me directly, and my breath hitches in my chest, a guttural sound revving in my throat. In her eyes is a simple challenge as clear as day—*You don't own me. You don't control me.*

And there's more.

*You don't scare me. Give me what you promised*—Mischa alive, a bloody war subverted.

She's right, but for a second, I forget why. I'd allow for an entire bloodbath if only to clear my fucking head. In her eyes, I lose track of everything...

Until they narrow, cutting away from me toward a figure watching us both.

"Donatello Vanici," Gregori says, now holding the cigar between two fingers, each capped by a fat gold ring.

Shit. I grab her hand purely out of instinct—a response to the possessive stare I sense grazing her body from head to toe.

Unlike his son, this man knows better than to openly show his unease. He forces a smile instead, revealing a missing front tooth beneath his graying mustache. Word on the street is that a rival knocked it out in his early days, and despite his wealth, he never had it fixed.

Perhaps for the same reason Giovanni openly sported a scar on his throat, left by a would-be murder attempt. *If anyone ever manages to get that close to you, they deserve to leave a scar,* he used to say. *Let it serve as a reminder—don't let it fucking happen again.*

I'm suddenly aware of the marks on my face, left by a writhing hellcat. They burn in her presence, and I feel the animalistic urge to return the favor. Mark her. Make her bleed...

"To what do I owe this visit?" Gregori asks. With a wave of his free hand, he sends his companion scurrying, but at least four men appear nearby to replace her. They merely watch.

For now.

Every passing second enhances the tension in this room. My gun is a lead weight in my jacket pocket, my fist a useless display. Forcing the fingers of that hand open, I tighten the opposite one, trapping the fragile digits caught within it. In essence, *she* is the only weapon I need.

"Don't tell me you came for the hell of it," Gregori taunts when I remain silent. "Or maybe you wanted to enjoy the show? Though, you always seemed too high and mighty to have your cock stroked—"

"I'm here about Mischa Stepanov," I correct, stepping forward to take the hand the old man offers me. I shake it once, but when he turns to the woman, I decline for her. Who knows where that hand has been.

"Dear Mischa?" Gregori raises an eyebrow. "You have my attention."

"I'm sure Mischa's already come to you with some sordid little story meant to provoke you into joining his crusade against me," I say, cutting to the chase. "What was it? That I'm a kidnapper? Attempted child-murderer? Outright asshole?"

"Among other things," Gregori says offhandedly. He leans back against his leather seat, inhaling from his cigar. A gold ashtray sits next to him, and he casually flicks a heap of ash into it. "Though who the fuck cares what the truth is? Mischa has money and power on his side. What do you have?"

Always to the point he was. Our dealings weren't many, but after every one, I distinctly remember the feeling of being fleeced, and the sudden need to take a shower.

"I'll tell you—" the old man pauses to take a puff from his cigar. His next word punctuates the cloud of smoke he exhales. "Nothing. Your harbor just went up in flames. You have no ties to the *famiglia.* From what I hear, you're a wanted man with a price on your head. Stepanov promised to make it worth my while if I helped him find you. I just never thought you'd stroll right up to me and present your fucking neck." He snaps his fingers, and one of his men takes a menacing step forward.

I think my laugh is what startles him into backing down. Hell, the sound startles *me,* so rich it's damn near genuine.

"Is that all? 'Worth your while'?" I parrot. "I think I can do a bit better than that."

"Oh?" Gregori inclines his head, his beady eyes narrowing. "You seem rather confident for a dead man walking, Vanici."

"Confident, yes," I counter. "Dead? Well, the devil must be shit at his job because as far as I know, I'm still fucking alive."

Painfully, goddamn *alive.* Even while Vin treads somewhere in limbo, wasting away while I waste more time.

"Hmph," Gregori huffs. "You and I both know that fact depends on how long you manage to stay out of *mafiya* hands." He drags on his cigar before tossing it aside for good. With both hands braced over his knees, he sits forward, his beady eyes suddenly flashing with interest. "You think you can offer me money? I doubt you have enough to outbid Mischa. Besides, I wouldn't be fool enough to stand with you alone. Even your reputation isn't quite that fearsome. Stand against the *mafiya,* and you'd be dead before you opened that smart fucking mouth."

"Funny," I snap. "My mouth is open now."

"Smart-ass." He goes red, his cheeks puffing. I glance at his men, but none of them move—a fact that doesn't comfort me one damn bit. I've already boxed myself in, and I'd bet my ass that Mischa Stepanov is on his way here.

It's killing me not to grab my gun. Desperate to do *something,* I grip my tie and tug. As I do, the hand in my other grasp flutters as if to remind me of what little power I do have.

"You're right," I admit. "I don't have a lot of time, so hear me well, Gregori. You say I have nothing? You're wrong—I have all of the *famiglia* at my back."

"The *famiglia?*" Gregori snorts, slapping his thigh. "Even after all these years, your sense of humor is legendary, Donatello. Antonio's a stupid cunt, but he's not that stupid. No way would he welcome you back."

I smile wide. "You're right. It's a damn good thing then that Antonio Salvatore is dead."

The reaction couldn't have been scripted to have more impact. The entire room goes silent. You could hear a pin drop—or Mateo Saleri grunt as he rushes to stand beside his father. Gone is his smug sneer. His eyes home in on mine, openly suspicious.

"You?" He laughs. "I don't buy it."

"You should," I say, letting my voice carry throughout the entire room. "Antonio took money to 'buy' a hit on the Stepanovs. He set me up, and I have his patsy on video admitting it all. Mischa has it as well, by the way," I add. Predictably, Gregori pales with horror. Whether he believes me or not is beside the point. If Mischa didn't confront him with this information, there had to be a reason.

Smiling, I voice it out loud, "Do you really think he'll believe Antonio acted alone? Like you said, he was a stupid son of a bitch. Too stupid to come up with something like that without help. Now his father-in-law? I don't think anyone would call you *naïve*, Gregori."

He sputters, his cheeks turning even redder. I think he'd launch himself at me if he could, which makes the fact that he isn't more glaring. Another telling sign is that his men still don't make a move.

"If Mischa's not suspecting you now, it's only a matter of time," I say. "We both know Antonio was too greedy for his own fucking good."

"Where is your proof that he's dead?" he demands, throwing his bejeweled hands into the air. "Are we just supposed to take your word for it?"

"Go to his mansion and see for yourself," I say. "His body should still be there."

"What?" Gregori nearly falls out of his seat. "You went to his home?" Suddenly, something seems to dawn on him. His eyes go wide, his jaw slack. "Kisa—"

"Your granddaughter is alive," I say. "For now. I shouldn't have to add that threat, but if you wanted a reason not to attack me, there it is."

The man sputters, turning five fucking different shades of red all within the span of a few heartbeats. "You bastard! I should—"

"I have a man with a blade at little Kisa's throat, waiting for my signal. If he doesn't hear from me, the knife bites deep. I can assure you, you won't find her in time."

His eyes bug as he mulls whether I'm bluffing or not.

I am. But he doesn't know it.

Neither does the woman. Her fingers buck against mine, desperate to wrench away in disgust. I have no doubt that she'll whirl on me, brandishing those hellcat nails with righteous indignation.

"Trust me," I hiss through my teeth loud enough for only her to hear.

She goes still, and I barely refocus on Gregori in time to catch the moment he nods toward one of his men, who finally reaches inside his suit jacket. *Shit.*

"You can kill me," I say quickly. "Or you can prove that you're smarter than Antonio. I don't want a war. Not even with Mischa."

Mateo raises his hand, and his man stands down. "So what do you want? You think Mischa will take the time to hear your threats before he runs you through?"

I force a harsh laugh. "Mischa needs to stop and ask himself why he truly attacked me. Faulty intel? Or the pride of a man too stubborn to admit that he can't even control his own daughter?"

The father and son share a glance. Mateo returns his attention to me first, an eyebrow raised. "From what I heard, you dragged that daughter from her own fucking birthday party and did what men like you do."

I laugh again even as the fingers in my grasp turn to stone. "And what was that?"

He demurs with a smile that doesn't reach his eyes. "I'd rather not say in front of the lady."

"*This* lady?" I tug her forward, surprised when she obeys, coming to stand before me. "You mean Willow Stepanova, unharmed and un-assaulted?"

Even before the words finish leaving my mouth, my eyes go down to her neck, but the bruises I expect to find have vanished. Makeup, I realize, even before I settle over that red mouth, unable to suppress my own confusion. She covered them. Why?

Belatedly, I remember my warning to her—*Play your role.*

"You are a fool," Gregori snarls, lurching to his feet. "To parade the girl here—"

"Parade?" I grab her shoulder, feeling the delicate bones flex beneath my grip. It's not a restraint—but a warning to the men who advance. Sure enough, they stop short, but one of them finally draws a pistol from his jacket pocket. I'm painfully aware of the time it would take to grab my own. Too long. *Fuck.*

All I can do is keep playing the long game.

"You believed Mischa's fairy tales without stopping to ask yourself how I could break into his manor and drag the girl out not once but *twice*," I point out, thinking fast. "You've been to Stepanov manor. I'd need an army, which you just pointed out I don't have."

The two men share another searching look, but I don't miss the overriding emotion they both sport in the end. Greed.

"But you know what I do have?" I add, sliding my hand over the soft collar bone beneath it, grazing a trembling throat. "I have Mischa's daughter, in love with me despite her father's disagreement."

I don't look at her face as I spout that bullshit lie. Instead, I slip my fingers into her hair, controlling her scalp. Despite the contact, I still expect her to run. Wince, anything.

Anything but remain by my side, seemingly endorsing the lie.

"Love?" Mateo sneers, drawing my attention. "Isn't she a bit too young for you?"

"The last time I checked, nineteen wasn't the age of a child," I counter with a confidence I don't feel. Against my palm, the brush of her skin contradicts me—soft. Fresh. Innocent. My throat goes dry, and I force a swallow. "Mischa's pride has made him desperate to start a war. Do you really want to align yourself with him all in the name of a petty feud? I'm not asking for your loyalty."

"So, what do you want?" Gregori demands.

"It's simple—stay out of my way."

Mateo hisses. "And if you're the liar? How the fuck do we even know you're telling the truth? I'm of mind to think you did rape the girl—"

My pulse surges, drowning him out. I can't resist the allure anymore—my eyes are on her. Her mouth. Those lips. If only I could make them talk to parrot whatever I want. Her silence is my limitation, and a paranoid part of me wonders if the little witch was banking on that.

I can't make her say the right words, so what use is this ruse?

I'll always be the monster in comparison. Perhaps I should fall back to plan B instead? Make it known that she's my captive, my hostage—her life is mine until my demands are met.

But then I see those eyes. They flit up to mine, smugly aware of my shift in thinking. She's too coy to smile in triumph or savor her victory some other way. She just stares, a corner of her mouth tilted in silent admonishment.

*You were wrong,* she taunts with that expression. *Wrong. No one would ever believe I'm in love with you. No one.*

My hand is against the side of her throat before I can stop myself. *Good.* Choking her out would be a decent step toward plan B. Her eyes widen as if she's reading my mind, and I can only stare as she comes up with her own strategy on the spot.

It's so predictable. I called her maturity into question. So, like any child desperate to participate in a round of chess, she clumsily reaches for the nearest piece she can touch, knocking over everything else in her path.

In this case? Her piece is me.

Her fingers splay against my wounded cheek. Before I can even tense to avoid her attack, she lunges, lurching onto the tips of her toes, narrowing the distance between us.

My breath hisses through my teeth. *Damn her.* I know her aim the second her eyes go to my mouth—but I'm even more sure of the fact that she won't carry through. She'll cower in the end. Slap me. Try to run.

Those lips won't brush mine with a hesitance that fractures my resolve more than a bullet to the head would. It's like I *have* been shot. My mind goes blank. Her breath is on my skin, her mouth so soft it's like fucking silk…

My lips part, drinking in her taste however faint it is. Like fire and spice—the very embodiment of the lighter fluid I doused myself in at Havienna. Only in this instance, she's both an accelerant and a match.

An inferno.

A drug.

A low grunt catches in my throat, my fingers grasping for a slender hip to steady her as I inhale, our lips a breath apart. She deliberately lingers here, daring me to react.

Because I've already failed. Her scent is a poison, made ten times more effective by her nearness. I'm struck by both. Defeated. A surge of lust overwhelms every other thought. I want more. Crave it.

Until I remember who she is. What she is.

I recoil from her so violently she staggers. I only have a second to remember where I am. What I'm doing. Reflexively, I snatch her arm, keeping her close, but it's too late. I'm off balance.

Any second, the Saleris will attack, unconvinced by the charade.

But they don't...

It takes me a second to realize why. She may have been foolish, but her childish, idiotic move did what I don't think I could have achieved short of snapping her neck—it got their attention.

"I'm warning you now, you don't want part of Mischa's family feud," I rasp, looking up to find them still watching. "Stay out of it."

"Or what?" Gregori purses his fat lips, grasping for another cigar from an ornate box beside him.

"Or you'll get the same treatment as Antonio," I reply without a hint of irony. "Little Kisa's already lost so much… I'd hate to see her suffer any more."

"Bold words," Mateo snarls. "What's to stop me from ordering my men to put a bullet in your brain now, taking the girl, and calling your bluff?"

*Nothing,* I realize. Still, I smile.

"I'll tell you what you stand to gain instead—leverage. Mischa went after me out of spite and nearly killed my nephew in the process. Do you really think that you can stand in the way of what he truly wants? He aims to cement power for himself. Seize the moment and seat himself at the head of the table. By staying neutral, you can leave two men to settle our differences and keep him in check."

"Don't tell me peace is what you're after," Gregori spits. He's fully righted himself, his brow furrowing. If he didn't believe at least half of what I've said, I doubt I'd still be standing here. "What do you really want?"

My brain spins its own answer to that question—*Dark eyes on mine, the scent of roses in my lungs, the taste of spice on my tongue. Her. As much as I can take…*

What the hell? Blinking, I swat the images aside. "I want your men to stand down so I can return to my operations at the harbor," I insist. "I don't want an alliance—but I do want reassurance and the ability to move freely throughout your territory. Your voice alone can sway the less powerful factions."

"That can't be all," Gregori spits.

I nod. "I want you to put out the word that Mischa is reckless, and you're staying out of his fight. Let the *mafiya* stand on their own. You can see for yourself that his crusade was based on a lie—" I jerk my chin toward the girl.

The action should seem performative at best. There's no way in hell we've convinced them. No way.

But Gregori's eyes betray none of the doubt they should. Scowling, he strokes his chin. "So what? You fuck Mischa's daughter and expect to fend off a war? I heard you were one of the few men who *don't* think with your cock."

When I snatch the woman's hand this time, it isn't for show. I crush her fingers. If she had a voice, she'd cry out.

"I'm going to marry her," I declare. The conviction in my own voice shocks me, but there's no point in playing coy now. "Let's see how far her father is prepared to go. He can hunt me down, but she'll be in the crossfire."

My voice bellows throughout the room as if I suspect the *mafiya* is already lurking inside, listening to every word. I hope so. I hope Mischa has a bird's eye view.

"And," I add. "If Mischa is willing to own up to his mistake and aim for peace, I'll be waiting."

Gregori is the one smiling now, but it's one of grim admiration. A wolf in grudging respect of another who took down a prey item everyone else was too afraid to.

"You twisted son of a bitch. You have balls, I'll give you that."

I force my lips into the shadow of a smile. "I'll send your invitation in the mail."

He sputters, and I have enough sense to read the room. *Times up.* I spin on my heel, heading back through the showroom, woman in tow. During our friendly conversation, the place has all but cleared out. It's a bad sign. If I were a betting man, I'd suspect that if the *mafiya* isn't already outside, lying in wait, they're not far off.

*Fuck.*

"What about my granddaughter?" Gregori asks as we near the exit untouched. Apparently, that threat hit its target. "If you touch her, I swear to God I'll gut you like a pig—"

"You can see her at my wedding," I counter from over my shoulder. "Have a nice night. In the morning, I expect your men to stand down. I'll send your regards to little Kisa."

Only now do I realize how big a fucking gamble I took by coming here—and for nothing. That show alone shouldn't have been enough.

Any second, I'll feel a bullet in my back…

But I don't. Not when we enter the lobby and not even as I push through the main doors, finding the street beyond deserted, but devoid of *mafiya* soldiers.

There's always the chance for a sniper. Taking cover should be my primary concern—not vengeance. The longer I remain sober, the less my brain seems inclined toward logical thinking. Rage wins out.

Growling, I tug the girl closer, bringing my mouth near her ear. "Don't you ever do something like that again. *Ever.*"

Fuck the game. She's banned from playing. My mouth stings with the remnants of that little stunt, and I know damn well why she did it. The answer glints in her gaze even now.

*I'm going to play,* she seethes. *You motherfucker, I'm going to play, and make you regret ever letting me touch a single piece. You can't control me.*

I shove her away, heading toward the car without bothering to see if she follows. She will. After all, she's made herself a vital pawn. My willing little fiancée.

It's one thing to taunt her with that future. Torment her with it.

It's another thing entirely to have her turn the tables. The worst part? It could fucking work...

Mischa can't hide behind the shield of being a vengeful father anymore. To anyone on the outside, he'll appear to be merely an obstacle, lashing out at a man he doesn't like over the affairs of his young daughter's heart.

It's the shit tragedies are made of. Giovanni Rossi himself couldn't have come up with a better cover story.

And I hate the mere thought of playing along. Why?

It's her doing. *Her* game.

The little bitch attempted her own fucking checkmate. To keep the ruse going, I need to play my part, though admittedly only in public.

In private, she's still what I want her to be—an enemy. A captive. Mine. Bruises aren't all makeup can hide…

"Where to now, sir?" Sanders prompts. I almost forgot the man's been here all along. To his credit, he's done his job—having my back and staying unnoticed. "I don't like being out in the open."

He's right.

"We'll be followed, so we can't go back to West Helm," I say, crossing the street to where the cars are.

But there's a better option.

"I know where we'll go. Have Luciano meet us there with the Salvatore girl—" Approaching footsteps consume my notice. *Her.* Good. I want her to hear this especially. Inclining my head, I look dead in her eyes as I say, "We're going home."

# 16

## WILLOW

A reprise—the repetition of several notes—is a hallmark of most musical compositions, one I always admired. When properly placed, the effect is a perfect illustration of the entire piece coming full circle.

I just never realized how horrible a concept it can be to endure in real life. To repeat, re-live and experience the same dramatic series of notes all over again.

Different and distorted but the *same*.

It's a vicious, twisted reprise to be here after seven years. Inside this house. In this small pink room that feels like a stranger's. In some ways, it is. Safiya no longer belongs to me.

She's become the creation of Donatello Vanici. Jealously, he hoards all memory of her. I can't even recall a single one without feeling like I'm intruding on someone else's life.

Someone else's pain.

Her room feels equally foreign, and that's exactly why he put me here. To hurt me. To force me to view the old, narrow mattress propped against the wall, and the bed frame coated in dust. To make me realize what he's done.

He owns her, reducing that little girl to nothing more than a series of stacked boxes. They take up a single corner and aren't labeled, but I know what's in them before I even peer inside the topmost one.

Toys, dolls, clothing—all of it.

The sight hits like a punch to the chest, and I grapple for stability, bracing my hand against the wall. These things…

He kept them all, letting them fester in this old, abandoned house, collecting dust and cobwebs. Why? My eyes water as I view this place for what it really is—my grave. *This* is his shrine to a dead girl.

This entire house has become nothing more than his crypt. Around me, the structure rattles to life, forced to accommodate living beings again. The walls are as ineffective as tissue paper against the sounds betraying the presence of at least a dozen strangers, picking their way through the various rooms, including the one next to mine. Vincenzo's old room…

"No!" A tiny voice seeps through the barrier between us, but I doubt I'm hallucinating. It sounded too soft to be from a memory. Not Vin. "I'm not sleepy," they assert.

The little girl? She sounds louder, insistent on that one point. Amid this insane ordeal, she doesn't want to sleep.

"Quiet," a male shushes her, his tone gentle. "You gotta try, honey. Just close your eyes…"

The genuine note of kindness differentiates this baritone from Donatello. Which one of these men took it upon himself to care for her? The gray-eyed figure?

My heart breaks as I remember that I'm not the only one captive to the whims of Donatello Vanici. I can only imagine how she's coping. Though how would any other little girl? I think of Aljona and Marnie and feel my throat thicken. I left them asleep in their nursery, but how did they react to wake up and find me gone? And their mother and brother?

Creeping in circles is the only way I can drown out the thoughts, letting my feet noisily prod the old floorboards—but I'm not alone.

Another set of footsteps ring out to echo mine, sounding just beyond this room. They're too heavy to be a child's. Unsteady. Their familiar cadence instantly brings a suspect to mind.

*Donatello.*

He's pacing as well. Each heavy footfall echoes off the walls, reverberating through the thin barrier between us. It's as fitting a soundtrack as any to mark this moment—steady, relentless, violent noise. In a sense, another sort of reprise, recalling the twisted events that unfolded the last time we were here alone.

Fighting. Struggling. Almost burning alive…

I shudder, ghosting my fingers along my throat, feeling the bruises throb. Some sting more than the others, and I prod those spots the most. I want to feel that pain.

Maybe it can distract from my mouth. My lips still burn with the heat of his breath. They ache, though barely touched in reality.

*Damn him.* My eyes burn, spilling fresh hot tears—but I don't know why. It's harder to breathe this dusty air. Harder to think. Frustrated, I cross the room, hammering my feet against the floor to drown out his noise. Reaching the nearest window, I throw it open and lean out, gulping at the night air.

All the bracing cold does is highlight my searing cheeks, no doubt blushing red. Not because of shame. I did what he wanted me to do. What he all but *threatened* me to do. I played along.

And he pushed me away, scolding my actions as though I were a naughty child. Not because I refused to take part in his twisted charade…

Because I played too well. I kissed him—and in the process, I made Mischa look like a fool. Mischa… One of the few people who has ever truly cared for me.

My breaths come faster when I think of him. To distract from the guilt, I eye the moon above, partially obscured by gently swaying trees. I'd give anything to know that Mischa's men were out there now, creeping closer to this embodiment of hell. Evgeni, his charming grin flattened into a frown—he'd lead the charge to rescue me.

I *need* to be rescued.

*Ha,* a part of me scoffs. *Donatello needs to be rescued. From you...*

I hate him. God, I hate him. Hate so potent I can taste it. Feel it. I dig my nails into my palms so hard I jump, but the biting sting isn't nearly sharp enough to counter the remnants of him.

On my throat. My lips. *God,* my entire body hums with the aftereffects of Donatello Vanici in some way or another.

*Damn him.*

I bare my teeth, wishing with all of my soul that I could scream. He couldn't ignore me then. If I could throw his own silly hypocrisy in his face, he'd hear me. If I had a knife, I'd lash at his skin and carve my new name across his chest...

Perhaps he'd acknowledge the truth.

If either of us has a right to torment the other, it's me. I'm the one with the right to strip *him* naked and subject him to torture. The one with the right to shove a blade in his hand and taunt him with how far he's willing to go.

I'm the one with the right to hate him.

*Damn him!*

I push away from the window, glaring at these pretty pink walls with even more disgust. Once, they made me feel so safe. So protected.

It horrifies me to remember that he even painted them himself.

And now? They make for the worst kind of prison. Bars would be preferable. Locked in a cage, I'd have an excuse for staying this long.

My heart pounds with renewed purpose as I scan the room in a different light. I should run now, taking the girl with me. Traversing the woods on foot should be a fate preferable to Donatello Vanici any day. The window is an option, but risky in the dark.

The easiest way out is right through the front door.

Let him try to stop me.

I take a step purposefully toward the hall. At that exact moment, a different set of footsteps advances in my direction. The ominous thud stops me cold. A coincidence? I tiptoe closer to the door, only to hear those same footsteps echo me in tandem.

Step.

Thump.

Step.

We're in a silent game, my noisy shadow and I. By the time I reach the door, the tension is palpable. My racing heartbeat ticks the seconds down like a metronome.

*Tick, tick, tick...*

Feeding on the anxiety, my opponent waits until I brace my hand against the doorknob to finally speak. "Now, you want to hide, little hellcat? Don't tell me you've changed your mind."

I stiffen. *Changed my mind.* Like I ever had a choice.

"You weren't afraid before," he adds. *Before*—standing in a realm of strange men with him at my side. Performing the very damn act he wanted me to. *Play*, he said. And I did.

But it wasn't good enough for him.

"You don't get to hide now," he warns. "So you've changed your mind? Come and face me."

His taunt slithers through the barrier of the door and into my head, impossible to ignore. "You've stayed this long," he points out softly. "But it's good if you run now. I've scared you. At least let me see that fear for myself."

The door flies open without an attempt on my end. Donatello stands behind it, still dressed in the pristine suit he wore to the club—but his expression? His eyes blaze, set in his skull like burning coals.

I shock myself by meeting those eyes without flinching. Outwardly, at least. For once, intimidation isn't his aim. Narrowed, he drags his attention lower, fixating on my chest. I flinch. It's like he sees through flesh and bone right down to the rapidly beating heart beneath.

"Do you want to know why I brought you here?" he asks.

I make my entire body rigid, depriving him of an answer.

"As proof," he says simply. "You may look like Safiya. You may share her memories—but you are not her."

Each word lands like the cruelest foundation of a sick joke. That perfect, innocent little girl he knew once upon a time. The one who loved him so damn much. The one whose innocence he shattered.

*This,* I realize, is his method of punishment for my actions at the club—using memories as his cudgel. Not only will he deny me my past identity. He still cherishes her.

"You can't be."

He's in front of me before I can fully recover. Throat tight, all I can do is stare as he reaches out, cupping my chin against his palm. Without warning, his thumb shoots along my lower lip with a precision that stings.

"She wouldn't kiss me," he declares.

So that's what this is really about. I kissed him, and he makes it sound so vile an act. As though I wanted to. As though I enjoyed the feeling…

I almost can't process the sickening insinuation. My mind goes blank as I try. Thoughts shut down.

"Do you deny it?" His eyes trace my mouth as if the flesh alone contains the truth. *No.* "Don't tell me that was your first kiss. Wasted on a silly little stunt."

The reproach in his voice comes as a shock. I grit my teeth, glaring in a way that I hope conveys the obvious—*no.*

"Liar," he scolds. His nostrils flare, eyes narrowing a fraction of an inch. I've angered him. "I was the first man to kiss you. Wasn't I?"

The first man to kiss me. To see me naked. To taunt me with the nature of my sex and lord my ignorance over me. He's the first, alright. The first to force his way inside me to test my purity.

But when utilized against *him,* my maturity is a step too far.

Poor Donatello. I've insulted his sense of decency.

"Did you think that was funny?" he demands. "A little game? Next time, I suggest you not flaunt yourself in front of goddamn sex traffickers. Did you hear me?"

He's closer. Too close. Distractingly, his thumb returns, drifting up to my cheek. With a subtle bit of applied pressure, he manipulates me into facing him fully.

"You realize what you've done? Don't ignore me," he warns as my eyelids threaten to lower. "Don't hide from it. You can't. I should know. I've spent nearly a decade hiding."

It's the first time he's directly referenced the past without hate or pain in his voice. Just emptiness. *Damn him.* He doesn't get to do this. Ask probing questions as if he's entitled to any answers.

I wrench away from him to eye the wall. His laughter, however, chases me.

"You think I've gone insane," he declares, once again worming his way into my skull unbidden. I can feel him in there, slinking through my thoughts as boldly as he pleases. His fingers seem determined to do the same to the rest of me. One captures my chin while the other strokes the hair from my face, leaving nothing to obscure my view of him.

A stern frown makes his point painfully obvious—my body is *his* tool to utilize. Not mine.

"Don't you? You think I've lost my mind, but you haven't stopped to consider the obvious, little hellcat? You're just as insane as I am," he says with a venom reserved for the nastiest of insults. "I can smell it on you. That anger. The rage. You feel it creeping through your soul no matter how hard you try to ignore it. That pretty life as a safe little musician never suited you, did it?"

Hooded, his eyes toy with my frame, hovering over the parts of me that make my cheeks flame more than when he had me strip for him.

Not my breasts or my hips, but my hands. He inspects them in that way only he has ever been capable of—this peeling, constricting ability to reduce anything before him to the barest bones.

"These hands…" He moves too quickly to counter, grabbing one of them. Deftly, he displays my palm, pressing his thumb against the center of it. His gaze cuts up to mine, ablaze with mocking. "These hands weren't made for music."

He manipulates my fingers as I watch, contorting them to press against his chest.

"I know how you really want to use these pretty hands, hellcat," he gloats as I struggle in vain to pull away. I can feel the coiling muscle beneath my touch, dangerous and thick. His warmth. The surge of his heartbeat, hammering against me as effectively as any weapon.

*Thump. Thump. Thump!*

"To kill," he says over the pulsating noise. "Maim. Rip me open. Go on. Do it."

I'm in that open room again, crouching near a puddle of blood as he shoves a knife into my hand. *You want pain,* he taunted. *You want him to suffer, just as you suffered. Am I wrong?*

Maybe he wasn't. In that brief moment, I had felt something stir to life inside me that I can't deny. Curiosity.

And I feel it now, building as he lets me go.

"Do it." Stepping back, he extends his arms in welcome while I stumble to find my balance. A smile shapes his mouth, but it's wild. Crazed.

"Don't tell me that you need your little weapon—" he reaches into the pocket of his jacket for an item I instantly recognize. My knife. He dangles it between two fingers before tossing it into the air and catching it by the handle. Smiling, he presents it to me flat against his palm.

"Don't be shy. Take it. Now."

I'm not given a chance to refuse. He lashes out, seizing my wrist. My breath sticks in my lungs as the edge of the blade grazes the flesh of my forearm. Gently, but the warning is unmistakable.

"You want to hurt me, hellcat," he goads. "So go on, then. I'm sure you could make a mark if you tried."

And he wants me to. I can see that desire flashing clearly in his eyes.

He wants the fight. The thrill.

But most of all, he wants me to forget the only weapon I've been able to effectively wield against him—*myself.*

The longer I face him, the more unsteady I feel. Like a fallen soldier lost amid a minefield. One wrong move may be my last, but I have no choice but to navigate a way out.

He wants me to stab him? I feel a desperate urge to do the opposite. Deny him the pleasure of predicting my actions. Controlling me.

He can't.

At first, I don't understand why I slide my hand along my waist, cinching a fistful of my skirt. The fabric is so thin that the excess material clings to me, enhancing my body's curves.

And he notices, recoiling a fraction of an inch.

"Enough!" Already, he's recovered, sporting that judgmental sneer. "You hate me, little hellcat. Don't go out of your way to claim mercy now. Finish me off. Now! Do it!"

He raises the blade again, offering it hilt-first.

I don't move.

"Take it!" He grabs my wrist, wrenching me against him. His other hand sinks through my hair, seizing a fistful to keep me in place as he lowers his mouth to my ear. "Any innocent, childish fantasies you still harbor? Forget them," he snaps. "I won't hesitate to hurt you."

And yet, his touch doesn't match his words. Firm but not painful. His fingers shake, entwined within the strands of my hair as if he wants nothing more than to pull away.

He can read me so easily, but I marvel at the fact that, even after all this time, I can still interpret some piece of him, however small. His heart doesn't lie. I reach out willingly this time, finding the same spot on his chest he made me touch a minute ago.

It thrums with a steady pulse, so strong my fingertips burn in the aftermath. This simple melody sparks a revelation inside me. No, he doesn't like it when I touch him.

He doesn't like when I kiss him.

He doesn't *like* when he can't predict me…

He craves it. All of it. More than the violence, he craves the chaos.

As if to validate that notion, he raises the knife, bringing it near my throat. Merely to watch me react, I suspect—and I reward him with a trembling breath. "You want to play? Then let's play."

Alarm grips my spine as the edge of the blade kisses the skin above my pulse point. He lets it linger there before moving it up, up…above my head entirely.

"A real game this time. Which one? I know, hide and seek," he decides, letting me go, knife in hand. "Let's play it now. I'll hide this blade, little hellcat—and you better pray that you find it. I'll even give you time to search. Turn around."

My breathing hitches, my knees locking in defiance.

He laughs, and this unsteady display of noise reveals his true feelings better than if he spoke them explicitly—he needs me unnerved. He needs me to fear him. It's the only way he can remain in control.

"Turn around, hellcat. Do it—"

I spin on my own, robbing him of the chance to fully voice the command. His harsh exhale betrays his disappointment. He didn't predict that.

Nonetheless, his steps track his journey across the room. Toward the pile of boxes in the corner. Curiosity itches my brain, and I have to dig my heels into the floor to keep from watching him.

Already, he's moving away, heading for the doorway. "Find it," he taunts. "I'll be waiting when you—"

I lunge so quickly the rush of air racing through my ears drowns him out. I practically throw myself in the corner he just vacated, preparing to rip open a box and hunt. I don't need to. *There…*

He left it out in the open, daring me to claim it.

I snatch the blade, shivering as my thumb grazes the name etched into the handle—*Mouse*. That sheltered, rescued girl, daughter of a crime lord. She's as distant to me now as Safiya. A mask. A role I had to play.

Stripped of both identities, who am I?

That question feels unanswerable as I whirl around to find a monster lurking in the doorway. As I brandish the blade, he smiles, and my stomach lurches. God, he craves to fight me so badly. To have me throw myself at him. Claw at him. Scream for his attention.

This time, I don't. I slash the blade at my own throat, and I couldn't begin to predict his reaction—rage.

"No!" He roars, lunging toward me. "What the hell is—" He practically skids to a stop when he realizes I'm not bleeding.

I didn't cut my skin…and yet, the cool air assaulting the left side of my chest stings just as much as any stab wound. The thin strap has been cut, letting the material dip without support. I shiver, hating my body's instinctive reaction. The bastard probably thinks it's because of him.

The goosebumps that prickle my flesh. The tightness in my chest.

All because of him.

I don't let myself think it through as I snatch the other strap of this dress. Meet his gaze.

Cut.

Triumph is a fitting antidote to fear. I'm in control of my own body again—and I intentionally let the dress slide from my body to pool on the floor. On trembling legs, I step from the material entirely. I'm naked before him all over again.

And the more I watch him…

The better I feel.

He teased me for thinking I had power over him?

Well, now I do. Power so fearsome he staggers back in the face of it. His throat works noiselessly, but the only sound ripping from it comes out too growled to be words. He can't fathom this form of defiance.

One by one, I force my fingers to release the knife and let it fall, unconcerned as it skitters across the floor.

And he nearly trips in his rush to back away, out into the hall. His lips part, eyes blazing. The sad part is that shock almost humanizes him. *Almost* makes everything he's put me through worth it. Almost…

Attacking him with a knife failed to get this reaction out of him.

Speechless, shocked, alarmed. Fearful, even.

But then he turns on his heel, breaking my hold over him, and nearly runs into another man whose arrival we both missed. Luciano. His gray eyes widen as he sees me, and I feel my cheeks flush. Frantic, I try to use my hands to shield what little I can.

However, Donatello goes rigid. A muscle in his throat works, and I think he might strike something. Me? Luciano?

When his hand lashes out, I'm holding my breath.

But all he does is snatch the doorknob and slam it shut, trapping me in here.

"What the hell do you think you're doing?" Donatello's voice resonates through the very walls. Only the physical barrier of the door between us gives me a reason to suspect he's not talking to me.

"I came to check on *Kisa*," a man replies, his tone carefully straddling the line between respectful and irritated. "Little girl. Saw her father die in front of her then got shoved into a trunk. Ring a bell?"

"Don't forget what I fucking told you—"

"About you being the only one to see your little friend? Touch her? Yeah, I remember. Though maybe you should tell *her* that? Having her walk around naked might make your little directive harder for the boys to abide by."

Tension crackles between the two men, palpable even isolated from them in here. In the resulting silence, my brain dwells on that choice of words—about you being the only one to see her? Touch her?

Would even someone as domineering as Donatello resort to such a base command? Yes, a part of me whispers. The man who rages when I kiss him wants me only to himself.

His toy to break.

To corrupt.

My cheeks flame at the thought, and I nearly miss what Donatello says next in a tone marginally calmer. "Just... Get her some fucking clothes. The girl too."

He must be responsible for the furious stomping that rattles the staircase next, followed by an exasperated sigh I assume comes from Luciano. He leaves next, traveling further down the hall. In the absence of defiance and fear, I sway, eventually leaning against the wall for stability.

Gradually, it sinks in that despite that stunt, nothing's really changed. I'm still here. I'm still naked, shivering in the night air drifting in through the still open window.

He's still in control.

But as footsteps advance in this direction, I lurch to my feet with a savage desire to face him again. If he thinks he can manipulate me, he can think again…

A soft knock rattles the door, and all tension deflates from my body. I can tell from the pressure alone that my visitor isn't Donatello.

"I brought you clothes," a man says, his voice vaguely familiar. "It's stuff I found in one of the rooms," he adds.

I wait until his steps finally retreat before I creep to the door and crack it just enough to spy a small cardboard box resting in the hall.

I drag it inside, bracing my back against the door as I close it. Even in the dark, I suspect who the owner of this clothing might have been. Her smell outlasts time, connected to a million different happy memories.

My connection to her wasn't as strong as it was to her husband, but I still remember her fondly. And I know that Donatello didn't send these items to me himself.

Like Safiya, this figure is another one he's claimed.

Olivia.

# EVGENI

Unfortunately for Briar Winthorp, she has to battle with another woman for my attention—though both present real threats to the Stepanov family. Just in very different ways.

Willow's fate remains at the forefront of my mind... Forty-eight hours into her disappearance and I feel no less responsible. Could anyone blame Mischa if that were his real reason for exiling me to the hospital?

It's my fault she escaped. *Again.*

Though maybe escape is the wrong word to use. I'm no fool. All of the signs point to one obvious conclusion—she left on her own. Willingly. The main question is, why? I suspect it has everything to do with Mischa's hostility toward Donatello Vanici, even before his so-called first assault on the girl.

It makes sense. She's drawn to him. Enough to forsake her home and protective family. Enough to have Mischa on edge, ready to go to war.

Enough to confront a madman by herself. If anything, Vanici seems to reciprocate that unsettling draw between them. What did he call her? *Safiya...*

No matter the reason for Willow's lapse in judgment, it's not like I can blame her. Temptation is an insidious thing, creeping into your thoughts and teasing answers to questions better left unasked. Such as why Briar Winthorp returned from obscurity after so long.

Or why I haven't mentioned said return to Mischa more than a day later.

His feelings on the Winthorps aren't exactly a mystery. I suspect he has no love for any member of that family, sister of his wife or not. No wonder she hasn't attempted to visit him directly.

Though Mischa certainly has his hands full.

It strikes me as funny that even while at the manor, Mischa still withheld information from me. Word of a fire at the harbor reaches my post in the hospital hours later—but that's the telling part. I had to hear it secondhand from a pair of nurses walking by rather than from my team. Mario doesn't answer his phone when I call for more details. I'm left to hunt for information on my own. Even before I look up the reports in detail, I suspect that it wasn't a freak blaze.

Key details from the headlines prove it—done seemingly at random. No witnesses. Carefully controlled burning and a fire that managed to stay contained to its target… It has all the hallmarks of a *mafiya* strike.

*Son of a bitch.* It's a bold move, coming from Mischa—but setting fire to a port is a long way from painting the town red with Vanici's blood. No, he's waiting for something. The real question is what?

Not that I can ask him directly. That much is made obvious when Mario finally sends me a text message, but it only conveys Mrs. Stepanova's current condition—no change—and nothing else. When I send a reply, prodding about the harbor, he doesn't respond. I decide to play coy, responding with a direct question about Vanici.

*Still looking,* is his reply. Nothing else. Sloppy on his part, but effective enough to get the point across.

Where Mischa is concerned, I've been cut out.

The feeling itches at my skin until I have to move, walk, run —anything to distract from it. Rather than rest before returning to my post in the wing, I patrol the building's outside perimeter on foot. As long as I keep moving, churning blood through my system, I can keep the irritation at bay.

Mischa's secretive planning aside, his attack turns the hospital into a topmost target should Vanici seek to retaliate. Begrudgingly, I wonder if that's why he really stationed me here—in anticipation of the fallout.

The only upside is that I doubt Donatello Vanici would be bold enough to mount a strike. Though hell, he might.

After all, madness has no boundaries.

Concern for Willow eats away at me in the rare moments when I'm not stewing over everything else. Such a situation should be handled delicately, but I suspect that delicate is the last attribute Mischa has in mind. The more I think it over, the harder I find myself running until I'm in a full sprint.

No matter how hard I breathe, I can't ignore one glaring fact—I'm worried. Violence doesn't scare me, but brutality does. Cruelty. I know firsthand the damage that can resonate when a man loses his soul—Mischa himself threw as much in my face.

I know the aftermath of vengeance.

And I know the limits of sanity. How far a man can be pushed to the brink before he snaps. Mischa? He's almost there, and I pray he doesn't cross that line.

If he hasn't already.

But he's not the only one acting out of character. I lied to him, obscuring the identity of the woman from the hospital room. Why?

Perhaps because I knew she wouldn't be satisfied with just one visit...

And, this time, I'll be ready for her.

After another lap, I reenter the building, dripping sweat beneath my gray jacket, breathing heavy. I don't bother to rest or change. I head straight for the private wing intending to take over for Danil. Even before I enter the hallway, I sense her—a presence that permeates the crisp, clean atmosphere of the hospital proper.

She infects this space, tainting the air with the stench of perfume. I don't have to see her to suspect she's near, but she's good. Subtle. As I draw up beside Danil, his expression doesn't reveal the stress it might if he'd dealt with an intruder.

He eyes my forehead with a frown, noticing the sweat drying there. "Ev. Did you rest at all?"

"I'm fine," I say, shrugging off his concern. "Any visitors while I was out?"

He shakes his head. "No, sir. The doctor's last update was an hour ago. After him, there's only been a cleaning lady."

"Good." I start forward, only to stop short. "Cleaning lady?"

"Yeah. Not one of the usuals, but they were out sick. There's a reason I noticed *her*, though." He chuckles, winking. "A bit too pretty for the profession, but who am I to judge?"

My breathing picks up in a way that has nothing to do with my run. "Is she still here?" Gritting my teeth, I can barely keep my voice steady.

He nods, frowning. "Is something wrong, sir?"

I head for Mrs. Stepanova's room without a reply, reaching for my holster. Paces from the doorway, my nostrils flare, confirming the suspicion building in my gut. *Perfume,* growing more potent with every step I take. I can taste it on my tongue as I round the corner and peer inside the spacious suite.

Mrs. Stepanova lies in bed, unmoving and unconscious but alone. Her progress from the other day is apparent in the color returning to her skin and the easier pace of her breathing. Even so, the relief I feel isn't enough to prevent me from continuing down the hall past the vacant rooms that make up the rest of the deserted suite.

As predicted, they're empty, and I hiss out a sigh, leaning against the nearest wall. Mischa's edginess has made me overly paranoid. And reckless. If the intruder is a spy or an assassin, I've given her more than enough time to wreak havoc. In blunter terms, I've been gambling with Mrs. Stepanova's life.

All in the name of what? Unraveling the mystery of a long-lost character from the Stepanovs' past?

I'm starting to believe that the lack of sleep has led me to spin my own fairy tales. Make my own mistakes, or punish Mischa by keeping him in the dark. Perhaps the boredom of this monotonous post is addling my brain?

To be on the safe side, I continue down the length of the hall, checking for anything out of place.

As I start to turn back, I see it—a metal cart of cleaning supplies positioned just beside a nearby door. Whoever put it there didn't even bother to hide it, and perhaps that's why I didn't notice it until now. It's bold. Then I hear a noise equally as blatant—faint whistling, musical and feminine. The song itself has no real tune, just random notes strung together.

Or the contented purr of a cat too arrogant for stealth. I wonder if she heard me, tearing up and down the hall while smirking at the brilliance of her hiding place—within plain sight.

I start to grab my pistol, but I round the doorway of the room without drawing it. She leans against the wall near a row of windows, presenting a far different picture than the other day. Her blond hair has been swept into a low bun, her expensive outfit replaced by a simple light blue uniform.

As Danil remarked, her beauty clashes with the disguise. With that bold smirk, no one would mistake her as someone accustomed to lurking in the background.

"I'm surprised you aren't pointing that gun at me," she declares, hands on her hips. Confidence radiates from her posture—until I reach her eyes, that is. They flicker nervously, taking stock of the nearest exit.

"You and me both," I retort.

She exhales, carrying on as if I never spoke, "Or launching into some cynical, threatening speech meant to send my poor heart into a flutter. Your man there—" She gestures in the vague direction of Danil. "He didn't recognize me. Not to mention my photo wasn't plastered all over the walls of this damn hospital. Don't tell me that you kept our naughty secret?"

Despite her smile, she doesn't sound thrilled at the idea.

"Does that upset you?" I enter the room fully, closing the door behind me—not all the way, just enough that she stiffens. That act alone tells me more than I think she realizes. She's smart for one, but guarded, all while maintaining the illusion of confidence. It's an act. But for whose benefit?

"It intrigues me," she says, addressing my question. "Why a big bad man such as yourself would be so lax in my dear sister's security. If my intentions were nefarious, you would have given me ample time to harm her."

She's right—and I don't know what irritates me more. The fact that she knows as much, or that I've willingly taken such a stupid risk.

Time to reconcile both failures. I advance another step, keeping her cart between us. "So, what are your intentions?" I ask.

"What else?" She shrugs but quickly inches back, disguising the motion with a yawn. "To reunite with my beloved sister and nephew, of course, especially in their time of need—"

"So you break into a private wing under the guise of being a custodian?"

"This?" She fingers the hem of her blue uniform shirt. "I did this for *you*. I thought you would appreciate the effort." Her eyes dart to her cart, and I suspect she has a weapon hidden there.

Aware of that, I position myself in front of it.

"By 'appreciate the effort,' do you mean alert Mischa of your presence and have you barred from the property?"

"So why haven't you?" Her tone stays entirely level, but I don't miss the subtle inflection. Or how she flinched at the utterance of a certain name.

So I say it again. "Mischa. You're afraid of him."

Her hard swallow tells me all I need to know. She is. Because she knows what I suspect—Mischa wouldn't welcome such a reunion. Not now. Which only deepens the mystery of why she chose to return at all.

And Ellen to target, unconscious or not.

Time to ask her outright. "If you intended to visit as you claim, then why not go through Mischa directly?"

Her eyes narrow. She doesn't like having her little game turned on its head. "Let me guess, he's lurking in that hallway behind you, ready to kidnap little old me? At least this time, he might get the right sister."

It's a reference to the events preceding the end of the *mafiya*-Winthorp feud—Mischa attacked the family directly, kidnapping who he thought was Briar Winthorp. In reality, he took Ellen, his now-wife, unearthing a wealth of family secrets in the process.

"Ah, so you aren't as ignorant as you look," Briar snipes. "I'm sure you know the stylized version of events. Your wonderful Mischa rescued his lovely bride from her evil half-sister and my vicious monster of a brother, raising the son of his enemy as his own—"

"You toy with me," I point out, ignoring her original question. "But you're smart enough to avoid notice. Why is that?"

Her smile widens, and devoid of the red lipstick, it's still disarming.

"Why not?" she asks. "Perhaps, I was 'smart' enough to do my research, Evgeni Volkov."

I can't resist the grin that contorts my mouth—or perhaps it's a snarl. "I doubt you could learn much from merely my name."

She laughs, inclining her head with a knowing smirk. "You'd be surprised what information someone can garner. Especially with a few greased palms—the right palms. You are a hard man to understand, but shrewd. No wonder you were drawn to Mischa. Working for a murderer is par for the course for you. Do you think you find peace in it? Serving one happy family when you've slaughtered so many others—"

"You don't know a damn thing about me." I grit my teeth before I can stop the reaction, sending her grin widening further. She won that round. But I've gleaned a revelation of my own. "It's not every woman who could come across such knowledge."

I'm being polite. The few people who could have enlightened her don't deserve the effort. Child killers.

Murderers. The kind of men I refuse to associate with. Anymore…

"Who are you working for?" I hunt her gleaming eyes, scouring them for any hint of weakness—and I find plenty. But not in the form I expect.

"I'm working in the interest of my own bleeding heart," she sneers, crossing her arms. Those eyes dart again, more wildly.

Especially when I take another step.

"Your bleeding heart," I echo. "Or an opportunity?"

Her tongue flits across her lower lip, stealing the smile in its wake. An answer to my suspicion is written across her face —*the latter.*

"You must like me, soldier," she says in a simpering tone meant to charm. "To risk provoking the wrath of the man holding your leash, not once but twice. Quite the feat. I'm starting to think you enjoy our little clandestine meetings."

"I'm starting to think you don't give a damn about meeting with me at all. And…you don't," I suspect out loud—her swift frown confirms it. "You *want* me to alert Mischa about you. Why?"

She shrugs with a sigh. One I'm now close enough to feel sear my cheek.

"Why would I want you to alert a dangerous madman that I've returned in my estranged half-sister's time of need, you ask? Word of advice, Evgeni, if something sounds as ridiculous out loud as it must when thought inside that devious brain of yours, maybe it's just that? Ridiculous—"

"Don't play coy." My hand is on her wrist before I even realize it, gripping so tightly I can feel the slender bones beneath. For all her bravado, she's slight. Weak. Just a woman.

A desperate one. The cadence of her breathing falters despite her confident smile. The stench of perfume can't hide the faint scent of sweat, and that pretty makeup can't disguise the dark shadows beneath her eyes.

She hasn't been sleeping. Judging from the pallor of her skin, she hasn't been eating much either, and even as brazen as she is, I doubt any woman in her position would prance into a hostile environment twice in as many days.

Not unless she wanted something. Desperately.

"What do you want from Mischa?"

She wrenches away from me while taking a step back, effectively placing herself against the wall. Her hand slips into her pocket, and I stiffen with the realization that she could have a weapon.

But even as her pulse flutters madly at the base of her throat, she doesn't draw it.

"Let me ask *you* a question. Why haven't you alerted your employer that your security has failed to protect my sister, more than once? You haven't dragged me before him kicking and screaming. Are you afraid of the punishment you might receive for such a failure?"

Her tone is sufficiently cutting. I figure any other man would miss the hitch in her voice.

She's more than desperate. She's terrified.

"What are you after?" I demand, taking another step toward her.

It's a mistake. She's thin enough to slip past me and pivot on her heel, betraying a lithe grace that reveals some level of training. Not in fighting, but something more feminine. Dancing?

"I told you," she says, her hand still in her pocket. "I'm here only to reunite with my dear, ailing sister, though maybe it is time I contact my brother-in-law directly? We're all so long overdue for a reunion."

Her threat would be convincing if it weren't for how she tenses, her right foot twitching against the floor.

With one shift of my stance, I move to block her in.

"Give me a reason," I demand. "Is it money you want?"

"Do I look like that much of a cliché?" she murmurs, insulted.

She doesn't. "Women like you typically sport tans this time of year, but you aren't," I point out. "Your nails are unpainted as well. Either you've come into hard times, or you are a very frugal heiress."

Or, she's been too busy for those small luxuries. Busy running from something.

Or someone.

"You soldiers, so astute," she simpers, batting her eyelashes. "Though should I say *mercenary*, in this case? Seeing as how the man you take orders from is no ordained government. This time. Though that means he's prone to chasing after dead ends. Ignoring the real threat until it's too late—"

"A woman who consults with child murderers and the criminal underbelly," I say coldly—the only people she could have learned this information from. "Those aren't the sort to populate some high-class ball."

"I haven't been to one myself in a long time," she counters in a softer tone. "But even I know when something seems too good to be true."

"So what are you saying? Someone else attacked Mischa?"

"No." Her eyes dart to the doorway and back to me. "I'm saying…what if Mischa was *never* the intended target?"

I feel my brow furrow. "Mrs. Stepanova?"

She scoffs, tarnishing her cool façade. "As if Ellen could ever make herself relevant enough to be targeted by anyone. I want you to think bigger, Mr. Volkov. Colder. Everyone in this business is no more than a snake—so slither into your deepest darkest impulses. Think of it this way—it all has an…*air* of mystery about it, doesn't it? Now, if you'll excuse me, I'm late for my next room."

As she starts past me, I snatch her arm, surprised when she darts out of reach. She's quick, and I feel the knife she pulls from nowhere biting against my wrist before I even see the blade itself.

"Play nice," she warns in a trembling voice. "I may not be a soldier, but I suspect that you wouldn't like it if I hit this security button and cried rape, sending the entire hospital running, now would you?" She wiggles her other hand, now in her pocket, presumably poised to strike the alarm.

*Son of a bitch.* She's smart, and I'm not in the position to assume she's bluffing.

"Fine." I step back, keeping my hands in view. "So you've done your research on me," I admit. "But I've done my fair share on you. I will say there isn't much news about the Winthorps recently."

She chuckles without any amusement reaching her eyes. "No. But I wouldn't be so naïve as to think the Winthorp name ended with my brother Robert. Don't tell me Mischa is? His wife had a child by another man, as did our mother. Surely he knows that husbands and wives stray from their marriages. I wonder if *he* has bastards running around behind my sister's back?"

"He may," I concede. "But I have to confess that it is odd behavior for a woman so concerned for her ailing sister to mock her marriage."

"Right you are." Pink paints her cheeks, and her nostrils flare. Her frustration is ugly. Raw. And yet, I can't help thinking the realness suits her better than the fake grins.

"So allow me to cut to the chase as any concerned family member would," she snaps. "While Mischa is chasing phantoms in the shadows, the real threat is growing stronger. The next time they attack, I can assure you, the victims won't land in a hospital. If there is anything left of them to bury, that is."

"Is that a threat?"

She laughs. "No. It is an honest warning. You're a bodyguard, aren't you? Shouldn't you be acting on intel like this to…I don't know. Guard bodies?"

Her seething rage hits a target. How ironic that she understands my job better than Mischa seems to.

"But let me guess," I say. "You're willing to divulge all you know of this mysterious threat, but only if rewarded. What's your price?"

That coy smirk returns. "My apologies, *soldier*, but I don't bargain with the help. Anything I know goes only to Mischa."

"Mischa, who would rather run you through with a blade than hear a word you have to say, is that right?"

The corner of her mouth falls, but the expression reveals another hint of the real woman lurking beneath her mask. Someone with so few options, she's already seriously considered that possibility. She's still determined to go down this route anyway.

"That's where you come in, dear soldier. *You* convince him not to."

"Tell me what you know," I suggest, making my tone softer. I try to, anyway. "And if it's convincing, maybe I'll let you take your chances."

"Oh no," she scolds, waggling a finger disapprovingly. "And spoil my own fun by letting you take all of the credit? I will speak to Mischa on my own—"

"But you need a way to get to him," I interject.

A muscle in her jaw twitches. Just as quickly, she disguises the unease behind another blinding smile. "Perhaps I do need to change my tack after all. While we're busy playing word games, the threat to all of you grows more real by the second. I can assure you that the next attack won't end in a near miss."

"Is *that* a threat?" I demand, reaching for her again.

She easily evades my grasp, pivoting on her heel. "No. Think of it more like a friendly warning. The game is only beginning, Evgeni. Will you let your employer be caught unaware simply because you have too much pride to act on the intelligence provided by a woman? I don't even know if I should waste my breath on stating the obvious of what will happen if you don't."

"*Intelligence* you don't find fit to share with just anyone but the person who destroyed your family?"

Her lips press together so quickly I almost miss it. That's the third time her mask has slipped. Sparkling blue eyes blaze with more than enough pride to outlast the mistakes, though.

If she's good at anything, it's acting.

"You don't believe me," she says calmly. "I wonder how your boss will feel if the worst happens and he finds out that his most valued lackey withheld information from him that could prevent it? Trust me, you have no idea as to the forces at play. What happened to my sister and her son? That was merely a gentle opening salvo. You can take that as a threat, if it will help you listen."

Her tone is convincing enough. Too convincing.

"You want an audience with Mischa, but I think he'd be more skeptical of you than I am," I say, turning on my heel. "As for me, I've decided that you have nothing. You think you can convince or blackmail Mischa? Do it. Maybe he'll give you the pennies your family left behind—"

"As if that bastard has any right to control my family's estate!" Real anger colors her cheeks red, and her free hand curls into a fist I doubt she's even aware of making.

"Give me something," I tell her, done with this game. "Something to pique my interest. Something other than vague, half-empty threats and a mysterious bogeyman. Then you can leave."

Slowly, she rebuilds her armor, swapping a glare for a stern frown. "Here—" She reaches into her pocket before I can stop her. Rather than a weapon, all she holds is a slim slip of paper.

"I'll do both," she snaps, shoving the paper toward me. It's a card, printed with the address of a nearby motel. "The name is Alexander, and his life is just as important as your precious Eli's. Do you want the lives of *two* children on your conscience?"

"Two." It could be a boast. A sick attempt at manipulation. If it weren't for her eyes. They blaze with a raw hint of an emotion I haven't seen in her until now. Honesty?

"Who is Alexander?"

"I gave you something worthy of piquing your interest," she says, pushing past me. "Now, you uphold your end of our bargain. Let me speak to Mischa. Keep him on a leash. I get what I want, and you can sleep peacefully at night knowing that you subverted a war."

"And if I don't?"

"The blood will be on your hands. Given your past, I don't think you can live with that. Can you?"

"Enough!" Anger flares, unfolding across my expression before I can suppress it, and she pales.

A good man would ignore the way she shudders. The sight wouldn't make his heart race, his mouth dampen. A good man wouldn't imagine how far such a woman's expression might transform when she's in the throes of true fear.

It's a way I haven't thought in a long damn time. Like a predator. To suppress it, I think of my freedom. My future. I think of sanity.

The feeling subsides.

"Did you hear me?" Briar asks. I blink and find her watching me, an eyebrow raised. "I must not be such a threat, after all."

She stands on tiptoe, bringing her face near mine. I should recoil. I don't, and she inches even closer, swiping her lips across my cheek. "Remember our bargain," she murmurs. "Once you decide to stop playing the obvious game, come find me. I think you'll know how."

She saunters from the room, leaving her cart behind.

"Wait!" I start after her, but she's already exiting into a stairwell. By the time I snatch the handle, it's locked.

"Sir?" Danil calls from the front of the suite. "Is everything okay?"

"Fine," I reply. I know that even if I were to run for the opposite stairwell and try to head her off, she'd be gone.

She's smart. I can't shake that assessment as I move to take Danil's place. Smart, coy, and—I rub my hand across my wrist—dangerous.

Her words keep echoing in my brain. *An air of mystery…* The way she stressed that word clashed with her crisp accent. An excess of emphasis, almost as if she meant another word entirely.

*Heir?* It could fit. Technically, Ellen would be heir to Mischa's fortune should he die, but the woman had scoffed at the suggestion of her being the target. Which would only leave…

*Eli?* He may be Mischa's oldest child, but—while it's not common knowledge—his father was another, as Briar so politely insinuated. Her brother, Robert Winthorp.

And given that as far as I know, the elder Winthorps are all dead, that would leave the boy as the sole heir of that particular fortune.

And a worthy target of someone looking to claim it.

"Sir?" Danil's voice chases me as I exit the suite before he can.

"I'll have someone sent to relieve you," I call over my shoulder, taking the steps two at a time. "Send word to the manor. I'm taking a break."

"No one can fault you for getting some sleep, finally," the man says.

But sleep isn't on my mind.

Briar Winthorp is, just as she intended.

# 18

# DON

Rage is addictive, a harsher vice than the cheapest alcohol. Pervasive, it overwhelms the body like a poison—or, to be more specific, like venom. One injected by a viper with a malignant aim—to penetrate deep and contaminate anything it contacts.

Thoughts. Feelings. Emotions. All become corrupted by the fervor sowed by one little witch.

The only antidote?

Get drunk off of it, in my opinion. Keep doing the same damn thing sowing the pain until you overdose. Drown in it. Then brutally smother every ounce of surviving emotion until it's finally gone. Snuffed out.

Only then can you find relief.

So by God, I drown out thoughts of *her* with dangerous fantasy. In the confines of my brain, I lose any sense of decency, envisioning every vile thing I could do to her.

Ways I could hurt her. Slowly. Methodically. The sicker, the better.

But not sick enough. Even in my mind, she remains unfazed by the worst shit my brain comes up with. Through the darkest thoughts, her eyes glint with a taunt—*You won't hurt me.*

*You can't touch me.*

And she's right. Hell, I gave her every chance to mount her own attack, get this hate out of her system. Rather than try, she stripped herself naked just to reinforce the hold she thinks she has over me.

And it worked.

When she stupidly offered up her body on a platter, I couldn't touch her, and she capitalized on that moment to wield a very different kind of weapon. It struck true, just like she wanted. The shock lingers even now as that scene replays inside my skull, over and over. Her defiant posture. Those slight curves and flawless skin...

An artist couldn't design a better body to both entice and repel. Because despite that beauty, every inch of her seems hell-bent on resisting me. Taunting me. Daring me to look away—but I couldn't.

My brain hoards that moment jealously, pouring over every damn frame. Breasts small enough to fit in the palm of my hand, hips so narrow they might snap if I mount her. Those eyes... How enticing might they be if I take her up on her dare, damn my own hesitation? I try clinging to my anger, that intoxicating rage, but biology betrays me. My cock throbs with each slow instant replay, and I lose track of the rest. Everything but her…

"Are you alright?"

The voice comes from the doorway, jolting me awake. At first, I don't recognize the room around me, trashed and covered in dust—my old study. I must have slept here, slumped over the desk, but the pale light ghosting through the windows is just enough to illuminate the aftermath of my last visit.

Oily splotches coat the desk's surface, and one of the chairs has been toppled over. That's not all. A pair of two distinct sets of footsteps mar the dusty floor, mine and a woman's. If I breathe in deeply enough, I'm sure I can still smell her. Roses and hate.

"You look like hell," Luciano adds, entering the room fully, dressed in a black shirt and slacks. "Don't tell me you're rethinking your fucking insane plan. I know I am."

"No." The only thoughts in my head center around a woman standing defiantly as black fabric pooled at her feet.

And Luciano's face when he saw her.

I eye him critically, wondering if he's stuck on the same memory. "You remember what I said about the girl?"

To his credit, he keeps his expression blank. "Off limits," he recites. "Yours alone. Am I missing anything?"

*Yeah. That I'll cut your eyes out if you so much as look at her again…*

*Fuck.* It's not jealousy. I write off whatever ripples through my gut as pure irritation. I'm sure she allowed him to see her on purpose, like a child playing with matches, hoping to see a spark. Fortunately for her, I am not the Saleris.

Sex isn't my preferred currency. For his sake, Luciano's better not be either.

"As for my insane fucking plan," I say, returning my attention to his original statement. "Did you make the arrangements I asked for?"

He nods, reluctantly if that. "I did. Though, I have to admit that I'm partially convinced you won't go through with it. I heard that you had balls, even back in the old days. But this…"

I have to laugh, though there's no humor in the sound. "Oh, I more than intend to go 'through with it.'" I'm no longer looking in his direction. The view from this window overlooks a muddy expanse of earth. Over the years, the yard has become overrun with neglect, choked by weeds. Not the grandest of venues for a wedding.

"Antonio's mansion, did you secure it?" I ask, picturing the gaudy property in the hills.

"Yes," Luciano says. "Though honestly, *famiglia* accounts pay for the damn thing. Antonio never had shit in his own name."

"Send your men to patrol the property. I want it ready to stay in."

I look over to see him raising an eyebrow. "I didn't take you as the decadent mansion type."

"Clear it out," I add. "Burn the shit inside if you want. The furniture doesn't matter. I just need the space."

"For what?"

My jaw aches before I realize why—a real smile shapes my mouth for the first time in days. "Just do it. And I want you to do something else for me. Fabio Botelli—" my smile falls flat. Fab—understandably—is beyond pissed. Only God knows what he's already learned, but it's time to face the music now and cut him in on the plan. I can't hide from him forever. "Track him down and tell him where I am."

"Is that smart?" Luciano replies. "Can you trust him?"

"Trust him, yes." As for the smart part, not contacting Fab from the outset was the dumb move. He won't like playing catch up, but there isn't time to feel guilt.

Speaking of which…

"Where is the Salvatore girl?"

Luciano juts his chin. "You mean, *Kisa?*"

I wince hearing her name spoken out loud. In addition to Fabio, she's another reality I'll have to reckon with. "Yes… Kisa. You seem protective of her."

He looks away, his jaw clenched. "Yeah, well, someone had to be."

I fixate on his tone—cold. Hard. "I'm guessing Antonio wasn't father of the year?"

Luciano scoffs. "I wouldn't use the term 'father,' to describe him—" He stops short, his eyes narrowing. He said more than he meant to, a slip-up he covers expertly with a shrug. "She's in one of the rooms upstairs, next to your…guest. I found clothing for both, by the way."

A part of me reacts to that statement with an unexpected sense of relief. Ignoring it, I refocus on the task ahead. "I'm going to need your help when I'm ready to head out," I say. "Bring as many men as you can while leaving the house secure."

"Can I ask where we're headed?"

I thread my fingers together, mulling over the plan. Finally, I say, "The hospital."

Enough games. It's time to test the Saleris on their own turf, and come through for Vincenzo. Sure, it's a risk, but the hospital is the one place Mischa wouldn't mount an outright attack.

That's the gamble, anyway.

"The hospital…" Luciano cocks his head, his expression carefully blank. "Do you think that's smart?"

"The Saleris will let me pass," I point out, though I'm not entirely convinced of that. Mateo and Gregori don't exactly have a track record built on honesty and goodwill. I have to trust that my bluff put the fear of God into them.

For now.

"No one's going to go against the *mafiya*," Luciano points out. "Whether you have proof of your innocence or not."

"You don't know them like I do," I counter. "Everyone has a price. Everyone."

And everyone has a breaking point. Mine feels imminent—that indeterminate action from which there is no turning back. She's pushing me there, that ghost from my past, mocking me with every breath.

We're both bound for hell, it feels like.

In the meantime, I might as well enjoy the ride.

Fabio arrives within the hour, driving himself in a black car identical to the one I stole and subsequently totaled. I make a mental note to cover the damages, but guilt isn't what churns my stomach as he parks paces from the house.

He's alone.

I don't know why I keep staring at the empty passenger's seat. Maybe I expected to see Vin sitting there, sporting a Band-Aid but lucid. Alive.

What a naïve fucking hope. Fabio's appearance unnerves me more than Vin's absence, though. He looks ten times worse than he sounded on the phone. A wreck. I've never seen his hair so disheveled, his chin coated in auburn stubble. His suit jacket is rumpled, the white shirt beneath stained.

I have no doubt that his lapse in self-care is a testament to his concern for Vin. The second he climbs from his car, he meets my gaze.

"He's alive," he says in a rush before he seems to realize where we are. His eyes dart around the yard strewn with *famiglia* vans and Antonio's red sports car. He's not stupid. I'm sure he recognizes them. Nonetheless, he turns back to me without saying as much.

"Hello, Fab," I croak.

He scoffs. "Vin's alive, but I don't know for how long I can say the same thing about you, you idiot!" As a credit to his resolve, he sounds only half as scolding as usual. "I almost didn't want to come. I'm sure Mischa is watching me now —" he shoots a glance over his shoulder as if he's afraid the *mafiya* will surge from the trees at any second. "You know it's only a matter of time before he finds you here, of all places... But I knew you wouldn't rest until I told you in person. He's still critical, but alive, Don. Vincenzo's still alive."

I wait for the news to affect me like it should. Only a few minutes ago, I would have assumed with tears. Unending relief. Gratitude. As it stands, I only feel the chill of the morning air on the back of my neck. I only see the empty car behind Fab. I keep hearing that goddamn word —*critical.*

"It's about damn time you told me where you were. Have you come to your senses, at last?" Fab demands, cocking his head to eye me critically. "It's not ideal, but if you give me an hour, I can get you out of the city and on a plane. Maybe to Mexico? I hear it's wonderful this time of year—"

"Not necessary," I say, turning to pace this small corner of the driveway. It's an overcast day, cold as shit. An icy wind cuts through the clearing, enhancing the grim fucking mood. What feels like a raindrop splashes on my forehead as the words I prepare to say ring truer than ever. "I'm done hiding."

"D-Done?" Fab sounds stunned as he blinks his bloodshot eyes. This close, I can smell the cigarette smoke wafting from him—he's fallen back on his old vice hard.

"You practically have scorch marks on your lips," I scold. "I think you should kick the habit."

Of all things, he laughs, but his eyes widen as if he's as shocked by the reaction as I am. "You don't get to crack jokes, you son of a bitch! After everything you've put me through. Like you look any better? You look…." His eyes narrow, scrutinizing me closer. "Sober."

He makes it sound monumental. More shocking than singlehandedly turning the entire *mafiya* against me. He makes it sound like something to be proud of.

"I am," I admit, though my mind sober isn't anywhere near the calm, logistical state of someone like Fabio. My brain *needs* impairment—something to weigh it down. Without that handicap, too many dangerous ideas seem possible.

Like tormenting a woman with golden hair in every way imaginable.

I forcefully shake my head to clear it. "Where's Vin now?"

"Vin..." His entire expression hollows out, becoming pained. "For now, he's in a private clinic somewhere in the suburbs. He's stable. I'll spare you the gritty details."

He doesn't have to; I can read in between the lines. Vin is stable but requires access to adequate care if he hopes to have a shot. I've been down this road before...

But this time? I can actually do something about it.

"Can you move him?"

Fabio frowns. "He's not up to go gallivanting to Mexico if that's what you mean."

"No. Can you move him to the hospital?"

Anger always looks so dignified on Fab. He doesn't snarl like I do or glare. He only has to incline his head to get his point clearly across. "For what? So you can taunt Mischa and have Vin die in a shootout for real this time?"

"No," I insist. Weighing my words, I try to pick the most tactful way of phrasing it. Something other than—*Fuck Mischa.* "So that he can be admitted and treated. I've already cleared it with the Saleris. Mercy hospital is in their territory. The *mafiya* can't do shit without Gregori's backing—"

"And Gregori Saleri is a deceitful fucking snake," Fabio snarls so forcefully spit flies from his mouth. "There's no way he would… You're serious—" he runs his hand over his face, shaking his head in disbelief. "Fuck, Donatello. How the hell did you secure something like that? Or *think* you did, at least. What did you do?"

I take in his gaunt appearance and jump to the conclusion that perusing the local gossip hasn't been at the top of his priorities. "You haven't heard." It makes sense—primarily explaining why he's nowhere near as edgy as he should be. Or as angry.

He doesn't know.

"Heard what?" He shoots me an incredulous look while smoothing his hand down the front of his suit as if hunting for something. A heartbeat later, he fishes a cigarette from his pocket along with a gold lighter. "You want to know what I do know? That I'm tired, Donatello. Every fucking waking moment that I'm not with Vin, I'm spending it on the phone trying to cover your ass with any neutral party I can. You know what that comes out to? Hunting down everyone that might be able to give you an alibi during the Stepanov attacks."

Apparently, he hasn't been completely out of the loop.

"So tell me, Don," he demands, propping the butt of the cigarette in his mouth. "What *don't* I know?"

"That I love Vincenzo more than anything, and that you might be a close second. You are my brother, Fabio, if not in name, then in every other way that matters. Do you trust me?" I hold my hand out.

With a heavy sigh, he takes it, shaking it firmly. "Of course I trust you, you dumb son of a bitch."

"Good. Then trust that I'm doing what needs to be done," I insist. "That's all."

"You always were so fucking sentimental." He scans my face while fumbling to light his cigarette. After taking a deep puff from it, he sighs, flicking the ash onto the pavement. "You scare me when you look like this, you know. It's been years… But I still recognize it, that dangerous gleam in your eye. Just like I recognize that these are *famiglia* men—" he nods to two figures lingering on the porch, standing guard. "I doubt Antonio Salvatore would join forces with you—or that you would let him. So what have you done?"

His eyes plead with me to reassure him. Lie?

"I need you to trust me, Fab," I say instead. "And I need you to have Vincenzo transferred to the hospital. I'll meet you there. No one will dare touch him or you. I promise."

He eyes the structure behind me with open revulsion. "I don't like that you're back here," he admits. "*This* house of all places—"

"It's safe," I counter. "Mischa wouldn't expect me to return."

"Bah!" He exhales a cloud of smoke. "I'm worried about *you*, Donatello."

"I don't need you to be worried." I try to grin, but I can't raise my lips high enough. So I shrug. "I need you to trust me."

"Fine." He takes another deep drag from his vice. "I'm too tired to ask questions. I'll just pray that you've made up with Mischa and all is well. You might be a crazy son of a bitch, but you'd never put Vin in danger. Never." He waits as if expecting me to counter that fact.

When I don't, he tosses his cigarette and grinds it into the dirt with his heel. "I'll meet you at the hospital. In the meantime, I think I'll do my own research. Though, something's telling me that I don't want to know half of what you've been up to."

With one last wary glance my way, he climbs back into the car and drives off.

As I head back to the house, I spot one of the men standing guard nearby, Sanders. "Tail him," I say, nodding toward Fab's retreating car. "Make sure no one else is. Have his back. If you see so much as a hair out of place, you call me, understood?"

He nods, setting off. Inside, Luciano lingers in the front hallway. His guarded expression makes me wonder if he stood here, purposefully listening in. Or… If he crept upstairs and into a certain room. Would the woman inside strip so eagerly again?

"Don?" Luciano waves his hand before my face.

"Get ready," I tell him, putting everything out of my mind but this—getting Vin to safety. "I want to be at the hospital within an hour."

"You're really going to go through with this?"

I don't bother to soften my tone. "Is there a reason why I shouldn't?"

He opens his mouth as if he means to say something else, but winds up nodding instead. "Okay then. Want me to retrieve your guest?"

I choose to overlook what could be eagerness in his voice. "No. Get ready to head out. I'll meet you near the car."

He retreats deeper into the house, shouting for the others as he goes. Belatedly, he calls back to me, "Someone will stay behind with Kisa."

"Good." I turn my attention to the staircase, but despite the urgency in the air, I take my time mounting it. In contrast to Antonio's, this house was always small. Modest. Just five rooms in comparison. *Hers* is near the end, beside Vin's.

A thousand different admonishments run through my mind the closer I come to it, warning me to turn back. Have Luciano drag her downstairs instead. Hell, I can smell her through the fucking door. Roses and sweat.

The aroma conjures an image of her in my brain before I can quash it. She's standing tall, I bet, waiting to face me. Her hair will be down, and Luciano probably found a dress for her. Tight, with a neckline that might display her throat. I can almost hear the thump of her heartbeat surging with every step closer I come.

I finally grip the doorknob, hesitating for a fraction of a second. Maybe she followed through on our little game and took the knife, preparing to use it this time? Of all things, a smile tugs on my mouth as I push the door open.

God, I hope so.

As predicted, she's standing near the bed, one hand tucked behind her back, the other at her side. If she's holding the weapon, I lose track of the ability to care.

"What the hell…"

Luciano gave her clothing, alright. A deep blue dress that fits her surprisingly well, far more modest than the black ensemble. The primal part of my brain drinks her in, noting how the color sets off her hair and those eyes…

But a different emotion from lust overrides the appreciation —shock. I grapple for the edge of the doorway, gripping it tight. That's no random outfit—I've seen it worn a million times, just on a different woman.

It was Olivia's.

"Take it off!" I barely recognize the voice ripping from my throat. "Now. Take it off!"

At the back of my mind, I know she didn't pick it—still, that doesn't matter. I start forward, intending to rip it from her, my damn self. "I said…take…it…off—"

She doesn't move, but I go still regardless. Those lips are slightly parted, her chin held high, and those eyes… They stare straight ahead, boring into mine like goddamn lasers, tempered by nothing. Not fear. Not hate.

She's daring me to break my own fucking rule. Touch her.

Luciano may not know the history of that dress, but she does. Wearing it is just the opening salvo in our latest battle of wills. Fuck me, she's already scored.

One round won.

"You…" I clench both hands into fists just to keep from reaching for her. Instead, I turn and enter the hall, descending the steps two at a time.

Before I know it, I'm in Antonio's red car, gripping the steering wheel so hard my knuckles are white against the dark leather. Without thinking, I put the engine into drive, ready to pull away. *Forget her.* Forget the plan. Forget everything.

The door opens before I can hit the gas, and I don't have to look to identify the culprit. She climbs in, settling quietly beside me, her scent a fucking vice around my throat.

I could tell her to get out, but that's what she wants.

To be acknowledged. To be seen. To take precedence in my mind, if only for a second…

So I deny her.

I just drive.

Luciano was right—it takes balls.

Not to come here—that could be explained by insanity. Or perhaps stupidity. No, as I walk through the main lobby, head held high, even I can admit that it takes balls to figuratively sport Willow Stepanova on my arm.

Like it's real. Like she's here of her own free will, and there's no threat of war hanging over our heads. It takes balls to go into battle with her and resist the urge to look over my shoulder every five goddamn minutes. Not for Mischa.

For the knife, I'm sure she still has.

To her credit, she doesn't bolt the second we're in public. She doesn't stab me either, but I'm not cocky enough to believe fear is what keeps her in line. No, her *pride* remains her strongest armor.

The only hint of unease is the slight quiver in her throat. Though, I can admit that her emotion could be caused by a myriad of other reasons. As far as she knows, her mother and brother are still under care in this facility, along with the latest Stepanov newborn. Should I feel some semblance of sympathy at that?

I'm too sober to care, entirely fixated on the layout of the building.

Surprisingly, Mischa *isn't* waiting in the lobby. It's spacious with plenty of room to maneuver in the event of combat, but apart from wandering nurses and the average visitor, it's relatively empty. We approach the receptionist without incident, but I'm more on edge than ever.

"Welcome to Mercy." The woman seated at the polished desk flashes a grin. "How can I help you?"

"I'm waiting for a transfer. Vincenzo Vanici."

She swallows hard, clearing her throat, and turns to a computer monitor. After a second of scanning the screen, she nods. "Yes, all of the arrangements have been made. You can head up to the fourth floor."

God bless Fabio. I have no doubt that this is all due to him. The real question is whether I can uphold my part of the bargain by protecting them both.

"I'll keep watch from here," Luciano says, Ash behind him. They're dressed so as not to arouse suspicion, any weapons discreetly hidden.

Assuming Sanders is still shadowing Fabio, that leaves just one man to cover me on the way upstairs. I'll be outnumbered when Mischa shows up—and it's only a matter of *when*, given that his wife and children are in this building. Luciano could be positioning himself to cut and run.

The second I see his face, the paranoia dies. The bastard's more alert than I am, darting his gaze suspiciously toward every potential entrance and exit.

"Alright. We'll head up now." Inclining my head toward the girl, I start for the elevator. "Let's go."

"I should go first," the remaining *famiglia* soldier says, surging ahead to claim the empty elevator. "To make sure it's clear."

I let him take the lead, waiting in the lobby with the girl for the elevator to return. When it does, she enters without resistance. Her silence feels heavier than usual. I look over, and she's facing forward, her shoulders squared. Is it the ruse that has her so wary?

Or the sliver of space separating us…

As the doors slide shut, the authority I have over her sinks in. By pure physicality alone, I could overpower her. Even if it's the dumbest fucking thing to do in this moment, I want to. Test her. Taunt her. Watch her squirm.

Regain the upper hand in this game.

"I warned you." I'm surprised how guttural my voice comes out sounding. Furious.

Does that startle her?

*Yes.* She keeps her face turned from me, but the elevator's polished door serves as a mirror. I can clearly see those eyes, glinting with stubborn pride. That pursed little mouth tightening, her defiant posture wavering.

"Did you hear me, hellcat? I mean…*wife.*" I grab her wrist before I can even process the motion, dragging her closer. "There are lines you don't want to cross with me."

Like stripping naked just to get a rise. Letting another man see her. Flaunting herself—not because she craves the attention, either. She's too fucking naïve to realize the enormity of the fire she's playing with.

That's it. No other reason could explain her boldness… Like *wanting* me to see her. She wouldn't even know what to do with me if I did lose control.

To prove it, I shove her back, pressing her small body into a corner. It's too easy. Just for a second, I let my brain off its leash, relishing her reaction—a shudder. A swallow. A wary glance at my hands.

I flex them, unconcerned by the threat the gesture might convey—the complete opposite of my "you're here willingly" spiel to her. This is a lesson she needs to learn. Power, and who between the two of us truly has it.

I do.

Aware of that, her teeth clip together, the only audible sound she makes as those eyes dart fearfully up to mine, her fingers flying to my chest to push me off.

"Do you think I won't do it? Touch you?" To prove the opposite, I reach out, ghosting the top of her shoulder. "Do you think that just because you're in on this game, I won't force you to play your role if I have to?"

Her eyelids flutter, her cheeks pink.

Satisfied, I start to pull back. "I thought so—"

Her fingers find mine before I've gone a full step. Boldly, they curl around the width of my hand—but her nails graze the flesh deliberately. Hard.

A grunt revs in my throat as everything leaves my skull, but this—she's testing me—*purposefully* testing me. I try to wrench my hand back. She bears down harder. Tighter.

A question rips from my throat, "Do you really want to fight me?"

I jerk my head around just to see her response—more defiance. She squares her chin without an ounce of fear.

It's the worst thing she could do.

My next reaction is born purely out of instinct. I snatch at her throat with my free hand, leveraging my weight against hers. A million warnings race through my skull, but it's already too late. Her chest slams against mine as she tries to push past me, but she's no match. I wrestle her body into submission with barely any effort.

But she fights me every step of the way. Kicking. Writhing. Struggling. *Fuck.* Every point of contact feeds the dangerous tension building in my abdomen. My slacks tighten uncomfortably. Too fast.

"Stop!" I snap, pulling back as far as I can while keeping her restrained.

She relents, breathing so heavy the cadence plays like a fucking song. Helpless, I flex my hand, sensing tender bone and delicate muscle beneath. I could choke her again. Strangle her finally and send her body to Mischa.

But the second those eyes meet mine, all other thoughts go blank. Her scent dominates, her heat so intoxicating I groan. My mouth is against her jaw, I realize, able to sense the tension coiled beneath that silken skin. I could kiss her now. Claim those pink lips for my own and show her how a kiss should be. With teeth. Pressure.

Hard enough to hurt. Bleed…

Another woman would let me have that moment. Seize it. Anyone other than this stubborn little princess so determined to not be relegated as a mere pawn in this game of power. No, she wants control by any means. Again, I can almost feel her grappling for it, figuratively wrestling for the upper hand.

My attention is the match in this equation, ripe for the taking.

Already, she's inclining her head, putting her mouth beyond reach, daring me to close the gap. Daring me to chase her scent. Daring me to ignore my own goddamn boundaries.

Those eyes meet mine fearlessly with an intensity I shouldn't find. She should be cowering, not confident, her pink lips glistening, so fucking tempting. Restraining myself is an exercise in self-control unlike any I've ever experienced—no other vice holds quite the allure she does. Not alcohol. Not heroin.

Just when I think I can withstand her, she flits her tongue across her lower lip. My brain goes blank in the aftermath. The next thing I know, is fire. That wetness is on my tongue, her heat like a match. I lurch forward, nearly crushing her against the wall just to seek out more. Take it.

But when a quivering tongue prods my mouth for entry, it hits me that I was never in control of this game…

Suddenly, the elevator doors part, and I barely have the sense of mind to let her go, staggering to put distance between us. It's like surfacing from underwater to snap back to reality. Focus. I'm in the hospital again, and the *famiglia* agent is standing at the mouth of the elevator, his expression blank.

"Sir." He nods respectfully. "They're here."

*Here.* His tone isn't quite grim enough to be referring to the *mafiya.* For the first time in days, the full extent of everything that's transpired hits me all over again. All of it. *Vin…*

My chest fucking aches at the thought of seeing him finally.

Ignoring the woman nearby, I start walking while hunting for what little positives I can find. This ward is secluded, for one, semi-private. Even the staff seems discreet, unsurprised by our arrival. Trust Fab to cover all the bases.

He stands near the last room, somehow seeming more exhausted than he did over an hour ago. A few paces back, I notice Sanders posted against the wall. Spotting me, he nods before returning his attention to the rest of the hall.

"Took you long enough," Fabio says with a sigh. "Now… You should brace yourself, Don," he warns as I approach. He already has another cigarette in hand, but a sharp glance from a passing nurse makes him shove it back into his pocket. "Most of…*the stuff* is just as a precaution. Once he has the surgery, they can stabilize him—"

I stop listening, entering the room without giving myself the chance to falter. This is it. Days of thinking the worst only to culminate in this moment…

My first thought is that the room is nice. Fab came through again, getting him one with a view of the city. It's large with calming white walls and a bed positioned in the center.

But the figure lying there, with tubes sticking out of him, isn't my boy. Not my Vin.

He can't be.

This figure is a ghost. A shell, so pale I can see through his skin to the blue veins beneath. A machine breathes for him in a slow, ghastly rhythm. His eyes are closed, his mouth absent that beautiful smile.

And all the lies I've fed myself fall flat.

Mischa Stepanov isn't the only one to blame for this.

I am.

This is *my* fucking fault.

# 19

## WILLOW

*I* never knew it was possible to actually taste the pulse surging in your throat. Mine carries the distinct flavor of copper, *blood*; I've bitten my lip, but I can't move. My entire body goes rigid, electrified as though I've just stuck my finger in an outlet—or witnessed the unthinkable…

Donatello Vanici facing a reality he can't sneer down or brutalize.

This moment humanizes him like nothing else, highlighting the gauntness of his once handsome features. Robbed of all bravado, he's a ghost, thriving on the darkness the shadows provide, clinging to life like a zombie animated by only one stimulus.

Pain.

At the sight of Vincenzo, he staggers, threatening to collapse. His hand shoots out, gripping the back of a nearby chair, but the weight of his body nearly topples it. Like an old man, he hunches over, helpless…

My legs twitch, lurching into motion without permission. I'm already reaching for his shoulder before I can process the cons of the action. Plenty.

His heat scorches me through the cotton of his jacket. Instinctively, I try to draw my hand back—but his clamps down on my wrist before I can. I stiffen, expecting him to shove me off, but he tugs me closer, using my body to steady his. God, he's heavy. Firm.

But his weight feels different when he isn't leveraging it like a weapon. He clings to me with an amount of care that shocks me. Gentle. When I finally see his face, I realize why —he's distant, miles away, too far gone to give a damn about me. I've never seen any man so lost. Vacant. For an instant, those piercing dark irises serve as a mirror, reflecting my own expression back—and it's terrifying to see myself as he does…

Devoid of hate in exchange for concern.

For him.

He blinks, seeming to realize where he is. Shrugging me off, he keeps moving, eventually sinking to his knees beside the bed. The sound he makes next… I'll never forget it—a wordless howl that floods the room.

No matter my feelings toward him, even I'm not immune. My heart aches, but for the wrong reasons. Is this how he mourned for his precious Safiya, after he left me—*her?* It's sick to think this way. Selfish. And yet…the thoughts keep coming.

Did he cry out like this? Sink to the floor as if every ounce of strength left him, driven out by sorrow? Did he crouch over those things in that pink room and sob openly?

Tears blur my vision, and I lose track of the comparisons. All I can do is watch the scene unfolding, as disconnected as an outsider. For as long as I can, I prolong my own reckoning with the figure in the bed.

Until I have no choice.

When I finally look at Vincenzo, I choke on another wave of conflicting emotion. It's strange how he looks the same, even after all this time. Even with his head wrapped in bandages, his skin so pale it's see-through in places.

"He hasn't regained consciousness yet," a man declares from the doorway.

Only slightly taller than me with a head of auburn hair, he's dressed in a tailored suit, his posture conveying authority. Another shocking wave of recognition hits me. Once, I called him by another name. *Uncle Fabio.*

He stares past me without an ounce of recognition, speaking to Donatello. "The doctor assures me that there is brain activity. He requires surgery to relieve some pressure on his brain, but if all goes well, his status will improve—"

"Whatever it takes." In the blink of an eye, Donatello is on his feet. He's cold and composed once more, but his hand still grips Vincenzo's, his thumb stroking the pale skin. "Whatever the cost. I don't care. You have them do it."

"Of course." Fabio nods. "But who did you…" He trails off the second he sees me, grappling for a nearby table just to keep his balance. Dismay constricts his features, and I'm sure that he knows who I am. "Jesus, Mary, and Joseph, Donatello Vanici," he croaks. "You didn't. Tell me you didn't!"

He spins to confront the taller man, his expression horrified. "Are you insane? After everything I've done for you? For Vincenzo? This is what you do? You bring the daughter of the *mafiya* here?"

I was right, I realize. He knows who I am—just not the identity I expected him to.

"As what?" he demands. "Some kind of fucking hostage! Have you lost your mind—"

"Look at her, Fab," Donatello says quietly. Despite his insistence, his eyes are on the wall. "Look."

"I'm not blind, you stupid bastard. I can see this situation for what it is—insanity—"

"I said *look at her*, Fabio!" Donatello lunges toward me. Snatching my arm, he spins me to face the other man's inspection. Gone from his touch is any of that previous warmth. His hand gripping my chin might as well be a manacle. "Look at her! Really look. I'm sure you see it now."

"What are you…" Fabio blinks, shaking his head. If possible, he turns even paler before finally exhaling a sound in between a sigh and a groan.

"You aren't blind," Donatello says in a tone so cold I shiver. "I'm sure you knew before I did. I'm sure you *always* knew who she really was. You just kept it from me. For what? You thought I'd go after her then?"

For what it's worth, Fabio looks shocked into silence, still eyeing my face.

Donatello grunts, unsatisfied. His fingers grip me tighter, his breaths searing my neck. "It doesn't matter. Fuck, you doubt me now of all times? I would die for Vincenzo!"

His voice rings out, and Fabio flinches, startled back to the present.

"I know that," he says faintly. "I know that."

"So trust me. I didn't kidnap her. In fact, I didn't do a damn thing to her!" One by one, he pries his fingers from me to illustrate as much. "Mischa jumped the gun. He struck first."

"So, what do you plan to do?" Fabio demands tiredly. "Threaten the girl as retaliation? Trade her life for Vin's? Is that the real reason you got safe passage here? Just to lure Mischa Stepanov?" Raw pain laces his voice, and Donatello flinches.

"I'm not going to hurt her." He returns to the bed, lifting Vin's limp hand with both of his. "I'm going to marry her, Fab, and end this feud before it even begins."

"You…what?" The man staggers to the wall, bracing his hand against it. Nonetheless, he sinks to his knees with a faint sigh. "Jesus Christ, you've gone insane—"

"I haven't," Donatello snarls. "Think about it for a second. Use your head and fucking *think*. I marry her—"

"And Mischa kills all of us!"

"No," he snaps. "I marry her and beat Mischa at his own game. The bastard thinks he owns this city. He wouldn't have come after me, otherwise. This is personal. So I make it so fucking personal he has to face me on an even playing field."

"And what about her?" Fabio gestures to me. "I'm sure you've threatened her. God, don't tell me you raped her—"

"I never have to touch her," Donatello declares. He sounds so damn confident of that. "I haven't, by the way. You want to know why? All I need to do is show her with me *unharmed*. All I need to do is make her my wife and dangle that goddamn ring before Mischa and the world. If it looks like she's willingly mine, he can't touch me."

"You realize how you sound," Fabio croaks, letting his mouth hang open. "Do you? You sound insane, Donatello. You sound like you've lost your damn mind—"

"I have." He sounds so calm. So unconcerned by the grit in his own voice. The coldness. "I have lost my mind."

For the first time, I hear his words—truly hear them. He's not proposing a marriage. He's not even proposing a twisted hostage scenario. He's proposing, in essence, a sick reversal of his original crime—throw me away again. Only this time? My soul is what gets sold. My humanity.

I'll be reduced to a lifeless husk sporting a ring, no better than Vincenzo.

As Fabio insinuated, a life for a life.

"What would you have me do, huh?" Donatello questions as if arguing directly with my thoughts. "Sit idly by and let Vincenzo die? Sit by and watch Mischa Stepanov lord his power over me as though I'm some patsy he can step on, even if he fucking crushes me in the process? No..." His laugh will haunt my nightmares. "I can't let that happen. I refuse to."

"So you what? Turn into the same sort of tyrant you used to scoff at? This isn't you, Don," Fabio pleads. "Not anymore. Trust that I love Vin as much as you do. I would have found a way. I would have done something. Something that doesn't result in you with your boot on the neck of Mischa Stepanov."

"Well, it's too late." Donatello faces him, his head held high, shoulders squared. "So what are you going to do now?"

"Damn…" The man sighs heavily, rising to his feet. "You swear on your life that you haven't touched her? Not so much as a fucking hair?"

Donatello makes a motion in between a nod and a shake of his head. "I haven't seriously harmed her—"

"And you won't," Fabio warns. "Not a hair. You don't harm her. You don't touch her. You don't fuck—do anything other than *look* at her. Promise me."

Donatello's eyes narrow. Finally, he nods. "You have my word."

"I better," the other man insists, wagging a trembling finger. "I mean it. Now, as for your insane, ridiculous plan that I in no way endorse…it just might be crazy enough to work."

He starts to pace, instantly transforming from frantic to composed. With one hand, he strokes his chin, mulling over the thoughts he proposes out loud. "I assume there's more to this—you'll need to catch me up on the politics of it all."

"You don't know the half of it," Donatello warns. "To cut to the fun bit, Antonio Salvatore is dead, I'm in control of the *famiglia* now, and I found proof that Mischa acted on faulty intel. Someone else wanted his family attacked."

Fabio sways, his expression shifting from alarmed, to horrified, and then resigned all within the space of a second. "Who?"

Donatello shrugs. "Didn't get that far."

"Typical," Fabio snaps. "You always jump the damn gun. Right. Aside from that, you might be on to something. Cooling things down now could ensure peace with Mischa and avert an outright feud. You make it known that you haven't harmed her. She's here of her own account. And you won't go any further than marriage as a show of good faith. It could buy you time. And, of course, I can help spin the narrative. Put things into motion. Spread the publicity. Mischa may control the criminal underbelly, but he has nothing on the public front. With a few well-placed phone calls, I can make this the talk of the fucking city. He'll be boxed in."

"I'm not asking you to make yourself a target, Fab," Donatello says.

"Stop right there—" Fabio raises his hand. "You don't need to ask me to do a damn thing. Everyone knows we're connected. I don't have a choice but to fix this mess. Now…" He folds his hands behind his back, continuing to pace. "A long engagement would be the best course of action. An actual marriage might not even be necessary—"

"The legal protections are what matter," Donatello interjects. "Mischa can rage all he wants, but there are rules that even men like us are forced to follow."

"What a twisted world," Fabio laments. "Maybe you're right, but only to buy enough time for you and Mischa to hash out your differences without putting bullets in each other's brains. In that case, a brief ceremony. We'd need to arrange for the right guests. The right optics to make this as convincing as possible. Even the *mafiya* can't challenge public opinion." He reaches into his pocket, withdrawing a cell phone. "I need to make some calls. Give me some time. And don't worry about Vin," he adds more softly. "That's been arranged too. Just try to stay out of trouble for five minutes."

He leaves the room, the phone attached to his ear.

In the resulting silence, Donatello returns to Vin's bedside, taking his other hand. "Don't look at me like that," he warns.

Considering that Vin's eyes are closed, it's obvious who he's speaking to.

"This way, you keep your family alive. Vincenzo alive. You get to go back inside your perfect little cage and—"

I back away from him so violently I nearly trip. I brace my hand against the nearest window to steady myself, overlooking a lonely gray parking lot, the city in the distance. The sight is surprisingly reassuring, a desolate landscape partially populated. It reminds me of a world far from the machinations of men like the one behind me.

If I really were the bird he mocks me to be, I'd fly away now.

Fast.

"Don't pretend like this isn't the best fucking option," he warns, advancing too quickly to evade. "You stay alive, and I get the best chance to save Vincenzo. Look at him—"

His fingers latch onto my throat, forcing me to face the bed. "Look at what your beloved father did. You want his blood on your hands? Then refuse to play along."

I grit my teeth, my eyes watering. Maybe he's right? In his cruel, sick sense of logic, this is probably the far less of multiple evils. Merciful. After all, he once sold me intending to let me die.

The only difference now is that he gets to inflict the damage himself. He gets to steal the pampered, polished life Mischa provided and relegate me to insignificance all over again.

His life becomes my new prison.

And I'd rather be left for dead.

I'm crying in earnest. Tears paint my cheeks in steady strokes, but inside I'm woefully numb. The medical machinery and noises around us create a twisted sort of melody—a mocking rendition of what I have to look forward to.

A dead-end—being technically alive, but in essence, just existing. Breathing. A shell.

"Don't you dare think you can run now," Donatello cautions as I remember how to move and wrench out of his grasp, staggering to put distance between us. "You wanted my attention? Well, now you have it."

I could laugh. Scream. Rip him open with my nails or stab him with my knife.

I could. But that's what he wants. To lord this prison over me. To gloat. To have me writhe on his hook so he can forget who truly caused this mess.

He did.

*Focus!* It takes everything I have to wrestle my rage into submission. I'm shaking with the effort, choking on the air in my lungs as more tears blur my vision. When I finally regain control over my breathing, I meet the gaze of the man before me, putting everything I have into my expression, if only to convey one point. One last threat.

I'll play his game, alright.

And I'll make him regret ever asking me to in the first place —not through violence. Something far worse.

I'll become *his* prison.

I'll make his life a living hell.

I'll make him writhe on my hook, and in the end, he'll be the one to turn tail and run.

I'll make him pay.

His gaze hardens as if he's aware of every plot and scheme taking shape. "Fair enough." His mouth flattens into a hard, stern line, but his raised eyebrow makes my pulse race. It's amused. A dare. I swear I hear him murmur, "You think you can try? I want to see you do it—"

"Sir!" A man staggers into the room. I vaguely recognize him as the figure stationed by the door when we arrived, now grim-faced, his hand ominously inside his jacket pocket. "*Mafiya* men spotted entering the hospital. They're on their way here."

"It was only a matter of time," Donatello murmurs, but I marvel at the levelness of his tone as he enters the hall with a galling sense of calm. I scramble after him, my brain struggling to reconcile his myriad of clashing responses. When I strip for him of my own accord, he rages, but in the face of a different kind of enemy?

He's damn near poised. The stark contrast highlights just how unsure I am of my own feelings. Doubt gnaws on my nerves with every step I take. Mischa is here… I should feel relieved. I *am*. My heart swells, and I ache to see him. Try to explain. Apologize.

Maybe I could end this just by facing him, finally?

The thoughts barely finish forming, when a commotion cuts the tranquil quiet of the ward, alarming the few nurses and medical personnel. Slamming doors. Shouting. My stomach contorts into knots as my head swivels along with everyone else's toward the source of the noise. Instantly, I'm forced to reconcile my wishes for what they are—childish fantasies.

Mischa *is* here, barging through a door that I assume leads to a stairwell, but instead of relief, fear floods my body. It's so strange how a few changes in demeanor and clothing can drastically alter someone.

Gone is the jolly fellow who I've witnessed read fairy tales to his young daughters and play tag with his sons. Hate strips any ounce of warmth from his features, and I'm not immune to the effect he has on those caught in his path. I stiffen, my eyes glued to him, my body tensing with instinctive alarm, sensing the danger in the atmosphere.

His blond hair is gathered loosely at the nape of his neck, enhancing the angular planes of his face and the dark eyes ablaze. If it weren't obvious until now, the piercing glare he sports makes it clear—this man isn't here to make nice. He's ready for war. Dressed head to toe in gray fatigues, he embodies the frightening image of the *mafiya* leader the world knows him to be.

But another figure stalks past me to meet him fearlessly, easily drawing my attention away. Remarkably, he undergoes the same drastic transformation as Mischa, but in reverse—from stiff with grief to electric. Wearing a black suit, his dark hair mussed, he seems like an unlikely match compared to Mischa's bulk—but no less intimidating. Shadow in contrast to fiery gold. Light against darkness. When viewed together, the effect they have is chilling.

Two equally powerful pieces fighting for control over a dwindling game board. The sole piece deciding said fate? A lone, insignificant pawn caught between both sides. That designation feels cemented by the way Donatello positions himself—near enough to grab me.

"Are you really going to shoot me here?" he demands of Mischa, outstretching his arms in a grand gesture. "Right here? Then do it, you son of a bitch."

The vitriol seems honed like a volley of arrows into an advancing army. Undeterred, Mischa merely slows his pace as a cruel half-smile tugs on his mouth. At least six men lurk behind him, a mere fraction of what I know his security force to be. At a glance, I only recognize a few faces, none of them Evgeni.

"You dare show your face here," Mischa growls, sounding more incredulous than enraged. "I should—" his gaze meets mine and his entire expression shifts, his eyes widening. "Willow…"

"Not so fast." Donatello places a hand on my shoulder, locking me in place before I can even think to move. "I want to hear you say it," he demands. "What are you here to do? Plan to shoot up a hospital? Finish Vincenzo off? Don't be shy with your plans for vengeance now."

A shadow darkens Mischa's expression, harshening the rage already apparent. "I'm the one who should be asking you that fucking question." He inclines his head, his eyes slits. "Let me hear you say it—are you threatening her?"

I shrink beneath the weight of attention as several pairs of eyes turn to me.

"You haven't heard?" Donatello scoffs, tightening his grip on me. Ruthlessly. His nails bare down on the thin material of the dress, threatening to pierce the tender flesh beneath. It stings, but I'm more alarmed by the suspicion that pain isn't his aim this time. For once, he *sees* me, but only as something to claim. Own. "I'm sure you have. Your friends, the Saleris haven't told you?"

He waits, but Mischa doesn't react—which is exactly what I think he was counting on. I glance over to see him practically levitating with arrogance. With a dark eyebrow raised, he says, "I plan to marry your daughter, Mischa. As a show of goodwill and to acknowledge her affections after you viciously mounted an attack on my family. Consider yourself lucky that I'm more interested in peace than revenge."

Silence falls with a deafening impact. All I can hear is my pulse racing as my heart pounds so hard I feel it jolt up my throat. I can't even look at him—but as I cut my gaze down to the tile flooring, I'm acutely aware of the man behind me. His touch is violent, his breath fire against my cheek. His stance unnerves me more than his hate does—it's possessive. *Confusing.*

Finally, he withdraws his hand, but the sensation hits like a slap. It's jarring, recalling the torment he put me through in the shower tenfold—unbearable heat switched to sudden cold.

"Threaten me if you want," he taunts, facing Mischa. "It will only serve to prove my point—you're too power-hungry, caught up in personal grievances to see reason. Don't tell me this all has to do with the harbor?"

That dangerous silence lingers for a second longer. Another.

"You know damn well what this has to do with," Mischa growls in a tone so guttural I feel it in my bones. Finally, I lift my head to face him, unprepared for the man I see. For a moment, I'm twelve again, viewing him as a stranger whose motives I couldn't fathom. Would he be just another monster?

As he sees me, however, the spell is broken. He's the man I've come to trust once more, though furious as he eyes the place Donatello held me. "How dare you even touch her—"

"Let's ask her if I forced her here," Donatello counters with a false sense of calm. "If she's so battered and broken, let her run to you. Go!"

His hand slams against my back, shoving me forward. I stumble, my eyes riveted to Mischa. God, I never knew how much my heart could hurt. Physically throb as if stabbed. Beaten. Broken. Deep down, I know exactly what will make the pain go away—run.

Hide. Forget Donatello, damn the consequences of what might happen. In this moment, I want nothing more than to do just that—go home to my family.

I even take a step, but then reality cruelly sinks in. The man on my heels didn't release me out of kindness. He's merely testing the invisible binds linking us together more tightly than any chains. Pride—I refuse now; I'm playing right into his depiction of me. That as a selfish little girl. And I'd prove him right, Vin's death would truly be on my hands.

And I would be *his* pawn to conquer.

If I were hoping otherwise, Mischa's expression gives a clear roadmap about how this will end. In violence. The sheer depth of the rage written across his features is breathtaking. So much anger. Hate.

As his hard mask returns in full, I barely recognize him.

"I guess that's settled," Donatello remarks, forcing me to realize what everyone else has. All this time, I haven't moved.

Smug, my captor appears at my side, snatching my hand—but I can sense the tension coiled in every thick finger. Despite his outward composure, he's wary.

As he should be.

"We should discuss this over lunch, like men," Donatello suggests. "I'll send you the information—"

"You go to hell," Mischa snarls, his eyes flashing. With every word, his accent thickens, coating each syllable in malice. "You want to hide inside a hospital? Use a woman as a shield? I knew you were a coward, but this… It's pathetic."

"Tomorrow," Donatello cordially replies as if never interrupted. "We can discuss my nephew's medical bills, which you will personally cover."

Mischa growls, sounding more animal than human. A wolf, snarling for blood. "You—"

"And, as a show of faith, you will have access to the Vanici harbor enterprise," a different voice interjects, throwing the tension on its head. Fabio. Almost comically, everyone whips around to find him standing in a doorway roughly in between the two men—a symbolic placement if there ever was one.

In his hands is a small notepad and pen. I have a strange thought of him patiently taking notes all this time.

"This will be a union of two families," he says, seemingly the voice of reason amid this unfathomable chaos. "As a show of faith, I'm sure we can come to other agreements. Donatello has assured me that your daughter has not been harmed in any way—"

"Perhaps you want to examine her yourself," Donatello interjects with a hint of menace. "At least before you go crying rape. Just know this—I have no intention of ever laying a hand on your precious daughter—"

"She has always been *my* daughter," Mischa snarls, his hands fists. "Always. Never will I forsake her. The same can't be said for you, can it?"

"No." Donatello's voice is unchanged. "But I guess I can take those words as your blessing?"

A ripple goes through Mischa's men as their leader cocks his head in warning. "My blessing?"

He seems to teleport; he moves so fast. Air whooshes past my ears, and I only see a blur of motion before a force shoves me aside, ripping my hand from Donatello. I crash against the wall, scrambling to spin around.

A sickening thud shatters the silence, followed by a masculine groan. Another. It happens so quickly I can barely track it all. Men scramble in every which direction, while—at the center of it all—Mischa grapples with Donatello, his hands around the other man's neck. With a violent thud, he shoves him against the wall, and I know in my soul he won't stop there.

"Enough!" someone shouts, their voice drowned out by another groan. "Not here! Jesus Christ—"

My pulse surges, deafening me. I'm only aware of moving blindly with no real aim in mind. Just shoving my way through the fray, against a wall of writhing bodies. Reaching out. Grasping at a muscular arm and tugging.

The figure in question jerks, his eyes finding mine. Mischa. A flicker of emotion flits across his gaze too quickly to track. The rage contorting his features doesn't diminish, but he steps back just enough for the man in his grasp to break free.

"It's about damn time you attacked *me*," Donatello rasps. He staggers to regain his balance, swiping at his nose. Blood flows freely from one nostril, speckling his chin and white shirt, not that he seems to care. He's smiling wide, his teeth painted scarlet. "Do it again. Hit me. Shoot me! You know you want to. At least we're finally man to man." Another manic grin contradicts any fear that he might be truly in pain. With a start, I realize this is the most animated I've seen him since that horrific moment in Havienna.

"Attack me," he hisses. "Not a *boy*. You're luckier than you know, Mischa—" his eyes cut to me, devoid of an ounce of warmth. "I could have killed her. God, the things I could have done to her…"

He sounds annoyed that he *hasn't* done those horrible things. Sure, he's considered them, going so far as to taunt me with the threat. But he hasn't crossed the line. The only sense of comfort I can find is that the other night I realized why—he's *afraid* to.

"You won't ever touch her again." Mischa surges forward, grabbing my arm to pull me against him. His strength is a battering ram, both a comfort and a restraint. "You're lucky I don't castrate you with my bare fucking hands," he says to the man watching us.

Donatello doesn't react, still sporting that gruesome smile. I can't escape the creeping sensation that he's in my head again, boldly reading my mind.

And whatever he finds emboldens him more. "Not being able to touch her might make our wedding a tad bit more difficult—"

"Marry her?" Mischa scoffs. "I'll kill you first—"

"Don't tell me you're making the choice for her?" Donatello's smirk widens as he licks the blood from his lips. "You don't trust your little girl, Mischa?"

"Come near her again, and I will kill you." To his credit, Mischa doesn't take the bait this time. Gesturing to his men, he conveys the reason why—this fight was never fair from the outset. "Stand down now, and maybe I'll let you live for the time being," he says. "I'm taking my daughter home."

He turns back the way he came, maneuvering me to follow. He's too strong. Too fast. It takes effort to dislodge my arm from him. Desperation. Wrenching on my shoulder isn't enough. He doesn't react when I paw at his wrist with my free hand, either. In the end, I have to grab the edge of a nearby doorway and leverage my body weight against him. He tightens his grip at first until, with a shocked grunt, he loosens it just enough.

The second I pull free, it's as if all of the air is sucked from the room. My skin burns in the absence of Mischa's touch, and this time I can't escape his expression.

He only stares, his gaze devoid of emotion. No anger. No hate. No pain.

And I'd prefer he shout. Yell. Rage at me.

In his silence, I break. Internally fracture, held up only by muscle and bone. Like a coward, I wrench my gaze down to his chest, but the sight isn't a comfort. I swear I can see his heart pounding madly beneath his jacket, assaulted by both shock and rage.

Or maybe a different emotion, one that softens his voice just a fraction as he asks, "Is this what you want?"

*What I want.* There are too many nuances to that statement to parse over. The only one that matters is the grim suspicion that, just like Donatello, he knows me too well.

My impulsive answer? *No.* I want to go home. See my family. Know for sure that Ellen and Eli are okay. Forget what's happened.

Ignore the past.

Instead, I look up and try to tell him everything I can through my expression. That I love him—so much. That I would never willingly turn against him…

He holds my gaze unflinchingly, every bit the stoic figure I've come to respect. For a second, I swear I see a grudging frown tug on his mouth. Acknowledgment that he at least understood, even if he doesn't quite understand…

But I'm too much of a coward to be sure. I look away and catch Donatello watching me, his mouth in a flat line. I'm struck by the sense that he knows what I'm planning even before I do. Gradually, I regain my balance and start toward him, but his blank expression doesn't waver.

Though he at least has enough tact not to gloat now. There's no point. As far as his twisted game is concerned, he's already won his round.

The pawn is his to claim.

Walking toward him is like wading through quicksand. I fully expect Mischa to grab me again. Lunge. Fight. But it's as if the world is paralyzed in this moment. I'm the only person alive able to move. Walk. Breathe.

And I can take some small shred of smug pride in watching Donatello's expression. The hard mask slips for a heartbeat.

I know he's holding his breath, cocking his head warily as I reach out, grappling for a fistful of his suit jacket. I raise it slowly, dabbing at the blood streaked across his face.

As I do, I meet his gaze, and I let him in. I let him see every thought circling my brain.

He thinks he's in control of this game? He's wrong. So wrong. Now more than ever, am I determined to punish him for everything he's done. Death isn't good enough.

I want him to thoroughly know the pain that comes from doubting your own identity. From having someone else consume who you are and spit out a mockery.

I want him to suffer just as I did.

And I make a mental note to do whatever it takes. I strip myself of any past hesitations or modesty, and I dive right into the only weapon I have that's ever truly seemed to affect him.

He vows never to touch me? Well, I didn't promise to show the same restraint. As our eyes meet, I let my thumb graze his jaw just once.

It's a warning. Unexpectedly, he nods, having understood me clearly. "Play with fire if you want, hellcat," he murmurs for only me to hear. "Play. I'll gladly watch you burn—"

"Willow?" Mischa's voice is ice.

I turn to him as Donatello shrugs me off, but gently, maintaining the ruse that I am his willing fiancée.

"Lunch, tomorrow," he says to the figure behind me. "Bring your fists if it will make you feel better. I'll make sure to find a place public enough to cause a scene—"

"Fuck you."

"Your daughter won't—the least I can do," Donatello says quickly. My cheeks flame at the rare note of honesty in his voice. I don't think he even realizes it himself. "Until our wedding, at least. Though maybe I should change my mind?"

The tension cracks, and I brace for another assault.

"Enough," a quiet voice demands. Fabio. "I suggest we settle this for now," he says, smoothing his hand down the front of his suit. "Not here. Both of you have family trying to rest and heal. Let's not forget that, shall we? Who knows what amount of stress this little argument might cause them? As Donatello suggested, you should meet tomorrow at a restaurant of my choosing. All necessary documents will be agreed upon then."

"You're just as insane as he is," Mischa growls.

"I am insane," Fabio says with a respectful tone and a slight nod. "I've spent the past three days trying to hold my nephew's brains in with bandages while hunting for a hospital safe enough for him to recover in. If you think Donatello is the only one with a grievance to leverage, think again. You've seen the proof of Antonio Salvatore's crimes. Maybe you should spend your time finding out who really set this mess into motion. *Both* of you."

Again that rare note of authority slips into his tone, hardening it.

"A wedding honestly sounds reckless and contrived, but damn it, if it keeps my nephew alive and puts an end to this before more damage can be done, I will shove them down the aisle myself. As you can see, the girl isn't a prisoner. I'll vouch for Donatello's behavior—she'll remain intact and safe before any vows are uttered. Now, again I suggest you leave while I try to head off any publicity that might arise, yes?"

I never actually hear Mischa acquiesce. Like a coward, I face the wall, and it feels like an eternity passes before the *mafiya* finally retreat. Their heavy steps are my only clue, along with Donatello's weary sigh.

"I owe you, Fab," he rasps with genuine gratitude. "I mean it—"

"You're damn right you do," Fabio snaps, jutting his chin. "Whether you put a fucking chastity belt on her or lock her in a room, she better be unharmed. I mean it, Donatello—"

"She's a child, Fab," he says offhandedly.

"Hmph." Fabio's eyes narrow to slits. "You almost sounded convincing. Now get the hell out of here. Think of all the bribes I'll have to hand out to keep the staff quiet, in addition to arranging for increased security—those *famiglia* aren't nearly enough."

"That's another thing I wanted to talk to you about," Donatello suggests. "Antonio wasn't exactly a champion of employee retention. I need help tracking down the old crew to replenish ranks."

"I did notice the entourage seemed a little anemic," Fabio says. "But this was never my realm, Donatello. Never. I always kept my nose out of *famiglia* business, and you never had a problem with that before. Why should I change what I think in hindsight was a very prudent decision now?"

"For me," Donatello says simply. I marvel at this vulnerability. This raw, open pleading. If he had asked me to participate in his scheme like this…

Would that have made any difference?

"I need you, Fab," he says, his expression stern once more. "I need you."

"Fine." Sighing, Fabio rakes a hand through his graying auburn hair. "I'll hunt down some old contacts—but my one stipulation is some new recruits. I think I know of a small outfit you might be able to absorb. They're scruffy and will need some shaping up, but I think in this instance, the more, the merrier."

Donatello scoffs. "Don't tell me you've been rubbing shoulders with lowly criminals, Fab."

"You don't know the half of it." The man shoots him a guarded look. "Anyway. Go get cleaned up. I'll stay here for a while. I think they'll schedule the surgery for tonight—but I don't think you should be here."

Donatello's entire posture shifts in the blink of an eye. He hunches, the color draining from his skin. I sense my heel twitch against the floor at the fear he might collapse again.

"You think I'll let him go under the knife alone?" he asks.

Fabio doesn't even flinch. "I think you should let the team work in *peace.* Let Vin rest without worrying about another visit from the *mafiya*, hmm?"

"Don't use him as your excuse," Donatello growls, drawing himself back to full height. "What? You think I'll be too emotional?"

"That's exactly what I think." Fabio crosses to him and places a hand on his chest. "You need to stay focused, Don. Keep your head clear. The best thing you can do for Vin is to make things as safe as possible for him. He should be your primary concern right now. Not Mischa. Not anyone. So go home. Wait for my call on his status. Don't drink, and keep your head clear. Think of the man you want Vin to see when he wakes up. You, covered in blood? Or you, dressed nicely in a suit, not smelling like drink for once, with a safe home for him to recuperate in? I'll leave you to make that choice."

He returns to Vincenzo's room, smiling weakly at the startled nurses and medical personnel peering from around corners.

"Fuck." Donatello eyes his bloodied hand, shaking off fresh droplets of blood. Shoving that same hand into his pocket, he meets my gaze and inclines his head toward the elevator. "Let's go."

He lumbers down the hall, leaving me to follow. At a glance, Mischa's men appear to be long gone—but my guilt isn't. It pools in my blood, growing stronger with each beat of my heart. I swear I can hear it, morphing from noise into a guilt-ridden taunt—*I failed him.*

*I failed him...*

There is no pretty way to say it. No heroic words to soften the blow. I chose Donatello Vanici over the man I love like a father. The man who saved me. Who has always protected me.

I turned my back on my family.

For what? The whim of a monster.

"You played your part, little wife," Donatello remarks from inside the elevator.

I flinch, hating how he can read me so accurately. He leans against the wall, his eyes unsettlingly dark. "I'm sure your Mischa will be angry, but I think you'll agree that it is better to be angry than dead."

*Is it?*

My body chooses to answer for me where words can't. I step back just as the doors start to close.

"No!" He's too fast, shoving his hand between the barrier before it can fully seal. Eyes flashing, he starts toward me, but I'm already turning my back to him, retracing our path through the hall.

He's hot on my heels, raging. "What the hell are you playing at?"

It's the wrong terminology. This is so not a game.

It's a war, and I'm tired of cowering behind the trenches.

Increasing my pace, I practically sprint to my destination, expecting to feel a wrenching hand on my shoulder at any second. Just when I swear I see movement in the corner of my eye, I enter a room where the only conscious inhabitant looks up, puzzled by my appearance.

"Can… Can I help you?" Fabio asks, rising from a chair beside Vin's bed.

"What the hell are you doing?" Donatello snarls, storming in a second later. He doesn't reach for me. Yet.

Ignoring him, I approach Fabio, making my expression as pleading as I can. Truth be told, I know nothing about him. He could be just as dismissive of me as Donatello, but when I raise my hands and mime for a pen and paper, he nods, fishing both from his suit jacket.

"Here." He gestures to a small table nearby, clearing a space for me to write.

"What are you doing?" Donatello demands as I start scribbling. I can sense him reading over my shoulder, but I don't bother to disguise my words. As I pen my first line across the page, he scoffs.

"A list of demands?" Fabio interprets.

I nod, gripping the pen so tightly it shakes, smearing ink. If this were a game, as he claimed, the rules could be easily broken. But in war? There are more rigid norms to follow.

Or so I hope.

"Does the heiress think she gets to stomp her foot and get her way?" Donatello mockingly snipes. The venom in his voice is a shock. Not entirely due to anger, I suspect. Fear?

Once again, he hates when I foil his expectations of me.

"You've had your say. Let's see her speak for herself." Fabio gestures to the page. "Well, let's see them then—"

"Fabio, are you seriously entertaining this?"

The man raises an eyebrow. "Is she your *willing* fiancée or not?"

Donatello says nothing, but I can feel his gaze boring through the back of my neck.

"Well then," Fabio says in the resulting silence. "Let's see her demands."

I only have four—just a small list in the grand scheme, composed with one aim in mind. In what way can I claw back a pathetic shred of power for myself?

The first step is to remember who I am—a Stepanov. Ellen and Eli are in this very building. I can't leave without seeing them, so I write.

*1. I am allowed to see my family.*

"Now?" Fabio sounds wary, but Donatello snorts.

Or maybe he growls. "No. Hell no——"

"Perhaps once everything is set in writing," Fabio says over him. His lips contort into a strained smile purely for my benefit. "I'll see to it personally."

"So she can go prancing back to Stepanov manor and return leading an army of guards?" Donatello snipes. "Hell no."

"If we make the proper arrangements, I don't see why not," Fabio says tacitly. He taps the paper, eyeing me expectantly. "What else?"

*2. I have my own guard stay with me. Evgeni.*

It's the only option that seems capable of making Havienna somewhat bearable—a piece of my new life. Someone to ground me in the world of Donatello Vanici. He may have consumed Safiya, but I refuse to let him destroy Willow.

"Think that's a proper 'arrangement'?" Donatello snipes.

Fabio furrows his brow in concentration but merely nods. "What else?"

My hand shakes, but I force myself to finish.

*3. I have unlimited access to my own financial accounts.*

That draws an even more violent scoff. Unbothered, I keep writing.

*4. I am allowed to pick my own clothing.*

He doesn't challenge that stipulation. For the first time, I look back to find him leaning beside me, his hand braced on the table, his eyes dark in thought. A shudder runs through me that I can't explain. Rather than inspect it, I turn back to my paper as Fabio gently takes it from my hand.

"These all look agreeable to me," he declares. "I'll have them drafted into the final agreement you'll present to Mischa—"

"No!" Donatello grabs for the page, but Fabio pulls it out of reach. "Have you lost your mind?"

"You want this to seem like an equal partnership, right?" Fabio eyes my list and nods, folding it. Meeting my gaze, he tucks it into his pocket. "These sound reasonable enough. Consider them done—" He turns his attention to Donatello, unfazed by the glower the other man shoots him. "I suggest you start making your arrangements. Think of it this way, Mischa has less to counter if it's clear she's let her own voice be heard in this matter. Which brings me to another point…" He eyes me as if considering whether or not to voice his concern. After a second, he squares his jaw. "The matter of her 'virtue.' Call me old-fashioned, but if you haven't touched her as you say, then we should codify that. Have it cemented in stone so that no one can accuse you of taking advantage. Besides, if your *love* is so pure, you should have no trouble waiting to consummate your union—"

"Knock it off." Donatello casts me a glance of disgust. "I have no intention of ever fucking her if that's what you mean."

My cheeks flame—a reaction I have no control over. It's purely instinctive and not at all a response to the sincerity in his voice. Sincerity that so vastly contradicts the way he touched me only a few moments ago. When his mouth had been inches from mine, and I could see it in his eyes…

He wanted more.

"Good," Fabio says. "Then put your money where your mouth is. You break that—in any way. If she winds up… scandalized in your care, you forfeit everything. I'm sure you have no trouble agreeing to that."

Donatello noticeably hesitates, his eyes flicking in my direction. Just when I think he'll argue, he nods curtly. "Fine. Let my little wife have her stipulations." Pushing back from the table, he stalks from the room, his voice a parting slap. "Come."

"I'll make sure these are drawn up," Fabio insists. He opens his mouth as if he means to say more. Instead, he nods. "Good luck."

I take a steadying breath before turning to the doorway, but a childish urge to linger here in Fabio's orbit swamps me. With every inch I stray from him, the shift in the atmosphere becomes more apparent. It's a feeling like that of being adrift in a boat with no oars.

And my destination is a waterfall certain to dash me to pieces.

More than that, Donatello Vanici is a storm unto himself, swirling madly just beyond the door.

I could run and cower from the resulting tempest. Or step right out into the thick of it, unbothered.

He stiffens when I enter the hall and find him waiting, standing tall as a nurse scurries past him, looking so small in comparison to his bulk. In his eyes, I expect to see that simmering anger—and I do. But mingled there amongst it all is an emotion I wasn't anticipating.

Grudging respect?

It gleams for just a second from the overall darkness before he blinks and inclines his head. "Come. Little wife."

I stiffen, inhaling a shaky breath. His tone says it all—he'll make me pay for my little play for power.

But this time?

I'm ready to do battle—and I have more than a knife to counter him with.

# EVGENI

*B*riar, in all her mystery, continues to surprise me. I expect the card she gave to lead to some grand hotel. A backdrop elegant enough to fit the allure of a disgraced heiress.

Instead, I find myself before a motel in the part of Hell's Gambit aptly called the "shitty end." In a city where crime runs rampant, it's only fitting that the district deemed the very worst fits all of the most glorified stereotypes.

Two women stand on the corner across the street, and their outfits make it obvious what wares they're selling even in broad daylight. Further down the block, a man stands wearing an oversized jacket, his gaze darting around the few people passing by.

Inside, the place's quality is even more apparent with peeling tile and creatures scurrying in the shadows. My my, the Winthorp heiress has fallen from grace.

Her room is on the second floor in a slightly better location that overlooks a vacant parking lot rather than the main street. I knock once, expecting a haughty silence from the other end.

Anything but a cheerful, purred, "Just a minute."

Amusement mingles with an emotion I can't decipher, and both make me raise an eyebrow with one realization—she's expecting someone.

Just as I start to wonder who, the door opens, ushering a cloud of perfumed steam into the hall.

"Oh," the woman remarks, sounding mildly surprised. "It's you."

I blink to find her standing on the other end with her back to me. Her bare back. A towel slung around her waist barely covers the curve of her ass and the rounded tops of her thighs.

Everything else is on stark display. Modest doesn't seem to be her default setting, so I suspect her appearance is entirely by design. To intentionally distract me.

Perhaps from the fact that a male was here. Recently. I mentally parse through the stern, gruff figures I passed entering this establishment, none of whom seem to be an aristocrat's preferred company. Perhaps this woman has fallen further than I realized?

"Do tell me you're here for a reason," she prompts.

"That depends. I hope I'm not interrupting something," I counter.

"I promised one of the girls downstairs some of my old clothes," she says coyly before slinking around a corner, presumably into a bathroom given the steam wafting from that direction.

I picture her tailored red dress and the janitorial outfit. "I don't think your style fits with their line of work."

She laughs, sticking her head out from around the corner. Her blue eyes gleam, and I'm once again struck by how similar she looks to Ellen Stepanova.

And how different. It's as if someone took Ellen and stripped the warmth from her gaze, leaving only cold, serpentine mystery. This woman is as similar to her as I assume Eli is to his murderous, bastard of a biological father.

*So tread carefully,* a part of me warns. *Even if your cock insists otherwise.*

I blame biology for the tightening in my abdomen. I'd have to be blind not to notice her beauty. Luckily, those same eyes spot the gun lying on a dresser across the room. I don't miss the distinctive hint of masculine cologne underneath her feminine smell, either.

The lone bed in the center of the room is empty, apart from rumpled white sheets. A few paces away is a closed door, I assume leads to a closet. Could the culprit of the scent be lurking there, waiting to spring an attack?

Though hell, I couldn't blame anyone but myself if this is an ambush. I'm the fool that blindly entered it without even alerting my men of my location.

Almost as if I know how stupid it would sound out loud. To come here on a whim. Even rookies know one simple rule—never meet an enemy in their den, especially not alone.

But here I am, so why wait for the tables to be turned?

The room is small enough to cross in just three strides. From here, I have a clear view into a narrow bathroom where she stands with her back to me, sans the towel.

Gritting my teeth, I rip my gaze away and wrench open the door, palming my own gun in its holster.

Inside, all I find is a leather suitcase and a simple array of clothing hanging. At a glance, none of the items, in particular, look like they could belong to a man, from the slender red dress to a simple coat and a few blouses.

"Don't tell me you intend to interrogate my luggage?" the woman purrs from the doorway of the bathroom.

I turn to find none of the playfulness reflected in her gaze. Her eyes warily track the return of my gun to its holster while her arms hold a thin towel around her. The dampness of her hair reinforces the fact that she took a shower, and I interrupted. But was she alone?

Unapologetic, I surge forward, surveying the narrow bathroom before glancing into the shower.

It's empty.

"Should you strip search me as well," she remarks coldly. I glance back to find she's pressed herself against the wall. "Maybe I have a weapon hidden on my person? Make sure you're thorough."

Sarcasm laces her tone, but I recall her trick with the blade at the hospital and back away, keeping her hands in view.

"Maybe I should?"

Amusement mingled with irritation flickers across her gaze. Then she shrugs. "Oh, all right." With an exaggerated sigh, she lets the towel fall, stepping into me with her arms outstretched. "Take your time," she taunts.

Something that could be alarm makes me grit my teeth, but I take another step, switching to the mindset of a man who can't afford to take a chance. Not even if it's offered mockingly.

I let my eyes sweep her body with a scrutiny usually reserved for the days I'd scan the landscape for enemy soldiers or active threats. Instead of underbrush and sky, I make a mental map of pale skin unmarred by so much as a pimple. The only flaw I find at all is a series of linear, faded scars along the inside of her wrist—which she quickly contorts from my view once she catches me staring.

Other than that, some men might deem her…perfect.

Perfectly dangerous in my book.

"Satisfied?" she snaps once it's clear that she doesn't have a weapon within reach. I wouldn't put it past her type to smuggle a knife in one of the few crevices available on a human body not visible to the naked eye.

A flush spreads across her cheeks as if she can read my mind, but her smile is shameless.

"I think you've seen enough." She stoops, grabbing her towel from the floor. Casually she drapes it around her, and I'm finally convinced that she's alone. "What brings you here? Let me guess. You intend to lure me into a trap at the behest of your employer?"

"No," I snap. "I came to listen. Who is Alexander?"

She laughs while slinking past me for the closet. From it, she grabs the red dress and drops her towel again in favor of it. From over her shoulder, she chirps, "Don't tell me you believe me, now?"

"I don't," I counter. "But even if you are lying, I'd still like to know your aim."

"But don't you already?" She whirls around and props her hand beneath her chin. Slowly, her eyes rake me over, and she nods once to herself. "Spoiled little rich girl, desperate for money. My aim is to fleece Mischa by threatening his wife or holding whatever information I may know about my family over his head, yes?"

She smirks knowingly when I don't respond.

"Oh, Evgeni, Evgeni…" Arching her back, she eyes herself in a dingy mirror hanging on the wall and runs a hand down her side. "Of course, there's always the possibility that I've already decided what type of man you are and have arranged everything perfectly to exploit that knowledge."

"Oh?"

Her smile widens. "That you are the bleeding-heart type ripe for the manipulation by some poor, downtrodden woman you deem in need of saving. That by luring you here with the promise of information, I've only managed to provoke that sense in you. Once you see my living arrangements, you'll be driven to protect me."

It's an unnervingly specific plan. "Then you've sorely misjudged me," I say.

"Ah, but did I?" She nods in the general direction of my gun—while I notice she's inching closer to the one lying on the dresser. "Don't tell me you bring that on all of your social calls."

"Only when I'm meeting with someone who has already proven themselves dangerous."

She shrugs and switches tack, throwing herself onto the mattress. Fluttering her lashes, she eyes me through them. "Well, I must have made quite the impression for you to come so armed just to meet one lone woman. If I do tempt you enough to take a shot at me, do use a silencer, or you might spook the drunk next door."

"A drunk, huh? Is *he* responsible for the smell of cologne in here?"

Her tongue flits across her lower lip—I caught her off guard. "As you can see, I'm all alone, soldier," she simpers.

It's a lie, but I can't fathom her reasoning.

"Right. One lone woman," I parrot.

"Ah!" Her upper lip quirks into a smug grin. "So you do have a sense of humor. You could have fooled me—"

"Talk," I demand. "Or lose your chance. Given your family history, I think you know a thing or two about loss."

Her smile falls, and something in my chest twinges. Regret? I don't decipher it.

With a heavy sigh, she hauls herself upright and spins to face me while still seated on the edge of the bed.

"You're right," she snaps. "I do know a thing or two about *loss*. Especially loss derived from the pissing contests of two arrogant men. Your Mischa? I've been on the receiving end of one of his grudges before. I'd rather not be in that position again—" the shudder she suppresses seems genuine enough. "So arrange a meeting between us like a good dog and everyone is happy. Trust me, I think he'll want to learn what I know."

"And what is that?" I demand. "You should be careful throwing around the term 'dog.' I've known some men who train their animals to rip their enemies limb from limb."

"And I'm sure Mischa has trained you well," she says softly. "But before you rip me apart, you should know one thing."

"What?"

"I'm the only person standing in between him and a bullet aimed for his skull—and not just his. Those sweet little girls of his. The boy? Eli? Would you see them all dead because you were too arrogant to listen to what I have to say?"

I take a step toward the bed. "I suggest you say it now."

She swallows, her eyes darting to my side again. "Alright. Mischa is in danger—"

"And how do you know that?"

I can't tell if the emotion flitting across her gaze is unease or pride. "Because I'm the one who brought the hoard right to his door."

Her words take a second to process. "What are you—"

My phone buzzes in my pocket, an occurrence so abnormal I reach for it automatically.

"Volkov?"

"You should get here," a man warns, his voice vaguely familiar. Usually, he isn't whispering.

"Mario?"

"Just get back to base," he insists. "Now. Mr. Stepanov is not happy."

His stern tone is the only trigger I need to lurch into action, heading for the door.

"Also, while this may not be the best time to mention it," he adds in a rush, "I found something you might be interested in. It's not much, but I think you're smart enough to make use of it. I'll send it all in an email. Keep in mind it won't lead back to me, and if anyone asks, we never had this conversation."

He hangs up before I can even question. For once, Donatello Vanici isn't at the forefront of my mind.

"Leaving so soon?" the woman simpers, crossing her arms as I open the door. "Don't let me stop you. I'm sure anything at all must be more important than—"

Pivoting on my heel, I snatch her arm, yanking her from the bed mid-word. She covers her fear easily, trying to pull her hand back with a smile.

"Let go of me—"

"You wanted your audience with Mischa?" I snarl, satisfied when she falls silent. "Well, you've got it. I'm taking you to him now."

Surprisingly, she doesn't argue as I haul her from the room.

And I can't resist the paranoid suspicion that she was ready for just this very scenario.

Ready for me.

*B*efore I even go through the main gates, it's apparent that security is at an all-time high. The typical detail looks to be at least doubled, with more men than usual milling alongside the road, eyeing me warily as I approach the house.

I drive straight to the front of the manor, sensing the urgency in the air. Mario wasn't exaggerating. Something is wrong.

My body feels electrified by the charged atmosphere as I park just beyond the front steps. For the first time, I have to resist the urge to grab my gun, sporting it out in the open.

"Stay here," I warn the woman huddling in the passenger's seat. "Though hell, you're stupid enough to run, try it—" I nod to the nearest agent standing guard near the entrance. "While I'm inside, I'll give them permission to shoot if you step so much as a hair out of this van. Got it?"

"Of course." She flashes a disarming smile, but I'm not the only one affected by the heightened mood. She seems paler than ever, her eyes glued to the manor house in a way that could be politely deemed as "disgusted."

"In the meantime, I'll run over my heartfelt entreat to the man who killed my brother and destroyed my family," she adds absently.

Real hate tinges her voice, and for the first time, I mull over the sheer stupidity of bringing her here. I didn't even think to blindfold her—a breach of protocol too glaring to interpret as of yet.

Instead, I leave the van and instantly feel all eyes fixate in my direction, but not in the typical greeting. They're on edge, eyeing me warily as I start inside.

"What's going on?" I ask one of the two men posted by the main entrance.

He shrugs, avoiding eye contact. "Mr. Stepanov is in his study—"

"Something happened at the hospital," another man interjects. "You weren't there."

Alarm runs down my spine, and I'm already lunging forward. "Mrs. Stepanova? Is everything alright?"

Rather than answer, both men push open the door, ushering me inside.

The trip to the study feels longer than ever, populated nearly every step of the way by a guard standing at attention. Either they're readying for something or…

They've just returned.

The answer is made clear the second I near the door to the study where Mischa stands, shrugging off his jacket.

"Where the hell were you?" His voice is chilling, bellowing throughout the room. I've never heard this tone directed my way before—a guttural baritone previously reserved only for Donatello Vanici.

"Sir. I had to step out. I informed the other men on duty…" One look at his face, and I sense the need to drop all protocol. If there were ever a time for honesty between us, this is it. "What happened?"

"Donatello Vanici strolled into the hospital where my wife is. Where my children are. *That* is what happened." He slams a fist against his desk with a sound like a gunshot. "Do you have any idea the danger they were in? Do you?"

But more than that is angering him, evident in his tense posture, crackling with barely concealed aggression. I only know of one topic capable of stirring this kind of reaction. "Willow," I say thickly. "She was there?"

"Yes." Mischa cocks his head, his expression suddenly ice. That look alone tells me that this reunion with his daughter wasn't a particularly happy one. "Do you want to know what that bastard claimed? Do you?" He hisses a chilling imitation of a laugh. "That he was going to marry her."

"What?" I feel my brows shoot up. "That's—"

"Sick," Mischa says with a grudging nod. "That's exactly why he thought of it."

"But Willow…" I bite my tongue, trying to choose my words carefully. If Mischa is this angry, but Vanici isn't dead, there can be only one explanation as to why.

"Did he threaten her?"

Mischa looks away, glaring through the window, and I have my answer.

"She stayed with him." It feels strange to say out loud, but in my gut, I suspect it's the truth even before I see Mischa's jaw tighten in acknowledgment. He whirls back to face me, and I'm struck by just how angry he truly is.

Not all of it might be directed at Vanici, I suspect.

"She didn't have a fucking choice, did she?" he counters. "Vanici threatened her. The bastard probably got a kick out of it."

"Did she look injured?" I press, trying to wrap my brain around how such a meeting went down. I can't imagine Mischa standing aside while Vanici pranced off with his daughter—and he wouldn't. Unless something convinced him to, and I doubt Donatello Vanici would have that sway. Only one person could make Mischa show that kind of restraint. Willow. Which means...

"She...wanted to stay?"

"I know her," Mischa insists. "She wouldn't submit to that motherfucker without a reason. That son of a bitch!" He slams a fist against his desk, and the conviction in his voice would be enough to convince anyone else. But I remember the way they interacted in that recording, how Vanici seemed to worm his way inside her head. It was obvious from day one—the bastard has a hold over her.

"I should have been there," I admit.

"Damn right you should have," Mischa growls, turning the full brunt of his gaze to me. "I hope your diversion was worth it."

A part of me reacts to that word choice. Diversion? Did he have me followed? Know where I'd been all along?

Or is his caginess feeding my own budding paranoia? Even so, one fact remains clearer than ever.

"I would have been there if I were on your detail," I point out. "Like I should have been. In fact, if you told me the connection between Willow and Vanici from the start, we might not be having this conversation."

"You don't know Vanici," Mischa warns, his eyes slits. "And I suggest you drop this topic. It's done. I've already sent Mario to replace your post at the hospital—"

"So you continue to shove me aside," I say, alarmed by just how much that angers me. Rage coils through my bloodstream, red hot and searing. "Vanici? Maybe I don't know *you*. I thought Willow was your focus. Not some childish feud." The words are out of my mouth, and it's too late to take them back.

"What did you say?" Mischa steps from around the desk, his head cocked in a warning.

Any other day I'd adhere to my creed. Bite my tongue.

Today? I'm too damn tired.

"I said you brought this on yourself," I say, holding my ground. "All because you were too damn stubborn to listen —" Within the space of a second, he's within striking distance, and I don't even see the punch coming.

My vision goes black as pain shoots through my jaw. Groaning, I blink to bring the room back into focus. Mischa's back is to me as he paces, anger radiating from him like heat.

"Get out," he growls. "You're done."

"So you won't even talk to me about this? What is really going on between Willow and Vanici? They knew each other, didn't they?" I taste blood. A lot of it. I have to spit at my feet just to keep speaking. "Mischa—"

"Don't make me rethink my leniency, Evgeni," he warns.

"I'm not doing anything but trying to reason with you." I spit again, fighting to ignore the fire lancing through my jaw. "Just hear me out. I'm sorry I left, but I think I learned another lead—"

"Get the fuck out." He isn't even looking at me anymore, marching toward the desk. "Now. Before I change my mind on letting you leave peacefully."

"Peacefully?" I scoff at the word, holding my ground even as he whirls around, ready to strike again. Anger simmers just beneath the limits of my control. I cling to every ounce of restraint I have, but when my lips part, I can't contain the words that spill out. "You call what you've done 'peace'? Vanici is no Saint, but if you would have listened to me from the outset—"

"You'd have me roll over like a fucking whipped dog," Mischa counters coldly. "Because that's what you are, isn't it? I knew you were gun-shy when I hired you, but there comes a point when 'peace' can't be fucking *wished* for. I won't sit by and let my daughter be taken from me."

"Because that's what I did? Sat by?" I don't even recognize the sound of my voice. I hear it as if I'm miles away, and for a second, I don't even see Mischa. I see blood. Lifeless faces staring up at me. I see death…

"Don't judge me," Mischa cautions in a voice so harsh it snaps me back. I blink and see him clearly again, his eyes like coals. "Don't you fucking dare. I'm no 'saint' either, but I never massacred women and children under the guise of following orders. These should be simple for you—get the hell out."

I say nothing, eyeing the man I've followed faithfully for over six years.

He's barely recognizable, but deep down, a part of me acknowledges the subtle changes. His coldness. The vicious tension lacing his posture. His rage.

Fear will do that to a man. Consume him until it's all he can see. I know that firsthand. It's why I've come to trust my simple creed before the Stepanovs, and it's the only thing I have left to rely on now.

*Loyalty first. Survival second. Never get too close.*

Still stroking my jaw, I head for the door, passing the man standing guard. My surroundings blur as I navigate the house, exiting what feels like an eternity later. Out front, my van still waits untouched.

"Don't tell me he's not home," Briar snipes as I open the door, climbing into the driver's seat. Her sly smile is comically easy to see through now. Fake. A thin veneer against her fear.

She's terrified. Hell, she reeks of it.

But I don't feel a damn thing. Just a persistent, pulsating sensation near my hip. Without thinking, I swipe my hand there, striking something hard. My phone?

"Evgeni?" Briar prods, her voice trembling slightly. "What are you doing?"

Her eyes are on the hand I slip into my pocket, but I don't answer, withdrawing my cell phone. I narrow my eyes at the notification flashing on the home screen—an email from an unfamiliar address. Belatedly, I remember Mario's parting words. He found something.

In the end, it isn't much—a single name that nonetheless triggers a wave of haunting recognition.

*Safiya Mangenello.*

I heard it before... When? I wrack my brain until the answer hits me—straight from Donatello Vanici's mouth. The name he called Willow.

"Where are you going?" Briar demands, her fear even more apparent. Her eyes are saucers, her lips pursed, her hand reaching for the door on her end.

Stowing the phone, I put the car into drive before she can get it open, slamming on the gas. As I peel down the driveway, I don't look back at the manor once.

Mario was right. Even a name is enough to set me on the right path. If Mischa won't listen to reason, then I'll follow another avenue if I have to. Anything to protect Willow.

At least I have two potential veins of information to tap—Briar Winthorp and Safiya Mangenello.

One of them holds the answers. Only this time?

I refuse to be restrained by any sort of creed.

# 21

# WILLOW

Returning to Havienna feels like leaving the real world for a shadow realm. One in which up is down and down is...

*Pain.*

As the sun makes one final stand against the evening cloud cover, the sunlight bathes the walls of the old house like firelight, and apprehension rips through my body, dissolving every ounce of resolve. I was wrong. Shadow realm might have been too kind a term—it's hell, a reality made perfectly clear the closer we come to it.

The devil himself sits beside me, itching to reclaim his domain.

He doesn't speak as he parks in the driveway, flanked by two vans. Without so much as a word to me, he exits the car, leaving me to follow as the men we went with fall into step behind us.

Inside the house, I shiver, hating the painfully familiar feeling that shoots through me as I cross the foyer. The past battles with the present, and I'm nearly overwhelmed by the conflicting emotions. All I can do is grit my teeth and dart my gaze without settling over anything for long.

I still notice when Donatello barrels past the stairs, heading in the direction of his study. Preferring to extend the distance between us, I scramble up the stairs, aimlessly wandering the hall, unwilling to enter that pink room just yet.

I stop short just beyond it, startled to find someone watching me from the doorway to Vin's old room. Not a ghost, though she's pale enough. My heart breaks at the sight of those wide eyes staring blankly. Someone found clothes for her at least, but I recognize them with a chilling jolt of *déjà vu.*

They were mine. Hers. Safiya's.

The little pink shirt has faded slightly with time, but it and a pair of jeans fit the girl perfectly.

I approach her slowly, all thoughts of Donatello forgotten. The same person who procured the clothing is presumably responsible for arranging the room as comfortable as possible given the circumstances. They made up Vin's old bed, and the small collection of toys scattered around also seem familiar.

The girl watches me warily, her thin arms crossed over her chest. Raising a dark eyebrow, she inclines her head. "I want to go home."

The pleading note in her voice breaks me. I wind up staggering toward the bed, sitting on the end of it, feeling more helpless than I did even before Mischa. It's not her fear that rips through me like a lance. It's her hope. Like I might help her achieve her only goal. To go home.

When in reality? I'm no better than the madman holding her captive. Unlike her, I always had a choice whether or not to be here.

I don't know what it is about my posture that draws her closer. Silently, she sits on the floor nearby and picks up a ratty doll with a sigh. "Luca said you can't talk," she says in a near whisper.

Luca? I picture the man always near Donatello with the watchful gray eyes. Luciano. Has he been taking care of her?

She doesn't say. When I nod to confirm her insinuation, she returns to her doll, absently twisting its stringy hair around her finger. Something in her dejected expression chills me to the bone. There's a familiarity in her posture. Like this isn't the first time she's had to submit to a horrific situation and distract herself with play.

I think of my sisters, Marnie and Aljona, even little Ivan. They wouldn't be half as calm as she is. Where did Donatello find her? I wrack my brain and recall a name he's said before. Antonio. Antonio Salvatore.

Was he a different monster than Donatello? I can't ask her. But as I watch her fiddle with the doll, I recall another memory—this time not one of Safiya's.

I had already shed that identity by the time I came under the care of someone other than Donatello Vanici. A gruff man with long, wild blond hair and flashing dark eyes. Early on, he proved himself different from the man I'd been sold to. He gruffly procured clothing for me and taught me how to braid my hair. He teased me with his rare smile and snuck me sweets.

In that short amount of time, he set himself apart from any other father I knew.

Without thinking, I reach for the girl, tentatively stroking one of her black curls. It's soft, the color a beautiful raven hue. She stiffens, her eyes cutting cautiously to mine. When I run my fingers through her hair, she doesn't withdraw.

So I stroke until she lets me inch nearer. Then, once I gauge that she won't withdraw, I braid her curls as slowly and methodically as Mischa once did for me.

*It's pitch dark when I startle awake, sensing a smaller body curled alongside mine. It takes me a second to realize where I am—still in Vin's old room. A sliver of moonlight drifting through the window illuminates the little girl, asleep near the head of the bed, her hair in a neat braid.

Whatever woke me hasn't disturbed her, at least. She lies still, her chest rising easily.

I can't say the same. My heart stutters, my breathing heavy. Anxiety eats at my fraying nerves, but I don't know why. Then I hear it—a faint noise resonating through the walls in addition to the typical creaking of the house. It's deeper, unsettling in pitch. Guttural. Howling.

An animal?

Cautiously, I rise to my feet, feeling my way to the door. When I open it, the hall is deserted but silent. I wait, straining my ears. Could the noise have been a trick of the wind? Just as I start to retreat into the room again, I hear it. Definitely a low cry, coming from the end of the hall.

Curiosity drives me forward. Or recognition…

The closer I come, the less that sound resembles random noise until I can clearly identify it. Human. A man. One crying out in utter agony.

Before I know it, I'm standing near a partially closed door, sensing the hair on the back of my neck stand on end. Every cell in my body throbs, warning me to back away. Better yet, take the girl and run for good.

I push on the doorknob instead, peering into a room I vaguely remember from another life. I rarely came in here, even back then. It was a mysterious realm where adults retreated at night and children were banished from.

It smells like him. Like pain and sweat, and other intangible scents collectively deemed *masculine.* Loud, his breaths rasp on the air, unsteady and disjointed, undercut by the creak of the mattress. He's moving, but I doubt he's awake, merely tossing and turning. Writhing.

"God," he rasps, shocking me into stopping cold. A frantic heartbeat later, I realize he's still asleep, shouting only at nothing. Just phantoms. "Fuck… No. No!"

I freeze, paralyzed by the same feeling I felt in the hospital. Helplessness, like a bystander forced to watch a tragedy unfold, unable to do a damn thing to help.

If I heard him, I'm sure the others in this house have as well. Preserving his modesty could explain whatever impulse drives me to close the door without leaving.

Or cruel voyeurism. For once, I get to see him tormented, but the sensation constricting my heart isn't anything close to pleasure. I'm not happy as he cries out wordlessly to no one. I'm numb.

He excels so well at turning his pain into rage that it's easy to forget what it stems from. *Pain.* An agony few can fathom. It marks those who suffer from it like scars.

My feet inch closer to that bed of their own accord, while my heart beats frantically as if protesting every step of the way.

*Go back.*

*Go back!*

Too late. I'm near enough to see the sweat glistening on his forehead and the sheets tangled around his frame. My bare foot strikes something soft, and I look down, making out the vague outlines of clothing. His suit jacket, shirt, and finally his pants. As my gaze flits back to the bed, my cheeks flame as I register the bold outline of his body.

He's naked except for a pair of boxers. His bare chest heaves as he claws at the sheets tangled around him, and I have my clearest view ever of the tattoo.

The name blazes as if on fire, the letters bold enough to make out in the dark. I don't know what possesses me to reach out, brushing the end of the final A.

He groans, his eyelids fluttering, lips moving wordlessly. A silly thought strikes me—braiding his hair won't soothe him.

But I don't know any other methods.

I should leave. Avoid him. Run. The same way I should have stayed in Stepanov manor the night I heard about Vin. The same way I should have avoided him at all costs from day one.

Where this man is concerned, I do nothing at all that I *should*.

So, instead, I sit on the end of the mattress with my back to him. Before long, my fingers shoot out as if of their own accord, landing over that telltale jagged strip of flesh so different from the rest of him. It's like I've already mapped it inside my head without meaning to, able to navigate every ridge and curve without having to see what the shapes form.

*Her* name.

Absently, I trace the letters over and over the way I would the notes printed on a sheet of music. And as if his body is my instrument, it plays along. His groans lessen while his heavy breaths paint the air in a twisted, unstable melody…

One so beautiful and so haunting it deafens me to everything else.

Even the part of my soul warning me to run.

# 22

## DON

This fucking house is a prison—both hers and mine. The calculus of bringing her here was that the environment would give me the edge, but now?

I couldn't give a damn about exerting my influence over the little Stepanova. I'm too tired. The kind of bone-melting exhaustion sleep can't fix. I've forgotten what it feels like to experience it. Or to dream, for that matter. Whenever I close my eyes, I do neither.

Instead, I get a taste of what true hell is. Emptiness. Loneliness. Nothing. A darkness where the loss of everything and everyone ever stolen from me looms, and I'm powerless to run from it anymore.

Who needs hellfire? Guilt is searing enough, blazing through my chest, impossible to douse.

*For Vin. Olivia. Safiya…*

I still see them, lurking just beyond reach. I can hear them calling for me. Condemning me. Dooming me. Their cries tease me on the edge of consciousness, impossible to escape.

Screw Fabio's praise of sobriety; I'd kill for a bottle. Booze would be enough to dull the clamor and let me sink into oblivion. It's gotten me through the past seven years, after all.

Damn, it's been so long since I've laid in this room. Fuck, this might even be the same bed I shared with Olivia, feeling her soft, warm body against mine, her voice in my ear. The memory feels more real than ever. I can hear her, *"Wake up, baby. It's late. I told you that another round would exhaust you, old man…"*

Her warmth breaches time and space, heating my skin. I swear I feel her hand on my shoulder…

But it's not.

I jolt awake, fully aware that the warm fingers grazing my chest are too small. Too textured. Olivia kept her hands manicured, but these…

They've been used. Worked, but in a delicate manner different from the callouses that harden mine. *Music,* a part of me suspects, even before I open my eyes.

Pale moonlight drifts through the singular window, adding vague definition to the master bedroom, though now emptied of everything but the bed. Bathed in the glow is a lone figure perched on the end of the mattress, her back to me even as her fingers trace the expanse of my bare chest. She could be a twisted figment of my imagination if it weren't for her smell.

Roses.

I sigh, eyeing the ceiling, too tired to mull over her motives this time. She could be a masochist, driven to find me always at my fucking lowest. Her mind is a landmine I'd rather not maneuver. Instead, I remember…

How it felt to have a body next to mine. A feminine scent flooding my nose. With Liv, I only felt a constant current of love. Trust. Obedience.

With her?

There is no warmth, just a cruel need to test her presence. Exploit it. In the absence of liquor, she's all I have—so I take it. She doesn't expect the second I snatch her hand, lifting it for inspection. There's always the possibility that she's not here. Experimentally, I flick my thumb across her palm, sensing the shudder that runs through her. She's real, all right. To her credit, she doesn't pull away.

Or to her detriment.

I've changed my mind. Fuck sobriety. Her fear is a fitting substitute for liquor, and I'm too weak to resist.

So, I tug, dragging her closer until she's almost lying on her side. Those eyes flit up to mine, but if I expect to find a motive in them, she denies me that much.

Her gaze is unreadable.

But I've already learned how to make her react. With a shift of my weight, she's beneath me, and I get my wish—her slender throat jerks around a hard swallow. Inhaling, I savor the slight tinge to her scent. How those eyes widen and her teeth seize her lower lip in alarm.

*Finally,* she gives me something to interpret—fear. I crave the shiver that wracks her spine as I deliberately run my finger across her chest, copying the same path she traced over mine. Her heat distracts me from everything. So warm.

But her scent is a gut-punch, so sharp I find myself leaning down, inhaling as much as I can. It's the wrong move. Intoxicated, I close my eyes, extending this dangerous position a second longer. Another.

Nothing compares to feeling her body against mine. For a moment, I can pretend I'm back there, with the weight of the world on my shoulders but a loving woman in my bed.

It's funny how that intangible concept can change every fucking thing. *Love.* One kiss can soothe the blood-soaked memories. The act of it can even make a new life.

And one fucking second can rip it all away.

When I open my eyes, the figure staring up at me isn't my sweet Liv. She's a different creature entirely, with dark eyes so huge they swallow me whole. Pink curved lips. A gaze that doesn't flinch.

Not from me, or the open hostility I don't bother to hide. She takes me in as though it's all entertainment just for her. She won't admit it out loud, but this is why she's here. Why she's *always* been here.

My descent into madness amuses her. Why wouldn't it? It's guaranteed vengeance, and she doesn't even have to wield a blade or pull the trigger to carry it out.

My own brain will destroy me in the end, and her presence is the catalyst.

I choke out a laugh, eyeing that pretty mouth. The least I can do is give her a good show.

"Do you enjoy your taste of power, little wife?" I'm surprised by how calm I sound. Inside? My heart is ramming against my ribcage, my breathing heavy.

Oh yes, she's enjoying this.

Instead of a verbal answer, she inclines her head, sending that hair fanning out around her. Her eyes flicker, processing the question, but she's unsure. Unprepared. Damn, there's something irresistible about catching her off guard. Making her squirm.

"You like to exert control over me?" I ask her, letting my gaze travel down her face and lower, glimpsing the flesh bared below the neckline of her dress. It's wrong. But what the fuck do I care?

This moment is a thin, fragile barrier keeping the past at bay. I'll deal with the consequences later...

When her breasts aren't separated from me by a thin layer of fabric. When I can't feel her heartbeat hammering away. Or every twitch and jolt of her muscles as she fights her body's own instincts to lie still.

My brain does what it does best and conjures up dangerous images—like of her splayed in her bed back in that perfect Stepanov manor, naked and alone. It brings up a very good question…

"Have you ever touched yourself, hellcat?"

That lone question has the same effect as gasoline dangled over an open flame.

Her skin ignites, flushing red in the silvery lighting, her lips twitching as she swallows again. Her fear is one thing, but this is the real addicting aspect of her—this supposed innocence. A girl who grew up in the heart of the *mafiya* but never saw a man's dick in person. Yet, she dangles her sexuality when it suits her.

Which brings up an irritating point—it suits her. Stripping naked when it gives her an advantage. Playing coy when it doesn't. Insisting on her own stipulations and most egregious of all…

Seeming offended by my insistence on one point—I don't want her.

Not this body. Not those eyes watching me grip her wrist, pressing the slender limb against the sheets. She stiffens, her breaths coming faster. *Good.* I should only want to push her this far.

Nothing more.

Until I do. It's like another part of me takes over, bypassing all logic, driven only by curiosity. How far can I make her go?

Her eyes track every movement of my head as I bring it near hers. Letting my lips brush her earlobe, I test that theory with a simple statement. "You don't know the first damn thing about what really happens between a man and a woman. You've never fucked…and I'm assuming the answer to my question is no. You've never touched yourself, either."

Her body always betrays her. That slender throat quivers as her heart beats so rapidly I can hear it. I could dance to the melody if I wanted—fitting given her music background. She may be silent, but terror makes her sing. A symphony of physical tells, too beautiful to resist.

I feel my grip on her arm tighten. Before I know it, I'm dragging that hand across the sheets, down to her waist. Then lower.

Sensing my intention, she starts to struggle, kicking with her legs. The pressure of one knee is enough to pin her down. She tries clawing at me with those hellcat nails, but if she pierces the skin, I don't feel it. I don't feel a damn thing. My entire focus centers on the thin wrist in my grasp, manipulating it against her will until her fingers brush her hip.

She goes still, her lip between her teeth, her cheeks flushing a deeper scarlet even in the dark. Beautiful. And dangerous.

I'm fully aware of the line I'm toeing. The risk I'm taking by playing this game. In another time, and another place, I'd heed the warnings blaring through my veins.

But I'm already addicted to this…

Her defiance. Even now, she doesn't shy from my gaze. She holds it, daring me to push her harder. Test her. Break her.

So I blurt the first thing that comes to mind, damn the risk. "Do you want me to teach you?"

*Bingo.* She sucks in a breath, though I realize I've done the same. Her fingers twitch, inching between us as I goad her on. My cock twitches, but I drag her hand right past it, urging her lower.

Lower.

Her eyes stare resolutely past me, up at the ceiling—but her body is an inferno. A rigid mass of twitching muscle. I close my eyes again, breathing her in. Her legs twitch, fighting to resist the pressure of her own hand inching between them. The air wheezes from her lungs, her pulse a fucking symphony.

My thoughts flash back to how she reacted as we stood before the Saleris. How she looked at me then. It wasn't her audacity to kiss me that irritated me. Still does… It was the way she did it. Her expression, so quick I doubt she was even aware of it.

The same brief glimpse of terror I saw in the study when I tried to strike a match, and again in the hospital with

Mischa. I don't care that she's the catalyst for my impending war with the *mafiya*—that's not what condemns her.

This one look has always been her original sin.

Concern for me.

"You still care about me, hellcat?" I croak, hating the raw pain in my voice. Because it's a lie. It has to be... But like any addict, I chase the illusion.

Even when it stings.

"Then show me what I'm missing," I rasp. "This is how you can hurt me. Show me what I'll never have."

I open my eyes just in time to see her eyelids lower as she registers that statement. Does it empower her? *No,* I decide. It annoys her. I'm giving her permission to torture me.

She hates being controlled, so fucking stubborn she'll do anything to defy any attempt to. Like stop fighting me, letting her hand settle exactly where I aim it.

Fire washes through my abdomen, heralding a volatile reaction. Fabio's warning echoes faintly through my skull, but I'm inclined to ignore him. If I pretend this is a dream, nothing that happens fucking matters. There are no consequences if I'm imagining all of this.

And I have to be.

Because otherwise, the little hellcat wouldn't look so... eager? Her nostrils flare, her eyes darting back up to mine.

I slide my fingers over hers, painfully aware of the searing heat building between us. Sweat slicks her soft skin, enhancing every little tremor to shoot through the tender muscles and fragile bones. If I weren't sure before, I am now—she's never done this.

So I bear down harder.

At the same time, our gazes meet again, but it's different. I'm inside her head, clearly seeing every thought to cross her mind. Confusion. Sweet, fucking *confusion*.

How could something so debasing feel so fucking good? It's a question I'm wrestling with myself. Finally, she takes over, resisting my grip.

"Do it."

Her eyes blaze, accepting the challenge.

And she does. Her lips flutter, pursed over gritting teeth, and it's all the proof I need. Damn. I'd kill to see her fingers make contact for the first time—but nothing comes close to watching the realization spark within her. The pleasure that can come from a simple touch. A sensation sharp enough to blind her to everything else. The world. Shame. Me…

"Look at me," I goad before she completely goes vacant. I'm here with her.

And, fuck, it's hell. It's heaven.

"Keep going," I grate through clenched teeth.

Her eyes narrow, but I sense her hips arch. Buck.

"More."

Her eyelids flutter as her head rears back against the pillow. Her teeth seize her lower lip, her breaths feathering.

I rock against her, torturing myself with the feel of her moving hand and twitching limbs.

I make the mistake of watching her again as those eyes go to my chest. Her throat jerks around a swallow, her hand moving faster as she traces the letters tattooed there.

I know the second she comes. She can't disguise it.

Her entire body radiates pleasure, her lips parting, body glistening with sweat.

It's incredible.

Terrifying. I'm struck through, mortally wounded the second she goes limp. Her scent teases the air, sharp with pleasure, and I'm dying a slow, vengeful death.

The little witch has won another round.

And she found a weapon better than a knife.

"Wake up!"

I startle to awareness, groaning as my head pounds. A cool, wet sensation hits me full in the face, snapping me awake. Water? I sputter, wrenching my eyes open to find Fabio standing over me, an empty glass in hand.

"What the fuck?" I croak, spotting the dampness coloring the sheets around me. He spilled something on me, alright.

"Considering the fact that your entire fucking life depends on you making this meeting with Mischa, I assume you don't want to be late. You wouldn't wake up." He leans over me and sniffs. "What? Did you drink an entire fucking bottle?"

"You're cursing," I point out—a rarer occurrence than even his smoking.

"Fuck you," he bites back.

"Fuck me," I rasp. My head pounds violently enough to be explained by a hangover—but even that can't explain the erection threatening to rip through the front of my goddamn boxers. It's an almost painful state of lust. Beyond blue balls.

I grapple for a handful of sheets to haul myself upright, and I remember the source of the discomfort…

Fuck, the sheets are still warm. Like she slept here afterward —my innocent little fiancée who fingered herself beneath me for the first time. Climaxed, her dark eyes so wide with the newfound sensation it's like taking an entire cask of whiskey straight into the vein.

"Jesus, Don!" Fabio's tone drips with disapproval, and he crosses to the window. With his gaze on the view, he fishes a cigarette from his pocket and lights it up in the same breath. "Just tell me—how drunk are you?"

"Not drunk," I admit, hauling myself into a sitting position.

"You sound like it," Fabio snipes. "You sound like hell."

"What time is it? How is Vin?"

"Vin is fine," he says, his tone softer. "He's recovering well. No complications. You can see him later. Now, I need you dressed, along with your pretty fiancée, and across town within the hour to meet Mischa on time."

"Fuck." I swipe my hand across my bare chest. The skin there burns as if ignited—all because a little minx wanted to see my scars as she came.

I groan, swiping my hand along my face as if I can physically wipe the memories away.

"Are you sick?" Fabio asks, a hint of sympathy leeching into his tone.

"No." But I am.

Sick enough to toy with fire and enjoy the searing burn. God, I can still smell her. Feel her.

"Well, if you aren't sick, we need to move. Here—" he throws a handful of fabric at me, dry at least. "Get dressed. I have a car waiting. You have five minutes. I assume your lovely fiancée is somewhere safe and sound in this house…" He trails off, his expression shifting from anxious to horrified. With a forced cough, he heads for the door. "I'll find her."

I wonder if he will, "safe and sound" in that pink fucking room.

I can't seem to move, eyeing the black suit Fab left as though dressing is a foreign concept.

My innocent little fiancée…

Even if I wanted to fuck her—hell. My cock throbs, and I drop the pretense, at least in my skull. I do. I crave her if only to get her out of my system for good.

But I can't touch her.

"Don? Change of plans." Fabio storms into the room, scoffing when he sees I'm still not dressed. Rolling his eyes, he inhales on his cigarette. "Mischa's called off the meeting—"

"Son of a bitch!" I lurch to my feet, already spinning toward the window. I expect to see a hoard of *mafiya* vehicles peeling down the driveway. If not now, then soon. "I should have known this fucking plan wouldn't—"

"Oh, the plan is still on," Fabio insists in that superior tone he rarely uses. The one that signifies when he's fully in "accountant" mode and the world around him becomes reduced to numbers and profit. "The arrangements are already being put into place as we speak. Your wedding, by the way, will be within a week."

My head spins, and I wish I truly were hungover. I'd be too numb to fully feel the consequences of those words and what they represent.

My wedding, to a woman I can't ever fully claim.

I grit my teeth so hard my jaw cracks, snapping me back to the present reality. "So why did Mischa call off the meeting?"

Fabio huffs on his cigarette and then sighs. "His wife is awake. I thought it prudent to allow him some time to help her…adjust."

Namely to the reality that her daughter is being married off and an attempt had been made on her life.

"So what now?"

"You still get dressed. I've been pulling some strings to help you get the *famiglia* back underway—"

"Thank you."

"Don't," he says. "If you do anything illegal, I don't want to know. But I figure keeping you busy minimizes the risk of you going on another killing spree."

"There's another thing," I say. "Antonio was set up by someone else. I need to find out who."

"That could be a nice way to segue your relationship with Mischa away from murder."

"It could," I admit.

A happy family on a mission of revenge.

It's the shit warm, fuzzy fairy tales are made of.

**~ The story continues in Shattered Throne, Book three in the Mice and Men Series ~**

AFTERWORD

You have finished book two of Donatello and Willow's story. Do you want to see where it all began? Check out the War of Roses Trilogy!

**XV: Fifteen: War of Roses Trilogy Book One**

Kidnapped, Ellen must do whatever it takes to survive her cruel mafia captor, Mischa. Will he break her— or will she outsmart him?

WHEN HATE BECOMES OBSESSION…
Mistaken for her beautiful half-sister, Ellen Winthorp is taken captive by a madman who declares that she will be his "fifteen": the fifteenth victim of a vicious mafia blood feud. Armed with only her instincts, Ellen must resist her captor for as long as she can—which is easier said than done the more she's exposed to the complex man beneath the beast.

Because Mischa Stepanov isn't a mindless monster—he's a wolf, and she's the unwitting doe caught in his midst.

Unraveling the torment of his past may be her only hope of salvation...

Or the secrets uncovered may destroy them both.

# CHAPTER 1 OF XV: WAR OF ROSES TRILOGY BOOK 1

*Noise…*
*Chaos…*
*Briar…*

The first thing I'm aware of is that I'm blindfolded—a fact that could be a blessing in disguise as my thoughts blur and jumble together. Only one coherent question escapes the fray: *Where am I?*

No answer comes to me immediately. My straining ears can make out only a few words muttered nearby in unfamiliar voices. Deep, *masculine* voices.

Various smells irritate my nostrils as well: sweat, body odor, male. *All* male. God, *where am I?*

I try flexing my shoulders only to wince. My hands are impossible to move, tied behind my back with something rough. Rope?

*Oh, God.*

Familiar terror gnaws at my belly as moisture gathers in my armpits and sweeps across my palms. At least, now, I have an inkling of my fate. I'm trapped in another one of his games. My nostrils flare with renewed purpose: seeking out *his* scent.

He must have hired lackeys this time; foreign body odor drowns out the stench of his cologne. I can't smell him.

*But you can survive this.* I fall back on the mantra that has gotten me through every day for sixteen years. *You can survive, Ellen. Focus, Ellen. Breathe, Ellen.*

Ten hours—that's how long I endured last time. My resolve had nearly splintered by the end. I'd almost given in. Almost.

But even psychological wounds eventually heal and leave tougher scar tissue behind. I can last another ten hours with Robert. My brain makes that distinction as the barrage of scents dissipates, revealing one that overpowers the rest: a man's. I taste the nuances in his stench rather than smell them—he's *that* potent, composed of a multitude of different things.

Cigar smoke.

Vodka.

One scent in particular makes my heart stop. Salty and sweet, it's almost as familiar as the flowery perfume wafting from my skin now. *Blood?*

Robert never smokes. He doesn't drink. Whenever he hurts me, he always washes his hands before and after. It is our routine, and he is nothing if not predictable.

No. This is someone new. Someone taller, whose shadow completely blots out what little detail plays across my blindfold. His footsteps are steady. Heavy.

"This her?"

I sense the outline of his fingers before the callused edge of one grazes my forehead.

"You made sure?"

His voice is deep. Almost *too* deep to be intelligible: a series of grated, rumbling notes. There's an accent tucked among them—something thick. Eastern European? Briar had a maid from there once. Sonja.

Sonja liked to read Jane Eyre. She liked scribbling love notes to Robert Sr.'s men before fucking them in the broom closet late at night when she thought no one was looking. Sonja liked a lot of things before Robert took a liking to her.

But another figure from my memory possessed this accent as well. Even though his words were hissed in a whisper, I still remember. *Breathe!*

"Bring her."

Those two words snap me back to the present. Unfamiliar hands grab my shoulders, cinching the soft silk of my blouse. *Briar's* blouse. She dressed me in it lovingly, remarking on how the color complemented my eyes. Our eyes, the same shade of light blue.

"Move!"

A tug on my shoulders hauls me upright and unseen hands shove me forward. Every sound echoes. Four footsteps, including mine. The biggest man takes the lead, I suspect, his gait rhythmic against creaking floorboards.

In contrast, the men holding me dig their nails into my skin and scurry toward an unknown destination. A rusty squeal seconds later conjures the image of an old door opening, and the footsteps trail off.

"Move!"

Something rams into my side and I stagger for balance until my cheek strikes a hard surface. It's warm. *Human.*

"Get her on the bed."

Those harsh hands return to my shoulders to fulfill the command.

"Sit her on the edge…like that. Cut her hands free."

A metallic hiss sends a shiver down my spine—then *pain!* Fire courses through my fingertips as circulation returns to them. I long to flex each one, but I know better. Instead, I keep them close, settling them onto my lap.

These men kept my skirt on, at least. Her skirt. The hem comes down past my knees, and I've never been so grateful for four inches of satin. It will buy me more time.

Ten hours. I've already lasted ten minutes. *You can do this,* the courageous part of my soul whispers. But then that voice dies in the wake of two more words uttered in that guttural cadence.

"Leave us."

The two smaller men scatter in the direction we entered—but it's all wrong. No. No. I don't smell Robert, and he'd never leave me alone with another man. Not his lackey. Not even his own father.

Most alarming of all, this man certainly is no Winthorp. His voice isn't familiar and this house doesn't smell like any property on the familial grounds.

*They took me from the motorcade…*

Fire sears through my skull as memories return in snatches. The clearest one is of her face. *Briar.* So beautiful, dominated by that pure, sweet smile. "I want you there," she insisted. "We're sisters, after all."

*Sisters.* I cherished how that word sounded in her soft cadence, tucking that moment inside myself like one of the trinkets hidden in my secret cache. Love was more precious than a button or rock I'd stolen away. Those four words meant everything. *I want you there.*

But the memory of that moment serves as a weak antidote to the terror paralyzing me now. More bits and pieces come back.

I was in the car—the beautiful limousine for once, instead of one of the servant vans that took up the rear. For part of the way, I was even sitting beside her while she braided my hair. "We look alike now," she wistfully remarked, beaming at our reflections in the polished windows.

*We look alike.* The phrase haunts me. As if I could ever look like Briar, with her lighter ringlets and her creamy skin. The only feature we truly share is our eyes. Our mother's eyes. Large, round, and blue. In every other respect, she takes after her father, with a beautiful aristocratic nose and a graceful neck. Every Winthorp possesses the same subtle characteristics—markings of the blood, they like to claim. Good blood. Blue blood.

I take after my father, whoever he is.

Briar loves to tout our tentative resemblance anyway—especially to her benefit. *I* am the one the maid saw sneaking out back two summers ago. *I* am the one who scurried out of the room of that visiting businessman one winter.

And now…

*We look alike.*

"Take off the blindfold." That voice…

I swallow hard, uneasy. Robert has found a new monster to play with. Someone who shares his flair for the dramatic. *But where is he?* My tormentor always relishes this part of the game. How he enjoys savoring my fear as I try to piece together where I am. Admittedly, it wasn't this hard before; he never strays too far from the property.

His favorite lairs are the boathouse, or the deserted crypt, or the east wing. I could always hear the bluebirds chirping throughout the grounds, no matter which corner of the estate he deemed my chosen cell.

My ears strain, searching for that faint, familiar song. This time of year, they're nearly deafening, able to be heard in even the farthest reaches of Winthorp Manor.

Two seconds. Three.

I hear nothing.

"Take off the blindfold."

The harsh rasp of syllables steals my breath away. I know anger on Robert. On Robert Sr. Even on Briar. They stutter. They shout. They scream.

None of them ever exude their impatience to the point where I can sense it in the air. Or taste it: copper on my tongue. This man isn't a Winthorp.

The realization coaxes my body into action. My sore fingers finally contort, trembling after what must have been hours of captivity. Whoever tied my blindfold snagged bits of my hair in the process and every tug on the knot at the base of my neck rips tiny strands loose from my scalp—comparable to my pathetic hopes being ripped from underneath me one by one.

I don't hear the bluebirds.

I can't smell Robert's favorite cologne.

When I finally get the knot loosened enough to uncover my eyes…

I see hell.

Mother used to say it was beautiful, forsaking the teachings of the local priest. "Hell is a rose," she used to murmur, her gaze turned inward, wistful and distant. "A flawless one, with all the life sucked out of it. The thorns have become knives. Its leaves have swallowed up the stalk. It's grotesque. It's deadly. But never forget that, underneath the violence, it's still beautiful."

*He* is beautiful. Or he was once. Blond hair draws my attention first—a sun-kissed gold in places, darkened with age in others. It's been clawed back from his face into a ponytail longer than mine was before Briar trimmed it. His eyes are that dangerous color between blood and brown. Like a flame, they catch the light filtering in through a sloppily boarded-up window beside him. His face is angular. Chiseled. Stone. Every feature is sculpted to convey just one emotion: determination. The way an owl might watch the mice scurrying underfoot in the stables. Or the way Robert used to look at me.

The way the devil looks, I presume, as if he has all the time in the world. More than ten hours.

An eternity to torture me.

**~ Continue Reading XV ~**

# A WORD FROM THE AUTHOR

Hey there!

Thank you so much for reading! If you enjoyed the story, please leave a review and recommend the book to any friend you think would love this twisted world. You'd have my eternal gratitude. Even a short sentence goes a long way!

Then, come join the rest of us dark romance lovers in my Facebook Group where you can get snippets, sneak peeks of upcoming books and even help vote on aspects of future novels.

**Come to the dark side:**
https://www.facebook.com/groups/lanasbeautifulmonsters/

**WANT MORE STUFF TO READ?**
Join my newsletter and get a **free book**! Plus, you get to stay updated with any new releases, random givcaways and exclusive sneak peeks!
https://www.lanaskybooks.com/newsletter

**Other Novels:** https://lanaskybooks.com/

# ABOUT THE AUTHOR

Lana Sky is a reclusive writer in the United States who spends most of her time daydreaming about complex male characters and parenting her Cockapoo Joey. She writes dark, twisted romance across several genres. Her titles include everything from mafia romance to vampires.

facebook.com/AuthorLanaSky

twitter.com/lanasky101

amazon.com/author/lanasky

pinterest.com/lanasky101

goodreads.com/lanasky

instagram.com/lanasky101

bookbub.com/authors/lana-sky

tiktok.com/@author_lana_sky

www.ingramcontent.com/pod-product-compliance
Lightning Source LLC
Chambersburg PA
CBHW071417190726
48292CB00001B/19

reaching out would pull me to my death—my fate would duplicate that young girl's.

Someone behind me pushed me forward. It was a deliberate attempt to sacrifice me—a brutal tactic going on up and down the line to draw an opponent forward. Sacrificial pawns, and now I was one. Then a tangled mass of bodies from both sides triggered an eruption of complete chaos everywhere. I ducked punches, rolled on the floor, scissor-kicked a man about to smash my head in with one of those retractable steel police batons.

I fought my way blindly toward the exit despite the hands trying to clutch me, fingernails clawing at my face, head, and clothes, and the fists swinging at me from all directions. I have never been so afraid in my life.

I made it to the doorway, gasping, my clothes ripped and hanging in shreds. I was bleeding wherever my skin was exposed. As I stumbled down that dimly lit corridor to the metal door leading to the alley, I sobbed in exhaustion. Whether it was hysterical laughter or sobbing, I couldn't have said then. I had the tunnel vision of a desperate man trying to save his life.

My last fear put ice in my stomach: would that door open? I rammed my shoulder into it so hard the force carried me into the alley where I hit the ground, rolled, and slammed into a dumpster that rang like a gong when I struck it. I picked myself up, smelled the putrid air, and staggered down the alley toward the street where that cab had dropped off Neci and me a lifetime ago.

It had to be close to three in the morning by my hazy reckoning. Even if there were cabs in this area at this time of night, no sane driver would pull over for something that looked like me at that time. I knew I had to get as far from that club as my legs could get me.

Maybe I could flag down a passing cop cruiser or an ambulance.

I walked for an hour at least. I didn't recognize any street names and just animal instinct kept me moving. I was a battered homing pigeon heading for the Bruckner Expressway. The East River wasn't far to my south, but I kept heading west, looking behind me every ten steps, then twenty, finally just moving ahead, hoping the sky would lighten in the east and save me. I heard voices in shadows and kept moving, fearful that I might attract attention from street predators or junkies looking for an easy mark.

I remember stopping to rest in a couple tenement doorways. Once, I fell asleep in front of a bodega, the first sign of civilization since I had left that madhouse, that carnival of violent freaks behind me.

Because I learned years ago to carry my wallet in my front pants pocket, I still had my wallet. As dawn broke, I found a taxi sitting near the corner of the Four-One precinct house. I intended to go straight to the front desk and report what I had just experienced and seen— probably one murder—and yet . . .

My numbed state, my cowardice, if I must admit it, led my weary legs straight up to the cabbie where I held a fistful of twenties in front of his window. He looked at the money; then he looked at me. He hesitated, finally nodded. I got inside.

The ride back to my apartment was a blur. I remembered nothing until he pulled in front of the lobby. The ride and tip left me broke but alive. I remember a couple tenants passed me in the lobby on my way to the elevators. Their heads swiveled on their necks. I stood rooted, unmoving, in front of the elevator doors when they opened and the early risers all heading downtown to their jobs in the banks, brokerage firms, and offices split in front of me like a bow wave. I sensed people behind me but I entered alone. No one was going to ride up with me in my condition. New York discretion. This is the same city where 38 people saw Kitty Genovese murdered in front of her own apartment and no one called the police.

I showered, slapped ointment on my scratches, checked out the purple bruising on my torso and the puffed left eye where someone had connected in my scramble to the exit. Even cleaned up, I looked like someone who'd been rolled out of a trash compactor.

I slept for ten hours, woke with a blinding headache, ate leftovers from the fridge and sat down to think. I called everyone I knew in Manhattan. No one knew Neci. I called a friend from NYU who, as best I could recall, had informed me of the party the night I met Neci.

"No, man, I don't remember her," Jonathan said.

"You must have seen me leaving with her," I replied. "We were holding hands."

"Shit, man, I was too engrossed in the film."

"What film?" I didn't recall any TV sets playing in the apartment, not with all that music.

"In the bedroom," Jonathan said. "The guy's got a fantastic collection of baroque films. *Freaks*, a remastered *Nosferatu*—"

"Jonathan, I don't give a shit about pinheads and vampires. I god-damned near got killed in a Bronx shithole packed with real freaks!"

* * *

Nobody had a clue who Neci was and no one at the party that night remembered seeing me leave with anyone. The one person who did see me leave saw me go alone, so I knew he had me mistaken for somebody else.

It gave me the shivers thinking of her holding my hand, leading me like a sheep to the slaughter.

After two more days of stewing and fretting, pacing a path in my rug, I finally decided I had to call the cops. I spoke to a desk sergeant at the Four-One, and he told me to come in at one o'clock to make a full report. He didn't sound convinced.

I called an Uber and arrived at the station exactly on time. I was told to wait on a bench for a detective to call for me. Forty-five minutes later, a uniformed cop led me up a flight of stairs to the detectives' bullpen. I was introduced to a Detective Mackey, who shook my hand, told me to take a plastic seat beside his carrel and tell him what I had come to tell him.

I gave him the account as I had rehearsed it the previous day. I kept my voice even and chose my words carefully. I started from the party on West 63rd and finished with my stumbling home to bed three days ago. He listened and took notes the entire time. He didn't look at me more than once or twice and the only thing he said was to ask me why I didn't report it right away if "this girl you saw was being beaten to death in this—in this 'corridor of death.'"

I blushed. "That's what they were shouting when the music started up," I said, "and I didn't call you right away because I was pretty beat up and exhausted."

"Uh-huh," he said in a tone that said I should try pulling his leg with the bells on it. If he'd called me a downright liar, he couldn't have made it plainer he didn't believe a word I'd said.

"Let's go," he said.

"Go? Go where?"

"To your"—he checked his notes again—"to your Club Ludillo."

I gave him precise directions as if I had a GPS in my head. I'd never forget that place no matter how much time passed.

"This it?"

"Across the street," I said. "See that alleyway? It leads to a metal door. The club's inside."

"You sure about that? There's nothing around here. It's a dump."

"Trust me."

"I don't trust nobody," he told me, getting out and locking his unmarked car. "I'm a cop."

I led him down the alley and even saw the same cardboard "house" where that pair of eyes had looked out from inside when Neci and I entered.

The door was locked. Mackey gave me a sour look, told me to hold the flashlight. He returned carrying a Halligan bar, the firemen's tool for breaching doors.

I stood back while he popped the upper end off its frame with the pick end. We entered with Mackey's flashlight beam leading us down to the main room of the building.

"Look at the shit in this place," he said; "it stinks."

I hadn't noticed it that night.

"This way. Right there. That's the door. Go through there and you'll see everything."

Mackey brushed past me and I followed.

The cop took a few steps into the main area and stopped in his tracks. He played the light around sweeping it back and forth.

My heart climbed into my throat. It wasn't simply different. It was empty, deserted, and the only furniture in the place were giant weaving spindles from a textile factory.

"So," Mackey said sarcastically, "did all this mayhem you described occur in and around these big machines? Those things must weigh a couple, three tons apiece."

There was no bar, no tables or chairs, no track lighting overhead—nothing. It was a factory that hadn't seen any human enterprise since the turn of the last century. I was left speechless, a stuttering wreck. In desperation, I told the detective to flash his light on the floor in the center of the room. Where that petite girl had fallen under a storm of vicious kicks and blows, there had to be a pool of blood.

"This your 'corridor of death,' huh?" The sarcasm dripped from his voice.

"I don't know how to explain it."

"You were drinking that night you said, right?"

"Look, I couldn't have drunk enough to hallucinate everything that happened to me that night! There had to be a couple hundred people here. I was nearly clubbed to death—"

"Yes, so you said. Well, there's nothing here. Look at the floor. See our footprints? How do two hundred people—'maniacs,' in your word—manage to tramp all over this place and leave no trace?"

"It was . . . clean when I was here," I said. "Maybe someone came in and cleaned the place—"

"Are you out of your mind? A dozen cleaning outfits working non-stop couldn't clean up a place that fast and then turn around and haul in a couple dozen machines and plant them around. Look at the dirt . . . the filth! Come on, let's get out of here. I've seen enough."

On the ride back to the station, Mackey never said another word to me. I could just imagine what he told his fellow officers when I left. My frazzled mind played out a scene of him surrounded by other detectives barely holding in his laughter as he described me telling him about the *Gilligan's Island* theme signaling the Corridor of Death. I was an instant stationhouse joke, maybe a legend in a city infamous for bizarre characters and wild stories told by cops in their favorite bars.

But it wasn't just the mockery that I would have to endure. I was served a warrant for filing a false report. I had to get a lawyer, go to an arraignment, plead "no contest," and pay a six-hundred dollar fine for wasting city resources.

I spent the next month dodging friends and acquaintances. I unplugged my phone for two weeks. Another month passed, I barely left the apartment. I stopped going to clubs. I stopped going out at night.

Jonathan left a dozen messages. I finally gave in and called him back.

"You sound like Mickey Rourke in *Angel Heart*," he said; then he did one of his bad imitations: 'I know who I am! I know who I am!'"

"Go ahead, make fun of me," I said calmly, although I was twitching with rage and frustration. "I know what happened to me that night."

I had a panic attack in a subway. I stopped going out altogether except for necessities. Another month passed before I returned Jonathan's calls.

"Congratulations. You're officially an agoraphobic recluse," he said; "you better get some help soon, my friend."

I took his advice. He gave me the number of a therapist in the east seventies who specialized in PTSD cases. I made an appointment for early September.

On my third appointment with him, he seemed different when we shook hands. He had a smug look on his face. He was going to solve the paradox of my confusing reality and fantasy, he said.

"First," he began, "Club Ludillo. Have you ever heard of Rio's 'funk balls'?"

"What you have described occurs there," he said.

"What?"

"Teenagers from the *favelas*, the slums. They attend these wild balls on Saturday nights. They meet in warehouses run by drug gangs. They have music until midnight and then the DJ plays the theme song to *Bonanza*. Do you remember that show?"

"It's a cowboy show from the sixties, right?"

"Correct." He hummed a few bars off-key.

"That famous TV theme song is the signal for rivals to meet in the center. The drug gangs have guards who patrol your 'corridor of death,' which is their term, by the way. They try to pull one another across. It's horrible, from all accounts. Many teens are killed. Even the girls participate in the murders. The guards throw the dead bodies into the hillsides. Only at dawn when it's safe will the police enter the *favelas* to pick up the dead."

"I didn't know anything about that," I said. I could see where this was going.

"Your *Gilligan's Island* is simply transposed. Your seventies disco music is their funk music from the seventies."

The look on his face was more irritating than the realization he didn't believe me any more than Detective Mackey had.

"OK," I said, "and before you start humming Black Sabbath at me, tell me how I could know this without ever having heard of these funk balls in Rio?"

"Your subconscious mind heard of it, I assure you," he said. He was all but gloating now. "Your mind,

410

however you came by the knowledge of the existence of these fight clubs, absorbed it like a teacher doing a grammar lesson on a blackboard and pulled it together to form your . . . *vision.*"

"And Neci?"

"Neci was a part it—the biggest part of it. Not one woman but a composite of girls you've known, with a touch of the exotic added by your sub-conscious mind as part and parcel of this fantastic narrative which you convinced yourself had happened."

"My wounds, the blood—the fact I was beaten black and blue?"

"In your fugue state, you had obviously wandered into one of those underground clubs where misfits—"

"Misfits?"

"Bikers, perhaps. A rough crowd, to be sure. You must have caught their attention. They beat you savagely. Your mind—"

"I had my palm read," I fumed.

"Yes . . . by Donna De Varona."

I watched him like a hawk for the slightest sneer or hint of contemptuous laughter.

He must have seen me bridle. Sensing me become calmer, he continued: "She's a famous person. You simply transposed her from the memory of that evening when you were browsing in your college library."

I was sick to my stomach. I excused myself and immediately ran to the small bathroom in his outer office. I threw up the coffee I'd had that morning until nothing but ropy strings of drool came up.

When I returned to his office, I was beaten, abject, ashamed. An even greater emotion welling up than what my humiliation had produced: *I was insane.*

He read my mind.

"Don't be alarmed," he said. "Trauma-inducing hallucinations are a byproduct of any severe emotional distress. You are a perfectly normal, young man. Do not be unduly alarmed. I can help you. We can work through this together."

I spent thousands of dollars over the next six months. I became familiar with his office décor and every inflection of light filtering through his Venetian blinds for the exact time of day. He said I was "improving" each time. We worked through my past, my parents' marriage, my mother's early death, and my random existence in the city, which garnered a huge amount of time; he pressed for even more details which I could not provide.

Finally, I was able to leave my apartment for longer and longer periods of time. It was a triumph for me to take the Second Avenue subway. I made myself stay on, ignoring the hideous press of bodies at the peak times, getting off at 72$^{nd}$, then at the 86$^{th}$ Street station, and finally making it all the way to the 96$^{th}$ Street terminus.

I was cured. My therapist convinced me that all the stress from my upbringing, hiding from the fact I was an unattached single male with no worthwhile occupation, and facing a lonelier future had eroded all my self-confidence.

Coming home one night from a pleasant reunion with Jonathan at his new bistro, I saw her: Neci. She sat at a table with a group of friends in a deli just across the street from my apartment.

*Goading me . . . sold me out, that dirty little bitch.*

* * *

What happened at the deli has been described by reporters as "pure mayhem." I didn't kill anyone, but I broke some bones and half-destroyed the place. They say I was babbling about "demons" and "freaks" as I smashed up the place.

The restitution the court ordered will break my trust fund completely.

I have a year and two months, six days left of my three-year sentence at Dannemora. It's not a nice place. Most of the inmates are extremely dangerous men, losers, and misfits. Several men in my pod are out-and-out sociopaths despite the fact they look "normal." Some of these grown men can barely read at a fourth-grade level. They run various cons on people like me. I'm a soft touch because I don't belong in their world. I have knife scars from three separate attacks because I refused to pay "tribute" to the enforcers of the gangs. I could request confinement in SHU, the segregated housing unit, but I've declined the warden's offer to relocate my berth. I'm not sure why. There will be more attacks and I might not get out of here alive. If I do manage, I might not have all my IQ points as some of these cons like to use pipes to the head. These men, so many of them look exactly like the men from Club Ludillo.

My lawyer stopped responding to my requests to locate Neci. He says the same thing over and over in different ways: "There was no such person named Neci among the people you attacked in that deli . . ."

When I get out, I'll find her. I know that because she found me twice.

THE END

# The Monster That Resides Within
### By Scarlett Lake

She steps out of the shadows, the figure of sophistication and grace, a stark contrast to the dark and grimy cobbled streets of London's East End. Her black heels click loudly on the cobbles as she pulls the collar of her cloak up high and ducks through the backstreets, trying to become one of the forgotten. But for someone like her, with her almost flawless, pale, porcelain skin, high sculpted cheekbones, dark, plump lips and wavy raven hair, going unseen is next to impossible. Her beauty shines in the dark, illuminating even the darkest of alleys and the shocking sights they attempt to hide. Sights that once appalled and rocked people to the core are now nothing but a whisper on the ocean. Especially when compared to those that Jack leaves.

Jack, the Ripper who haunts London's streets during the dead of night, stalking and hunting out those who he deems unworthy. Those whores who spread their legs for anyone with a dime to fling their way. Those who find themselves pushed up against the soot-covered alley walls with their bloomers pulled down around their ankles, sitting in the gutters with the rats. Whores just like her. Only Lilian, the beauty of the night who lights up the streets with her mere presence alone, spreads her legs on a warm comfy blanket filled bed and for far more than just a dime.

Turning down the alley on her right, Lilian disappears into the shadows once more. The hairs on the back of her neck stand to attention. As though hit by a bolt of electricity as she feels the eyes of someone upon her. Eyes that leer and ogle as she moves with grace in her tight-fitting dress that pushes her bosom up high. These eyes don't belong to the mysterious Jack; these eyes she knows. These eyes she fears. These are the eyes of the devil. Who parades around in the body of a man. Who seeks to claim her and make her his, to hide her from the world. Take her from her children; so that she can service him and only him.

He reminds her in every way of the man who haunts her dreams. The man who used and abused her like she was a piece of meat. The brand scar on her back burns as a constant reminder that she will always, in some manner, belong to Albert White, even as he lays in a permanent slumber several feet beneath the ground in his silk-lined wooden coffin. She will never be free of him. Even death couldn't take her away from the memories and torment. And now another seeks to do the same. Claim her as his own. To wrap his grubby fat fingers around her neck and squeeze while he pounds into her with the rhythm and grace of a rotten gate flapping in a storm. To carve his mark into her, making her his for all to see. To lock her up in his tower and never let her see the light of day again.

She turns, navigating the maze-like streets as she seeks to lose him like a rat fleeing a starving cat. Most nights, she avoids stepping out onto the dark streets, preferring instead to stay inside within the safety of the brothel she runs just a stone's throw away from London's docks. Most nights, her clients come to her, and she services them on her silk sheets, staying out of the dark shadows and away from the prying eyes of the beast. But tonight, another one beckons. One who demands she come to him and spend the night tangled up in a sweaty mess within his silk sheets. The only one who she would brave the streets for. The one they call Dorian Gray.

One more alley, she thinks as she steps into the abyss and focuses on the lamplights she can see at the other end. She knows the route like the back of her hand. Which twists and turns to take, which streets to avoid, the quickest route. One that avoids the dreadful foul-smelling asylum on the corner of Dean Street—his place of work. He who watches her yet has his pick of insane ripe fruit—if he were so to choose. Still, he wants her. But he doesn't know she is not as sane as she seems.

Her pace quickens as she sets her sights on the lamplight up ahead, flickering a pale orange in the night, barely creating any light at all. Just a few more steps, then she's there, on Dorian's street, a few doors away from salvation. She sucks in a breath. Her pace quickens once more to match the thump, thump, thump of her heart as she can feel him behind her, his beady eyes undressing her as she moves—his stale breath almost a tickle on the back of her neck.

She emerges from the alley, underneath the soft glow of the light, exhaling heavily and turning to look back into the abyss, seeing nothing but blackness and an empty space beyond.

He's not there, not tonight. He's just a shadow haunting her every waking moment.

Shaking it off, Lilian moves down the street, passing a series of grand townhouses, each one with a copper nameplate on the wall etched with a name. She stops outside the grandest one of all, one with 'GRAY', etched into its sign.

***

Within minutes of crossing the threshold, Dorian had her pressed up against his drawing-room door, the knob pressing into her back as he latched his thin lips onto her neck and sucked; hard!

"Dorian," she scolds the younger man as his lips travel downwards to brush against the brow of her ample bosom. He hums with a mouthful of skin but doesn't stop his assault.

"Dorian, the doorknob," she says as she squirms, pushing her body away from the door and further into the wet, warm mouth of the man who has hired her services for the night. He pulls her away from the door, his lips moving to hers as he walks them back into the grand drawing-room. The room is bathed in low light with several oil lamps and numerous candles scattered around the room. The walls are lined with portraits of every shape and size, each one depicting a face of nobility in their soft oil strokes. As beautiful as it is, it's a space that has always given Lilian a chill up her spine. There's something about being stared at by hundreds of pairs of glassy eyes that unnerves her, but not Dorian. The exhibitionist in him thrives on it, even if the eyes aren't real in every sense of the word.

He pushes her through to the centre of the room where a deep, blood-red chaise sits. Spinning her, he points her towards a large window and eases the velvet cloak off her shoulders, letting it fall to the floor to pool at their feet.

"Dorian…" she starts again as his lips once more latch onto the smooth pale white skin of her neck, and his hands reach around to pull lightly at the ribbon holding her black satin corset together.

"Ssshhh," he responds with a gentle whisper in her ear, his breath tickling her, sending shivers down her spine - the good kind of shivers. Sometimes she can't help but wonder how someone so young can be so talented when it comes to 'activities of the night'. It's one reason she comes to him; that and the extortionate amount he pays her for her 'personal' visits. It's his money that keeps her paying the rent for the townhouse, enabling her and her children to do their work away from the dangers of London streets. Keeps them safe from the Jacks of the world who deem them unclean and an abomination to society because they earn money the only way they knowhow. A way those same cretins use and abuse when it suits them. When they need a place to stick their manhood and thrust away all their frustrations.

The money she needs, but coming here is about more than just that; it's also about feeling alive. His touch sends sparks jolting through her entire being, makes goosebumps erupt on her skin and her nipples stand firm. No man has ever had that control over her before, not in the way he does. She's been controlled before. Spent most of her life being controlled by men who see her as an object they won in a prizefight, rather than a figure of beauty and desire. He almost, dare she say it, he almost makes her feel loved.

"Dorian," she sighs again, wanting to ask him to close the drapes over the window, even though she knows it's a futile request. Every time she asks and every time he denies. It's a dance they weave as he drops her dress to the ground leaving her in nothing but a pair of black lacy stockings hugging her shapely legs and the garter holding them in place. Placing one palm flat on her chest, he pulls her backwards till she falls into his lap on the chaise.

She turns her head towards him as he places her right where he wants her.

"The drapes," she gasps as he begins to move, his mouth sucking hard the junction between neck and shoulder as he ignores her request, just like she knew he would. It's all a part of his love of exhibition; to let those who were to glance in the window as they pass see him thrusting into one of the most stunning women of the city. Lilian is used to people watching, but with him, the one she avoids, stepping up his stalking game of late… she doesn't want him to see her, not like this. Not naked and vulnerable in the arms of another. Not when she refused to let him be the arms to hold her as he thrust into her and take her as his own. Yet she knows, as her right-hand reaches around to grip the back of Dorian's head tightly, that he's out there watching, waiting. Getting off on her nude body wishing it was he who could take her in the way Dorian currently is.

Glancing towards the window, she sees nothing but an empty street. Yet she can feel his eyes on her, as though he's standing right before her.

***

He steps out of the shadows, watching, waiting for his time to strike, knowing he has to hold off. That's the agreement they made. If he gets too greedy, steps in too soon, he'll lose.

His fists clench into tight balls, his knuckles turning white as he watches Dorian take the woman who will soon be his. The young man wanted one last night with her. He said no at first, but Dorian refused to let him have her until he agreed to one last night of sexual deviancy.

His teeth grind together as his jaw locks, watching her moan and groan while moving gracefully on his nude form.

Soon, he reminds himself. Soon, she will be his.

***

Lilian groans as her mind begins to rouse from a deep slumber. Her body feels heavy and sore, every muscle aching and throbbing. As much as she enjoys her nights with young Dorian, she's glad that they aren't a daily occurrence. Every time she wakes feeling like she's run a marathon, her middle-aged body no longer able to keep up or recover as quickly as it once did. He's insatiable; Dorian Gray, with his dark, slicked-back hair, lean structured build, high cheekbones and that little dimple in his chin. In his early 20s, the man is old enough to be her son. Yet has the strength and stamina to spend the night making love to her till she can't take it any longer and begs for him to stop.

Her eyes flutter open, heavy, as she struggles to push through the fog in her waking mind. She moves her fingers, the tips twitching like someone who has just awoken from a coma. Something feels wrong. She feels heavier, limp, like she cannot move her limbs. Her body aches, itches. Feeling out of place, odd, not of the norm. Not how she is used to her body feeling.

Blinking rapidly, she looks up to a dull grey ceiling instead of the crisp white, intricately patterned one found in Dorian's bedroom. She tries to lift her head but finds it glued to the base she lies upon, which she now just realises is cold and hard, not soft and light like Dorian's luxurious bedding.

Panic begins to set in as she struggles against the bonds, holding her down onto the ice-cold slab. Thrashing from side to side, they cut into her skin, ripping the flesh open as blood begins to ooze out of her, warm, red, almost hissing as it hits the cold metal beneath. Her eyes flick from side to side as she attempts to look around, trying to figure on where on Earth she is, but she sees nothing but dark unmoving shapes in the gloom.

"Easy, my love," a deep gravelly voice rings out coming from somewhere behind her head. A voice that brings fear and dread to Lilian as her heart begins to race, and her body starts to sweat. A voice she has been avoiding. A voice that haunts her nightmares. One that she prayed she would never hear again.

It seems God has abandoned her and let the devil come to play.

"Easy there," he says as he steps into view, his shadow hovering over her as his hand reaches out towards her cheek to graze his rough finger tips along the flesh. "We don't want you hurting yourself now, do we? My love."

She's rendered speechless as he moves down her body to gently grab her torn wrist. He unlatches the buckle, holding it down; he releases the appendage lifting it towards his face. A thin stream of blood trickles down from the rip, travelling along her arm like a thread caught in a wind. Her face scrunches up in disgust as he brings her hand towards his lips and bends slightly to place a soft saliva filled kiss upon the backs of her fingers. She looks away for a second, begging her voice to work, to yell, to shout at him to stop. To tell him she doesn't belong to him, she isn't his to own. To beg him to stop touching her and leave her be, to let her go. Part of her screams to ask why she's here? How she's here? When the last thing she remembers was falling asleep alongside the nude and lean body of young Dorian. But no matter how many thoughts and questions run through her mind, she cannot seem to get her mouth to expel anything other than a raspy pain-filled breath.

Lilian looks back at the man, begging her eyes to speak her anger where her voice cannot. Instead of scrunching and becoming hooded in a glare, they stretch and open wide in shock at what they gaze upon. There, along the join where wrist meets hand, is a scar, a nasty deep wound with deep stitches holding each end together. Several have torn from her struggles, causing the blood that flows an easy escape. The skin that forms the arm does not match the tone of that which encases the hand.

Looking further down her arm that is held up, still in the hands of the one named Victor, she sees another stitched wound that encircles her upper arm halfway up.

The hand is hers; she'd know that shade of glossy raven black on her nails anywhere. And her delicate silver band etched with roses still sits upon her middle finger. The shoulder half of her upper arm is hers; she can just about see the small white scar she has there from her married days when she was a toy for her husband to play with, and he liked to play with knives.

They truly are one and the same; her husband played with knives, and so does this man. The man, the city of London, fears, in a different way they fear the Ripper stalking the streets. This man, the one she fears above all others, is Victor Frankenstein, the creator of monsters and Father of the damned.

***

"You've had your time," Victor growls with clenched fists. He stands by Dorian's bed and looks down upon the nude form of Lilian, who lies asleep on her back, her bare breasts on display like a precious artefact.

Dorian climbs out of bed as naked as the day he was born and moves to stand alongside Victor. "Yes, I suppose I have," he says with a cheeky smirk.

"Do you have it?" the younger man asks as he holds out his hand.

Victor reaches into his pocket and pulls out a small vial filled with a purple liquid. He places it into Dorian's waiting palm which, immediately closes over the glass.

"If this doesn't work, there is nowhere you can run and nowhere you can hide."

"Do not insult me!" Victor growls out loud as his eyes flash in anger. His outburst startles the sleeping beauty on the bed, and her eyes pop open. Pulling something out of another pocket, he lunges forward, thrusting a long syringe into her neck. He forces a substance into her body before she has a chance to comprehend what's going on.

Stroking a strand of hair away from her face, Victor picks Lilian up in his arms, cradling her like a newborn child as he watches Dorian down the vial contents.

"What do you want with her?"

"It's time I took a new bride," Victor responds without a backwards glance as he carries Lilian out of the bedroom and out into the night.

***

The next time her mind awakens, the fog dissipates quicker, and her memories come flooding back in seconds as her mind flashes through her evening. Navigating London's dark and dingy alley system. The knob pressing into her back. Being pulled back onto Dorian's nude and waiting form as hundreds of pairs of glassy oil eyes ogle them, as they move together in a rhythm they've perfected over many encounters. Falling asleep amongst his soft luxurious bedding with Dorian's bareback staring at her, the portrait tattoo that fills his back, watching over her as she sleeps. One that she briefly notices looks different, as if the portrait is rotting away, but sleep takes hold of her before she can dwell too much.

Then waking up on a cold slab in a room filled with nothing but dark shapes and gloom that signals nothing good. Her arm flashes next through her mind as she remembers seeing a portion that doesn't match, that a tone darker than her pale white skin is connected by stitches to her upper arm and wrist. She doesn't remember anything after that. Nothing other than

Frankenstein's hulking form stood leering over her nude body as she lies on display for him. Bile rising in her throat as her voice box refuses to work, to even let out a scream of anger or one of fear.

Her eyes flutter open once more, and she finds herself faced with the same gloomy room on the same stone-cold slab. Her body beginning to shiver as the cold sinks deep into her skin and works its way down to her bones before settling into her core. She tries to move her head, but just like before, it sticks glued to the hard surface by a thick black band strapped over her forehead.

Lilian's fingers twitch on the mutant arm, the one that isn't fully her own, but something feels different this time. There's no band holding it down in place. Summoning all her strength, which isn't much as the cold drains her body, she flexes the muscles in her shoulder as she attempts to lift her new limb off the slab to hover in the air.

She manages a couple of inches before it crashes back down with a loud clang that echoes off the walls creating a deafening sound. She holds her breath and stills, pretending to still be asleep. But no one comes. Frankenstein doesn't appear at her side with his overweight figure and those eyes that originate in Hell.

Peeking her lids open, she confirms she is still alone and tries to lift the arm again. It raises several inches off the cold steel slab as she focuses all her might on keeping it there; one loud bang is suspicious enough. Two would most likely send him running to her side. The limb wobbles and shakes badly, but she manages to keep it up. After several moments that agonisingly feel like hours rather than seconds, she manages to move the arm, bending it in two as it reaches towards her head. Shaky tips graze against the skin at the base of her neck before pulling back as they edge along a bumpy raised seam of skin. She hisses as she touches the seam again, feeling a deep crevasse of exposed flesh followed by a thin wire-like line – a stitch!

Tears form in her eyes, clouding her vision as the shaking in her hand becomes almost uncontrollable. Pushing away from the fog that starts to creep into her mind, she forces her hand to feel around the band holding her neck down that sits above the seam she knew wasn't there last night. A tinkle reaches her ears as her nails scrap across metal. Scrambling, her movements becoming more erratic and clumsier by the second, she undoes the buckle, pulling the black material through one end of a metal loop and then the other. She sucks in a large gulp of air as the tension on her throat releases, and she feels like she can finally breathe again. She's dying at that moment to test her vocal cords, to see if it was the tightness of the strap crushing her windpipe that caused her temporary muteness - if it was temporary - but keeping quiet is the key to escape.

Now she's started; she daren't stop. Escape is on her mind as her body begins to wake, her muscles becoming used to moving again after being idle for how long she does not know. But it feels like a lifetime. Buckle after buckle, she reaches. The coordination and grace she had once now gone as it's replaced by a clumsiness that she isn't used to as she attempts to control limbs that do not look like her own, not completely.

Minutes tick by, feeling like hours as her heart beats erratically, threatening to thump its way out of her chest, snapping her ribs in two as it seeks to escape. Sure that any moment now Frankenstein will waltz back into the room with that trademark smirk of his, and THAT look in his eye. The one that shakes her to her core. The look that matches Albert's. She would almost think they were brothers with how similar they are in physical appearance and mental deviancy. The thought spurs her on as her body weakens by the second.

With a loud clank, the last buckle drops to the slab as Lilian rolls herself onto her side forcing her ice-cold body to crash to the stone ground. A hoarse, guttural moan emits from her throat, sending daggers down the internal flesh that feels as though it has been ripped raw. Her whole body screams in agony, pain emanating from every limb as she pushes herself to stand upright. Wobbling to her feet, Lilian tips backwards, her eyes rolling to the back of her head momentarily before she catches herself and straightens. Her vision blurs around the edges. She blinks rapidly, pushing away the haze as she takes a tentative step forward. Her feet wobble badly as she struggles to place them flat on the stonework beneath. She looks down, seeing several more unhealed scars held together by thick wiry stitches, her skin ranging in tones by a body that isn't entirely hers.

Something glints and shines in the corner of the room as it catches her eye. Lilian looks towards the corner and sees an overly large mirror that reaches well above her head with a few cracks in the corners. She moves towards it, making her feet pick up speed, the wobble being more pronounced the faster she tries to move. Her limbs feel heavy and sore, hard to control as she stumbles, drawn to the mirror-like a moth to a flame.

Reaching the grand glinting object, which reflects the stone-cold truth, she stands staring in shock at her body. A body which isn't her own. This mirror confirms that thought which had been floating around in the back of her mind. She's become another one of Frankenstein's monsters, a child of the damned.

There's a long-standing rumour about Victor and what he really gets up to while working at Eadon Hills Asylum for the criminally insane, the one that sits on the corner of Dean Street. A rumour that the constabulary has chosen to turn a blind eye to. Doctor Frankenstein and his experiments into life and death. Experiments which, if the stories are to be believed, see him create one man from another, the piecing together of human beings. As Lilian stands before the mirror looking at her nude form, she knows these rumours are based on fact and not rumours at all.

Her right-hand moves, lifting to the top of her chest as she runs her shaky fingers down, travelling along a jagged and bumpy line that stretches down between her breasts to stop just above her belly button. Tears begin to fall as she takes in her body, one she almost doesn't recognise. Her left arm has two stitched scars, one at her wrist and one halfway up her upper arm. Her right has one, just beneath her armpit connecting an entirely new arm to her body, one several shades darker than her pale skin tone. She holds both her hands up, side by side, noticing how they are not only different tones but how the right has shorter, stubbier fingers than the left, the left which she knows belongs to her thanks to those black nails and her silver ring.

Her legs have them too, the scars and stitches piecing bits of others to hers. A different foot on the left; hers on the right. Just below her knee, round the top of her thigh. She looks like a patchwork quilt of human skin.

Lilian is mesmerised by her body, studying the changes, her mind filled with shock and despair as she tries to work out why. It isn't until his warm, rough hand snakes around her waist and splays itself out on her stomach does she realise he's there.

"Why?" she whispers, a sound almost heard. She looks up into his eyes through the mirror. Those dark eyes belong to the devil.

"I want you to be mine," Victor says in his deep gravel with the lust in his voice as clear as day.

"I'm not yours to take," she says in agony as her vocal cords grate on the inside.

Victor's hand begins to move up her body, travelling over her newly formed bumps, the stitches pulling as his rough skin catches on them. She winces with a grimace at his touch, vomit forming in her throat.

"Don't try to speak. They haven't healed yet." Victor's hand strokes over her windpipe. His damage, it seems, was more than just external.

"Aren't you a vision?" His hand travels again, touching her in places she swore to never let him touch again, not after last time. Not when he went too far while soliciting her services as one of London's elite whores. "It's a pity no one else will agree."

He smirks at her, and everything clicks into place. He couldn't have her as she was when she was a strong, beautiful woman with almost flawless, perfect, porcelain skin. Now, she was a hideous patchwork beast with deep scars, mismatched skin and a voice that doesn't work properly. Now, no one will want her. Now, he can have her in his mind because no one else will.

Yet, if he had watched her close enough, he should have known, controlling her, claiming her for his own would not be that easy. He can turn her into a monster to keep her from the world, but Lilian is not the type to shy away and be told she isn't good enough. She lived her life for too long like that, and she refuses to play the victim ever again. If he had watched properly, followed her into the darkest depths of London's streets, to the places even the rats won't go, he would have seen. If he had watched with a brain that sought knowledge rather than one filled with lust, he would have seen the monster she already was. The monster that resides within. The monster Albert turned her into. The man who bought her as a child to be his wife.

She smiles as she turns to him, a plan formulating in her mind. Imagining the ways she can get him back for this deception, him and Dorian. She remembers now, waking briefly to hear Dorian make a deal for her, which he has no right to make.

When she was sold as a child, she went by another name, the name her parents gave her, Jacqueline Butcher. A name she reclaims - in the dead of night - only she's made a little change. Jack is the name of her monster, the monster that resides within. The monster that haunts the London streets, taking away those who do not deserve to breathe the same air as her. Each one betrayed her.

She smiles at the thought that soon, Jack can be released and rip the streets of those who think she is nothing more than a piece of meat to be played with and tossed away. The Ripper will rise again, just give her a little time to heal and then she will paint the city with blood.

-END-

# Final Notes
*By Sarah Cannavo*

*Intro*

A few stools down the bar from them some men were drinking and discussing the rash of suicides, unusually brutal but unquestionably self-inflicted wounds, that had recently erupted in Los Angeles: the girl who'd gashed her own wrists repeatedly, down to the bone; the man who'd filled a tub with drain cleaner and drowned himself; pills pumped from victims at rates extravagant even for the area. Seven victims so far, each leaving notes splattered with blood, tears, or both speaking to—screaming of—fears and desperations friends and family had no idea of. Debate raged: Was the heat wave to blame, societal backlash, was each inspiring the next? But Kali Winters was ignoring the debate and instead lamenting her love life to Mickey Grant and the remains of her third margarita.

"I'm telling you it's never gonna happen, Mickey," she said, pouting morbidly and tracing old initials carved deep into the dark scarred wood of the bar. "If I haven't found an actual lasting relationship yet—"

"It means you haven't found the right girl yet, not that you never will," Mickey said patiently, good-naturedly; it wasn't the first time either of them had said such things to each other. A writer, as well as an incubus, Mickey was more of a romantic than either of those things might have suggested, and with his easygoing, rock 'n roll-rumpled look he gave the impression of a stray waiting to be saved, what many of the women he picked up were looking for. If it wasn't, that was all right, too; Mickey's gift lay in desire, and he could sense exactly what someone wanted or needed and give it to them, even if his outward appearance—thick dark brown hair, a tall, lean, muscled body, a tendency for dark shirts and faded jeans—never changed. When he wasn't seeking someone to spend the night with, though, he tended to dampen that sense as best he could, lest he be constantly bombarded with the desires of everyone around him.

He didn't need a supernatural gift to read Kali, though; her loneliness was evident, and she didn't crack a smile when he said, "Hey, there's always that succubus in the Valley I could set you up with, if you wanted," merely sighed, and Mickey reached out and squeezed her shoulder gently. "You'll find somebody, Kali, or somebody will find you. I know it's been shitty going so far, but it'll happen someday."

Kali smiled then, patting his hand. "Thanks, Mickey."

432

"No problem, Short Stuff," he said, finishing his most recent whiskey, and she made a face and slugged his shoulder, though it was true: Kali was diminutive compared both to Mickey, who stood over six feet, and more average people, but as Mickey often said, she made up for it with her brassy personality and the throaty, husky voice she was never afraid to raise. "So just let it go, at least for tonight, all right? No pressure, no panicking; let's just have some fun. After all, nothing can cheer a person up faster than open-mic night at the Moody Blues."

Kali snorted. Occasionally the Moody Blues, the dive bar where the pair could often be found and whose blue-and-purple neon sign stained the cracked sidewalk outside, let local musicians showcase their talents—though the word often applied extremely loosely: Last month's act had been a man billing himself as John Beluga, who'd done a ninety-minute set of whale calls, uninterrupted sheerly because the stunned audience wanted to see how long he could go on for. "Sure," Kali said, and she and Mickey each ordered another drink to fortify themselves against whatever lay ahead.

The singer who stepped up to the stage—a rickety wooden stool and a microphone in a space that had been cleared of a few tables—was a woman, young, with the beauty of a nymph or *ingenue*, equally suited for a flower crown or evening gown. Pale pink plastic sunglasses, heart-shaped, were pushed up on her head; light brown hair tumbled long and loose around her shoulders; her full breasts were cupped by her white, flower-splattered sundress; her long legs ended in delicate sandaled feet, and her cherry-glossed lips glistened as she flashed her sparse audience a snow-white smile and said in a sultry voice, "Hi, my name's

Lexi Balcombe, and I'm honored to be playing for you tonight."

As she spoke, a thick tingling raced across the back of Mickey's neck and skull, stronger even than the one between his legs, and he ran a hand over the back of his head, recognizing magic when he felt it. "What's up?" Kali murmured, reluctantly tearing her eyes away from the girl tuning her acoustic guitar. "She something?"

"Yeah, but it didn't feel too strong," Mickey replied as the flash passed. "A hedge witch or something, probably." Kali gave a wordless sound in reply and looked back to Lexi, who was strumming lightly now and announcing she'd start with a set of covers; at her smallest movement, the air around her filled with a scent, some perfume, sweet as fresh flowers and sharp as the sea. Everybody watched her, waiting, wondering.

And Lexi started singing.


*Verse*


All other activity in the bar ceased. Jaws dropped, eyes locked, and from a corner Mickey heard a clatter and crash as a glass slipped from a slackened hand but he didn't look, nobody did, as Lexi's voice flowed like a warm breeze through the bar, a golden voice, a honey voice, rich and raw and smooth, alternately low and smoky, mournful, and high and sweet, teasing.

She sang classics, spun "Love Reign O'er Me" into "Nights in White Satin," did with a wink "California Dreamin'." She smiled all through "Summer Wine" and Mickey's head swam, his blood searing, churning; his bones felt restless beneath his skin. A demon of desire he was, and if she went with him, alone in the dark... He

434

swallowed his drink, ostensibly to steady himself, but he barely tasted it and didn't bother to signal for another.

She did "Dream Weaver," Sinatra's "Witchcraft," Bad Company's "Ready For Love." "If she pulls out some Zevon, I'll marry her," Mickey said hoarsely.

Kali didn't answer, though, even to warn Mickey he'd have to get through her first. Her eyes were riveted to Lexi's red lips as words dripped, slipped, flew, floated from them, familiar lyrics made new by all the tricks and turns of Lexi's voice. The sound of it wrapped around Kali, flooded through and filled her; her loneliness, her sadness, slid from her like a shed skin and faded from her memory, day after numbing day selling sex toys at the Leather and Lace, ex-girlfriends and messy patch jobs on her broken heart, the unshakeable sense that she was going nowhere fast—the music eased all that, sparked some hidden hope left in her. *There's still a chance,* it said to her, no matter the actual song, *and here it is, right now.* Never mind the shrinking part of her pointing out that she didn't know if Lexi Balcombe even went for girls or, if she did, that she would go for Kali— she was peddling happiness as well as her voice, and Kali was willing to buy.

Nor was she the only one, Mickey noticed, looking around the bar as Lexi introduced her next song. Expressions were glazing over in a way that had nothing to do with drink; whatever problems the other patrons had come into the bar with, they'd clearly forgotten them now, Lexi's performance soothing, like a lullaby, a love song. Something shifted in the back of Mickey's mind, but he clamped down on it as if swatting a fly, silencing the irritating buzz and ignoring the brief sting. *Something I forgot? What? Fuck it, it doesn't matter.*

Lexi bounced into "Excitable Boy," played "Paint It Black" with such ferocity Mickey was surprised she didn't snap a string—or all six—and finished the set with a haunting "Heart-Shaped Box." After the last note faded there was a moment of pure silence, and then a tidal wave of applause roared through the bar and Lexi smiled and bowed, leaning her guitar against the stool and standing, her flowered dress rustling.

"You're all too kind," she purred, tucking a lock of hair behind her ear. "I'll play a few more songs for you, I promise, but first—" she winked and flashed another white grin— "I need a damn drink."

*Bridge*

Lexi was polite to those who clamored to compliment her as she made her way to the bar, but she showed not a spark of true interest until she slid onto the stool next to Kali and looked her and Mickey over after ordering a tequila. "Are they always this appreciative here?"

"More so when the singer isn't calling Shamu for a booty call," Mickey replied, "but you *were* damn good. Props for the Zevon, by the way; you did him proud."

Lexi grinned. "Thanks." The scent was stronger now that she was closer, sweet and stinging, some kind of island flower. As she leaned on the bar, she was so close to Kali that Kali could feel the heat rippling from her skin, like sand warmed golden by the sun, and Kali felt this heat suffuse her, shifted a bit on her stool and hoped her own tan cheeks weren't flushing too profusely. *Damn it, pull yourself together, woman.* "So, are you two together?" Lexi gestured to Mickey and Kali.

Kali snorted. "Nah. I like 'em with bigger boobs."

Lexi laughed; the sound ran like warm fingers up the back of Kali's neck. "Well, that's good. I'd hate to break up date night." She looked closer at Mickey. "Hey, aren't you that writer? Mickey Grant?"

"So it says on the book jackets," Mickey replied easily. "You've read my stuff?"

"Some of it," Lexi said. "But I also saw you on TMZ last year when you got into a fistfight with that— producer, was it?"

"I'll have you know I was defending my honor," Mickey said. "The asshole accused me of coming onto his wife, which was untrue." He paused. "She came onto me."

"Sir Galahad, everybody." Kali rolled her eyes. "I'm Kallista, by the way—Kali. The long-suffering best friend."

Lexi waved for more drinks, eyes sparkling, tossed back her next shot and said, "Listen, I really don't want to step all over something here, but I was wondering if, after I finish up my next set, you wouldn't mind leaving with me, Kali?" That glamorous grin again. "If you don't think I'm too forward, that is."

Kali started, though not unpleasantly. Beneath the bar Mickey squeezed her left hand, and she knew him well enough to translate: *Have fun.* "Forward is good," Kali said, hating the surprised crack in her voice; she took a breath and added, "Where did you feel like going? Because I know some spots we could hit—"

"We could do that." Lexi shrugged, and then Kali felt Lexi's smooth warm hand slip high on her right thigh and start stroking; Kali fought back the urge to shiver and purr like a cat being petted. "Or we could just go back to your place."

"It's not exactly the Chateau Marmont, I'm warning you now," Kali said, amazed she managed to speak. "Hocking scented lube and vibrators doesn't exactly bring in the big bucks."

"I'm sure it'll be fine," Lexi said. "But I promised a few more songs and I better get to it. Don't leave without me, okay?"

"Wouldn't dream of it," Kali said, and Lexi, smiling, slipped her sunglasses from her head and slid them into Kali's long black hair, kissed her cheek, and sauntered back to her "stage" amid rising excited murmurs from the crowd.

"Look at you, snaring the mildly witchy woman." Mickey lightly elbowed Kali, grinning. "And they call me the chick magnet."

"Yeah," Kali said, looking dazed and rubbing lightly at the spot where Lexi had kissed her.


*Chorus*


"And you're sure you aren't pissed that I'm ditching you to hook up with a hedge witch?" Kali asked Mickey as they stood outside the bar, Kali waiting for Lexi to pack up her guitar and finish signing autographs for a few newly-minted rabid fans.

Smoke curled from between Mickey's lips as he laughed; he tapped the ash from his cigarette's cherry-red tip onto a nearby parking meter and said, "Yes, I'm sure I'm not pissed, Short Stack. I took you out tonight to cheer you up, help you have some fun. And if taking this singer home with you will make you happy, then—" he bent and kissed her forehead— "you have my blessing. Go. Tap that ass."

"Classy. But also appreciated. Thanks, Mickey."

Lexi emerged from the bar and slipped an arm around Kali's waist; shadows and neon stained her skin, and in her free hand she carried a gleaming black guitar case. "Are you sure you don't want me to drop you off?" Mickey asked, but it wasn't far to Kali's apartment and the day's heat had broken somewhat, so the women decided to take their time and walk. "Be safe, then. And don't do anything I wouldn't do!" Mickey called after them, waving.

"Lotta leeway, then," Kali called back, smirking, and Mickey cheerfully flipped her the bird before grinding his cigarette out beneath his boot heel and heading back into the bar.

"So, are you from Los Angeles originally?" Lexi asked as they walked, her arm still snaked around Kali's waist.

"L.A. woman, born and raised," Kali replied, "though I *did* spend some good times with my aunt Val out in New Jersey, so I guess you could call me an L.A. woman-Jersey girl hybrid. Not that it's a life story bound for the big screen any time soon, I don't think. Came out as a teen; my parents took it so well my mom calls every week to berate me for not having settled down with a good girl yet; a string of relationships of various lengths, and now I work at what's genteelly called an 'adult store' and my best friend's an inc—incredibly good-natured fuckup. Not much blockbuster material in any of that. But what about you? You a local girl?"

"A bit farther away, actually. But I've been traveling for a while now, just playing my music, living off that as best I can." Lexi grinned. "Singing for my supper, you could say."

"Well, you're incredibly good at it." Lexi's second set had been original songs, revealing a further depth of talent as a songwriter as well. Kali had been enthralled, even more so than before, and remembering that now Kali added, "Hey, I don't want to jinx myself here, but out of everybody in the bar, what made you pick *me?*"

They were outside Kali's apartment now—had the walk really gone by so fast?—and as Kali fumbled her key from her pocket Lexi said, reaching up and running her fingers slowly through Kali's hair, "I just…sensed something about you, I guess, something different, something I liked…. I don't know, maybe I'm better with words when I'm singing."

"I think you're doing fine," Kali said, slipping the key into the lock. Out came Lexi's smile; Kali smiled back and stretched up to kiss her. Their mouths, their bodies, pressed together and Kali smelled flowers, the sea, a scent that made her feverish; one of the women turned the doorknob and they tumbled, still kissing, into Kali's apartment, slamming the door behind them.


*Hook*


Mickey didn't stay at the bar much longer, and he chose to leave alone. He lit another cigarette—a perk of being hellspawn, never having to worry about annoyances like cancer—and started his car, another beat-up black one in a long line of POS cars he bought cheap and rode into the ground. The radio worked, though, and he was drumming on the steering wheel along to Lynyrd Skynyrd as he drove home to his apartment, his mound of accusingly-blank notebooks, and his cream-colored French bulldog, Warren Zevon.

He was halfway home when his head cleared and his senses snapped back with a vengeance. The truth hit him then like cold water: the singing, the dazed patrons of the bar, the magic powerful enough to throw off even him.

Lexi wasn't a hedge witch.

"Fuck. Fuck. *Siren,"* Mickey said.

And he'd sent Kali home with her.

He whipped into a sharp, squealing U-turn, ignoring the shrieking horns and insults to his parentage that erupted all around him, and headed for Kali's place, praying that his protesting car would hold out and get him there in time.

"Mm. That was amazing," Kali said, stretching languorously in her rumpled bed and looking at Lexi, who was sitting naked next to her amid the sheets they'd rolled in, heated, until they seemed near to melting, wax-like. At some point along the way—time and action had blurred, and Kali couldn't quite say when—they'd lit a few candles, and glow and shadows dappled Lexi's skin as she ran a hand along Kali's exposed leg, expression catlike, and agreed, "That it was, baby. There's nothing like going out with a bang."

"I—wait, what do you mean?" Kali asked, pushing damp hair back from her face, her heartbeat still unhurried, unworried.

Lexi kneaded harder, pleasantly so, and a low, happy noise rose in her throat; it plucked at Kali and she relaxed further, half-ready to fall apart. "Kali, honey, you told me yourself you don't really feel like you're living for anything. So why bother?"

Kali struggled to make sense of what she was hearing, couldn't break through to the surface. "Lexi, I don't understand…"

"Of course you do, Kali," Lexi said soothingly—or was she singing again? There was something about her voice, growing as Kali listened, compelling Kali to listen, and these lyrics spoke to her even more than the last. She sat up and stared at Lexi, who said, "You might have Mickey to hang around with, but that's not what you really want, Kali. We both know it. You want somebody to love and somebody to love you, but you're alone now and you'll always be alone. It's harsh, maybe, but it's true. So what's the point of dragging out the ordeal? Just go ahead and end your suffering."

Speaking or singing? There was music in the room, spilling from Lexi, still beautiful but far colder, darker, with marked notes of dissonance that jabbed at Kali like needles, and as the harsh melody swirled in her skull the truth in Lexi's words sank in and gripped her; picturing her future she only saw a maw of emptiness yawning black before her, years of pain and loneliness, and she let out a whimper and started to shake, clutching her blankets in rigid fists. Every long, desolate night, empty hookup, and attack of desperation returned to haunt and mock her, her greatest fear rearing up stronger than ever before, scraping her raw and freezing her blood and her bones.

"Oh, God," she moaned, voice cracking, tears rolling unfelt down her face. "Oh God, what…what am I supposed to do?" She was alone, so alone, except for the music, the truth—and Lexi, singer, truth-bringer, who smiled and got out of bed, pulled on her dress and hunted around the room until she found some paper and a pen, which she handed to Kali.

"Write a note, first of all," she said. "It's the polite thing to do. Just write what you're feeling, Kali, all of it."

*Write a note, yes.* To Mickey, so he'd know, so he'd understand. Kali picked up her pen, hand shaking so badly her words cut the paper in places; her tears splashed and made the lines bleed. In her purse her phone was ringing repeatedly, but the dark song drowned it out, drowned everything out but her thoughts.

*Mickey, I'm sorry, but I can't do this anymore....*

"Good, Kali," Lexi said when she finished, the note fluttering from Kali's hand to the bed and coaxing notes still rising from Lexi's throat. Kali felt empty, scraped hollow to the core; she was sobbing in self-loathing as Lexi went to the mirror and shattered it with a blow, searching among the shards until she found the biggest, most jagged one, which she presented to Kali like a goddess bestowing a gift. "It's all right," she sang. "You can end your pain now. The music helps, but you have to do the rest yourself. It's easy, though, I promise." She smiled as Kali's trembling fingers curled around the glass. *End it, yes, I want to do it, no more pain...* "Just go ahead and slit your throat."

Relief rather than hesitation made Kali's hand shake as she raised the makeshift blade. She pressed it just barely into her throat and blood bubbled up from the nicked skin, and Lexi was smiling and singing, encouraging her, and it was almost over, and Kali closed her eyes—

—and in the other room there was a crash, a bang, and a moment later Mickey ripped the bedroom door open and Lexi hissed and jumped off the bed, song shattered. "You need to get the hell away from her right fucking now," Mickey snapped, putting himself between woman and siren. "You okay, Kali?"

She didn't answer, not soothed by the song any longer but still snared by the fear it'd awoken. With horror

Mickey noted the small wound on her neck and turned to Lexi, anger licking his features. "Siren."

"Incubus." Lexi shrugged. "See, I know what you are, too. Big fucking deal."

"It's you," Mickey said, muscles tensed, ready to swing if Lexi so much as looked at Kali. "I put it all together. Those suicides in the news—you got them to do it. You went home with them and used your song to convince them to kill themselves, and I'm guessing you fed off their energy as they were dying. Right?"

"Girl's gotta eat." The siren shrugged again. "Who are you to get so high-and-mighty, Grant? Don't your kind fuck 'em to death?"

"Not me, and personally, I find that assumption a little racist." He shifted closer, skin prickling.

"Sue me." Lexi's smile wasn't charming now but cold and harsh, a predator's grin. "You use pleasure, I use fear. That's the secret, baby; that's what makes the feeding even better: the fear. Like the look in a sailor's eyes after his ship hits the rocks and he realizes what's about to happen." She licked her lips and shivered in sadistic pleasure.

"And because those seven poor bastards killed themselves, you got to slip away scot-free each time to do it all over again. The perfect crime." Lexi laughed, self-satisfied; Mickey's fingers curled into fists. "You made a mistake this time, though, sea-bitch."

"Yeah? And what's that?"

"You fucked with my friend."

Mickey's punch caught Lexi off-guard and she stumbled back, head snapping to the side. She snarled and Mickey's human façade rippled, his back to Kali still; for a moment his face was that of the demon beneath the genial mask, but Lexi seemed unfazed by the change and caught his fist before his next punch could land. "I can do that, too," she said, and her irises turned yellow, pupils slit like a cat's; she grinned with teeth like needles and flicked a long forked tongue between her lips, and with a shriek of laughter she flung Mickey across the room. As he tried to right himself amid the broken glass Lexi opened her fanged mouth wide and tendrils of song started issuing from her throat, cut off abruptly when Mickey slammed into her and they both fell hard to the ground. "That's enough of that," he grunted, clapping a hand over her mouth.

But she fought, writhed and bit and worked her way free, snapping like a crocodile all the while. The moment she broke his hold she opened her mouth but didn't sing; she screamed. The sound spiked through Kali's skull and cleaved her scrambled thoughts, Mickey covered his ears and bent double in pain, and the bedroom window shattered, and when it did Lexi rushed for it, apparently not feeling the glass that cut into her bare feet, and leapt onto the sill lithe as a cat, sparing a glance and grin back. "You've been a lovely audience," she said, and flung herself out.

Mickey ran to the window and looked out. Moving at incredible speed, Lexi was almost out of sight; even so, he figured he could catch her, but he had one foot on the sill when behind him came a groan. *Kali.* He turned and found her stirring from her enthralled state, looking around at her trashed room, down at herself, trembling fingers finding the wound on her neck, a few more beads of blood welling up at the light pressure. "Mickey?" she said, and it all came crashing down on her. "Oh my God, Mickey, I…I was going to… She almost made me…"

"I know," Mickey said, grabbing Kali's closest clothes and keeping his voice steady. "But she's gone now. It's all right." Not exactly; Kali was shaking harder now and her state was raw as an exposed nerve, and Mickey knew that was the last time she'd be coherent for a while. "Come on, let's get you out of here. You can stay at my place tonight." Gently he helped her dress— she flinched when he first touched her, skittering back on the bed like a frightened animal—and then he carried her out to the car, tears streaming down her face all the while. "It's all right," he kept repeating, not sure she could hear him. "It's all right. It's gonna be all right."


*Refrain*


A month later Mickey and Kali were back at the Moody Blues for another open-mic night, their first since their scrape with the siren. Mickey worried at first about Kali, who'd been more withdrawn lately, but she'd laughed and said Lexi'd at least given her a longer yardstick to measure bad dates by.

"If it helps, I would've done her, too," Mickey said, swishing the whiskey in his glass.

Kali patted his hand. "It does. Thanks." She eyed him as he stood. "Where are you going?"

"I've got a surprise for you."

She groaned. "Please, not a John Beluga CD."

"Hopefully better than that. Watch my booze, will you?"

Mickey left her and headed to the empty performance stool, his guitar already waiting, and realizing what he was doing Kali lifted her glass to him; he grinned and saluted her as he settled in. "My name's Mickey Grant; most of you have tried to punch me out at one point or another, but if there are any new girls in the bar tonight,

I'm a Pisces, I enjoy long walks on the beach, rock 'n roll, and Jack Daniels, and I'm single, but it's okay if you're not."

Kali rolled her eyes. Strumming, Mickey said, "The first song I'm playing also happens to be for a special woman in my life. She's been going through some tough shit lately, but she shouldn't give up on herself just yet. I sure as hell haven't."

Kali tried to look nonchalant despite choking up, glad nobody seemed to notice; while not a siren, Mickey could hold an audience, she'd quickly learned, and without needing to dip into any extra incubus charisma to do it.

The brutal rash of suicides had stopped, its abrupt end causing as much speculation as its start. Kali was relieved and aware of how narrow her escape had been; she touched the spot on her throat where she'd cut herself, though it'd already healed, and shook her head to clear it, pushing thoughts of Lexi down and looking back at Mickey. "'Carry on; love is coming to us all,'" he was singing.

"Romantic bastard," she muttered, but she was smiling and dabbing at her eyes as she did.

When Mickey finished his set and came back to her, Kali hugged him tight, and they sat and drank in companionable silence until Kali ventured, "You think she's still out there, Mickey?"

Slowly he set his glass down. "Maybe. Sirens aren't easy to get rid of. Then again, maybe I sent her running right back to the sea. It's possible. Could be getting found out was enough to make her want to cool her heels, keep to herself for a bit."

Kali raised her glass. "I'll drink to that." They clinked their glasses and drank and sat there hoping, though for the rest of the night the other possibility ran like an unshakeable snatch of song through the backs of their minds.

*Coda*

It was a glitzy club near the San Francisco Bay, and on this Friday night it was a packed house. On a speaker-heavy stage the performer was setting up, this time a beautiful young woman in a long loose skirt and airy beaded top, a pale pink pair of heart-shaped sunglasses pushed up into her light brown hair. The club's rainbow lights swirled over her as she stepped up to the mic, making her appear ethereal, evanescent, and looking out over the writhing ocean of warm bodies packed tight on the dance floor, she smiled and licked her lips.

"Hi," she purred into the mic. "My name's Lexi Balcombe, and I'm honored to be playing for you tonight."

END

## OTHER HELLBOUND BOOKS

# The Toilet Zone: Number Two
### *"Restroom reading at its most terrifying!"*

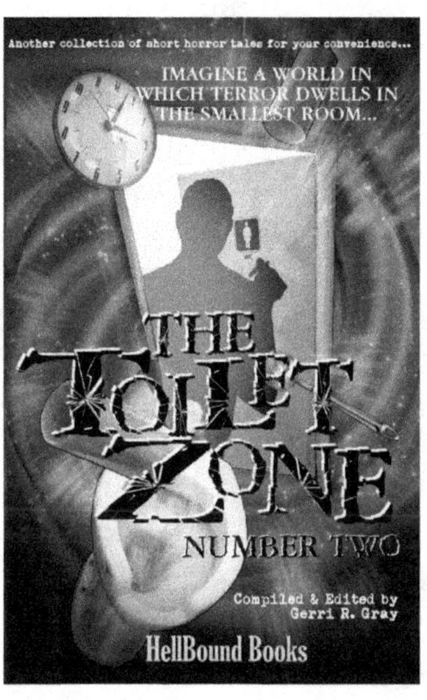


Imagine, if you will, you're traveling through the unknown, hellbound, with no roadmap or stars to guide you. The light fades as you descend into a shadow realm where supernatural terrors make their lair and evil lurks at every turn. Here, dead things don't always stay dead, for this is a world where things that shouldn't be… *are*, and things that should be are not.

In this world, it takes between 2,500 and 4,000 reading words to pay a visit to the smallest, but terrifyingly necessary, room, and stories are written precisely to chill the bones as you wait for nature to make its call.

You open up the book, and one of the 32 tales skulking within its hellish pages chooses you…

It's too late to turn back now.You are about to set foot into another dimension, so best watch out for that signpost up ahead...You've just crossed over into... The Toilet Zone

# Blood and Blasphemy

If you enjoy your horror dipped in buckets of blood and sprinkled with generous amounts of blasphemy, then you've come to the right place!

Blood and Blasphemy is a collection of over thirty of the most sacrilegious horror stories ever written.

Within these irreverent pages, you will encounter a priest that keeps his deformed spawn chained in a root cellar, a convent where a poisonous species of salamander is worshiped, a demonic altar boy, possessed religious relics that kill, blood-drinking clergymen, a Son of God who feeds on sin, an unsuspecting couple who run afoul of religious lunatics in a small town, the divine (and deadly) turd of Christ, and other terrifying tales guaranteed to make church ladies faint and nuns clutch their rosaries.

## Schlock! Horror!

An anthology of short stories based upon/inspired by and in loving homage to all of those great gorefest movies and books of the 1980's (not necessarily base in that era, although some do ride that wave of nostalgia!), the golden age when horror well and truly came kicking, screaming and spraying blood, gore & body parts out from the shadows...

This exemplary 80's themed/inspired tales of terror has been adjudicated and compiled by one Mr Bret McCormick, himself a writer, producer and director of many a schlock classic, including *Bio-Tech Warrior*, *Time Tracers*, *The Abomination*, *Ozone: The Attack of the Redneck Mutants* and the inimitable *Repligator*.

Featuring stories from: Todd Sullivan, Timothy C Hobbs, Mark Thomas, Andrew Post, James B. Pepe, Thomas Vaughn, Edward Karpp, Jaap Boekestein, Lisa Alfano, L. C. Holt, John Adam Gosham, Brandon Cracraft, M. Earl Smith, Sarah Cannavo, James Gardner, Bret McCormick, and James H. Longmore.

## Graveyard Girls

*Female authors + Horror = something spectacularly terrifying!*

A delicious collection of horrific tales and darkest poetry from the cream of the crop, all lovingly compiled by the incomparable Gerri R Gray! Nestling between the covers of this formidable tome are twenty-five of the very best lady authors writing on the horror scene today!

These tales of terror are guaranteed to chill your very soul and awaken you in the dead of the night with fear-sweat clinging to your every pore and your heart pounding hard and heavy in your labored breast…

Featuring superlative horror from: Xtina Marie, M. W. Brown, Rebecca Kolodziej, Anya Lee, Barbara Jacobson, Gerri R. Gray, Christina Bergling, Julia Benally, Olga Werby, Kelly Glover, Lee Franklin, Linda M. Crate, Vanessa Hawkins, P. Alanna Roethle, J Snow, Evelyn Eve, Serena Daniels, S. E. Davis, Sam Hill, J. C. Raye, Donna J. W. Munro, R. J. Murray, C. Bailey-Bacchus, Varonica Chaney, Marian Finch (Lady Marian).